D0594154

THE TRUTH LIES HERE

Also by

LINDSEY KLINGELE:

The Marked Girl

The Broken World

THE TRUTH LIES HERE

LINDSEY KLINGELE

HARPER TEEN
An Imprint of HarperCollinsPublishers

HarperTeen is an imprint of HarperCollins Publishers.

The Truth Lies Here
 For information address HarperCollins Children's Books, a division of HarperCollins Publishers, 195 Broadway, New York, NY 10007.
www.epicreads.com

Library of Congress Cataloging-in-Publication Data
Klingele, Lindsey, author.
The truth lies here / Lindsey Klingele. —First edition.
pages cm
Summary: Arriving for summer in her Michigan hometown, aspiring journalist Penny learns that her father, a tabloid journalist, is missing and charred dead bodies are being found in the woods.
ISBN 978-0-06-238039-5
[1. Missing persons—Fiction. 2. Murder—Fiction. 3. Journalism—Fiction. 4. Extraterrestrial beings—Fiction. 5. Supernatural—Fiction.] I. Mystery and detective stories.
PZ7.1.K655 Tru 2018 2017034539
[Fic]—dc23 CIP
AC

Typography by Erin Fitzsimmons
18 19 20 21 22 PC/LSCH 10 9 8 7 6 5 4 3 2 1

First Edition

Dad: There's a monster in the lake.

He's a big ole thing and he eats little girls for breakfast.

Me: No, there's not.

Dad: Well, how do you *know*?

Me: . . .

(Thanks, Dad)

THE TRUTH LIES HERE

THE BOY AND GIRL HAD EVERY REASON TO THINK THEY WERE ALONE.

After all, they'd been here many times before. In this open truck bed, under this dense canopy of leaves, miles and miles from town. It was the perfect place to disappear from the world for a while. Or to make out before curfew on a school night.

But on this particular night, they weren't as alone as they thought.

"Did you hear that?"

The girl pulled away from the boy and pushed a sweaty lock of hair over her forehead, half rising to scan the darkened woods. She tried to focus on the noise she'd heard—not the chattering of small animals or the rustling of dead leaves, but something distinct. Like someone saying *hush* into the wind.

"Did I hear what?" the boy murmured, trying to pull her back down to him.

There it was again—slightly louder now, almost like a sheet sliding over dry grass. The girl twisted her body, her legs straining against the zipped-up sleeping bag.

"That noise. You can't hear it?"

The boy sighed and sat up. He looked out over the edge of the pickup truck's open bed and peered into the shadows.

"I guess I hear something. . . ."

The girl exhaled. "What do you think it is?"

The boy turned to her, his eyes hard to make out in the moonless dark. "An axe murderer."

"Stop. I'm serious."

"So am I. Axe murderers are a big problem this time of year." The boy grinned. "Or was that deer ticks . . . ?"

"Ha-ha."

"I better do a body check, make sure none of them got you."

The girl laughed as the boy leaned in again. When his lips met the skin of her neck, her eyelids slowly dropped downward, almost closing . . . and through the crack she saw a bright, fleeting light.

The girl's eyes snapped open, and she pulled away from the boy abruptly.

"What? What now?" He no longer hid the exasperation in his voice.

"Did you see that?"

The boy sighed and twisted again toward the woods. After a moment, his back straightened. He leaned forward.

"What the hell?"

The light was bright and whitish, like a star. Its rapid movement through the trees gave it the appearance of a strobe.

"Hello?" the boy called. He got to his knees and signaled for the girl to stay down.

"What kind of flashlight is that bright?"

"Shh."

The light moved closer. Fifteen feet away, maybe less.

Something in the air smelled like burning. Burning leaves, burning trees, burning meat.

"Who's out there?" The boy gripped the edge of the truck bed, his knuckles turning white where they clutched at the metal.

The light burst through the trees, and it was too, too bright. It blocked out shadows, trees, everything. The boy and the girl both put their hands up to their eyes to shade them from the glare. The girl screamed, then choked, hot air lodged in her throat.

The light came closer. The boy and girl could feel its heat now. Radiating energy. The metal of the truck underneath them began to grow hot.

The girl screamed and screamed, her throat going raw. She pushed herself backward as far as she could go, until her spine hit the hard edge of the truck's cab. She could feel the boy next to her, but she could no longer see him. Even with her eyes closed, all she could see was whiteness.

The light had somehow managed to get into the truck bed with them. It was close, just inches away now, and moving so fast. The skin of the girl's hands began to bubble as she reached up to protect her face.

Just as she stopped screaming, the girl thought she heard a faint noise—a *click*—coming from the woods. It sounded like the shutter of a camera, snapping a picture.

After that, she heard nothing.

ONE

IT'S EASY TO remember the exact moment I stopped believing in my father. It happened right before I discovered that Bigfoot wasn't real and right after I was nearly mauled in the woods by a full-grown black bear.

So yeah, kind of hard to forget.

I was ten years old and lying on my belly in the vast woods of the Upper Peninsula. A pair of too-large binoculars were pressed up against my eye sockets, and through them I could make out the texture of the bark on some oak trees in the distance. Any time I moved the binoculars just a little, I saw only dark blurs and the magnified tips of my own eyelashes.

Dried, yellowing leaves brushed up against my arms and legs, and I longed to scratch the skin there. But moving was not an option. My dad only let me come on his Bigfoot hunting trip on one condition: that I remain absolutely silent and completely still.

Dad squatted in the dirt next to me, partially hidden behind a bush. I took shallow breaths, hoping not to distract him. Finding Bigfoot was an important mission for my dad—more important to him than almost anything else in the world, except for me. It was even more important than being home to celebrate his wedding anniversary with my mom. I knew, because I'd heard Mom saying that exact thing to my grandma on the phone a couple of days earlier.

But I figured it was Mom who was being unreasonable. Dad had adventure in his blood, and Bigfoot was on the move. How could a stupid anniversary compare with the chance to get a once-in-a-lifetime sighting? One that could make his entire career? Knowing what a big deal this was, I'd begged to go with him, and he'd finally agreed.

At that age, I believed in everything—Bigfoot, ghosts, alien abductions, werewolves, giant anacondas, boys who were really bats, bats that could turn into moths, moths that were really from Mars. I even still believed in—and you have no idea how much it pains me to admit this—Santa Claus. For as long as I could remember, Dad had told me stories about incredible beings. Through the bars of my crib, he whispered to me about the Fair Folk of Ireland. On car rides to visit my mom's parents in Fort Lauderdale, he'd tell me about the time he almost saw the Loch Ness Monster in Scotland.

He spoke about these creatures with a kind of hushed excitement, as though one could pop around the corner at any moment. That was the thing I wanted most in the whole world—for us to see one of his larger-than-life creatures, together. Even if it meant lying very still in a pile of scratchy leaves for hours on end.

"Penelope, stop fidgeting," my dad said without turning around.

I froze.

"I wasn't—"

"Shh." My dad put one hand up to quiet me. The other he ran absentmindedly over his short blond beard. "Do you hear that?"

I cocked my ear, willing myself to hear. It was a windless day, almost completely silent. No rustle of leaves, no swaying trees . . .

"There!"

And that's when I heard it: a soft crackling sound. I pressed my binoculars harder into my face, but all I could see through them was the orange, brown, yellow, green of the trees.

"Oh my God, Pen. That's him, that's *him*."

My heart raced as I swiveled the binoculars around. I was moving them too fast, and all I could see were blurs. A panic went through me. I couldn't miss this.

"Do you see it, Pen?"

Everything in me wanted to say yes. But I couldn't see it. I'd come all this way, and I was *missing it.* Tears sprang into the corners of my eyes, and I swallowed hard.

Dad leaned down and adjusted my binoculars.

"Here. He's by that oak; see him? Big and hairy and, oh man, I've got to get this."

Dad moved his hand away to reach for his backpack, but just before he did, my binoculars finally locked onto a spot in the distance. I saw a hulking, dark object partially obscured by a shaggy bush. The creature moved into the frame of my binoculars, and I could see the bulge of a hair-covered muscle. I inhaled sharply.

"I see it! I see it!"

"Shh," my dad said. He took out his camera with the telephoto lens and started taking pictures. "I can't believe I'm getting this." He spared a moment to grin down at me. "You must be my good-luck charm."

I couldn't keep the grin from my face if I'd tried.

Until the creature moved.

"Umm . . . Dad?"

The beast came out from behind the bush, slowly revealing its face. It had rounded, fuzzy ears, button-black eyes, a long snout . . . it wasn't a Bigfoot at all.

It was a black bear.

The disappointment I felt was swift and crushing, but I didn't feel it for me. I felt it for Dad, who had come alive with a kind of contagious glee. Who had called me his good-luck charm. But Dad didn't appear to see that his long-sought-after Bigfoot was really just a midsize bear. He kept snapping picture after picture.

The bear swung its head toward us and sniffed the air. Without dropping the binoculars, I began scooting backward on my stomach.

The bear took one step forward, then another, in our direction. I took the binoculars down from my face, and even with my naked eye, I could see it. Just a few hundred feet away.

"Dad?" I asked. I hated the shaky fear in my voice.

Dad put his camera away and stood up slowly. He motioned for me to do the same. I got to my knees, but was too scared to do anything else. Too scared to brush the dry leaves from where they clung to my elbows. Too scared to run.

The bear ambled forward, picking up speed as it moved toward us.

"I need you to do exactly as I say," my dad said in a low, stern voice. He kept his eyes on the bear.

I nodded, then realized that he couldn't see me. "Okay," I whispered. The bear was moving faster now.

"Don't make any sudden movements, and don't run. As much as you may want to, *do not run*. Do you hear me, Penelope?"

"Yes," I said, my voice sticking in my throat.

"Now, very slowly, start taking steps backward, moving behind me."

Working against the fear that wanted to lock my limbs to the ground, I forced my right leg to move backward, and then my left. The bear was close enough now that I could see its black eyes, could make out the claws on its massive paws.

"Go into my backpack and take out the blue container," Dad said, speaking almost too quickly for me to understand.

My fingers fumbled with the zipper of the backpack. I couldn't help but look around, wildly, for some place to run or hide. There were bushes and trees, of course, but even I knew you weren't supposed to try to climb a tree to get away from a black bear—we'd learned in school they could climb up after you.

With shaking fingers, I pulled out the blue Tupperware container that held our lunch and handed it up to Dad, nearly dropping it as I did so.

The bear was maybe twenty-five feet away from us now, its massive body picking up speed, its breath huffing out in short bursts. It made a frustrated noise halfway between a growl and a roar, and I could see the tops of its thick, yellowed teeth.

Dad ripped open the Tupperware container, revealing the pieces of fried chicken that were supposed to be our lunch. He took a piece out and threw it, hard, over the bear's head. I heard it land in a pile of leaves several feet away. The bear looked backward, following the noise. Dad pulled out another piece of chicken and threw that, too. Then another, again and again.

For a long moment, the bear continued to watch us. I

clutched the strap of Dad's backpack, wanting nothing more than to squeeze my eyes shut and pretend I was anywhere other than in these woods.

But I kept them open.

Slowly, the bear swung its massive body around with a heavy grunt. It sniffed the air and followed the scent of cold chicken to where Dad had thrown it.

Dad leaned forward with a shaky sigh. When he turned to face me, he was grinning.

"That was a close one, huh?"

But fear was still squeezing my throat closed, and I could only nod. Dad wasn't waiting for me to say something, anyway.

"Follow me."

Keeping our eyes on the bear, we slowly walked backward. Soon, the bear's matted hair and snorting noises were yards away. Then we turned and ran toward the car. Once safely inside, Dad pulled the doors closed tight. His smile widened, and then he was laughing loud enough to fill the entire space of the small car. He banged one hand against the steering wheel and let out a whoop.

I laughed, too, relief flooding through me. We'd made it. We were alive. The tips of my fingers were shaking, and I could hear buzzing in my ears.

Dad picked up the camera that hung from a strap around his neck. He started clicking through the images, his smile still big on his face. "Some of these will definitely work."

The buzzing stopped. I shook my head, confused. "Work for what?"

"The column! *Single Bigfoot Sighted.* How does that sound?"

I didn't get it.

"Some of these pictures are a bit blurry; that's perfect," he continued. The glee was creeping back into his voice.

"But, Dad," I said, sure I was missing something, "those are pictures of a bear. It's not really Bigfoot."

Dad didn't look up but continued to scroll through the images. Then he angled the camera screen up to show me one of the pictures. I could just barely make out the blurred shape of the bear as it charged. But its head was angled away in the shot, its claws hidden. I saw its torso, its muscled shoulders. If you squinted, it really could be Bigfoot in the woods.

"But . . . it's just a fuzzy picture of a bear."

Dad reached out and patted me absently on the head without removing his eyes from the camera screen. His finger tangled in my hair, pulling it a little. He didn't seem to notice.

"You gotta expand your mind, kiddo. Sometimes, reality can *be* a bit fuzzy."

I looked off in the direction of the bear, which I couldn't even see anymore.

Dad grinned again. "This trip worked out better than I thought."

In that second, my whole worldview shifted. It was like when I'd go to the eye doctor and he'd make me look through a machine with different lenses. A new lens would click into place, and what I saw in the room changed. *Click*, and everything was blurry. *Click*, and a bright *E* would shine out from the poster across the room, its edges so clear and bold it was almost startling. In that moment with my dad, it was like a whole series of new lenses were dropping in front of my eyes, changing what I knew about everything.

Click, Bigfoot wasn't real. Had never been real.

Click, my dad knew it. And he didn't care.

Click, I was an idiot. But I'd never be one again.

Seven years later, the lessons of that day were still with me. It's painful to remember sometimes how much of a sucker I used to be, how I used to eat up every fantastical lie without question. I collected outlandish stories the way other kids collected comics or Barbie accessories. But I'm not that person anymore. I've known for a long time that reality isn't fuzzy—something either is true or it isn't—and it's not that hard to get to the actual bottom of things if you just try. Which is actually how I found myself climbing over the dingy counter of a tiny snack kiosk at the Cherry Capital Airport in Traverse City, Michigan.

To be fair, I'd been waiting in line in front of an empty counter for ten minutes, clutching the same quickly warming bottle of water in my hand. A line of people from my flight had already formed behind me, many of them tapping their feet and giving loud, exaggerated sighs as they looked in vain for a cashier who was nowhere to be found.

The man right behind me uncrossed and then recrossed his arms for the eighth time. “Does anyone even work here?”

The woman behind him shook her head and shrugged, her shoulders touching the bottom of her blond bob. “Who knows?”

Something in her wide, pale eyes irked me. I wondered how long she’d just stand there and wait.

“*Someone* knows,” I replied. Then, without waiting another second, I pulled myself up onto the counter and swung my legs over to the other side. I marched over to the door behind the counter labeled *EMPLOYEES ONLY* and opened it. Inside, a young woman with thick eye makeup and a name tag that read *Dayna* was sitting on an unopened box of Mountain Dew, playing on her iPhone.

“Excuse me,” I said, trying to sound older than I knew I looked, “Did you know there’s a few people waiting out here?”

She looked up at me and blinked. “No.”

“Well . . . there are. Could you please help us out, maybe?”

Dayna stared at me, but then shrugged and walked over to the register. The woman with the bob smiled as I swung myself back over the counter.

“Huh,” she said. “I never would have thought to do that.”

I paid the surly cashier for my water and rolled my baggage away from the counter. On my way out of the store, a shelf of fresh newspapers caught my eye. I scanned the headlines, taking in the familiar, important-looking fonts of each major publication. Then a flash of bright yellow stopped me in my tracks.

The font on this cheap newsprint was an even more familiar—if a less welcome—sight than the others. It had bold blue lettering against a neon yellow banner that read *STRANGE WORLD* in all caps, like it was shouting at me. Down at the bottom of the page was smaller type, featuring the headline *Tips for Believers*, the popular column by Ike Hardjoy.

Of course this airport would carry *Strange World*, the only print publication still in circulation that catered to the nation's most hard-core conspiracy nuts and UFO seekers, as well as the only one that would still print my dad's column. I could just barely make out the type under my father's name—"Everything the government doesn't want you to know about alien sightings in North America."

I shook my head and walked quickly away from the store, setting my stuff up next to the wall-length picture windows in the baggage area and settling in to wait. I pulled up the Notes app on my phone and looked through everything I had written down on my own latest story idea—it wasn't as flashy as "alien sightings in North America," but at least it wasn't a lie. I still had a few months before I had to apply to Northwestern's undergraduate journalism program, and I wasn't going to waste them. I wanted a story that would grab the attention of the college admissions office. Something important and true.

My story notes were all on economic difficulties in the

Midwest following the closure of plants in the auto and plastics industries. They contained statistics, reports, and previously written articles. Lots of research, but all of it dry. My journalism teacher said I still had to find the human element from inside one of those towns that had suffered greatly after a plant closure.

Bone Lake, Michigan, population 2,300, fit the bill exactly. And it just so happened to be the place where I was born.

I looked out the giant window of the airport's baggage area. Past the parking lot, I could see the basic signs of northern Michigan in early summer. Blue-gray sky, dense trees, two-way blacktop. That pretty much covered it. About an hour down that road was Bone Lake, where Ike Hardjoy still lived, wrote the occasional completely fabricated article for cash, and parented a few weeks a year. Though this time he was getting me for a whole summer.

I glanced back down at my phone, this time checking for missed calls or texts. Nothing.

Dad was a half hour late.

I dialed his number as I looked down to where my luggage sat in a pool of fading sunlight. His phone rang five times and then cut off with a *beep*.

"Dad. Me again. I'm at the airport, waiting for you. I'd ask if there's traffic, but"—I looked out over the completely empty roadway leading from the parking lot—"well, you know. Please call me. Or better yet, please be on the way?"

I hung up and rested my forehead against the cool window. Strands of thick black hair escaped from my ponytail and landed softly against the glass. My reflection stood out against the blankness of the airport behind me. The dark hair and eyes were all from Mom, but the freckles were a gift from Dad. Or really, from Dad's own mom, who was also born and raised in Bone Lake. My family tree on both sides had roots that ran to the very foundation of the town.

That's partially why it made me uncomfortable to come back here, where so many people knew not just my story, but my parents' and grandparents' stories as well. It could be suffocating, having all those eyes on you. And after years of living in Chicago with my mom, I wasn't used to it anymore. Which is why I usually spent my mandatory summer weeks in Bone Lake holed up in my dad's house, watching TV and avoiding going into town. But this year I'd have to change up that strategy if I wanted to get good quotes for my story. I'd have to suck it up and venture into the fishbowl again. Getting into Northwestern depended on it.

Of course, before I could go interview the residents of Bone Lake, Dad had to actually show up and *get* me there.

"Come on, Dad," I whispered. "Come on." But all the hoping in the world didn't matter.

He wasn't coming.

THE PHONE RANG only once before she picked up.

"Hello?"

I smiled at the warm, familiar voice, which, as usual, sounded a tiny bit like it was shouting into the phone.

"Hey, Cindy. It's Penny."

"Penny! My gosh, girl. I forgot you were coming in today."

"Yeah, well, you weren't the only one."

A pause as Cindy breathed out loudly. "Your dad flaked, huh?"

"I don't really know why I'm surprised."

"Go easy on him. The old man's had a lot on his plate lately. But I know he's really excited to see you."

I didn't have a good response to that. Or at least, not a polite one. "Yeah . . . well, do you think you could maybe check next door real quick, see if his truck's in the driveway? Maybe he just forgot to set his alarm or something."

As a freelancer, my dad kept his own hours. Which was just a nice way of saying that he often slept through the day and stayed up late pounding on his laptop keyboard.

"I can't, sweetie. I'm at the shop right now, swamped with this cupcake order. . . ."

"Oh, okay."

"But I'll send Dex over to the airport to come get you. You flew into Traverse City, right?"

"Yeah, but really, Cindy, you don't have to—"

"Oh, it's no trouble."

"I don't want Dex to go out of his way—"

"Penny, stop. You're practically family." Cindy's voice grew distant and then was overtaken by a rustling of what sounded like fabric. "Dex! Grab the keys. Got a job for ya."

A voice in the background yelled, "What?" I imagined Cindy's skinny son, Dex, standing in his too-big apron behind the ice-cream shop's counter, maybe mopping the floor or refilling the Moose Tracks tub.

"He's on his way, Penny. Hold tight."

"Thanks, Cindy. I really appreciate it."

"Like I said, it's nothing. And Penny . . . go easy on your dad tonight. He's gonna feel really bad when he realizes he, you know . . ."

"Forgot me?"

"Yeah."

I smiled, though she couldn't see me, said goodbye, and hung up. I knew it would take Dex an hour to get to the airport from Bone Lake, but I didn't feel like waiting in the air-conditioned chill of the baggage area anymore. I grabbed my luggage—yanking it a little harder than I maybe had to—and headed outside.

The sidewalk was empty, so I sat down cross-legged on the cement and tilted my head upward to soak up the remaining sunlight. I started to lean up against a cylindrical cigarette butt receptacle, when a piece of paper stuck to the metal caught my eye. It was a flyer. My mouth parted slightly as I read the headline: *MISSING.*

Two black-and-white pictures were printed underneath the main header. One was of a smiling, blond teenage girl. The other was of a teenage boy kneeling on the grass in his blue-and-gold football jersey, squinting, as though he was facing directly into the sun. Both of them looked familiar.

The flyer identified them as *Cassidy Jones and Bryan Ryder, missing since May 25. Last seen driving west on M-66. $$$ reward for any information.*

My heart beat faster as I read over their names again. I did know them—another side effect of growing up in a fishbowl town. Cassidy was a year younger than me, so I didn't know her especially well. But Bryan had been in my grade before I moved. He used to play peewee football on the field behind the elementary school every summer. Sometimes my best friend, Reese Harper, and I would pack up a bag full of juice boxes and Pixy Stix and go watch the boys scrimmage. Reese always thought Bryan was cute, and I had a crush on his best friend, Micah. It took us months to work up the nerve to go talk to them for the first time.

Of course, that was before Reese stopped talking to me.

I had no idea what Bryan Ryder had been up to in the last few years. But if he and Cassidy were both missing, maybe they'd decided to run away together. That wouldn't be a first for Bone Lake.

I turned back to the parking lot and the road beyond, looking for Cindy's familiar red Beetle and Dex behind the wheel. It would be strange to see him driving; I'd known Dex for as long as I could remember, and he'd always seemed both shorter and younger than our age. We'd lived next door to each other since we were born, which practically guarantees best-friend status when you're a kid. But we drifted apart once we got to middle school, and I'd seen him only a handful of times over the past few years, usually holed up in the tree house behind our houses, reading old sci-fi paperbacks.

After about an hour, a white Geo Metro jerked its way into the airport parking lot and pulled into the nearest empty spot. After a moment, the front door creaked open and I watched as a pair of long, skinny legs climbed out of the car. They were connected to a lanky frame in a T-shirt that read *Skynet is already here*. The boy looked at me and squinted, then gave a half wave.

"Hey, Penny."

I peered at Dex, trying to reconcile this lean-faced teenager with the boy I once knew. Unlike me, Dex had always taken after just one parent—his mom, Cindy. He had her exact light brown skin and dark hair, though she was 100 percent Chippewa and he was also half Irish on his dad's side. Dex had also always shared Cindy's same wide smile and thoughtful eyes. But the Dex standing before me had definitely changed over the past year. For one thing, there was . . . *more* of him. He'd finally gotten some of his dad's height. And the lines of his face were harder, more definite. The old chubbiness around his cheeks was almost completely gone.

I got up from the sidewalk and brushed off my jeans with my hands. As soon as I stood up straight, I saw Dex's eyes widen.

"Whoa," he said, in his newly deep voice, "you got . . . bigger."

I cleared my throat and crossed my arms in front of my chest (which, to be fair, had grown about two sizes since the past summer).

"Excuse me?"

Dex's eyes snapped back up to my face, and his cheeks reddened. In that moment, I saw the old awkward Dex peeking out from behind his newly sharpened features. "No, I didn't mean . . . I just meant that you grew. Um, up. Not . . . out."

Yep. Same old Dex.

"*I* grew up? You're practically a giant."

Dex relaxed. "Last-minute growth spurt. I blame the genetically modified corn."

"Right. And you got a new ride, I see."

Dex leaned down on the hood of the Geo Metro, which creaked under his weight. "I bought it off Mrs. Morrison. You don't even want to know how much ice cream I had to scoop to afford it."

"It's . . . nice."

Dex jumped away from the car, moved around me, and reached for the handle of my suitcase. He jerked it toward him, rolling it over the sidewalk. "So Ike got caught up, huh?"

"Who knows? I can't even reach him."

Dex froze, and the suitcase slammed into his legs. He didn't seem to notice. "Wait. What?"

"I mean he's a no-show and he's not answering his phone. Probably forgot I was coming."

"No, he didn't. He talked to me about it yesterday. He was really excited. . . ." Dex's eyes narrowed. "This is bad. This is potentially, probably, really bad."

Dex took out his cell phone and dialed a number quickly.

"What's bad? And who are you calling? My dad's not answering."

Dex hung up the phone and stared down at it in his palm. When he looked up at me, his expression was instantly serious.

"Oh man, this is bad. Really, really bad."

"Would you stop saying that? What are you talking about?"

"Your dad. Something must have happened to him."

My heart thudded in my chest. "Wh-what do you mean?"

"He was looking into something really big," Dex rushed on. "Like, world-changing big. And I know he wouldn't have just left you here without calling."

All at once, the rush of momentary fear I'd felt in my stomach swooped out of me, leaving a hard ball of irritation in its place. "Wait, that's your reasoning? You *know* he wouldn't leave me here? How do you know what my dad would or wouldn't do?"

Dex shifted uncomfortably, and his eyes slid away from me.

"Are you telling me you know my dad better than I do?"

Dex opened his mouth to respond, but then caught the look on my face and closed it again.

"Because you might be buddy-buddy with *Ike*, but I've known the man my whole life," I continued, "and let me tell you, this is exactly the kind of thing he would do."

Dex chewed on his bottom lip. "Look, how about we get in the car and I'll explain on the way?"

Dex looked relieved when I reached down to pick up the rest of my bags and hauled them toward the car. By the time everything was loaded and we got on the road, the sun was sinking on the horizon. The inside of Dex's car smelled like gym socks and cinnamon gum, and I moved my feet gingerly away from the crumpled food wrappers and pop cans on his floor.

"Look, I didn't mean to make you mad," Dex said. He spoke in a measured voice, as if he were carefully picking his words. "I just . . . I'm kind of worried something might have happened to Ike."

"Okay," I said, forcing a journalist's neutrality into my voice. "I'm listening."

Dex ran a hand through his hair, which only made it stick out farther from his head. I turned my eyes back to the gray, cracked asphalt of the road as we sped over it.

"We've been investigating . . . well, actually, your dad's been investigating and I've been helping . . . but anyway, your dad thinks he knows something about these kids that went missing in town—"

"You mean Cassidy and Bryan?"

Dex's eyes shot over to me. "You heard about that?"

"There was a *MISSING* flyer at the airport."

"Oh. Well, yeah. Your dad thinks their disappearance is connected to this story he's been chasing."

"Of course he does," I muttered.

"He has all this evidence. Mysterious findings, lights in the woods—"

"Oh my God," I interrupted. "Is this the alien thing again?"

Dex kept his eyes on the road. "Ike calls them the Visitors."

"I know what he calls them."

"So you don't believe him?"

"Not since I was ten."

Dex pursed his lips together.

"And trust me, Dex, my dad doesn't really believe in any of that stuff, either. I mean, I hate to break this to you, since it sounds like you've become, like, his apprentice or something, but Ike is a fake. He wants people to think he believes, but it's all a hoax, and he knows it. So even if he is out chasing some 'story,'" I said, making air quotes with my fingers, "I assure you, he's perfectly safe."

Dex shook his head. "I know Ike has to . . . stretch the truth sometimes to make a living. But it's different this time. It's been different since he found that body of a missing hiker in the woods."

"Wait," I said, putting up a hand. "When did this happen?"

"February."

I slumped down in my seat. I'd spoken to Dad maybe five times on the phone since then. He'd never mentioned it.

"That's horrible. But I don't see—"

"It all connects! That's what Ike's been looking into. He thought he had a solid lead on the Visitors, finally. He has proof they killed that hiker."

"Proof?"

"Well," Dex said sheepishly, "he has this picture. And yeah, it's kind of blurry—"

"Blurry pictures are my dad's specialty. That's not proof of anything."

"You haven't even seen it! He has a picture of something *not human*. He took it in the woods near where the hiker died. And it might be connected to Cassidy and Bryan's disappearance, too."

I rubbed my fingers over my eyes. "Oh my God. Dex."

"You don't believe me?"

The question settled around me. I had once believed in everything so effortlessly. The Visitors in the woods were ingrained into my childhood, one of my first bedtime stories. I'd even written a report about them in second grade. I'd gotten an F, and in bold red letters on top of my report my teacher had written, *ASSIGNMENT MEANT TO BE ON MICHIGAN WILDLIFE. PLEASE REDO.*

"Ike is really on to something, Penny," Dex said.

The strain in his voice sounded achingly familiar. It sounded like the way I used to talk about my dad, before I knew the truth. Proud. Defensive. In on a secret that the rest of the world was too blind to see.

And it was all crap.

"Look, Dex, I'm sorry you think something's happened to my dad. But I promise you, he's fine. Maybe he's out in the woods 'hunting aliens.' Maybe he brought a case of Bud with him and passed out somewhere."

"That's a little harsh."

My nostrils flared in frustration, but I forced myself to bite back my first response—*what would you know about it? What do you know about my dad at all?* "Whatever. He'll probably show up tonight or tomorrow morning. It's not like he hasn't disappeared for a story before."

"But it's never been this serious before. I mean, what about Cassidy and Bryan? They're *gone.*"

I looked out the window, watching the dark woods flick past. "I'm sure there's a perfectly logical explanation. There always is. Maybe Cassidy and Bryan took a trip to Myrtle Beach. Or went to Windsor to gamble or get drunk or get married."

Dex scoffed. "That's dumb."

"It's not dumber than they were *kidnapped by aliens.*"

"I never said they were kidnapped. I just said it's connected. That's what Ike thought."

I sighed. "Can we just . . . not talk about it anymore? Please?"

Dex's jaw clenched.

We didn't speak another word until Dex pulled into my dad's driveway forty minutes later. The single-level house stood just as I remembered it. Its brown wood paneling looked faded by years in the sun, and its lawn was just slightly overgrown, as if it hadn't been mowed in a couple of weeks. Beyond the house, I could see the dark outline of the woods, and next door was Dex and Cindy's place. In comparison to my dad's dark house, it looked bright and warm, its porch light reaching out into the dawning twilight.

Dad's driveway was empty. Dex shot me a meaningful look as he let the car idle.

"It doesn't mean anything," I said, suddenly feeling tired.

The day of travel was starting to catch up with me. "He could have taken the truck anywhere."

Dex shook his head slightly, his eyes on my house. "I'm still going to drive around and see if I can find him. I'm worried."

I shrugged. "Suit yourself."

Just as I reached for the door handle, he spoke again, his voice soft. "You really have changed, Penny."

I pursed my lips, wanting nothing more in that moment than to be home, in my bedroom in Chicago, lying down on my familiar sheets and reading the news on my iPad. Not here, in front of this house filled with so many memories I wanted to forget.

"You're right," I said. "I have."

Dex looked at me with disappointment, maybe even a little sadness, but I didn't feel any loss over the girl I used to be. To believe blindly is to get burned, and I was smarter than that now. I knew better.

"Have fun chasing aliens, Dex," I said, turning my back on him and heading toward the house. "I have work to do."

THREE

I LET MYSELF into the house and dragged my suitcases in behind me. The living room was exactly the same as the last time I was home—same orange, seventies shag carpeting, same fifteen-year-old TV set sitting in a wooden cabinet. The windows looked out over the yard and the trees beyond, but it was too dark out to see anything through them.

I walked through the house, flipping on lights as I went, and finally reached my room. It had been mostly untouched since I was twelve years old, and every summer that I came back to it, I was further from the version of myself that used to live in it full-time. This room had the same floral wallpaper that was put up when I was five, while my room in Chicago had recently been painted a dark blue gray. Here, the back of the door was papered with posters of Zac Efron and the cast of *High School*

Musical; there, my room was covered with two large corkboards that held my calendars, assignment information, and articles I liked. Here, the small secondhand desk had been painted all white and was still covered in bits of glue and glitter; there, my sleek IKEA desk usually held only my laptop, some pens, and a stack of female war-correspondent biographies that my mom had given to me for Christmas.

I quickly peeked into Dad's room—just in case—but there was no one there. His bed was unmade and his curtains were pulled shut. His office was a mess, but that wasn't anything new. The desk was covered in papers, the walls lined with corkboards chock-full of ideas for stories. I skimmed them—*prehistoric lizard spotted in Daytona. Crop triangles = the new crop circles?*—and shook my head.

Framed against one wall was the very first article Dad had ever written for *Strange World*. Published when I was only a year old, it was about the supposed alien landing in Bone Lake. The beginning of Dad's obsession with the Visitors. That year, a meteorite had landed in the woods outside of town. It was slightly larger than most meteorites, so it drew some attention from the local and state news, and even brought some scientists to town to check it out. But it was just your garden-variety—or rather space-variety—hunk of rock, and the story quickly faded away.

For everyone except my dad, that is, who claimed he'd noticed some "strange occurrences" in town that year and thought they might be connected to the meteorite crash. So he drafted up a story about the alien "Visitors" who'd come down with the space rock and who were now living in the woods outside of his hometown, and he sold it on spec to the fledgling *Strange World*. The piece hit big, putting the paper on the map and ensuring Dad would have an income forever—or at least as long as there was a section of the tabloid-reading public that cared more about batboy sightings than *Bachelorette* proposals.

As a kid, I thought my dad's article on the Visitors was a brave piece of genius; everyone in town rolled their eyes and huffed about the added attention Dad had brought to Bone Lake (this time from wild-eyed tabloid junkies rather than scientists), but I knew the truth—the Visitors were real and lived in the woods just beyond my house, and everyone except for my dad and me was too dumb to see it. That, or they'd been brainwashed by the aliens.

Later, of course, I realized the only real draw my dad had felt toward the meteorite was the pull of potential cash. He learned how to spin a story for a quick buck, and from there he never looked back. To this day, he wouldn't admit he'd made the Visitors up to anyone—not even me.

Turning away from Dad's framed article, I switched off the light in his office and wandered to the small kitchen to look for food. My dad's entire diet consisted of what my mom used to jokingly call "summer barbecue staples." He would rather eat grilled meat morning, noon, and night than even think about buying a vegetable. Which was one of the few things we had in common anymore.

"Thank God," I murmured as I popped open a fresh bag of ridged potato chips and popped one in my mouth, savoring the taste of salt. Mom typically ordered in healthy dinners for the two of us, but she'd been on a particularly intense kale-and-proteins kick this past spring. I think she felt guilty for leaving me to go on a sabbatical to Barcelona. Her trip was the reason I was stuck in Bone Lake for the entire summer, rather than the usual three weeks. On the bright side, at least I wouldn't have to eat a single leafy green while I was here. Plus, I'd have more time to work on my article.

Back in the living room, I sat down with my chips, opened up my file labeled *Bone Lake story* on my laptop, and started to read through my notes.

In the 1980s, Bone Lake was a midsize town for northern Michigan—not huge, not even Traverse City big—but respectable. Most of that was due to the plastics plant outside of town, the one that employed a large chunk of Bone Lake's high school graduates. They became line workers, technicians, managers, secretaries, security guards, janitors. The plant, Tevis Manufacturing, molded parts for the insides of large and utility vehicles, though its biggest contract was with the military. A lot of the interior pieces of military Jeeps—pretty much anything that was plastic, anyway—were made right in Bone

Lake. But in 2005, all that changed.

A local worker named Hal Jameson—a security guard—died while on night duty. There was an investigation, but the death was ruled completely accidental, apparently a human error on Jameson's part. But it didn't matter. The incident made state news and put a spotlight on the government's contract with the plant. Someone at some point had cut some corners, and now fingers were pointing blame. The state news soon became national news, and the plant accident was sliding into scandal. Rather than stick around and see the mess through, the government pulled their contract entirely. After that, the plant's other clients fell like dominoes. Its doors closed for good by 2006.

Half the people in town lost their jobs. And it wasn't like there was another plant just around the corner—with the auto industry sending its manufacturing overseas, shuttered plants were a dime-a-dozen experience in Michigan. Bone Lake became another statistic.

That was the summary of what I had so far. But I knew there was more to the story than just the numbers and dates in my research folder. Finding and adding in a more human element would be just the thing to get me into Northwestern. I started typing up a list of anyone I could interview during my summer at Dad's. The first name to flash through my mind was Micah Jameson, Hal Jameson's son (and my first crush).

Even though I hadn't seen him in a couple of years, just the thought of him sent a familiar ripple through my stomach. I used to get that same feeling whenever I heard Micah laughing in class, or whenever I saw him throwing around a football after school, his hair turning golden under the late-afternoon sun. Maybe first crush feelings just stay with you like that, like the residue of past emotions that fade but never evaporate entirely.

Even though I'd been friendly with Micah in middle school, I'd never asked him about his dad or the accident before—it had happened when we were so young. I hesitatingly typed his name onto my list, following it up with other people who stayed in town after the plant closed. Many—like Dex's dad—had moved away to try to find new work.

After working on my list of who to talk to and what to ask them for a while, I shut my laptop and looked around for the TV remote. I couldn't find it in its usual spot on the coffee table. In its place instead was a shiny, new-looking digital camera. Dex's words from the car flashed through my mind—about how my dad had taken a strange picture as part of some new "story." Before I could think through what I was doing, I picked up the camera, clicking it on with my thumb.

A photo popped up in the camera's preview screen. It was a simple shot of a group of trees in the woods. It looked like it had been taken a few months earlier—the trees were just starting to grow buds, and their dark, spindly limbs stood out starkly against traces of snow on the ground.

I flipped to the next picture. It was the same grouping of trees, but this time they were shrouded in darkness. In the next picture, they were lit up with dazzling morning sun, and the bark looked almost orange in the light. I kept clicking over to see more pictures, but they were all of the same stand of trees at various times of day. Sometimes the picture would feature a bird or a squirrel in the frame, but mostly it was just the trees. Picture after picture after picture.

"What the hell, Dad?" I murmured.

And then I came to a photo that was different from the others. It had clearly been taken in the same place, but half the image was blurred out by white, as if the flash had failed, or as if someone had shone a bright flashlight right into the lens. I peered closer. Right in the middle of the picture, where the whiteness met the black outlines of the tree trunks, was a thin, dark shape. It stood out starkly from the white glare, a black line perpendicular to the ground that bent in the middle, angling off in a different direction and ending in a few shorter, stubby lines that splayed out from one another. If I squinted, it could almost pass for a long, spindly arm, bent at the elbow, its fingers reaching out as if grasping for something. . . .

I shook my head and pulled away from the image. Certainly, I could imagine Dad spinning it so the dark shape seemed ominous—this was the man who'd once passed off a bird as a flying saucer, after all. But no matter how many lies he told or how many people believed him, it wouldn't change the truth—that thing caught in the light was nothing more than a tree branch, likely broken by the winter snow.

I sighed and thrust the camera into the coffee table drawer. A few minutes later, I found the remote control under the couch cushions. Pushing the bag of chips aside, I lay back on the couch and flipped on the TV, turning the channel to a nineties sitcom, an episode I'd already seen at least three times. It was the perfect thing to turn my brain off.

After a few minutes, I felt my eyelids begin to droop. I had the fleeting, selfish thought that when Dad came home, the first thing he'd see was me on the couch, surrounded by chip crumbs, a living, breathing reminder of what he'd forgotten to do today. I almost wanted to be conscious for that moment.

Instead, I was asleep before the first commercial break. I dreamt I was walking in the woods, lost and surrounded by black and broken trees, their branches ice-covered and catching at my clothes as if trying to keep me from going any farther.

FOUR

DAD DIDN'T COME home during the night. His room was still empty when I looked in the next morning, his bed unmade in the exact same way it had been the day before. When I looked into the driveway and saw his truck was still gone, my stomach felt uneasy. But I brushed the feeling aside—no matter what Dex had said, I knew Dad would walk through the front door any moment. He wouldn't apologize for forgetting to pick me up, but I could guess what he would say instead—*I was really on to something, Pen—you know how it is.* Or, *It all worked out, didn't it? You made it here! Now stop pouting and let's get some breakfast.* And then he'd grin that sheepish grin that made it impossible for anyone to stay truly angry with him. I knew that grin like I knew my own reflection.

But just because I knew how the conversation would go

down didn't mean I had to sit here and wait around for it to happen. If Dad wasn't worrying about me, I wasn't going to worry about him.

I showered and got dressed, then made my way to the garage. Sitting in a corner near a pile of cardboard boxes and some scattered tools was my ten-speed bike. I quickly pumped some air into the deflated tires, wiped a layer of dust off the seat, and hopped on.

I biked slowly down the driveway and then across the street, and I could feel the tension in my shoulders easing. The breeze lifted up my still-damp hair as I pedaled harder. I didn't have a bike in Chicago, and it was this feeling—this sense of weightless movement through the fresh, pine-smelling air—that reminded me of my childhood summers more than anything else. It was my dad who taught me how to ride a bike, long ago. I could still remember how he'd reacted when I made it down the driveway without falling off—he'd thrown his hands up in the air and ran up and down the driveway, yelling at the top of his lungs like I'd just won an Olympic gold medal instead of simply managing to keep my butt on a plastic purple bike seat. His excitement was contagious. I'd felt so proud of myself I thought I'd burst.

I biked the two miles into town, passing more and more houses as I got closer to the main shop-lined street, most of them tucked away from the road, closer to the woods. Many were old, and some were falling into disrepair. Seeing Bone

Lake only once a year like I did gave me a fast-forward view of its decline, one that moved doggedly forward in normal time for everyone else. Every year, when I came back, there were one or two more closed businesses, five or six more foreclosed houses, seven or eight more dilapidated lots.

A few of the remaining businesses popped up as I neared the main part of town—a post office, an antiques shop, a breakfast place that had been run by the same woman for forty years. There were more cars on this section of the street, but not many. Bone Lake had exactly five stoplights.

I finally pedaled up to a white clapboard store, with a pink-and-white striped awning, that was nestled in between a Goodwill and a barber shop. Most of the front of the store was taken up by a giant plate of glass, which was painted in gold letters that read *SWEET STREET.*

After leaning my bike up against the side of the shop, I pushed open the front door and walked inside, where the scents of chocolate and caramel immediately overwhelmed me. The smell—and look—of the store was exactly like I remembered. I'd spent a lot of time there as a kid, and sometimes Cindy had even let me "help out" behind the counter. I was hoping Cindy might let me help out for real this summer. After all, writing a story to get me into Northwestern wouldn't exactly help *pay* for Northwestern. Scooping ice cream for a couple of months might help me cover at least five weeks of a meal plan, which, hey, was something.

"Hey, Cindy."

Cindy's head popped up, and she smiled wide. The sunlight shining through the main window highlighted the warm brown color of her eyes. They were the same shade as Dex's.

"You're here!"

Instead of moving around the counter to greet me, Cindy leaned over it, giving me a tight hug that lifted me a bit off my feet and smashed my ribs into the counter. This close, I could smell the *Cindy*-ness of her—the sugar that dusted her hair and the cinnamon lingering on the faded Pearl Jam T-shirt she often wore instead of an apron.

Cindy shook her head as she released me, then looked me up and down. "Would you get a look at yourself? Dex didn't mention how much you've grown . . . and you've gotten so pretty."

I didn't know how to respond, and instead just gave an awkward shrug-squirm combo move.

"I mean, you were always a pretty girl," Cindy continued, "but every time you come home, you look more and more like your mom."

I laughed, not commenting on the "home" remark. Bone Lake hadn't been my home in years. "That's funny. She says I'm starting to look more like Dad."

Cindy straightened, and the smile slipped from her face. "Speaking of, I noticed Ike's truck was still gone this morning. Dex is real worried about him."

I waved my hand. "I'm sure he'll turn up any second.

Probably just went camping or hunting or chasing a story—you know how he is."

Cindy nodded, but I could see the worry in her eyes. "Still, if he's not back by tonight, and you need a place to stay, you're welcome with us. I don't like the thought of you in that house all alone."

"Thanks, Cin. But I'll be fine. You know what I *could* use? A job."

Cindy blinked, looking surprised.

"If you need the help, I mean," I continued. "I know summer's your busiest season, and this time I'll be home till August—"

"Of course!" Cindy interrupted. "I could definitely use a summer hand, especially now that Dex spends so much time with his *X-Files* club—"

"His . . . what?"

Cindy laughed and waved a dismissive hand. "Oh, he started this club at school, they're supposed to look into proof of extraterrestrial life and that sort of thing. Mostly they just eat pizza and watch *X-Files* reruns."

"Oh, that's . . . huh," I said. At least that explained why Dex was suddenly Ike Hardjoy's number one fan.

"Anyway, I'd love to have some extra help here. Maybe afternoons and weekends? That's when we're busiest."

I grinned. "When can I start?"

"How about tomorrow? I gotta deliver a wedding cake to Traverse City. The couple seem to really hate each other, but then again, they were smart enough to order my cheesecake frosting, so who knows? You can help Dex run the store while I'm gone."

I smiled, but then thought again about Dex's disappointed expression when he'd dropped me off the night before. I wasn't looking forward to another argument about my dad, aliens, or any combination of the two. "Yeah . . . sounds good."

"So that gives you, what? One whole day of summer to waste before you get to work," Cindy said with a wink. She was joking, but her words echoed in my mind. I didn't even have one day to waste, not if I wanted to get my Northwestern admissions article as strong as possible.

"Actually, Cindy, I was hoping you might help me with something else? If you have a minute?" I straightened up, pulling a small notebook and pen out of my purse.

"Ooh, looks serious. What's up?"

I explained to her about the article I had to write, and why I wanted to focus on Bone Lake's economic decline since the plant closure.

Cindy's mouth puckered in distaste. "Now, why would you want to write about something so depressing?"

"Well, I'm hoping 'depressing' will catch the eyes of the admissions officers. Plus, I want to write about something important. Something true. And true things are usually kinda depressing, right?"

Cindy looked at me with concern. "You don't really believe that, do you, hon?"

I shrugged and smiled, like I might have been kidding, and Cindy's expression relaxed.

"Okay, shoot."

I jumped right in. "How do you think your business has been affected by the plant's closing?"

"Oh, it hasn't, I don't think," Cindy said quickly, waving her hand as if I was being silly. "I mean, there are up years and down years, but people always want ice cream. And cakes."

"Okay . . . but what about the town? Have you noticed any changes here in the past ten years?"

Cindy took a deep breath and looked up at the ceiling, as if the answer might be written there. "No," she finally said, drawing out the word. "Well, Molly's Antiques burned down, and now it's a consignment shop. That's different. Plus, the church finally repaved the parking lot."

I smiled thinly, trying to hide my disappointment. I wondered—just for a second—if I should ask about Cindy's husband, Mark. He'd left when Dex and I were in the sixth grade. He'd gone looking for work since he couldn't find any here after he lost his job at the plant, but he hadn't come back since. I knew bringing up Mark would cause Cindy pain. Maybe it's what a *real* journalist would do, but . . .

"Okay," I said instead, "let's talk about the actual plant closing for a second. Do you remember anything about when it happened? Or the accident with Mr. Jameson?"

Cindy blinked once, then twice. Then she shook her head.

"What a tragic thing that was. And a shame, too. It's best not to think too much about it."

"Sure, but could you maybe try to say *something* about it? It's just that the article is really important—"

"I'm sorry, Penny," Cindy said, shaking her head. "My memory just isn't what it used to be. You know who you should talk to? Hector at the hardware store. He knows everything that goes on in this town. And he was a manager at the plant before it closed, you know."

"Oh yeah! That's right. But do you remember even a little—"

I was cut off by a ringing phone.

"Gotta get that; might be an order," Cindy said, pushing herself away from the counter. "So you'll be in tomorrow?"

"Definitely," I said, a bit jarred by Cindy's sudden shift as she raced toward the ancient landline. I waved goodbye, deciding to take Cindy up on her advice.

Hector's Hardware was just two blocks away.

When I made my way over to the shop and pushed open the front door, I once again felt like I was in a time warp. Just like Sweet Street, nothing in this room had changed since the last time I'd been in it. It had the same scratched linoleum, the same inappropriate pinup calendar hanging behind the counter. Hector looked the same, too—tall frame, thinning hair, and wide-set eyes that bulged a bit when he laughed.

"Well, if it isn't the littlest Hardjoy, back for the summer already," Hector said, putting down his phone and grinning widely when he saw me. Hector had been one of my dad's friends growing up. He was one of the few people who didn't seem to mind Dad's weird obsessions and stories and would still grab a beer with him from time to time. "You here to pick up something for your dad? He ordered some screws a while back, but they were on back order. I think they came in, but I'll have to check. Our stock boy just went missing, and everything's gone to heck. You heard about that? Bryan Ryder? His parents are real upset. Probably he just ran over to Windsor with his girl, that's what I think. Anyway, he didn't exactly call in before he up and left, and now I got packages coming in left and right, and I'm sure your dad's screws are around here somewhere—"

"Thanks, Hector, but I'm not here for Dad," I interrupted loudly. Hector was capable of carrying on a one-sided conversation for hours, if you let him. "I was actually just at Cindy's, and—"

"Did you try the new ice-cream flavor? Berry Vanilla Whip. It's no Mackinac Island Fudge, but then again, what is?"

"Oh, uh, no. . . . I was there to get a part-time job, actually—"

"Nice! I've been needing a man on the inside. Been trying to get hold of Cindy's maple candy recipe for years, but she always says—"

"—it's a family secret."

"Yup. But if you should happen to find that secret lying

around in a drawer somewhere . . ." Hector gave an exaggerated wink.

"Uh, sure. I'll keep an eye out."

Hector's eyes widened as he grinned. "Excellent."

Something else occurred to me before I could get to my article questions—Cindy was right, there wasn't anything that went on in Bone Lake that Hector didn't know about.

"Hey, Hector, speaking of my dad, you haven't seen him around, have you? He didn't show up to pick me up at the airport, and I was wondering . . . did he tell you he was going camping or hunting or anything?"

Hector's mouth pulled down in an exaggerated frown as he shook his head. "He didn't mention it. Actually, haven't seen your dad around too much lately. A couple of times over at Vinny's, we played darts, but I don't remember him talking about a trip."

"He was at Vinny's?" I asked, hearing a beat too late how all the friendliness had dropped out of my voice, leaving it flat and cold.

Hector blinked, confused. "Yeah . . ." He studied me a moment, as if trying to figure out what was behind my abrupt shift in tone. I quickly smiled and waved my hand.

"That's okay, don't worry about it. I actually came over to ask you about something else. . . ." I quickly laid out for Hector the same pitch I'd given Cindy, though this time it took three times as long to get out with all of Hector's interruptions. But at least, unlike Cindy, he conceded that Bone Lake had changed.

"Yeah, I guess things are kinda different around here," he said, tapping his fingers on the counter and nodding his head in thought. I quickly started taking notes as he continued. "What with the recession and everything."

"The recession?" I asked. "Don't you think the plant closing had something to do with it, too?"

"Oh sure, that was bad business, bad business. People were real upset when it happened."

"What do you remember from then? You worked at the plant, right?"

"Yep. Got a job there right outta high school. Worked my way up to manager in six years, you know."

"So, how did you feel when the plant closed?"

"Terrible! It was hard times. But now I got my store, make my own hours. Course, running your own business isn't always easy, either. Like now I gotta figure out if I should hire a new stock boy or wait for Bryan to show back up—"

"Right, but, about the plant," I said, worried we were getting off track. "I haven't found a ton of concrete information from the time it actually closed. Do you know much about the accident?"

A cloud seemed to pass over Hector's face. "Now, that was a real tragedy," he said, his voice faraway. "A real shame. Human error is all it was, which is the worst part. But it's best not to think too much about it. . . ."

My pen stuttered a bit over the page as I wrote down Hector's words, but before I could ask Hector to repeat himself, he'd moved on.

"That was a real bad time, Penny. But I think we've moved past it, if you want my honest opinion. You can write that down. Say, *Hector Correa, a successful, upstanding businessman, is optimistic about the future of his town*—do you think *upstanding* is the best word? Or maybe *honorable*?"

"Um, they're both pretty good," I said, reluctantly putting away my notebook. As Hector went on to talk about the new brand of paint he was stocking and how the newspaper didn't deliver on Mondays anymore, I began to realize how hard a task I'd set for myself this summer. Why was it so difficult for Bone Lake's residents to talk about its obvious decline? Or maybe they just didn't want to talk about it with *me*? I'd always be Ike's daughter, the littlest Hardjoy, whenever I came back to Bone Lake. But I was also an outsider now, too.

The front door opened with a dinging noise, and Hector excused himself to go help the new customer. I took the opportunity to look through my hastily scribbled notes. I stopped when I got to one particular line—*It's best not to think too much about it.*

Putting my finger there to mark the spot, I flipped back a couple of pages to my interview with Cindy. Written there, at the bottom of the page, was the same line. The *exact* same.

It's best not to think too much about it.

A coincidence? Probably. It was a pretty common expression. But why had Hector and Cindy both been so reluctant to talk about the specifics about what happened to Hal Jameson at the plant? It's not like what happened was a secret town shame or anything; at the time, the accident had made it into newspapers around the state.

Frowning, I closed my notebook. When I looked up, movement on the other side of the shop's glass window caught my eye, and I froze. Standing right there on the other side of the glass, the afternoon sun lighting up the gold ends of his hair, was another Jameson. One with blue eyes and a Clark Kent jawline that a younger version of me had memorized a long time ago.

Micah.

My stomach dropped, and for a moment I felt like I couldn't breathe.

Damn. First crushes really *did* leave a mark.

By the time I was able to inhale again, Micah had looked up through the window. He spotted me, squinted, and then his face broke out into its trademark wide smile. I was smiling back before I could help myself, the notebook in my hand all but forgotten.

I STEPPED OUTSIDE the hardware store, blinking in the early summer sunshine.

"Penny? Is that you?"

Micah's smile stayed fixed on his face as he crossed the distance between us in two giant steps and gathered me up in a hug.

"Hi," I squeaked, my face pressed against his letterman jacket.

"I almost didn't recognize you," Micah said. "It's been forever."

He pulled back, and I tried to regain my balance as gracefully as possible.

"I know."

"No, seriously," he said. "When's the last time we saw each other?"

"Hmm . . ." I said, pretending like I was trying to remember. In truth, I remembered the last time I'd seen Micah Jameson very clearly, but he hadn't seen me. Last summer, Dad had sent me on an early morning grocery store run to get more bread and mustard, and I saw Micah pulling a gallon of milk from the dairy fridge one aisle over. But I'd been wearing pajama bottoms and flip-flops, and was too embarrassed to go say hi.

"Wasn't it Reese's birthday party?" he asked. "In like eighth grade?"

Seventh.

"Yeah, that sounds right. Wow, you look the same."

"Thanks. I think." He laughed. "So you back for a little bit?"

"A few months, actually. Practically the whole summer."

Micah smiled again, like he was genuinely pleased to hear I'd be around for a while. My stomach swooped again.

"Sweet. You got any plans while you're here?"

"Um . . ." I became aware again of the spiral notebook in my hand. It contained, along with my laptop, pretty much the entirety of my summer plans. I thought about the list I'd made the night before, of potential interviewees. Micah's name was at the very top of that list. Getting him to talk on record about his dad was essential. But as I looked into his face, with his dark blue eyes squinting in the sun, his long lashes casting shadows over his cheekbones, it was like my entire project just flew from my mind, leaving a gaping hole behind. I scrambled to say something—anything resembling human speech at all—but the gears in my head had ground to a stop. Nothing worked.

"I, uh . . . nothing really. I'll be helping out at the ice-cream store a little," I managed.

"Cool," Micah said.

"Yeah. Ice cream's the best."

Ice cream's the best? What the hell was I talking about? Where was my head? Micah smiled so wide that for a moment I wondered if he was making fun of me. But no—that was just how he smiled.

I scanned my brain for something rational to say.

I used to write your peewee football jersey number on the back cover of all my notebooks. No.

Remember when we played spin the bottle at Reese's birthday party, and my spin landed on you, but I was too nervous to kiss you, and I think you knew that, so you just kissed my hand instead? Probably not.

Hey, wanna talk about your dead dad for a minute to help me get into college? Definitely no.

If I couldn't even manage a regular conversation with Micah at the moment, asking for an incredibly personal interview was probably not the best move. I'd have to work up to it. And if "working up to it" required possibly hanging out with Micah this summer, well, then that was a sacrifice I'd just have to make.

For journalism.

"So, um . . . what are those?" I asked, trying to keep my

voice bright as I motioned to a bundle of papers in his hand.

Micah's expression darkened. He angled the papers so I could see. The black-and-white faces of Cassidy Jones and Bryan Ryder stared up at me.

"I'm just hanging up some more flyers," Micah said, his voice low.

"Oh, right. I can help with a couple if you want."

"Thanks, Penny," Micah said, handing me a thin stack. "That would be awesome of you."

"So there's still no word?"

Micah shook his head. "It just doesn't make sense, you know? Everyone's saying they maybe just skipped town, but we've got summer practice starting tomorrow. No way Bryan would miss that. Not for anything."

I nodded hard, not sure what to say. It made total sense to me that someone would give up on the glory of summer two-a-days to get away for a while. Maybe even start over somewhere new.

Micah shrugged. "Or maybe I'm just overreacting, and they'll show up tonight, ready to party, acting like nothing ever happened."

I continued nodding, as though I had any idea what Micah was talking about.

"Now that you're back in town, you're coming to the party, right?"

"Um . . ."

"You should definitely come. It's out at Millers' barn. You know it?"

"Oh. Yeah. That's . . . a good barn."

Micah laughed, just a little bit harder than the nonjoke really warranted. I joined in.

"Cool," he said. "I hope I see you there."

"Oh, you will. If I go. Which I probably will. So you probably will. Um. See me there." I cleared my throat and held up the small stack of flyers in my hand. "Anyway, better get started on these."

"Yeah." Micah nodded, then reached out and touched me lightly on the shoulder. "Thanks again, by the way."

"Oh yeah, no problem," I responded, giving him a thumbs-up.

A thumbs-up?

But Micah just cocked his head a little to the side and laughed. "All right. Well, see ya later."

I just nodded. Nodding was safe—I should just stick to nodding.

Micah crossed the road then, and I watched him saunter off, while I clutched the flyers in my hand. I couldn't help smiling a little as I swung my bike around on the sidewalk, already wondering how I would get to the barn party. I was barely paying attention to my surroundings when I looked up, and my heart froze.

Reese was staring at me from a few shops down the street.

She'd grown out her wavy blond hair and was a few inches taller, from what I could tell. But her expression was exactly the same as the last time I'd seen her. She's the only person I've ever known who's looked at me like that—with an actual hatred. As we made eye contact, the look morphed into one of cold indifference. She tore her gaze from me when the door of Vinny's Bar opened behind her. Reese's mom, Julie Harper, stepped out into the sunshine. She looked up and saw me, and if her daughter's face was a mask of coldness, Julie's was one of shock.

God, this really was a small town.

I willed myself to pump my legs forward and ride away as quickly as possible, but I felt stuck like a butterfly under glass, pinned in the moment by Julie's stare. Reese took her mother's arm and turned her toward a car that was parked on the curb.

I tried to push the Harpers from my mind as I hung up a few flyers in the window at Sweet Street and put a few more up on the bulletin board at the post office. By the time I started pedaling home, my thoughts swung back to Micah. I remembered how genuine he'd looked when he invited me out to the Millers' barn party—like he wasn't just being polite, but really did want me there—and I felt a smile cross my face again.

I wondered what I'd wear to the party, and whether or not I'd find an opportunity to ask him for an interview. My notebook was heavy in my purse, pulling down on my shoulder as I pedaled. I hadn't really gotten any new information or usable quotes; I'd gotten weirdly *similar* quotes from Cindy and Hector, but not useful ones.

I turned onto the cracked pavement of my quiet street, and my eyes automatically went to the driveway. Dad's truck was still gone. But another car on the road nearby caught my attention. It was black and sleek, so new-looking that it stood out against the dusty street. I didn't recognize the car; it didn't look like something anyone in Bone Lake would drive. At first, I thought it was parked across the street from Dad's, but as I pedaled closer I realized it was actually moving, just very slowly. It rolled inch by inch past our house.

I swerved out of its path, and as soon as I did the car picked up speed, kicking up a pebble that flew into my bike rim with a small pinging noise.

"Hey," I said angrily, looking up at the car as it moved past me.

I tried to see inside, but the windows were tinted almost black. It had a blue-and-white license plate—definitely from Michigan—but the plate itself was spotless. No rust, no dirt. It looked like it had just been taken through a deep clean. Or just been issued.

The car braked as it turned the corner, and then it was practically gone.

"City jerk," I muttered after its retreating taillights. The words sprang automatically to my lips, and a half second later I realized with a cringe that they weren't mine at all—they were my dad's. That was the expression he'd use whenever someone cut him off in traffic or sped by in a hurry. To him, it wasn't the "jerk" part that mattered—it was the "city." The ultimate insult in his eyes. He continued to use it all the time, even though his own daughter had been living in a city for the past four years.

But maybe four years wasn't long enough, I thought as I put up the kickstand on my bike and started toward the house. After all, I'd been home only a day, and already my dad's expression was coming out of my mouth as naturally as if it belonged there. It shook me, hearing myself repeating his words like I used to when I was small.

I pictured my bedroom in Chicago, my school, my unfinished college applications. *That* was who I was now, the real Penny Hardjoy. Bone Lake Penny was just a kid. A kid who believed everything her father ever told her.

Good riddance to that Penny.

But as I unlocked the front door and turned the handle to walk inside, the motion of it felt like second nature, like a muscle memory too deep to extract. No matter how many years had passed or how much I'd changed, my body still knew this was what it felt like to come home.

SIX

A COUPLE OF hours later, I was deep into a daytime *Law & Order* marathon when I heard five sharp raps on the front door. Dex. He had the same manic knocking style he'd had as a kid.

I pushed myself up off the couch with a sigh and opened the door. Dex bounced anxiously a couple of times on the balls of his feet and ran one hand through his hair, which was already sticking straight out from his head in several different directions.

"Okay, I feel like we got off on the wrong foot yesterday," he said. "And I just wanted to come over and say sorry."

I sighed and crossed my arms, then uncrossed them. Dex didn't look like someone ready to pick a fight. He just looked like a stretched-out version of the sweet kid I used to know.

"I'm sorry, too," I said, opening the door a little wider. "I was angry about my dad bailing on me, and I think I took it out on you."

Dex shrugged. "That's okay. You were probably right."

"Really?" I was surprised by how nonchalant Dex was being, especially after he'd been half-ready to launch a UFO search party the day before.

"Yeah," he said. "I drove around town and couldn't find Ike's truck anywhere. So maybe he did just take off after a lead and forgot what day it was."

"Figured as much," I said.

"You haven't heard from him, have you?"

I shook my head. Dex's lips pressed together, and for a moment he looked uneasy. But then his expression cleared.

"So . . . Mario Kart and Popsicles?"

I couldn't help but laugh. "Are you serious?"

"Why not?"

"Well, I haven't played that game in, like, five years."

"Which is your mistake, because I've been spending all that time practicing. So now I'll finally be able to take you down, Princess Peach."

"In your dreams."

I held the door wide, motioning for Dex to follow me inside. My dad kept a Wii in the cabinet under the TV, and years ago, Dex and I had spent many, many summer hours trying to beat each other at Mario Kart. When we'd gotten too good at the game, we added the Popsicle challenge, which necessitated either playing one-handed or risking brain freeze (both of which I was way better at handling than Dex). But I hadn't really touched the Wii since Dex and I stopped hanging out.

Dex turned the system on while I went to get two Popsicles from my dad's collection in the freezer.

"Grape still your favorite?" I called into the living room.

"You know it!"

Dex and I played while the afternoon wore on, and it was amazing how easy it was to lose myself in the game and forget the events of the day. Dex *had* gotten much better, and I found I had to concentrate to keep from losing (and from getting melted Popsicle all over the front of my shirt).

Eventually, I leaned back against the couch, spent.

"That was fun," Dex said, his eyes fixed on the controller in his hand.

"You know I let you win, right?"

"Yeah, and I appreciate it," Dex said without missing a beat. "Really makes up for all the times I let you win when we were kids."

"Oh, *please*," I said, and tossed my Popsicle stick at him.

Dex just barely dodged it. "Ah, now, *this* is the Penny I remember. Throwing garbage at me. Just like old times."

"Yeah, before you went and got all emo on me."

Dex reached down to get the stick from the floor and laid it carefully on the table. "Hey, I'm not the one who changed.

You're the one who started spending all your time with Reese and her drones."

"You used to like Reese, if I remember correctly."

I looked out the window at the darkening sky and the long stretch of lawn beneath it. We were in that same yard when an eleven-year-old Reese had dared Dex to kiss me. Which he did, even though we both knew it was *her* he wanted to be kissing.

"Not like *that*," Dex said, but I could see red creeping up the side of his neck and flashing across his cheeks. "And that was a long time ago. Before . . ." He trailed off.

I knew what it was before. Before Dex's dad left. After that, he started pulling away from me bit by bit, pouring more time into sci-fi movies and his Tumblr. And I wasn't exactly beating down his door to keep our friendship intact. I no longer wanted anything to do with make-believe. It made more sense to me to hang out with Reese in the land of the real; even if "real" meant obsessing over who sat where at our lunch table. Reese started making more noise about how weird Dex was getting, and I didn't fight her on it. I just . . . let him go.

"Well, things are different now," I said, trying to make my voice lighter. I stood up and started putting away the controllers.

"One more rematch?"

"Tempting. But I have plans."

"Really? *Law & Order* marathon?"

I turned my head sharply toward Dex. "How did you know . . . ?"

"I could hear the *duh-duh*s all the way over at my house."

"Oh. Well, no more TV for the night. I was invited to a party at Millers' barn."

Dex jumped straight off the couch, knocking the coffee table with his knee. He didn't even seem to notice.

"What? You can't go there!"

"Why not?"

Dex's mouth opened and closed a few times. I could see him struggling to choose his words.

"It's not safe."

I rolled my eyes. "Just because the football team gave you a few wedgies in the sixth grade . . ."

Dex waved his hand, impatient. "No, it's not that. I mean, yes, those guys are asshats, but Millers' barn, that's too close to where your dad—"

"And here I thought we were just having a nice time, *not* talking about my dad."

"No, wait. Please, listen," Dex started. He moved around the coffee table until he was standing in front of me, his hands out like I was a wild animal that might bolt at any moment. "Look, I know I told you I didn't think your dad was in trouble anymore, but that was just because you got so angry yesterday and I figured you wouldn't believe me until I found more proof."

I crossed my arms again and stared at him coldly. "So you lied?"

"Kinda."

I scoffed. "Of course. You *have* been hanging out with my dad, after all."

"What's that supposed to mean?"

"It means he's a liar. He lies, Dex. All the time. And about really dumb things, too."

"I don't think that's totally fair. Your dad knows the truth about a lot of weird stuff in this town. Even if no one believes him about the Visitors—"

I took a step closer, and Dex inched back, his hands still up between us.

"I'm only going to say this one more time. My dad did not get abducted by aliens. Because there are no aliens in Bone Lake. Aliens. Are. Not. Real," I said, getting louder on each word.

Dex's lips pressed tightly together. He exhaled loudly through his nose, as though he was trying to stay calm. Apparently, it didn't work. Because the next instant, he threw both of his hands up in the air.

"You can't possibly know that!" he burst out. "No one can know that. Do you have any idea how big the universe is? And how much we still don't know about it? I was reading this book the other day called *The World Unknown*, and the author says it's statistically likely that alien life has found its way to our planet at some point—"

"Oh my God, let me just interrupt you with all the ways I *do not care.*"

"How can you . . . not care?" Dex looked genuinely confused.

"Because there's already enough *actually* going on in our planet without having to make stuff up or think about what *might* be true! Have you ever read a newspaper? Do you know what's happening in the Ukraine right now? Or in Mexico City, or in our own freaking town? *That's* what's important, Dex. That's what I care about."

I didn't even realize I was yelling until I stopped and the room fell abruptly silent. I was breathing heavily, and so was Dex. His face was contorted in anger and concentration, like he was trying to decide just the right comeback. His eyes were fixed on me like I was the only thing in the room. I blinked and looked away, then took a step back, crossing my arms.

"Okay, let's just . . . agree to disagree," I said. "Sorry I got upset. Again." How was it possible Dex was able to get under my skin this much in one twenty-four-hour span? I didn't remember him being *this* annoying as a kid.

"I'm sorry, too," Dex said. "I'm just really worried about Ike."

I nodded. "I guess it is weird he hasn't called yet. How about this—if my dad doesn't turn up by tomorrow morning, we'll go to the police."

Dex shook his head. "I talked to the sheriff this morning."

That took me aback. "You did?"

"Yeah. I told him I thought something must have happened to Ike while he was chasing down this story. But he didn't believe me, either," Dex said. "I don't think the sheriff likes your dad very much."

I choked back a snort. Of course the sheriff would hate my dad, and I couldn't exactly blame him, either.

"I just need more evidence," Dex continued. "To convince him, and you. But in the meantime, you can't go out to that party tonight."

"And why not?"

"Over by the Millers' barn is where your dad found that body . . . the hiker."

The room seemed to dim for a moment. I didn't know what to say, as I imagined my dad stumbling through the woods with one of his cameras, coming across a shape in the leaves. . . .

"Oh."

Relief flooded into Dex's eyes, and I realized he was misinterpreting my reaction.

"I'm still going to the party, Dex."

He shook his head. "But—"

"It's horrible that my dad found a body. But that doesn't mean I'll be in danger tonight," I said. "Sometimes, hikers die in the woods. They get lost, they get hurt. . . ."

"That's not what happened to him. He was murdered."

"Really?" For a moment, I felt it—a flicker of fear.

"Well . . ." Dex took a deep breath. "The official report was an 'accidental fire,' but your dad swears it was more than that."

I exhaled. "I'm sure he does."

I reached out to grab my hoodie from its hook by the door. As I did, Dex quickly grabbed hold of my arm. I raised an eyebrow at him.

"Please, Penny. If anything happened to you, I'd . . ." Dex's voice wavered. He was looking into my eyes again, and for a moment, all I could focus on was the heat of his skin against mine, the pressure of his fingers around my arm. I was suddenly very curious to hear how he was going to finish that sentence.

"You'd what?" I asked.

A red flush began to crawl up Dex's neck. He looked down at his hand and seemed surprised to find it on my arm. He lifted his hand up quickly until it was clear of my skin.

"Your dad would never forgive me if I let you get hurt," Dex stammered, his eyes now averted from mine. "What would I tell him?"

And just like that, my curiosity vanished. "Tell him that I can make my own decisions. I've been doing it for years."

I pulled open the door and stepped out into the night, glancing back at Dex only long enough to see a look of surprise on his face. It felt satisfying to get in the last word, to get him back for only caring about my dad, to close the door hard between us. I walked quickly to where my bike stood on the lawn. The faster I could get away from that house, the better.

SEVEN

PARTY SOUNDS FLOATED down the two-lane highway as I pedaled harder and worried about sweating through my hoodie. I heard the rise and fall of the occasional call for more beer, the halfhearted laugh of a girl pretending to like a bad joke, and tinny music pumping through a speaker.

As I crested the hill, I saw the Millers' barn a few hundred yards away. It was tucked back from the main highway, down a small dirt road and nestled against the woods. Once owned by the Miller family, it'd been empty and crumbling for years. Far down at the other end of the hill was the hulking shadow of the abandoned plastics plant, looming like a distant specter at the edge of the makeshift party.

A fire was already crackling in a circular pit in front of the barn's faded wooden doors. About twenty-five high school kids surrounded the fire, some of them sitting close by on logs or old lawn chairs. A keg sat on the flatbed of someone's pickup truck.

I left my bike at the edge of the dirt road and walked closer to the party, nervously wiping my hands on my sweatshirt as I went. Micah was standing on the other side of the flames and talking with a girl with bright blond hair, whose back was to me. Micah said something, and I heard the girl's trilling laugh. She put her hand on Micah's arm, and on her finger was a single cherry-red Ring Pop. I sucked in a breath.

Reese had made Ring Pops a part of her signature style way back when we were still friends. At first, she just liked the taste of them. But then she started wearing them to school dances and to parties. When other girls started wearing Ring Pops, too, Reese should have been flattered. But instead she demanded that they stop. They all did.

The candy ring on Reese's hand was half-gone, and I could only imagine how red, red, red her lips would be when she angrily demanded I leave the party. If she deigned to speak to me at all, that is.

I steered quickly in the other direction, almost walking right into Emily Jennings. She was leaning against the side of the pickup truck, near the keg, with a phone in one hand and a full-to-the-brim red cup in the other. When she saw me, she grinned and jumped up, her brown bob bouncing around her chin, her drink sloshing over the edge of her cup and spilling to the dusty ground.

I could tell it wasn't her first drink of the night.

"Oh my God, Penny, is that you? You look so different!"

Emily came over and gave me a hug, and I had to duck a little to the right to avoid her sloshing drink.

"Hey, Emily. How've you been?"

"Good! I made senior cheerleading this year. Everyone thought I'd stay on the JV squad, but I've really been working on my high kicks—wanna see?"

"That's okay. I believe you."

"Also, my dad just fixed up this kick-ass speedboat. We're gonna take it out on the lake this summer." As Emily spoke, she moved her arms emphatically, dangerously close to sloshing her entire drink onto both our shoes. Still, I couldn't help but smile at her. Take away the cup of beer, and she was the exact same Emily Jennings I used to sit next to in the cafeteria in sixth grade.

"You should totally come with us!" Emily continued. "Do you water-ski? If not, it's okay. You can go tubing, too—"

"Emily," a sharp voice called out. Emily swung around to face a figure that was moving toward us, silhouetted against the flames. I went still.

"What are you doing?" Reese asked, stepping up to Emily and grabbing her arm.

"I was just saying hi to . . . oh." Emily's face fell, and she shot me an apologetic glance. "I forgot."

"You forgot?" Reese hissed. She wrinkled her nose at the boozy smell coming off Emily's breath. "Jesus, it's not even 10:00 p.m. Get it together, Em."

Emily's eyes remained fixed on the ground, like a puppy who knows it's done something wrong. Like I used to do whenever I said something that made Reese angry in middle school.

But that was a long time ago.

I stared in Reese's direction. "There's no need to talk to her like that," I said.

For a moment, Reese was completely motionless. Then, slowly, she turned her head to look at me. "I'm sorry, who even invited you here?"

Before I could respond, Micah stepped in, swinging one arm loosely around my shoulders. "You made it!"

Reese's eyes went wide and her jaw clamped shut, but only for a moment. By the time Micah looked over at her, she'd forced her features into a more relaxed expression.

"Micah, I didn't know you were still tight with Penny," Reese said, her voice carefully casual.

Emily, who looked completely confused by Reese's sudden personality shift, just lifted her cup up to her mouth and took a huge swallow.

"I ran into her today while I was hanging flyers. I know Penny only comes to town for the summers, so I figured I'd invite her out."

"And I figured I'd come," I said.

Reese's eyes flicked over to me briefly before she aimed another smile at Micah.

"That was really nice of you."

Micah shrugged and grinned that giant grin at me. Despite being the soberest person in the circle, I felt just a little wobbly.

"You know what they say," Micah continued. "*Mi* keg party *es su* keg party."

"Huh?" Emily asked. She pulled her empty cup down from her mouth.

"Here," Micah said, moving his arm from my shoulder and taking Emily's empty cup. "How about I get us all another round?"

"I'll help," I said quickly, eager to get away from Reese.

I walked with Micah to the pickup truck, and could feel Reese's eyes boring into my back the whole way. It occurred to me that things between us might get even more unpleasant now that she'd started speaking to me again.

So that was something to look forward to.

"What'll it be?" Micah asked, climbing into the truck bed and then reaching back to help me up. He pointed to the keg and to a couple of half-empty fifths. "Cheap beer or cheap liquor?"

"Beer, please."

He filled up a cup and handed it to me, and I nervously brought it up to my lips. I'd never been to a bonfire party before, but when I was younger I'd heard about the kinds of things that happened at them. These parties had been going on for years, for longer than I could guess. In fact, the very truck I was standing in was likely passed down from someone's father; it had probably seen more partying than any of the kids standing around the fire.

Like a lot of small towns in northern Michigan, Bone Lake didn't have a ton of places for high school students to hang out. A couple of gas stations, a couple of fast-food restaurants, a movie theater thirty miles away. It was completely different from what I had grown used to in the Chicago suburb of Evanston, with my overstuffed academic schedule and extracurricular activities. When my friends and I wanted to hang out on the weekends, we could go to concerts or comedy shows in the city. But our trips downtown were closely monitored. Our parents weren't just afraid of us doing drugs; they were afraid of us getting mugged, kidnapped, run over by the El train. My mom drove me most places and strictly enforced my curfew. It wasn't that my friends and I had never tried sneaking drinks before, but it was riskier, less tempting, and easier to get caught.

In Bone Lake, the rules were different. As kids, we weren't afraid of being kidnapped by strangers because, well, Bone Lake *had* no strangers. We'd traipse through the woods unattended, run around all day in roving packs, come home at sundown or even later. We grew up knowing that no matter where we went, we were safe, and never that far from home.

Of course, we also grew up bored. Hence, the parties in the woods, in someone's backyard, at the beach, near an abandoned barn. The location changed, but it was always the same party. Not that I'd ever had the chance to go to one. Back when we all still lived together as a family in Bone Lake, my mom would warn me about the parties and tell me I'd better not ever be caught at one when I got to high school. But it wasn't the drinking or the drugs that offended her. "I expect you to have a little more imagination than that, Penny," she used to say.

Her voice was in my head as I raised the red cup to my mouth. But it was soon replaced by Micah's.

"So it must kind of suck for you to have to come back here every summer," he said.

"What? No, it just, um . . ."

"Sucks."

I laughed awkwardly.

"Don't worry," Micah continued. He leaned in and faux-whispered, "I don't think it's a secret that there's not a lot going on around here."

I could feel his breath on my face when he leaned in, but it was brief. He sat up against one edge of the pickup truck bed, and I took the other side.

"So what do you do for fun in Chicago?"

I shrugged. "I write for the school paper."

"And that's fun?"

"I think so."

Micah smiled, and I felt myself smiling back. I knew my main objective should be getting him to open up to me about his dad and what had happened at the plant, but I couldn't really think of a way to steer the conversation in that direction. Or maybe I didn't want to, not yet.

"Chicago's just a place, really," I said, sticking to an easier topic instead. "Just like any other place. It has more people, I guess."

"But it's *Chicago*," he said. "It's got the Bulls, the nightlife, the food—"

"It does have great pizza."

Micah grinned. Then he looked down at his drink, and his face fell a couple of inches. "Man, I'd love to live somewhere like that."

"You can in, what, a year?" I said. "When you graduate, you can go wherever you want."

Micah kept his eyes down. "Yeah," he said, but his voice was low. "A year seems like a long time, though."

"I get that. I'm ready to be at Northwestern, like, yesterday."

Micah looked up again, all traces of sadness gone. He smiled. "Northwestern, huh? I got a recruitment letter from them."

"Really?"

"Hey, don't act so surprised," he said. "I'm not a *total* idiot."

"I know that! I didn't mean . . ." I sputtered.

"Relax," Micah said, grinning. "Just giving you a hard time."

And I *did* relax as I looked at the firelight reflecting off

Micah's face. I took another small sip from my cup. It was nice how calming it felt to be around Micah. My stomach butterflies still gave the occasional flutters, but overall, being with him was . . . pretty easy.

Still smiling, Micah stretched his leg out so his foot was right next to mine, and then he tapped the toe of his shoe against my sneaker. *Tap, tap.* Pause. *Tap, tap.* This felt different, somehow, from the way he'd hugged me outside of Hector's or the way he'd thrown an arm over my shoulder when I got to the party. Micah always had that effortless familiarity with everyone. But this, this *tap, tap* against my foot, it was something else. Something deliberate.

I felt my whole body get warmer. For a moment I wondered if the bonfire had grown bigger, large enough for its flames to heat me up way over here at the far edge of the circle. But when I looked at it, it was the same size as when I'd arrived. I took another sip from my cup.

I forced myself not to look at Micah's foot, still resting against my own. I cleared my throat. "Do you think you might go? To Northwestern?"

Micah shrugged. "It's a Big Ten, but I don't know. . . . Even if I get a partial scholarship, my mom can't really help that much."

I nodded. Tale as old as time.

"Been thinking about MSU, maybe. Bryan and I were talking about both going there. . . ."

Micah trailed off, his smile slipping from his face again.

"I'm sure he's okay," I said, hugging my arms to my chest. "Probably just took a road trip, right?"

"Yeah, well, that's the thing," Micah said, running a hand through his hair. "Apparently, the cops searched Bryan's and Cassidy's places, and nothing from their rooms was missing."

I lowered my cup, sitting up straighter. "What do you mean, nothing?"

"I mean they didn't take any clothes with them. No suitcases, nothing. Isn't that weird? If they were just going on a trip without telling anyone?"

Yes. It was weird. If it was true, it was very weird.

"It still doesn't necessarily mean something bad happened," I said, though in my mind I was picturing a truck mangled at the bottom of a ravine, a boat tipped over in Lake Michigan, Bryan and Cassidy wandering lost through the woods in the Upper Peninsula. Another image popped into my head—the strange picture on my dad's phone, the flash of light and the armlike branches—but I quickly pushed it away.

"Maybe it was a spur-of-the-moment thing, and they bought clothes wherever they were going," I said, trying to sound convincing.

Micah nodded his head slightly, like he was considering. "That could be." He took a sip of his drink, and then he nodded harder, his face brightening a little. "Yeah, it could definitely be. Bryan was always talking about how sometimes he felt like he just had to get out of this place. Maybe he just . . ."

"Took off."

"Yeah. Yeah, maybe."

Micah smiled again. I could sense an opportunity to ask for an interview rising up; Bryan and Cassidy wanting to get out of town was right in line with the heart of my article—how Bone Lake was an economic black hole sucking even its most promising residents down into the muck. I could ask Micah more about his own limited prospects, about his mom's finances, about his dad. . . .

But again, I didn't want to. The moment just didn't feel right. I didn't want to see Micah sad right now, or hear that bleak tone in his voice. Instead, I just wanted to see that smile on his face, the smile that made the air feel ten degrees warmer. I wanted to be the one who kept it there.

This time, I lightly tapped the toe of my shoe against his.

Micah's smile stretched farther.

"It's really not *so* bad here," I said, taking another sip of my drink. "I can think of a few nice things, anyway."

Micah's grin returned fully, and my stomach flipped. He tapped my foot back.

"Yeah? Like what, city girl?"

"Like . . ."

Tap. Tap. Tap.

"Yo, Micah!"

Micah pulled his foot back abruptly and looked over at a

kid in a letterman jacket who was calling him. I recognized the red hair and freckles of Kevin Abnair.

"Stop flirting and come play flip cup," Kevin called. His face twisted up into a half grin that looked like a leer in the firelight.

I felt my face heat up as I pulled my own abandoned foot back to my side of the truck. Micah flashed me a sheepish smile and hopped off the truck bed.

"Looks like I'm needed. Talk later?"

I nodded, hoping that he couldn't see my flushed cheeks in the darkness.

I wandered around the outskirts of the party for a few more minutes, wondering if there was anyone else here Reese hadn't forbidden to talk to me. Two girls I remembered, Jen B and Jen H, both averted their eyes when they saw me coming. I looked around for Emily and saw Dylan Rosen, another football player, hook his arm around her waist and whisper in her ear. She giggled and followed him back to the edge of the party and into the tree line.

I sat on a vacant log, nursed my same red cup of beer, and pretended to text on my phone. After a few minutes, I felt someone sit down on the other end of the log. I looked over, and Reese was staring me down, her jaw clenched. Her Ring Pop–stained lips looked comically red in the firelight.

"Okay, seriously? Are you just going to glare at me every time I see you for the rest of our lives?" I asked, turning to face her.

"I'm trying to make a point. That you're not welcome here. Was that not clear?"

I breathed through my nose, trying to push down the rising anger. I motioned to Micah, who was standing near the barn. "Some people seem to think differently."

Reese snorted. "Please. Micah's overly nice to everyone. He can't help it—it's like a nervous tic or something. But he wouldn't give you the time of day if he knew what you are."

"And what is that?"

Reese's eyes became tiny slits. "A lying attention whore."

I breathed out, wishing I was anywhere else in the world other than on that log. Reese stared at me until I forced my eyes away.

"Admit it," she said, sliding closer.

I shook my head.

"Just admit out loud that you're a liar, that you love attention, and I'll leave you alone. All summer."

I considered it; I honestly did. I'd forgotten how potent Reese's anger could be when she turned it on full blast. One time in sixth grade, Stacey Fenick told everyone in the girls' locker room that her brother had seen "Reese's pieces," and that he'd been "unimpressed." It only took two weeks for Reese to turn almost every girl in the sixth grade class against Stacey. We were all instructed to ice her out, to ignore her when she talked to us, to chew our gum and stick it in the handle of her locker every morning. And we all did it, too. Everyone knew not to cross Reese.

So I did consider it, just saying the words *I'm a liar* out loud. Maybe Reese would stop glaring at me whenever we passed by each other; maybe she would go back to leaving me alone. . . .

But I couldn't do it. I thought of my dad, of all his lies. I never wanted to live my life that way. The truth was always better than a lie—no matter what that lie might be, no matter how good it might sound, or how many problems it might fix. Reese could do whatever she wanted to me, but she wasn't going to force me to say something that wasn't true.

I turned around and looked her straight in the eye.

"I'm not a liar."

Reese's eyes widened with disbelief. She opened her mouth to respond, but her words were drowned out by a loud, piercing scream.

We both turned our heads toward the direction of the scream—the woods behind the barn. I jumped off the log and followed a few of the others who were moving toward the noise. The screams continued—it was definitely a girl, and she sounded terrified.

I moved quickly to the woods, briefly catching Micah's eye as he headed there, too. His face was tight with worry.

We moved past the first line of trees, following the sounds of the screams. After a few feet, the concerned murmurs of the kids back at the party were swallowed up by the woods. We were in pure darkness, a place where the glow of the fire didn't reach.

A bright, whitish light bounced against the ground and trees in front of us. Over the sounds of the girl screaming, I could hear someone trying to calm her down.

Then the light shifted and I recognized what it was—the focused beam of a flashlight app from a cell phone. It moved up from the ground and into the terrified, openmouthed face of Emily Jennings.

Dylan Rosen had hold of her arm, and he was trying to get her to stop screaming. His method of shaking her and saying, "Stop, stop," over and over didn't seem to be working.

"Dylan, what . . . ?" Micah said.

As I moved closer, I could smell something horrible, but couldn't exactly place it. It smelled like something burned, but also like . . . meat?

I went over and put a hand on Emily's shoulder. She immediately crumpled into me and started to hiccup as she gulped for air. "I thought . . . it was . . . a person."

Dylan swung his arm around, maneuvering the phone so that its light hit the ground a few feet away from us. I gasped.

There, lying in the dirt and leaves, was a body. It was completely blackened, as if it'd been thoroughly burned. At first glance, it almost did look like a human torso that was missing its arms and legs. Only when I stared closely at its head did I see the elongated nose, the tiny nubs of horns. It was a deer, completely charred. Under its cracked, blackened hide and skin were a reddish interior and glints of bone. It smelled as though it'd been lying there for some time.

"It's okay," I managed to say to Emily, who was still struggling to catch her breath.

Dylan turned to Micah, his features grim. "What the hell happened to it?"

Micah's eyes were glued to the dead deer. He slowly shook his head.

The deer's face had been completely burned, but somehow its eyes remained, big and round as black marbles. It seemed to be looking over our shoulders, as though it were staring transfixed at something in the woods beyond, something it was still scared of, even in death.

I SHOT STRAIGHT up in bed, my heart beating fast. For a moment I thought I was hearing Emily's screams again. But it was just the phone, ringing in the next room.

I stumbled out of bed, grabbing the now-warm glass of water on my nightstand and taking a gulp. There was a putrid taste in my mouth, probably a remnant of the cheap beer I'd drunk the night before. I trudged into the kitchen and picked up my dad's old landline.

"Hello?" My voice came out both groggy and cracked.

"Yeah, is Ike there?"

"Oh, uh . . . no," I said, leaning back against the wall. A faint pounding noise was drumming at the base of my skull—drinking that water so quickly might have been a bad idea.

“Who is this?” the gruff, impatient voice on the other end of the phone asked.

“This is his daughter. Who is this?”

“His editor,” the voice barked.

I closed my eyes against the light streaming in through the kitchen window.

“Do you know where he is?” the voice continued. I heard the light clicking sound of typing on the other end of the line.

“He’s been gone a couple of days. I think he’s out working on a story.”

“He’d better not still be working on it. His column was due three days ago.”

“Oh, well . . .” I struggled to think around the pounding in my head. “He’s not here, so . . .”

The gruff editor exhaled loudly into the phone. “Tell him Mac called, and that he better get his ass in gear. No more excuses. Got it?”

“Got it.”

Mac hung up without saying goodbye. The dial tone sounded like a horn, piercing its way into my skull. I quickly put the phone back on its cradle. It wasn’t weird for my dad to flake out on me for work. But for him to flake out on work, too? That was odd. A shiver of worry ran down my spine. What if Dad had been out chasing a story, and he’d gotten into some kind of accident? I remembered the scenarios I’d pictured the night before about Bryan and Cassidy. I saw them again, but this time with Dad's mangled truck in place of Bryan's. Dad lost in the woods . . .

Stop it, I thought to myself, shaking my head. No good would come from imagining the grisliest, worst-case scenario. Jumping to the most sensational conclusion was straight out of Dad's playbook, not mine. In almost every situation, a bear was just a bear, nothing more. And in this case, the most likely scenario was still that Dad got caught up chasing some story and forgot to charge his phone—or forgot to call at all.

I checked my cell again—still no word from Dad. But there was a text.

> Hey Penny. Nice talking to you last night. Except for the whole deer thing, haha. Hang soon?

Micah had asked for my number after driving me (and my bike) home from the party the night before, pretty much right after we found the deer. I composed three texts and deleted them before sending a simple smiley face and a *yeah, ok.* Then I brushed my teeth, swallowed two aspirin, and took a shower, which helped to make me feel a little bit more alive.

I had a quick breakfast of stale potato chips, then threw my shoes on and rode my bike over to Sweet Street. Dex was already inside, opening up the shop. As soon as I opened the main door, his head snapped up out of the ice-cream case, and the metal scooper he was holding dropped to the ground with a clatter.

"Hey. What are you doing here?"

"Your mom asked me to help out today."

"Oh. Right."

I walked around the edge of the ice-cream counter and into the back room to get an apron. Dex followed, his face pulled into an expression of concern.

"So, are you okay?"

I pulled the apron over my head and tied it behind my back. "Got a pretty bad headache, but other than that . . ."

"I heard what happened. With the deer."

"You heard it? Where?"

Dex waved his hand impatiently. "Heard it, saw it on Snapchat, whatever."

"Someone *posted* it?" I asked, incredulous.

Dex just shrugged. I moved past him, looking under the sink to see if the fresh napkins were in the same place they used to be when I was a kid. They were. I pulled out the napkins and headed to the counter again. Dex followed.

"It was the big news of the night. Well, aside from Emily puking in Jen B's car. That was posted, too."

"Gross." I sighed and started refilling the dented silver napkin dispenser that sat on top of the ice-cream counter.

"But you actually saw the deer? In person?"

"Unfortunately."

"Oh man. Oh man, oh man." Dex ran one hand through his hair, once again making it stick straight up from his head.

"What now?"

"I have to show you something."

With that, Dex spun on his heel and raced into the back room.

"Wait!" I called after him. "Aren't you going to help me open the store?"

I heard the back door slam shut. At the same moment, the front door opened and a woman shuffled in. She was barely clearing five feet, even in her sturdy heels. She wore a blue housedress over sweatpants and was carrying a large purple quilted purse.

"Hi, Mrs. Anderson," I called out, pitching my voice higher. Mrs. Anderson had been forgetting to turn on her hearing aids since I was a kid.

"Penny!" She screamed across the room. "Shouldn't you be in school?"

"It's summer, Mrs. Anderson."

She turned and looked out the window, widening her eyes in mock surprise. "Well, look at that. You're right." She grinned as she came up to the counter.

"How have you been?"

"Oh, lovely, lovely." Mrs. Anderson reached across the counter and patted my hand lightly with her own. She was one of the oldest living people in Bone Lake—my dad claimed that she'd babysat *his* mom once upon a time.

"One scoop of Superman ice cream, please," she said.

"You got it."

I took a small Styrofoam bowl from under the counter and

began scooping the blue, pink, and yellow ice cream into it. As I placed the bowl into Mrs. Anderson's small hands, an idea occurred to me. Mrs. Anderson hadn't been on my list of potential interview subjects because she had no direct connection to the plastics plant or its closing, but she *had* lived in this town longer than almost anyone else.

"Can I ask you something, Mrs. Anderson?"

"Sure," she responded brightly, handing me a folded, slightly torn five-dollar bill.

"I'm writing a news story . . . for school . . . and it's all about Bone Lake—"

"Well, how nice! Just like your dad?"

My jaw tightened as I rang up the ice cream and handed Mrs. Anderson her change. "Not exactly."

Mrs. Anderson didn't say anything, but I thought I noticed the corners of her mouth pull up slightly in a smile. She took a large bite of the ice cream, not even bothering to wipe off the blue streaks it left at the edges of her mouth.

I didn't have a notebook with me, but I pulled a napkin from the dispenser and a pen from a cup next to the cash register. "I'm writing my story on the plastics plant, and the effects its closing have had on Bone—on our town. Do you remember anything about the plant closing? About the accident?"

Mrs. Anderson looked off to the side, her cup of ice cream dropping a few inches. "I remember the accident. Tragic. How sad that was. Human error, they said."

"Who said?"

"Who said what?"

"Um . . . maybe let's try getting a bit more specific. Do you remember what you were doing when you found out about the accident? Or what happened that day?"

Mrs. Anderson looked off to the side again, as if trying to remember. Her eyes unfocused a bit. "It was very sad, I remember that. But it's best not to think too much about it."

My hand jerked, tearing a small hole into the napkin.

"What was that?" I whispered, my heart thudding in my chest.

"Dear, are you okay?" Mrs. Anderson leaned in, so close I could smell the ice cream sweetness of her breath.

I nodded, straightening. I moved my hand away from the napkin hole and continued writing Mrs. Anderson's words—*it's best not to think too much about it*. The exact same thing Cindy and Hector had both said. Two people were a coincidence. But three?

"Are you sure you're okay?"

"Um, yeah," I said, struggling to regain composure. "So . . . what else can you remember about that time in general?" I asked, trying to keep my voice level. "Were people angry that the plant closed?"

"*Angry* is a pretty harsh word, I think."

"Uh, okay. Do you think the town has changed much since it happened?"

"Well, we lost all that business," Mrs. Anderson said. "But we carry on, you know. And now here we are."

I sighed and then forced myself to smile.

"Thanks, Mrs. Anderson," I said, tucking the napkin into my pocket. "That's . . . really helpful."

Mrs. Anderson smiled, dropped a quarter into the tip jar, and winked at me. As she took another bite of the ice cream, she closed her eyes, savoring it as she headed out the front door.

I ran my finger over the edge of the napkin in my pocket. *It's best not to think too much about it.* Had the whole town gotten together and decided to collectively suppress one of its biggest tragedies? That seemed ridiculous, a conspiracy on par with something Dad would make up. But that line—it wasn't just similar, it was verbatim.

It's best not to think too much about it.

But why?

Before I could sort through any plausible theories, I heard a light shuffling noise coming from the kitchen. I headed that way and saw Dex pacing by the open back door. He held a piece of paper in one hand, and he was mouthing something too low for me to hear.

"Are you talking to someone?" I asked.

Dex jumped. "Oh, uh . . . just you. Sort of."

"What?"

"I mean, I wasn't talking to *you*. More the you in my head."

Dex ran one hand through his hair and scrunched up his face in discomfort. "I was trying to run through ways to say this without you getting mad."

I leaned against the kitchen doorjamb, torn between being annoyed and wanting to laugh. "Did you find one?"

"No."

Dex loped over to me, then thrust the piece of paper into my hands. It was thick and folded into quarters. "Look at this."

I looked closer at the paper, which had *March 2018* scribbled onto the top corner in my dad's handwriting. I straightened.

"Where did you get this?"

"Your dad's office."

I fixed a glare on Dex. "And how, exactly, did you get into his office?"

Dex bit his lip. "Uh . . . okay, so here's the part where you might get mad."

"I'm listening."

"Yesterday, when we were playing video games, you got up to go to the bathroom, and I kinda . . . stepped into Ike's office. Just to look around—"

"And steal his stuff?"

"I just wanted to see if there was a clue, or something. This was lying right on top of his safe. I heard you coming back before I could look at it, so I just . . . stuffed it in my pocket."

My hands tightened around the edge of the paper. "If you

wanted to see my dad's office, you could have asked. You didn't have to skulk around."

"I figured if I asked you'd say no."

"Dex," I started, my voice rising again, "You can't just come over and take what you want from our house." A small, unpleasant thought wiggled up through my brain. "Wait, is that the whole reason you came over yesterday?"

"No! I also wanted to hang out. Trust me."

I held up the folded paper. *"Trust you?"*

"I'm sorry! I really am. Just . . . just look at it. Please, that's all I'm asking."

In that moment, I didn't want to give Dex a single thing he wanted. But with every second, my curiosity about the paper grew stronger. I already knew I wanted to see what it was. I gritted my teeth and unfolded it.

On the other side of the paper was a blown-up color photo. It took a moment for my brain to process the image, but when it did, I sucked in a breath. I was staring down, once again, at charred remains. A body was lying on the ground, only instead of lying on fresh leaves and dirt, it was surrounded by melting snow. And in place of missing deer legs, it had two legs, two arms, and a head. A human head.

I thrust the image back at Dex.

"What the hell is this?"

"It's a picture of the body your dad found. The hiker in the woods."

I took a step back from Dex and the piece of paper. But I could still see it, upside-down and charred black. A human man. I could even make out his fingers. . . .

"It looks exactly like—"

"The deer? I know. That's what worries me."

I shook my head. "I don't understand."

Dex gently folded the paper up again and set it down on the counter. He took an eager half step toward me. "This is what set your dad off on his new story. He found this body in the woods and took a photo. The cops ruled it an accidental death, but your dad thought they were wrong, or they were covering something up. Like I told you the other day."

"I remember. It sounded like my dad was trying to make a story out of nothing. Again. Or did he have an actual reason this time?"

"There was a reason." Dex bit his lip and looked back at the folded piece of paper. It seemed as though he wanted to open it up again, but another glance at my face convinced him not to. "Did you notice anything unusual? In the picture?"

"Aside from the dead body?"

"The body was burned, and burned completely. Thoroughly. If the hiker had accidentally started a fire that got out of control, then where was the fire? Why were no trees around him burned? Your dad said he looked all around where the body was found and couldn't find a trace of anything else that had been burned."

I put my hand up to my forehead. The pounding was coming back with a vengeance. I couldn't get the image from the photo out of my head.

"The deer . . ." I finally managed. "There was no trace of a fire around it, either. I mean, it was dark, but I didn't see anything else that was burned."

Dex nodded vigorously, as if this proved his point. "I know. When you said you saw the deer last night, I knew I had to show this to you. Even if it meant you'd get mad at me for taking it. It's just too big a coincidence to ignore."

"I don't know, Dex. Two fires in the woods? It's not *that* big a coincidence."

Dex shook his head. "You're not listening. There *was* no fire. At least not where the bodies were found. If something killed that hiker, it placed the body there. Maybe the deer, too."

"Some*thing*?" I leaned heavily against the ice-cream case and shook my head. "You still think it's aliens."

"Maybe. I don't know. That's what your dad thought."

But the way he said it, I could tell that's what Dex thought, too.

"There was another picture," Dex said, talking quickly as if trying to spit all his words out before I could shoot them down. "The one I mentioned to you when I picked you up from the airport? *That's* the photo I was looking for in Ike's office, but I couldn't find it. He showed it to me once, though. It was of this . . . okay, I won't say *alien*. But this *creature*, glowing in the woods—"

"I saw it."

"You did?" Dex's expression turned eager.

"Yeah, but it's not a picture of an alien, Dex. It's a tree branch, caught in a flash of light. An overexposed photo, or a flashlight glare." I sighed, trying to make my voice gentle. "Whatever's going on here, it's not aliens. I don't know what happened to this hiker or the deer, but I'm sure there's a perfectly reasonable explanation. Have you ever heard of Occam's razor? The simplest explanation—"

"Is often the truest one," Dex said, rolling his eyes. "Of course I've heard it. Do you *know* how many times I've watched *X-Files*?"

"Um, no. But I do believe in the simplest explanation. When you hear hoofbeats, think horses, not zebras."

Or when you hear growling in the woods, think bear, not Bigfoot, I thought, but didn't say.

"Okay, but sometimes it *is* zebras. Or a recording of hoofbeats. Or something else weird. The simplest answer isn't *always* the true one."

I groaned, rubbing the palms of my hands against my temples. Talking with Dex was more frustrating than trying to argue with a wall. A wall that believes in aliens.

"Okay," Dex said, putting his hands up in submission. "Okay, let's take a step back. Forget about aliens for a second.

Let's say some*one* did this. Someone killed this hiker. Burned him and left him in the woods. And your dad went out looking for clues to find that someone. And now he's missing."

Suddenly, I found it a bit hard to breathe. I couldn't stop picturing the charred deer with its glassy black eyes. The dead hiker's burned body. Those were very real things—not just hypothetical visions of Dad's truck wrapped around a tree, but real dangers he'd likely been out chasing. And he was still out there, somewhere.

Black dots swam at the corners of my vision.

"Penny? You okay?" Dex's voice sounded faraway.

"I need air."

I rushed past Dex and out the front of the store. Once I got outside, I took large lungfuls of breath, urging those images out of my brain.

Dex came outside and stood by me. He pressed his lips together but didn't say anything.

"Okay, so . . . let's say you're right, Dex. Maybe Dad is out looking into this whole thing right now. Maybe . . . maybe something's even happened to him," I finally said. "Not aliens, obviously. But . . . something potentially bad."

"Potentially really, really bad. Like I said."

"Still, I don't want to start going down that road until I rule out every other possibility first. You don't get to the truth by making wild assumptions and then trying to prove they're true. You start by asking the right people the right questions."

Dex let out a relieved sigh. "Okay. So, how do we do that?"

I took a deep breath. "If my dad did take off, to chase this story or for another reason, there's one other person in town he might have told."

"Who?"

I looked across the street, to Vinny's Bar. Its front door was closed, its *OPEN* sign still dark. But I knew there was already someone inside. Someone who might know exactly where my dad had gone. Even if I really didn't want to ask her.

"Julie Harper."

NINE

THE HEAVY WOODEN doors at the front of Vinny's Bar were decades old and covered from top to bottom in scratches and dents. I knew what I had to do, but I struggled to reach out and grab the door handle. Instead, I bounced up and down on the balls of my feet and looked around the mostly empty street. I was stalling. Three soft thudding sounds pulled my attention back across the street. Dex was standing on the other side of Sweet Street's big front window, knocking on the glass. He made *go on* hand gestures and gave me an encouraging smile.

Go on. Right.

After all, wasn't this just another interview, really? I'd asked people hard questions before for the school newspaper. Julie Harper was just another person. I straightened my shoulders and pulled open the door of the bar quickly, before I could change my mind.

Inside, it was dark and quiet. Very little light came in through the main windows, and the single-room bar area was lit by a handful of overhead lamps. A few worn booths and tables were scattered on the right side of the room, along with some pool tables and a jukebox. The wood-paneled walls were hung with Red Wings posters. A long wooden bar and stools took up the left side.

I made my way over to the bar and hoisted myself up on one of the stools. The bartender was a man I vaguely recognized, though I couldn't remember his name. He was older, with silver sideburns and a handlebar mustache. His muscles practically busted out of his faded Zeppelin T-shirt.

"Diet or regular?" he growled.

"Uh, excuse me?"

One bushy eyebrow rose a half centimeter. "I know you ain't twenty-one, and our kitchen's not open yet. If you sit at the bar, you gotta order. So will it be diet pop or will it be regular?"

"Oh," I said, swallowing hard. I darted my eyes past the bartender to the door leading off to the kitchen, wondering if Julie might pop her head out at any second. "I'm actually here to see Julie. . . . Is she at work yet?"

The bartender blinked but didn't move.

"And I'll have a diet, I guess."

The bartender reached for a glass in a steady, unhurried

movement and started to pour my drink. Over his shoulder, he said, "Julie's balancing the books. I'll tell her you're here." He pushed a full glass of pop across the bar at me. "One fifty."

I put two dollars on the bar, and the bartender scooped it up and pushed through the door leading into the kitchen. The anxiety in my stomach was growing by the second, and the pop tasted acidic as it slid down my throat. I couldn't forget the last time I'd gone through that door behind the bar, even though I'd tried. Many times.

It was the summer after seventh grade, and I was supposed to be spending the night at Reese's house. But after ordering pizza and watching movies, we'd gotten bored and decided to take our bikes for a midnight ride. No one was there to stop us or tell us it was too late to ride around the empty streets; Reese's dad was working late and her mom was closing down the bar.

So we got on our bikes and started riding around the neighborhood in our pajamas, giddy to be doing something we weren't supposed to be doing. We were rounding the corner onto the nearly empty Main Street when Reese bounced off the curb and toppled onto the pavement. If she'd been wearing a T-shirt and jeans, she might have gotten off with a few light scrapes, but her thin nightgown didn't provide any protection. Every part of her skin that hit pavement—elbows, hips, knees—was torn.

Reese screamed with the shock of the fall, but after that she went silent. I could see her pain in the ghostly whiteness of her face. Blood trickled through the newly formed holes in her skin, and I didn't know what to do. So I set Reese on the curb and ran to where I knew I could find the nearest adult—Vinny's Bar.

The bar was dark and empty, and all of its chairs were flipped over on top of the tables as if someone had walked away in the middle of mopping. But the kitchen light was still on, and I heard a woman's laugh. I wove my way behind the bar and through the kitchen, past wiped-down stainless steel counters and cardboard boxes full of bottles. The sound of the woman's laughter got louder as I neared the office.

I put my shoulder against the door and pushed it open without thinking. But when I crossed the threshold, I froze.

Julie was standing in front of her desk, her back to me. Her blouse was untucked and her hair tumbled wild down her back. Her face was pressed up against a man's, but she pulled back and turned at the sound of my entrance, and she gasped. I did, too.

The man she was kissing was my dad.

The three of us stood silent for a moment, our mouths all hanging open. I remember waiting for them to give me an explanation for what I was seeing, waiting for them to say the words that would put the image to rights in my mind. *It's not what it looks like.* Or, *Wait, just let me explain. . . .*

But neither of them said anything. Julie backed away, wiping smudges of lipstick from her mouth with the back of her hand.

My dad sighed and put his hands to his temple.

The first thing I was able to feel after shock was the hot rush of betrayal. But it wasn't betrayal at their actions, which my brain was slowly beginning to process. It was betrayal at their *lack* of a reaction. They were the adults. They were the ones who were supposed to say something in this moment, something that would make everything make sense. But they didn't, and the seconds dragged on.

Finally, my dad stood up straight and looked me in the eyes for the first time.

"What are you doing here?"

I felt something heavy falling down through my chest as I looked at my dad then, something that I hadn't felt since that day a couple of years earlier when he'd tried to pass off a black bear as Bigfoot. Disappointment so total I didn't have a word for it.

"Penelope? Why are you here?"

"It's Reese," I said. "She crashed her bike outside, and she's bleeding."

"Oh my God," Julie said. "Where is she?" She was tucking her shirt back in as she ushered me out the door. I didn't even spare my dad a backward glance as I followed her through the bar's kitchen.

After telling Julie where she could find Reese, I biked back home alone, let myself into the darkened house, and went straight to my bedroom. I tossed and turned. I wondered what

I would say to my dad, whether or not I should tell my mom. I hated the thought of lying to her, but I was terrified of where the truth might lead. If Dad was kissing Julie Harper, did that mean my parents would split up? Then what would happen? I was still awake as the sun crept out over the edge of the tree line through my window, and suddenly I knew what I had to do. It was so clear, so blindingly obvious. I had to talk to the one person in the world who knew me best, the one person who would help me understand what to do next. I had to talk to my best friend.

Reese was lying propped up in her bed when I got to her house the next morning. Her right arm and right leg were heavily bandaged, and there were even some angry red rash marks against the right side of her face. She looked miserable and hot, lying on top of her comforter and sucking on a red Ring Pop, strands of her thin blond hair matted to the sides of her face.

"How are you?" I asked, as I sat gingerly on the edge of her bed.

Reese shrugged. "Crappy. But I look worse than I feel. That's what my mom says, anyway."

For a second, Reese looked so small and vulnerable lying there on her bed that I wondered whether or not I should tell her what I saw. But then she pulled the sucker out of her mouth with a popping noise and grinned.

"Way to leave me in the middle of the road, by the way."

I smiled back, and my confidence returned. This was

Reese—strong, capable Reese. If anyone could help me figure out what to do, it would be her.

So I cleared my throat and started talking. Reese was both riveted and horrified, her eyes never leaving my face as I explained what I'd seen in the office of Vinny's Bar. When I was done, she swung her legs over the edge of her bed, wincing only slightly as she did so.

"I have to tell my dad. Right now."

I gulped. "You think?"

"Absolutely. Are you kidding? And you have to tell your mom, too. This is ridiculous. How could they just . . . ? Ugh."

Reese's face twisted up into disgust. That's when we formulated our plan. She'd go to the bar and confront her parents together, and I'd go home and talk to mine. We'd meet back up later that night to discuss how it went. That was the plan.

But things didn't exactly go down that way.

When I told my mom what I'd seen, she stood absolutely still for three seconds before her whole face tightened in anger. But I didn't know if her anger was because the affair was news to her, or because I had seen it. I think she might have suspected that something was going on—or maybe even known—but I never had the guts to ask her, not that day or since.

It was, my mom said, the final motivation she needed to get out of Bone Lake once and for all. When she told my dad that, the two of them started to fight—really fight—in a way I hadn't seen before. It was as though they didn't care that I was there and could hear every word they were saying. They didn't go down into the basement or the backyard to try to put distance between me and their words.

At first, they argued about me. My dad said there was "no way in hell" she was taking me away from him, and my mom responded that he hadn't really been there for me in years, anyway. He was always off researching a story or on one of his camping trips. He accused her of jumping on "a nothing kiss" as an excuse to finally abandon him and leave for somewhere "better," something she likely would have done years before—if it hadn't been for me.

I sat on the front stoop of our house, covering my ears lightly with my hands. My stomach curled up in knots, and I wanted more than anything else to not be hearing the things they were saying. I pulled myself up off the wooden stoop and rode my bike fast to Reese's house. When Reese opened the door a couple of inches, and her light blue eyes stared at me through the cracks, I could tell something was wrong.

"Reese, are you okay? What happened?"

Reese just stared at me for a moment. The right side of her face was still scratched up, red and angry. It had started to scab.

"I thought you were my best friend," she said, even and cool.

I shook my head. "What? I am. What do you—"

"How could you do that to me, if you're my best friend? I just don't understand." And that's when I heard it, the hitch in her voice, as though she was swallowing back tears.

"Do what?"

"So you're going to deny it? That you just made up this humongous lie and tried to hurt my family for no reason?"

My brain spun as I tried to make sense of her words.

But Reese was just picking up steam. "What is wrong with you, anyway? Why would you do that?"

I shook my head. "I didn't do anything. I saw your mom and my dad. . . . Didn't you talk to your mom?"

"Yeah, I did. And she said nothing happened. And I didn't believe her at first, you know? I thought, you're my best friend, and why would you lie to me?"

"I didn't," I said, and my voice sounded small to my own ears.

"But my mom wasn't alone at the bar that night. She was there with my dad. He remembers you coming in, too."

My mouth opened, but no words came out. I thought back to what I'd seen the night before. It had been awful but clear. I hadn't gotten it wrong.

"That's not true; I saw—"

"Stop lying!" Reese screamed, and I took a small half step back. Her voice was screechy, almost crazed. Her cool demeanor had completely cracked.

"Why did you do it, huh?" she asked. "Just because your parents are messed up and your life's miserable, you thought mine should be, too?"

I sucked in a breath. I couldn't believe these words were coming out of Reese's mouth and that they were directed at me. I was always on her side, in her corner. And she was in mine. Now she stared at me with eyes that burned.

"Get away from me," she said, "and don't ever come back."

She slammed the door closed. I waited a few moments before I just got on my bike and rode, not paying attention to where I was going. And I followed Reese's orders completely—I never went back. At the end of the summer, my mom made good on her threats and moved us to Chicago, where she'd found a job at Northwestern. The divorce was finalized at the end of the year, and as per the custody agreement, I was to spend three weeks every summer with my dad. During those summers, I'd avoided Reese almost completely, and Julie, too.

But I couldn't anymore.

So as I sat at the bar stool and sipped on my Diet Coke, I felt my stomach curl up in familiar knots. I hated that feeling, the nervousness and anxiety. *You just have to ask a few questions*, I told myself. Asking questions was easy.

But the thought of seeing Julie again twisted me up, pushed my insides back through time. Like I was twelve years old again, waiting for an explanation that wasn't coming, no matter how much I wanted—needed—to hear it.

The kitchen door swung open and Julie shouldered her way into the area behind the bar, flinging a hand towel over one shoulder. When she saw me, her steps faltered for a moment.

But then she smiled and moved forward as though nothing had happened.

"Hey, Penny, long time, no see," she said, sounding too upbeat. "What brings you by?"

"I came to talk to you, actually. I wanted to ask you a question."

A flicker of alarm briefly crossed Julie's face, and then it was gone. She gave another forced smile.

"Shoot." Julie raised her eyes expectantly, and I once again thought about how to phrase what I wanted to ask her. But the question that kept trying to push its way to the tip of my tongue wasn't about my dad at all. Suddenly, I knew exactly what I wanted to ask Julie Harper.

Why did you lie to your own daughter? Why did you make her hate me?

But that's not what I said when I opened my mouth. Instead, I said, "It's about my dad."

Julie's features hardened, and her eyes darted down. She opened her mouth to respond, but before she could speak, the front door of the bar opened. Julie looked upward with a grateful expression, which soon turned to controlled panic.

I turned to see who'd entered the bar, and felt a little bit of panic rise up in my throat as well. Walking into the dim light, dressed in his freshly pressed uniform, was Julie's husband.

The sheriff.

SHERIFF BUD HARPER had a much better poker face than his wife. He put on a tight smile as he stepped forward and shook my hand.

"Back for the summer, Penny? Little young to be hugging that bar, aren't you?"

I managed a smile in return. "Hi, Sheriff Harper."

The sheriff leaned over the bar and planted a quick kiss on Julie's cheek before taking a seat on the stool next to me. He was only a little bit taller than Julie, really not that much taller than me. His dark hair was combed neatly over his head, revealing a perfectly straight white line of scalp at its part.

The sheriff nodded down at my drink. "Hope it's just pop and ice in there."

Julie swatted him lightly in the arm with a towel. "Of course it is. What kind of establishment do you think I'm running here?"

The couple smiled at each other, but I thought I noticed a tenseness in his eyes, in her smile. Their words and actions felt a bit exaggerated, like they were putting on a show.

"Penny just dropped by to ask me a couple of questions," Julie said. "About her dad."

The sheriff swiveled in his seat. "Oh?"

I suddenly felt outflanked, with Julie standing in front of me and the sheriff sitting to my left. But I decided to charge ahead anyway.

"He's been missing for a couple of days," I said, trying to get the words out quickly. "I know he comes to this bar sometimes, so I was just wondering if maybe he told Julie anything. . . ."

"Huh," Julie said, furrowing her brow. "Wish I could help, but I don't think I've seen your dad in more than a week or so."

"I think I can help you out," the sheriff said, keeping his eyes on me. "I'll tell you what I told your little neighbor Dex yesterday. Charlie Randall down at the army surplus said Ike came in about a week back and picked up some propane. Said he was planning a camping trip."

I exhaled a breath I didn't even know I was holding. I felt a flash of irritation at Dex for keeping that detail from me. What the sheriff said made sense. My dad went camping all the time . . . except, *except* . . .

The image of the burned body floated through my mind

once again. I knew the sheriff would laugh off my dad's conspiracy theories and stories, just like everyone else in town did, but what my dad had found was genuinely disturbing.

"The thing is," I said, looking the sheriff in the eyes and trying again, "I guess my dad had been looking into a new story, one about that hiker in the woods."

The sheriff gave a grim nod. "Awful thing. Your dad was real shook up over that."

"He was?"

"Of course. Finding a body like that, it can be a real shock. Especially for someone like your dad."

My head turned sharply at the sheriff's words. "What do you mean, someone like my dad?"

The sheriff took a deep breath and exchanged a quick look with Julie. "Well, I've known Ike all my life. And he's always been a bit . . . goofy when it came to weird stuff. Paranoid, almost. Heck, Penny, you know what I mean."

I pursed my lips together. I did know what he meant. But hearing those words come out of someone else's mouth made my fists involuntarily clench.

"He was a bit of a mess after that hiker," Julie put in. "He came in here almost every night for a couple of weeks."

"Then he started going out in the woods, setting up cameras, taking pictures. . . ." The sheriff trailed off and gave a little shake of his head, as if to say, *Isn't it a shame?* "I couldn't exactly stop him," he continued. "It's not against the law or anything to set up a camera in the woods. And it's not even deer hunting season, so it wasn't like he was putting himself in danger."

I nodded as the sheriff continued, "I bet that's where he went this time, too. Out there playing with his camera. Course, if you're feeling worked up enough to want to file a missing persons report, you just come down to the station and let me know."

I looked down at my half-drunk glass of pop. The ice was all melted, and it had gone flat. The facts bounced around and around in my mind—my dad hadn't picked me up, he'd been taking weird pictures of the woods, he was planning a camping trip, he'd found a dead body, his truck was missing. Was it possible he'd gotten so caught up in a potential story that he'd completely forgotten about me? Yes. I could see him out there in the woods, taking photo after photo, so focused on his work that everything else in the world faded away. But if there really was someone dangerous out there, like whoever maybe killed the hiker, and my dad was after them . . . how long should I let him investigate on his own before getting really, really concerned?

I turned to the sheriff again. "I think I'll give him just another day or two to come home. If he hasn't shown up by then, I'll come down to the station and file a report."

The sheriff's features hardened just a bit, as if he was displeased with my answer. But he hid it quickly and reached out to squeeze my shoulder.

"Of course," he said. "And if you need a place to stay in the meantime . . ."

"Oh, no," I said quickly. "I'll be okay, and Cindy's right next door if I need anything."

"Well, all right, then."

I slid off my stool. "Thanks for your help," I said, as I walked toward the door. "I'll let you know if . . . well, I'll let you know."

"Take care, Penny," Julie said, right before I opened the door and stepped back into the sunshine. Before leaving, I looked back once more, and I could swear I saw sadness on her face as she watched me go.

Later that evening, I walked through the front door to find the house still empty. I went to the basement stairs and flicked the light on before running down, taking the stairs two at a time. When I was a kid, my dad had convinced me that ghosts lived under the stairs, and they could reach through the slats and grab your feet to make you trip and fall. I no longer believed in stair ghosts, obviously, but running down the basement stairs became such an ingrained habit that I still did it without thinking.

The basement was half-finished, with plywood walls and a concrete floor. Over on the far side of the room was a metal shelving unit that usually housed my dad's camping supplies. His camouflage sleeping bag was missing, as were his orange hunting vest and emergency kit. So part of the sheriff's story checked out. Dad had at least planned to be out in the woods overnight. But it was still nagging at me that he'd be gone for this many days without checking in. Every time I tried to brush it off, the picture of the burned hiker pushed its way to the front of my mind.

I bit my lip, frustrated at this dead end. If only there was some way to know where, specifically, my dad was chasing his story in the woods . . .

And then I realized there was.

I ran back upstairs and into the living room. Dad's camera was right where I had last seen it, in the coffee table drawer. I grabbed it and clicked through the photos of the woods again. But as hard as I tried, I couldn't tell *where* those specific trees were. Aside from the weird armlike branch, there was nothing distinct about the trees, nothing that could tell me what part of the woods they were in. I checked Dad's office next, but his desk had nothing in it related to the hiker in the woods or his "camping" plans, and the safe he kept against one wall was shut up tight with a combination lock.

I quickly texted Dex. Hey, it's Penny. Are you sure you didn't take anything else from my dad's office? Any other pictures from the woods?

After a moment, I added, I won't get mad, promise.

I only had to wait a few seconds for his reply. No other pics. I looked for them but couldn't find. Want me to come over and help you look?

I considered for a moment. On the one hand, it would be nice to talk all this out with someone. On the other hand, that someone was *Dex*. If I told him Dad's camping gear was missing, he'd probably say that it was part of a conspiracy, or that they'd been stolen by wood gnomes or something. I needed to focus on logic tonight, not fantasy.

No thanks.

If the sheriff and Dex were right about my dad setting up lots of cameras in the woods, that meant he might have more than one lying around at home. As a last resort, I checked the cabinet under the TV, where I knew my dad kept his printed pictures in an old shoe box. The box had a thick layer of dust on top when I pulled it out. It didn't look like Dad had so much as glanced at it lately. But I lifted the lid off anyway, then sat cross-legged on the living room carpet and started going through them.

The photos weren't organized in any particular way. A picture of me covered in blue icing at my first birthday party was stacked in between a picture of me on my first bike and one of my parents on one of their first dates. In that photo, both of my parents looked impossibly young, just a few years older than me. They were standing side by side on a pontoon boat in North Lake. My dad's blond hair was shoulder-length, and he was wearing a flannel shirt and ripped jeans. Next to him, Mom was wearing a sundress covered in little flowers, her hair just a little longer than Dad's. They were beautiful and grinning, holding on to cans of beer and on to each other. I set the picture aside.

The photos soon absorbed all of my attention, and I started to sort them by date. By my left knee was a pile of photos from when I was seven, including a couple of me and Dex roasting marshmallows over a campfire and smiling down from the tree house, and one of Mom and Dad with Cindy and Mark playing euchre at a picnic table. By my right toe was a pile from the years before I was born. It had pictures of my dad standing next to his brand-new truck, my mom grinning at her high school graduation. My parents had both gone to Bone Lake High, but were a couple of years apart. They didn't meet until the summer Mom graduated. She was working at a Denny's one town over to save money for college, and Dad used to go there to work on his horror novels. A few deep talks over waffles eventually led to a few dates, which eventually led to me. I used to hear the story of how they met all the time, though it had been years since either of them had recounted it to me. Probably they never would again.

In the right-toe pictures, my parents looked young—familiar and yet like strangers at the same time. They looked happy. But in the pile of photos that was growing to the left of me, things were noticeably different. In them, I was eleven and awkward, with thick, unruly hair. In half of the pictures, I was scowling at the frame, whether I was sitting on the dock with my dad or glaring up from the couch. That year, my parents made fewer and fewer appearances in front of the lens. But I could see them in the backgrounds of photos—my mom frowning into the camera (or at my dad) as I struggled to set up a tent on one of our last family camping trips, my dad staring out over the lake as in the foreground Reese and I mugged for the camera. Through the piles of years laid out before me, I could trace the disintegration of their happiness. They weren't just thin-lipped and angry in that last bad year, but for years before. I was surprised to see they both looked stressed out in a picture of my fifth birthday party, a party I only remember because Dad started a water balloon fight with my friends. How could I have missed the tense lines in their faces, the forced smiles? The pictures told a story I didn't fully remember living.

I turned over another picture, one of me at age eight, perched on Dad's shoulders and smiling wide. He was standing in front of a giant bridge, a bushy mustache on his face. On the back of the photo was printed *Penelope at Mackinac Island*. My mom must have taken the picture, though I didn't have a clear memory of the moment. It was certainly my dad's handwriting on the back—he always called me by my full name, Penelope (or Pen for short) but never, ever used Penny the way my mom and everyone else did. Dad said that Penelope was a strong, historic name, while Penny was the name of a girl who would have to be rescued by superheroes in a comic book. My parents used to argue about my name in a half-joking way. Or at least, I thought it was half-joking at the time.

I looked back at the younger photos of my parents, when they were smiling and in love. When had things started to go wrong? I'd always thought it happened around the time of the Julie Harper mess, but what if there were signs before then, things I'd missed? I suddenly felt further away from the people in those pictures than I ever had before.

A knock at the door caused me to jump, nearly knocking over a stack of photos at my feet. I carefully stood up, edged my way around the pictures and went to answer the door. Micah was standing there, his perfect, square jaw partially lit up by the cool glow of the porch light.

"Hey." He smiled, revealing a few deep-set dimples.

My stomach jumped, and I felt embarrassed by how glad I was to see him just show up at my front door.

"Um, hi."

"Sorry to just come over, but I wanted to make sure you were okay in person, after that weirdness last night," he said.

"That's . . . really nice of you." I remembered what Reese had said the night before, about Micah being nice to everyone. But surely coming over to my house out of the blue was more than just being nice?

"I'm doing fine," I added. "Just, you know, staying away from venison."

Micah smiled and cleared his throat. "Can I come in?"

"Oh! Yeah," I said, and jumped back from the door to let Micah inside. I forgot all about my sad family album scattered around the living room carpet until Micah stepped fully into the room and raised his eyebrows.

"I was just looking through some pictures," I said. "Nothing on cable." A half-assed explanation.

But if Micah thought that was weird, he didn't remark on it. Instead, he gave a small exclamation and jumped toward the pictures, picking one off the stack next to the leg of the coffee table.

I edged closer to see, stopping just a few inches from Micah. His jacket still smelled like smoke from the campfire the night before. The picture he held was of me, Reese, and Emily getting our faces painted outside the church carnival in fifth grade.

"I remember this day," he said, excitement in his voice.

"You do?"

"Of course. I got my face painted like a cheetah. I wanted to leave it on forever. I remember being so pissed when my mom made me wash it off."

"Oh, I remember you being a cheetah," I said with a small laugh. And suddenly I could picture it—fifth grader Micah running around with orange and yellow spots on his cheeks, growling to make all the girls squeal.

I remembered being one of the squealers. I remembered that feeling when cheetah Micah turned his attention on me—like I was chosen, special.

Micah chuckled and took a seat on the couch. I sat down

next to him, careful to leave a few inches between us.

"Good times," Micah said quietly, setting the picture down. "So . . . is your dad around?" He looked behind him, as if he expected my dad to come around the corner from the kitchen at any second. And did he seem . . . nervous?

"No, he's not here. He's . . ."

My words died in my throat. As soon as I'd said the word *no*, Micah grinned and scooted nearer, closing the gap of inches between us. He gave a crooked grin. "Sorry, what were you saying?"

"Uh," I responded, my head swimming. "My dad's . . . gone, actually. Kind of MIA at the moment."

"MIA?"

"He was supposed to be here when I got in from Chicago, but . . . he's not. Camping trip or something."

"You don't know?"

"He didn't exactly leave a note. But his camping stuff is gone, so . . ."

I wondered for a second if I should tell Micah about the dead hiker in the woods, my dad's weird photos . . . but no. Already he was looking at me differently. A few moments before, I'd been a girl on the couch he was trying to get close to. Now I was a girl with an absentee dad. I didn't need or want his pity.

"It's okay, though," I added, shrugging like I really didn't mind. "I'm used to taking care of myself."

"Yeah," Micah said, and I was surprised by the sudden

sadness in his voice. His gaze drifted away from me, over to the piles of photos on the floor. "But I know how much that sucks sometimes. Having to take care of everything yourself."

And I realized it probably wasn't just pity on Micah's face.

I'd never known much about Micah's home life. When we were younger, his mom rarely came out to community events, and no one ever went over to Micah's house. Everyone assumed Mrs. Jameson was still grieving her husband's death. I didn't know how to ask if that had changed or not in the past five years.

"It does suck a little," I admitted, not sure what else to say.

Micah smiled and gave his head a little shake then, as if pushing the bad feelings away. "Makes us tougher, right?"

"Definitely," I said, feeling like it was true the moment the word came out of my mouth. I *was* tough. I was used to handling things.

And I wasn't just going to sit around and wait for Dad to show up when he felt like it.

"And I have a plan," I said impulsively. It wasn't totally true, but as soon as I spoke the words aloud I realized it *could* be.

Micah turned toward me, interested. "Really?"

"Yeah. I'm going to go into the woods and track my dad down. Find him and ask him why the hell he didn't think to call or leave a note, and what possible reason he could have for making me worry like this."

"How are you going to do that?" Micah asked, and I thought

he might have sounded a bit impressed. Those dark blue eyes were focused on me, alert.

"Well, I don't know for sure where he went. But I do know some of his favorite camping spots. I'll go check them out tomorrow, see if he's there or if he left anything behind." As soon as the words were out of my mouth, I felt better than I had all day. I had a plan.

Micah smiled and nodded, and now I knew I wasn't reading into things—he looked impressed. "Taking things into your own hands. I like it."

"Yeah," I said, taking a deep breath. *Speaking of taking things into your own hands* . . . "Want to come with?"

I spoke the words quickly, so I could get them out without losing my nerve. But then there were a few beats of silence, ringing loudly in my ears, and I realized how dumb the proposition must have sounded. "I mean, I get if you already have plans or something—"

"Just football practice," Micah said. "But maybe after?"

"You . . . really want to come?"

"Yeah," Micah said, and his grin spread wide, his teeth glowing white even in the low light of the room. "Could be kinda fun. Like a mission."

"A mission on bikes."

"I could borrow Kevin's truck if you want. Cover more ground."

"That'd be great. If it's no trouble."

"None at all. Dude owes me. And I could bring some food for us, too."

"Food?"

"Well, going from spot to spot in the woods, we might get hungry." Micah smiled again, and my stomach flip-flopped. "Might need to take a break." *Flip.* "Or two." *Flop.*

"That's . . . very practical," I said, grinning back at Micah. Tomorrow, I was going to actually take action and look for dad. With Micah. And food.

"Tomorrow, then," Micah said.

"Yeah, tomorrow."

He waited a beat, still so close, before giving a gentle laugh—more an exhalation, really—and standing up from the couch.

"I hate to leave, but I should get going if I want to get up on time for practice," he said. "I'm glad you're okay."

"Thanks for coming by and checking on me. That was really cool of you."

"Not *that* cool. It was really just my excuse to come over and work my way up to asking you out." He grinned. "But you beat me to it."

I didn't know how to respond to that other than smiling like an idiot.

"See you tomorrow," Micah said, still grinning.

My heart was pounding as I walked him to the door and waved goodbye from the porch. As I turned to go back inside, I saw that the living room light was on at Cindy and Dex's place.

A figure moved away from the window, retreating back into the brightened room before I could see who it was.

I walked back inside and, even though I gave an honest try, I couldn't stop smiling for five whole minutes. It occurred to me that this summer might have more possibilities than I'd ever realized. It might even be nonterrible.

As soon as I found Dad.

"YOU'VE BEEN WASHING that ice-cream scoop for ten minutes."

Dex's voice interrupted my haze of daydreaming, and I blinked before looking down into the store's kitchen sink. My fingertips were starting to prune where they had dipped the metal scoop into the sudsy water over and over.

"Worried about your dad?" Dex's tone was gentle as he moved closer to me.

I felt a jolt of guilt as I pulled the scoop up and dried it on a dish towel in two quick moves. I hadn't been thinking of my dad—not exactly, anyway. I'd been thinking about my upcoming mission/plan/date(!) with Micah. And before that, I'd been thinking of my morning trip to the tiny Bone Lake Public Library, where part-time librarian/nursery school teacher/real estate agent Ms. Ledden had shown me the library's collection of newspaper articles on the plant closing. My latest theory on the weird sound bite that Cindy, Hector, and Mrs. Anderson had parroted was that they'd all read the same line in an op-ed or something, and it'd just stuck around in their minds. But I couldn't find any editorial telling Bone Lake residents that it was "best not to think about" the plant accident. Maybe they'd seen in an on-air news report instead.

Either way, my summer research project was turning up zilch so far. I was 0 for 3 in interviews, and honestly, I probably should have been more worried. The more time that passed without getting a strong "human perspective" on my article from someone else in town, the more imperative it became to get Micah's story. And that was a problem, too. Because every time I was around Micah, needing to ask him important journalistic (and probably painful) questions about his dad, I was too distracted by . . . well . . . his eyes. And his smile. And just his whole face region in general.

"Penny?"

"Um, yeah," I responded to Dex, trying to reorient my thoughts to Dad.

Dex leaned up against the wall, crossing his arms. "I've been thinking. Even if your dad did take his camping gear—"

"He did."

"Right, right. But anyway," Dex said, not skipping a beat, "he still probably took it with him to go look into his story.

And I just keep thinking that there must be a way to figure out where he was planning to go."

"Way ahead of you. I looked for his cameras last night, but I couldn't find any more in the house. No pictures with clues to where he might have gone, either."

"Oh," Dex said, deflating a bit. "Did you check his office?"

I shot him a *Come on, seriously?* look and took the clean scoopers to the front of the store. Dex followed, whirling around so fast his tennis shoes squeaked against the tile floor.

"Okay, but like, how *well* did you look? Because Ike has *lots* of files. I barely had time to look around when I was at your place, but I know there're more somewhere in that office. Plus, he has that safe. Seems more like a two-person job to go through it all." He bounced a little on his feet as he waited for an answer.

"You're really not going to let this go, are you?"

"What'll it hurt to be as thorough as possible?"

"Fine," I said, sighing. "If it will make you feel better. We'll go through my dad's office again. We'll try to figure out how to open the safe."

"Tonight?"

"No, not tonight. I have plans."

Dex made a surprised face. "Plans?"

"Don't act so shocked. You're not the only person I talk to in this town."

"So . . . you have plans with my mom, then?"

"Ha-ha. You should be excited, actually. I'm going out to go check out some of my dad's usual camping spots to see if he's there."

Dex's eyes lit up. "That's a great idea! What time should we go?"

"Well, I sort of have plans to go with someone else."

Dex stopped bouncing. "Someone else?"

"Micah Jameson."

"*That* guy? You're going to spend the night looking for your dad with . . . *Micah Jameson*?"

"Yeah. What?"

"Why would Micah Jameson want to help you find Ike?"

"Um, maybe so he can hang out with me? Or just because he's nice?"

Dex scoffed. "Nice. *Too* nice, more like."

"'Too nice' isn't a thing. That's like saying brownies are too fudgy. More is always better."

Dex shook his head. "I don't trust him. It's like he needs everyone in town to like him—and that goes double for every girl in our grade. He's just too . . . yeah, I'm sticking with 'too nice.' I mean, what's he got to hide?"

"Amazing biceps?"

Dex rolled his eyes. But then he crossed his arms and leaned against the ice-cream case, looking away from me.

"Have fun, I guess. But be careful."

"Dex, I'll be perfectly safe with Micah."

"If you say so. But I meant be careful going out in the woods at night. Remember the deer. And the hiker . . ."

Dex trailed off as he looked out the window, his eyebrows scrunched down.

"What is that?"

I followed Dex's gaze through the window. The two-lane street outside the ice-cream shop was completely empty, except for what looked like a small purple heap lying in the middle of the yellow line. I moved out from around the counter and closer to the window. The purple heap was a handbag, and just a few feet away from it, sitting upright with her legs sprawled out in front of her on the pavement, was Mrs. Anderson.

My apron flapped in the breeze as I ran through the door and out into the empty street. Dex followed close behind, and the store's glass door shut behind him with a soft *hiss*. We both reached Mrs. Anderson in a matter of seconds.

She looked oddly serene, sitting there in the middle of the street. Her expression was placid, almost vacant.

"Mrs. Anderson?" I asked as I knelt down to her level.

She looked at me, her eyes blinking under the shade of her orange sun hat.

"Hello, dear," she responded with a smile. "Do you know where I've placed my pie?"

I exchanged a quick look with Dex, who shrugged.

"I had it just a moment ago, hot out of the oven. I used those fresh blueberries from Hank's yard—they're better than they are in the store, you know."

"Mrs. Anderson, do you know where you are right now?"

Mrs. Anderson's brow wrinkled. "Of course I know where I am," she said. "I just don't know how I got here!"

Dex bent down and put one hand under Mrs. Anderson's elbow. "Why don't we get you up out of the street?"

I bent down to lift Mrs. Anderson from the other side. Together, we walked her over to the sidewalk in front of Sweet Street. When we stopped, Mrs. Anderson looked first at Dex, then me, up and down.

"What are you both doing in your aprons? The store doesn't open for another two hours. . . ."

"Mrs. Anderson, it's noon," I said.

She shook her head. I pulled my cell phone out of my pocket and showed her the time. Mrs. Anderson gave a small gasp, then put one hand up to her temple. "Well, I . . . I don't . . ."

"Can we call someone for you?" I asked. "A doctor, or maybe the sheriff?"

Mrs. Anderson blew a raspberry, her lips smacking wetly. "And what's that moron going to do, write me a ticket?"

Dex and I both stifled a laugh.

"I just need to get home, I think. Lie down for a bit."

"Why don't I take you?" I said.

"I don't want to trouble you—"

"It's no trouble. Dex, do you mind watching the store on your own?"

Dex shook his head. "Of course not. I'll see you tomorrow, Mrs. Anderson. Take care."

He went inside, and I handed Mrs. Anderson her handbag. We started to walk slowly down the street, my arm still locked under her elbow.

"What's the last thing you remember?" I asked as we passed the post office.

Mrs. Anderson took a moment before responding. "I was taking my morning pie out of the oven," she said. "And I thought I should bring it to . . ." She gave an angry sigh. "Oh, I can't remember."

"That's okay."

But Mrs. Anderson's mouth stayed firmly bunched up, and she continued to shake her head in frustration as we passed by the buildings at the end of Main Street. When we neared the corner, I saw a black car idling at the curb across the street. It had tinted windows, and its engine was so quiet you could barely tell it was on. It was the same car I'd seen in front of my dad's house the other day.

The sun bounced off the car's shiny exterior, nearly blinding me. Just as I shielded my eyes, it peeled away from the curb and maneuvered into the road with a squeal.

"Mrs. Anderson, do you know whose car that is?"

"What, dear?"

"Never mind. It's gone now." I turned back to the sidewalk

in front of us. "You're still on Waterbury, aren't you?" I asked, raising my voice.

"Yes, but you really don't have to walk me all the way home."

"I don't mind. It's not that far."

Mrs. Anderson smiled and patted my hand with her own. "You remind me of your father. He was always so sweet."

I swallowed, caught off guard. "I don't think that's how most people would describe him," I said.

Mrs. Anderson surprised me by laughing. "Oh, I'm sure he's lots of other things, too. But he's always had a soft heart." She loosened her grip on my arm as we turned onto Waterbury and started to pass by the one-story houses that lined the street. "He comes over to rake my yard in the fall, and shovel my driveway every winter."

I blinked, surprised. "I forgot that he did that."

"People forget small kindnesses," Mrs. Anderson said. "They're often the first things they forget."

A familiar bubble of anger rose up inside of me at Mrs. Anderson's gently chiding tone. First Dex and Cindy, now Mrs. Anderson—why were people so intent on telling me what a great guy my dad was? *I* was the one he had forgotten about to go on a last-minute camping trip to hunt down aliens or whatever—didn't I have a right to judge? To be even a little pissed off? And who cared if he was the type of person who shovels his neighbors' sidewalks? He was also the type of person to leave his own daughter in the lurch.

"My dad has a way of making you forget his kindnesses," I finally said. "He's pretty good at it, actually." I heard the sharpness in my tone a moment too late. I instantly regretted snapping at Mrs. Anderson, whose arm still rested, frail and light, above mine.

But Mrs. Anderson just smiled and kept walking. "Oh, I'm sure he does," she said.

"I'm sorry, Mrs. Anderson, I didn't mean—"

"It's okay, dear," she said. "I don't offend that easily. Besides, you're right. Your dad can be kind, but he can also be a bit of an asshole."

My eyes widened as Mrs. Anderson chuckled, her voice sweet and cracking and old. "It was true when he was a little boy, and it's true now. Good parts and bad . . . Oh! Maybe it was banana bread?"

"Mrs. Anderson . . . ?"

"They were going soft yesterday—I saw the dark bruises. I'm pretty sure I used them up, but then I remember picking blueberries. . . . Anyway, your mom was the best thing that ever happened to your dad, and also the worst."

"Uh, I'm not sure I follow. . . ."

We reached the base of Mrs. Anderson's yard and started to walk her up her gravel driveway. A row of pink roses lining her lawn were just starting to drop their petals, and she stopped to look at them.

"Or maybe it was *apple* pie. That does make more sense . . . but then what did I do with the bananas?"

Mrs. Anderson looked up at me as if she expected an answer. I shrugged helplessly, and she smiled. She opened her front door, which was unlocked, and stepped inside.

"Are you sure you're going to be okay?"

"Oh yes," she said. "I set my DVR up to record *The Price Is Right*."

"Well . . . okay, Mrs. Anderson. See you later."

"Bye, dear." Mrs. Anderson started to close the door, but then stopped just before I turned away. She looked at me, her eyes clear and blue. "Try not to stay too angry with him, okay? Summer's so short." She gave a vacant smile. "Summer. That's right. Yes, it was definitely the blueberries. But it's best not to think too much about it."

She shut the door in my face with a loud *click*, leaving me alone on her porch among the dying roses, feeling a chill run down my spine even in the midday heat.

I SPENT THE rest of the afternoon pacing around the house, feeling uneasy. I couldn't get Mrs. Anderson's words out of my head. It wasn't just her repetition of that one phrase that kept popping up all over town—*it's best not to think too much about it*—but also what she'd said about my dad. And then there was seeing that same black car driving slowly by again. I knew there had to be some reasonable explanation for all of these things, but I couldn't see it yet. It was like a puzzle with too many pieces missing, and I didn't know where to start looking to fit everything together.

But when Micah pulled into the driveway in Kevin Abnair's truck, my unease was replaced with resolve. I didn't know where to go next to find the missing puzzle pieces. But at least I could start looking for my dad.

Three hours later, my resolve was starting to fizzle out. The sun had already set behind the trees by the time Micah and I made it to our last stop, one of my dad's favorite camping spots at the far end of North Lake.

North Lake wasn't the biggest lake in town (that would be the actual Bone Lake, which our community was named after). But it was the deepest. If you swam out to the middle and looked straight down, all you could see was blackness stretching beyond your own legs. It looked like it went on forever, a bottomless hole. Dad loved it.

But when we got there, I found no hints of Dad. No tire tracks, no sign of a recent campfire.

"Sorry to drag you all around the woods for nothing," I said as Micah maneuvered the small truck through a dirt road at the edge of North Lake and parked at a patch of the narrow, rocky beach that was lit up by moonlight. The spot was familiar in a deep-down way; I'd spent many childhood nights out here with Dad, staring out at the water and waiting for a lake monster to rise up from its depths. I'd imagined how it would happen so many times, it practically felt like a memory—how the dark object would bubble up from the surface, breaking the water into small waves. First its glossy head, then its humped back, dripping water down shiny scales. Then the hollow eye sockets, the claws, the teeth. Even now, unable to help it, my eyes scanned over the water, looking for a ripple.

"I wouldn't say it was for *nothing*," Micah said, pulling my attention back to him with an easy grin. "Besides, this looks like the perfect spot to stop and eat, doesn't it?"

I forced myself to smile back, pulling my gaze away from a lake that I now knew was filled with nothing but seaweed, amoebas, and empty beer cans.

"Yeah, perfect."

We sat on a blanket in the open bed of the truck and unwrapped the food we'd brought with us—potato chips, packaged cheese slices, and rolled-up lunch meat from me, and homemade leftovers from Micah.

Micah looked down at my contribution and laughed. "Not much of a cook, huh?"

"Hey, these turkey slices didn't come prerolled, I'll have you know. I put many precious seconds into putting this together."

Micah laughed, and I picked up a piece of the pie he'd brought. "And you don't expect me to believe *you* made this?"

"Much as I'd like to take credit, you're right. This is pretty much all my mom."

I bit into the pie and nearly sighed with how good it tasted—I hadn't realized how much the days of hamburger buns and chips had deprived my taste buds of home-cooked food until that moment.

"Well, tell your mom she's an amazing cook," I said, wiping berry juice off my chin.

"Oh, she knows," Micah said. "I only wish she wouldn't make so much. She gets into this mode sometimes where she makes three meals a day like she's cooking for a family of four, instead of just . . . us."

Micah shrugged one shoulder, like this was no big deal, but his eyes were faraway as he took another bite. I struggled to find the right response.

"My mom's kind of the opposite," I finally said. "She *hates* cooking. For her, going to the grocery store is like getting a tooth drilled. She uses our oven as another place to store books."

"So what do you eat?"

"We order in, mostly. There's this vegan restaurant on our block that my mom loves."

Micah made a face. "Vegan? As in, no meat?"

"As in, no meat *or* cheese."

Micah's eyes widened. "Oh man," he said, pushing a Kraft Single in my direction. "Here. You need this more than I do."

I laughed, and in that moment my whole body felt like it could just float up out of the truck bed. It wasn't just that I was enjoying hanging out with Micah; it was also that he seemed to be enjoying hanging out with *me*. It felt partially unbelievable and partially intoxicating to have the full wattage of his attention focused solely on me. Well, me and pie.

"I know, right?" I continued, wanting nothing more than to stretch this conversation—this whole night—out for as long as possible. "This whole last semester I thought if I never saw another piece of spinach again, I'd be happy. But I've only been here a few days, and already I kind of miss it."

"I don't think I've ever missed spinach."

I looked down at the corn I was slowly picking at and gave a small shrug. "Well, maybe I just miss *her*."

As soon as I said the words, I knew they were true. I wondered if maybe these past few days alone had gotten to me more than I'd thought. Because I did miss Mom more than usual—I missed her steady presence, her way of centering things. I even missed the dumb kale juice in the fridge.

"I know what you mean," Micah said, his voice low. He got that faraway look again, and I saw clearly how I could swing the conversation back to something light—like the pie, or the fact that Kevin's truck smelled like someone had doused the whole thing with Axe body spray.

Instead, I put the corncob down and leaned a bit closer to Micah.

"You mean . . . your dad?"

Micah sucked in a breath, and I felt a small pang of guilt. I really hadn't planned to steer the conversation to Micah's dad, not tonight. But even though I'd asked out of concern, I couldn't deny the trickle of anticipation running through me at the thought that I might finally get some answers about Hal Jameson.

But instead, Micah shook his head. "No, I meant my mom, actually." Then he was the one playing with his food, picking small bits off a piece of fried chicken without eating it. "She hasn't really been the same since . . . well, since everything happened. I mean, she's okay most days, but she's not like she was before."

"I didn't know that," I said softly. "I'm so sorry."

Micah shrugged again. "It was a long time ago, but she just can't get over what happened to my dad, not really. The football helps, though."

"Football?"

"My games. They like, give her something to look forward to? Sometimes they're the only reason she gets out of her pajamas at all." Micah's hands moved on from the chicken and started crumpling up a napkin in his lap. "It's nice to be able to give her that, especially after . . ."

"After what?"

"Well, I don't know if you remember, but after my dad died, people weren't exactly . . . nice to us."

"What do you mean?" I kept my focus on Micah, ignoring how my fingers itched for my notebook and pen. And there was the guilt again, that my first instinct was to get Micah's words on record. I moved my hand under my thigh so I was almost sitting on it, as if I could hide what I wanted to do with it—not just from Micah, but from myself, too.

"Just that . . . you know my dad died in an accident at the plant?" Micah continued.

"Yeah," I said softly, my heart beating faster.

"Well, everyone blamed him for what happened. He used to drink sometimes, and they said he did it on the job. . . . I never believed it, but that didn't matter to anyone. Human error, they said, which basically meant it was his own damn fault. And that was it, case closed. Anyway, then the plant shut down and everyone lost all those jobs, and suddenly people weren't really sad about my dad anymore. He was, like, a pariah. No one even talked about him." Micah shook his head, and I could see he was still angry about it, after all these years. "You know I didn't even have friends until I joined peewee football? No one would look at me."

"I didn't know that," I finally managed. I'd never thought about how much pressure must have been on him, to make up for his dad's perceived mistakes in the eyes of all of Bone Lake.

"No one really does. I don't talk about it much," Micah said. "Not really sure why I brought it up, actually. Not exactly great first-date material."

"It's okay. I'm glad you felt like you could tell me about it."

Micah turned to look at me, and his eyes were soft. "Yeah. So am I."

The insides of my chest suddenly felt warm, and I *was* glad that Micah felt he could trust me enough to tell me something so personal. Of course, my next thought after that was how much Micah's story about his dad would add to my article. There it was again—a jump of excitement, followed by a flash of guilt. He'd opened up to me not because I'd asked him questions as a journalist, but because I'd asked him questions as a friend—as maybe something more than that. Suddenly, my decision to put off telling him about the article felt less strategic, and more like a lie. Like I was taking advantage of his trust. If he'd been so honest with me, it was time for me to return the favor.

"Micah, I should tell you something. . . ."

When I looked up, I saw that Micah's face was closer to mine than I'd realized.

"What's that?" he asked, his voice a low rumble in his throat. His eyes focused on me, and I could practically feel his gaze lighting up my skin. His eyes roved over my face, and my head cleared of everything except for the sight of him.

"Um."

Then Micah was leaning closer. His features turned blurry as my eyes half-closed, and I could feel his breath hit my lips. I lowered my eyelids completely and closed the centimeter of space between us. . . .

Crack.

I jerked back. Micah's momentum brought him forward a little, but then he caught himself and opened his eyes.

"Did you hear that?"

Micah looked around. "What?"

"That noise?"

I looked out into the darkness around us and heard another snapping sound—it sounded closer this time. Micah's eyebrows knit together, and I knew he'd heard it, too. He scanned the space outside the truck bed.

Another cracking noise, then another. They weren't just coming from one location, but from all around the truck, from every direction. And they were getting closer. I reached out and gripped Micah's hand without even thinking about it. He squeezed back but didn't look at me. His head whipped from one side to another, trying to track the sources of the noise.

Then we saw the lights. Bright, white circles that caught on the ground, on tree trunks, on the surface of the lake. They moved and spun, beams of twirling light.

"What is it?" My voice was high and strained, and I moved closer to Micah's shoulder, pressing into him. When one of the lights flashed across his face, I recognized his tight, clenched expression as fear.

A dark figure stepped toward us. It moved between the truck and the lake's edge, and was coming closer. Soon, another joined. And another. In the swirling, chaotic motion of the lights, they appeared to move slowly, and I could only make out pieces of them at a time—a torso, a leg, a hood.

Panic pumped through me, a stream of it, a flood. I screamed.

Then, I reached down to the bottom of the truck bed, grabbed the first object I could find, and hurled it out at the figures with all my might.

"Ow! What the hell was that?"

I recognized the voice. The pounding in my heart didn't lessen, but all of the fear that had coursed through my muscles transformed into something else—anger. Next to me, I could feel Micah's shoulders relax.

"Seriously, what the hell did she throw at me?"

One of the lights came up off the ground and focused on the figure in front of me. His face was half-hidden behind a dark hoodie, which I could now see read *Old Navy* in faded type. He was looking down at the ground, half smiling.

Kevin.

He knelt down and picked up a half-eaten corncob.

Someone else behind him laughed, and my spine went cold.

"Reese?"

She moved the flashlight up to her face, illuminating it from beneath.

"Boo," she said.

Two more figures moved from the darkness, though they didn't hold their flashlights still long enough for me to see who they were. Like Reese and Kevin, they wore dark pants and hoodies. They laughed as they drew near.

"Did we interrupt anything good?" Kevin asked. "I can't tell. Micah, is her shirt still on, man?" His smirk banished the last bits of fear from my system. I could feel my face starting to flush red, and from the gloating expression on Reese's face, I knew she could see it, too.

"God, I hope so," she said, her voice low. "No one needs to see those floppy things."

"*I* do," Kevin said. "Least I deserve for loaning out my truck."

Micah made a light sound next to me, and at first I thought

he was going to defend me, or tell Kevin to shut up, or to ask what they hell they were doing out here. But as the flashlights flicked over his face, it was clear he wasn't about to do any of those things.

He was smiling. It was a sheepish kind of smile, a *come on guys, be cool* kind of smile. But it was a smile. It occurred to me, in one blindingly humiliating moment, that Micah's friends must have known we were coming out here tonight; they must have planned this whole thing. . . .

"Micah?" I choked out.

He looked at me, and he must have seen the confusion and anger on my face. For a brief moment, he looked concerned. But then he bumped his shoulder into mine, playfully, and laughed.

"Come on, Penny. They're just playing."

I scrambled out of the pickup truck bed so fast, I scraped my shin on its edge. I bit down on my lip and tried to ignore the pain as I pushed through the circle of hoodie-wearing figures and started to run in the opposite direction from the lake.

"Hey, where's she going?" I heard someone say, but I couldn't tell who.

"Penny! Wait!" Micah.

I didn't turn around.

"Come on, stop!"

"She never did have a sense of humor." Reese.

I ran without thinking or planning, my only instinct to get

away. I moved through the trees until I could no longer hear their voices behind me, and I kept going. In the daylight, I might have been able to find the path that led around to the other side of the lake, but in the darkness of night I saw only branches and shadows and fragments of the night sky. The old fear crept back into me, the one instilled through years of stories of lake monsters and boogeymen and aliens with smooth, domed heads.

Hollowed eye sockets.

Claws.

Teeth.

But I pushed it all down. None of that stuff was real. There was nothing out in these woods except for trees and bushes and dirt.

And assholes, apparently.

I could still hear Micah's small laugh in my ear. I remembered his lips, moving closer and closer to mine, and my face burned. I ran harder, slowing only when branches scraped against my face or when I stumbled against a root.

"Penny!" I heard Micah scream out, but his voice was a long way away. Was he following me, or was he still at the lakeside, laughing with his friends?

I pushed forward, though I knew it would be smarter to stop and catch my bearings. But I would rather run through the woods alone than turn around and head back to that truck.

After a few minutes, I began to feel a little winded. I slowed my pace and tried to hear whether someone was following me. I heard only crickets and wind, the rustling of leaves.

I started walking again, trying to pick out a deer path in the woods. I'd been back here a million times with my dad, and I knew if I just kept going I'd eventually run into something familiar. I crested a ledge covered with a fallen log, and there, sitting across from me in a clearing, was a small two-door truck.

My breath caught in my throat. I wondered if maybe this truck belonged to Reese or one of the others. But I knew if the truck was here, the road couldn't be far away.

I climbed over the fallen log and started across the clearing. I hadn't made it two steps before I stepped on something that crunched softly under my foot, its edges poking up into the bottom of my shoe as it broke. It felt hard yet oddly fragile, like a stick covered in ice. Except there wouldn't be any ice out here, not now. Not in June. I looked down and saw the object illuminated in the moonlight.

It was a human hand.

Charred, burned, and gnarled, but unmistakably human, with five fingers twisted toward the dirt.

I jumped back, and my hands flew to my mouth. The hand was connected to a dark, misshapen mass that was pushed up against the fallen log I'd just climbed over. I stumbled backward and away, but not far away enough that I couldn't make out the figure lying there. I tasted chicken and corn and bile rising up in my throat, pushing against the sides of my mouth.

"Penny!"

Hearing my name yelled out in the clearing, so close, set off my jagged nerves. I jumped and whirled around. Micah was pushing through the woods into the clearing, close to the fallen log. I could only see his dark outline as he moved closer. I wanted to call out to him, to warn him, to scream, but when I opened my mouth, I felt bile rise up instead. I hacked and coughed, my hands on my knees.

I straightened and moved toward Micah, hands out, to stop him in his tracks. Instead, I tripped over something else on the ground and fell down, hard. I landed on my hands and looked behind me to see what I'd stumbled over. It was another body, charred black, nearly hidden in a small recess in the grass.

How many bodies were out here?

"Penny, what . . ." Micah stopped on top of the fallen log. He was looking down at the form lying below. In the darkness, I couldn't see his expression.

I finally heard a noise escape from my throat, but it was only a whimper. I scrambled to get up, to get as far away from the second body as possible. As I pushed myself up off the ground, my arm slid against something hard and scratchy. Another hand.

The ball of terror in my throat finally loosened, and I went down again, retching into the grass. As everything inside of me came up onto the forest floor, I could still see the charred hand through the corner of my eye. This one still had fingernails, painted blue and gold.

THIRTEEN

HOURS LATER, I could still taste acid in my throat.

I sat on a plastic chair under a set of stark fluorescent lights. A thin gray blanket was spread over my shoulders. It scratched my neck whenever I tried to crane my head to see what was happening around the corner in the small workspace shared by the town's deputies. The room was full now; it looked like every deputy and secretary in the force was on hand; plus, Julie Harper was pouring coffee in one corner, and a few townspeople milled about, having wandered in to see if they could lend a hand—or just to find out why the sheriff had been called to the woods at ten o'clock at night.

Sheriff Harper himself was on the phone, calling in for more reinforcements to scan the woods near the "scene." And to collect the bodies.

He hung up and made his way over to the small hallway where Micah and I were sitting. Micah was hunched over in his own plastic chair, staring at his tennis shoes with wide, unblinking eyes. We hadn't spoken a word to each other since he'd picked me up off the clearing floor and led me to the small access road by the lake. He'd been the one to call the police and explain what we'd found. He'd stood silently by my side as we waited for the squad car to drive up the dirt road and take us back to the station.

Micah barely glanced up as the sheriff came our way. Micah's face was bone white against the shadows made by the harsh lighting of the hallway. The anger I'd felt toward him just an hour before felt so far away I could barely remember it, like trying to recapture the emotions of a dream. I had an idea of what was running through his head because it was the same thing running through mine—the smell, the darkness, the misshapen lumps on the forest floor that used to be parts of people. People he knew.

Sheriff Harper looked to me, then to Micah, then back again. He had bags under his eyes, and I wondered if he'd been sleeping when the deputy's call came in. I pictured him on the brown La-Z-Boy where he used to fall asleep watching baseball games while Reese and I played in her bedroom as kids. Maybe the jangling phone call had startled him out of sleep, or maybe it had been a gentle nudge from Julie, waking him to let him know what had happened.

Either way, he couldn't have been prepared for it in the slightest. Teenagers never died in Bone Lake. Not like this.

"Your mom is on her way to come get you," the sheriff said to Micah. He turned to me. "And Cindy Wallace is coming for you."

I gave a small nod.

"We have your full statements, so the best thing you can do now is go home and try to get some rest," the sheriff continued. When neither of us responded, he cleared his throat and shuffled awkwardly in my direction. He put one hand on top of the gray blanket on my shoulder and patted it once, then twice.

"It was Bryan and Cassidy, wasn't it?" Micah's voice was flat and lifeless.

"We can't know anything for sure until we identify the bodies."

The sheriff's words bounced around my skull. *The bodies.*

Micah just shook his head, slowly. "It was Bryan's truck. I recognized it." His voice lowered, so I could barely hear him when he added, "I was there when he bought it."

The sheriff inhaled deeply before speaking. "I know you've both been through a trying experience. But we should really be careful not to jump to conclusions on what happened tonight until all the evidence from the woods is collected. There's no need to upset folks until we know for sure, do you understand?"

Micah didn't move or say a thing. I couldn't stop seeing that burned hand, the one with the blue and gold nail polish. The colors of Bone Lake High School. The colors worn by cheerleaders like Cassidy.

For a moment, I thought I might be sick again. But some of the sheriff's words got caught among the swirl in my brain and stuck there.

. . . until all the evidence from the woods is collected.

I thought of my dad's photos. Shot after shot of trees, grass, and sky. And my dad was probably out there, right this moment. . . .

I shot up out of my chair, barely noticing when the gray blanket fell from my shoulders. Surprised, Sheriff Harper took a step back. Even Micah whipped his head up, seeming alert for the first time in hours.

"My dad," I croaked. My voice sounded stiff. "He's out there. He took his camping stuff. He's in the woods—"

"Now, Penny—"

"Sheriff, what happened to those . . . what happened to . . ." I couldn't bring myself to say *Bryan and Cassidy.* Even more, I couldn't bring myself to say *the bodies.* ". . . And then, the hiker that was found a few months back, and the deer . . ."

"Slow down, now," the sheriff said, reaching out for my arm. I yanked it back, feeling panic course through me. Blackness swirled at the corners of my eyes, and a vibrating noise grew louder in my ears. If I didn't sit down soon, I knew I would fall.

Sheriff Harper reached for my arm again and helped me down into my seat. Dimly, I could tell the workspace around the corner had gone quiet, and I wondered how many people had heard my little outburst. Micah reached out with one hand, his long fingers brushing briefly against my shoulder before falling away. I sat back in my chair.

"I understand you're upset, Penny," the sheriff said. His voice sounded smooth, his words logical. "We're going to have to close off North Lake while we investigate this, and bring in reinforcements from other counties to search the area. We'll find your dad."

He sounded so sure. I managed a small nod, but the blackness stayed in the corner of my vision.

"I've known Ike for a long time, and I'm sure of one thing—that guy can take care of himself. I'm sure he's over in Cheboygan or even up in Mackinac as we speak. He's probably popping open a cool beer, sitting by the fire—"

I flinched at the word *fire*, and the sheriff caught himself.

"Don't you worry about it," he said.

But I was already beyond worry.

"Penny?"

I turned to see Cindy half jogging, half walking down the hallway. She was dressed in flannel pajamas and an orange robe, and her tennis shoes slapped against the linoleum floor. She gathered me up in a hug, squeezing me as if she hadn't seen me in weeks.

"Are you okay?"

"She's had a pretty big scare," Sheriff Harper said. "Thanks for coming to get her, Cin."

"Of course." Cindy kept one protective hand on my arm. She lowered her voice. "Any luck reaching Ike?"

My stomach twisted.

"We'll get hold of him soon. I was just telling Penny," the sheriff said. But he was looking down at his hands instead of at Cindy or me.

Cindy nodded, then looked to Micah. "Do you need a ride, hon?"

Micah shook his head. "My mom's coming." His voice was stilted, robotic.

Cindy looped an arm through mine and led me away from the room, keeping me close to her side as if I were suffering from hypothermia and needed body heat to survive. I looked back at Micah to say goodbye, but his eyes were once again open wide and fixed on the ground. He seemed far, far away in that moment. Too far for me or anyone else to reach.

Dex was waiting up for us to get home. As Cindy and I came in through the front hall, I saw him pacing the living room in an old T-shirt and Spider-Man pajama bottoms that were at least three inches too short. He noticed us come in and took two giant steps in my direction, as though he was going to pull me into a hug. But right before he reached me, he stopped abruptly, his arms falling awkwardly to his sides instead of wrapping around me. He cleared his throat.

"Are you okay?"

I nodded. "Yeah. I think so."

Cindy put one arm on my shoulder. "Penny will be staying with us tonight." She looked down at me. "No arguments."

I wasn't about to argue. The thought of going home and sleeping alone in my cold bedroom, worrying about Dad and trying to shut out the images of the night, was less than appealing.

"Is it true?" Dex asked. "Was it Bryan and Cassidy?"

Cindy's brow furrowed. "Where'd you hear that?"

"They said on the news that two bodies were found in the woods with a truck. They didn't give names, but . . ."

"That was fast," I said. I doubted the sheriff would be happy that the discovery in the woods was already part of the news cycle.

"So . . . was it them?"

"Dex," Cindy warned. Her hand tightened on my shoulder.

"It's okay," I said. "I mean, it's not okay, but . . . there's no use hiding from it. I'm pretty sure it was them."

A sound escaped from Dex's mouth then, something between a sigh and a gasp. Like the air was being involuntarily pushed out.

"I think maybe it's time we all get some rest," Cindy said. "Dex, why don't you sleep on the couch and let Penny take your room?"

"No, really—" I started.

"Of course," Dex said, already heading toward the linen cabinet in the hall.

"You don't have to go to any trouble. . . ."

But Dex and Cindy were already moving in tandem, taking sheets out of the closet and arranging pillows on the couch.

Then Cindy's hand was on my back and she was ushering me into Dex's room. Though I hadn't been here in years, it was almost exactly the same as I remembered it. A small television sat in one corner, surrounded by a variety of game consoles and clusters of wires. The walls were covered in posters from sci-fi and fantasy television shows and movies. A line of dusty action hero figurines lined one shelf near the door.

Dex's bed was the only thing that was truly different. Instead of a narrow twin bed covered with a bright Pokémon spread, there was a larger queen with a dark blue bedspread pulled aside to reveal twisted maroon sheets. It didn't look like a child's bed anymore, but like somewhere an adult would sleep. It was disconcerting, suddenly, to picture Dex in that bed. Alone, or maybe even with a girl . . .

"You'll be okay in here?" Cindy asked me gently. I turned to look at her and managed a smile. I wanted to talk—about what I'd seen, about how scared I was for my dad, but she looked so tired in that moment as she pulled her robe more tightly around herself.

"Yeah, I'll be okay."

Cindy nodded and left, easing the door half-closed behind her.

I sat down on the edge of Dex's bed and looked around the

room. There was no way I was getting any kind of sleep tonight.

A shadow passed by the door.

"Dex?" I called softly.

After a moment, Dex stuck his head in.

"Everything okay?"

"It's my dad," I blurted.

Dex's features softened and he stepped into the room, lightly closing the door behind him.

"People are showing up dead in the woods, and he's out there. I don't know if he's camping, like the sheriff said, or chasing down a lead like you seem to think, but he *is* out there. Somewhere."

Dex took a step toward me and sat down next to me on the edge of the bed. He smelled like shampoo and sleep and boy.

"Before tonight, I was worried about Dad. But I was also mad at him. I really thought I might be able to find him, and he'd have some lame excuse . . . but what if something happened to him? Something really bad?" I asked. It felt awful, saying the words aloud. It gave them more weight, more meaning. More of a chance they were true.

Dex was silent for a long moment.

"You think something did happen to him," I pressed. "You said that from the beginning."

Dex sighed and shifted on the bed. "I know . . . but I am wrong about most things, remember? You've said *that* from the beginning." He gave an attempt at a smile. "I'm sure he's okay."

"Do you really think that, or are you lying to make me feel better?"

Dex sucked in his bottom lip and fixed his eyes on the floor, as if he was seriously considering my question. Finally, he shrugged. "Maybe I'm lying to make *myself* feel better."

I thought his answer would make me feel worse, but it did the opposite. The sheriff had done little more than shrug off my concerns, but Dex was here, sharing them. He was just as worried as me.

"Do me a favor, okay?" I asked. "No lying. Not even to make us feel better. If something did happen to my dad, we have to face it. We have to figure out how to find him."

Dex nodded enthusiastically. "Deal." He paused. "Does this mean I can talk about the Visitor theory again?"

"No."

"Because if what happened to Bryan and Cassidy is the same thing as what happened to that hiker—"

"Dex," I said, my voice a warning. "Let's stick to the facts."

"Facts. Got it. I can do that."

He didn't sound totally convincing.

"I mean, I can try," he said.

I smiled a little despite myself.

"So what are we going to do?" I asked, pulling my legs up so I sat cross-legged on Dex's crumpled sheets. "The sheriff said he's going to look for my dad, but I can't just sit around and wait."

"How about first thing tomorrow morning, we stick to our plan of looking through your dad's important files, the ones in the safe. I don't know the combination, but maybe we can figure it out together. And maybe there's something he left behind, some clue to tell us which direction he went in at least."

"Okay." I sat up straighter, my breathing more normal. "It's a place to start, anyway."

Dex sat next to me in silence for a few more moments, as if unsure what else to say. His fingers drummed a beat against his knees. "Do you want some company for a while? We can watch a movie or something. Something light. Like Pixar, maybe."

It was almost tempting, and I wasn't eager to be alone. But I didn't want to lose myself in a fantasy world, either. I wanted to stay in this one. I wanted to sort through all the weird facts twisting through my head until they came together in a clear pattern. Until they revealed something true.

"I'll be okay, Dex. Thanks, though."

"Right," he said, pushing himself up from the bed. "Good night."

"Good night."

As soon as the door was closed again, I lay back down against Dex's pillows. I shimmied out of my jeans and put them on the floor next to my purse. I took out my phone and checked the time—1:13 a.m. I wondered if it was too late to text Micah. He probably wasn't sleeping, either. But what would I say?

Thanks for getting me out of that pit full of bodies?

Sorry your friends are dead?

Are you okay?

He wouldn't be okay, I knew that. And no text could make what happened tonight any better. I set my phone down on the floor and leaned back in the bed.

I kept telling myself to reach up and turn off the lamp on the nightstand, but dreaded the moment that the room would plunge into darkness. I left the light on. But my mind kept going back to the woods, to the leaves and darkness, to the charred skin and fingernails of kids I once used to pass on the playground every day.

To my dad.

I drifted in and out of consciousness, but didn't really get more than ten minutes of sleep at a time. The light burned red dots through my eyelids, but still I didn't reach up to turn off the lamp. After what felt like several hours, I heard a familiar chiming noise and jumped nearly a foot in the air. I reached over the side of the bed and picked up my cell phone, sighing heavily when I saw it was only 4:00 a.m. The chiming noise had been my email notification.

I lay back on the pillows with my cell phone in my hand. It wasn't like I was going to get any real sleep that night, anyway.

I clicked open my email to see I had one new message. And then I stopped breathing.

It was from my dad.

FOURTEEN

Penny,

I'm so sorry I haven't been able to reach you these past few days. I really meant to be there to pick you up from the airport, but this story I'm chasing in Saskatchewan turned out to be bigger than I expected, and I had to stay for longer than I meant to. Like an idiot, I forgot my phone charger, and my cell died on day two. I've been out in the backwoods, far away from civilization. But I finally drove forty miles just to find internet to send this to you. I'll be in touch soon to let you know when I'm coming back.

Love,

Dad

"Well . . . that's a relief, at least," Dex said, rubbing his eyes and leaning back on the living room couch, which was covered in sheets and blankets. He smiled up at me, where I was perched on the cushion next to him. It was still dark out, but I hadn't been able to wait to show him the email.

"This is great news, Penny. Ike's okay."

My eyes ran over the first line of the email again.

"I don't know where my dad is, Dex. But he is most definitely not okay."

Dex sat up, blinking. "What do you mean? He says right there—"

"Read it again. Really read it." I thrust the warm phone into his hands and watched as his eyes skimmed the screen.

"Does that sound like my dad to you?"

Dex just scratched his neck as he read the email. I sighed in frustration.

"First of all, my dad would never start out an email like that with an apology. If he knew he'd let me down, he'd find some way to frame it like it couldn't be helped. And he wouldn't get angry at himself for forgetting his phone charger; he'd get angry at his phone for dying in the first place."

"Yeah . . . that's probably true. . . ."

"And look at this," I said, pointing out the first line in the email. "*Penny.* He said he named me Penelope for a reason, and he hated Penny, remember? He and my mom used to argue about it sometimes."

"I remember. . . ."

My eyes locked on to Dex's, which were filling up with confusion and fear.

"Oh my God," Dex said, jumping off the couch. He started to pace back and forth in front of the coffee table. "So what does this mean? Maybe . . . maybe the email is in code, and he's trying to warn you of something? Or maybe someone broke into his email account so you'd stop looking for him. Or maybe . . ."

The more Dex spoke, the more uneasy I felt. It should have been easy to dismiss his half-baked theories, but when I'd opened the email, I'd wondered the same things myself. I'd had the same thoughts as *Dex*, someone who had five—*five*—different books on Area 51 on his bookshelf.

But there *was* something wrong with that email. And it wasn't a hunch—it was a fact. Dad would never call me Penny, not ever.

Dex was still pacing in front of me. His blue-and-red Spider-Man pajamas passed by in a blur. I reached out one hand to stop him, and he came to a halt right in front of me, his knee hitting the palm of my hand.

"Dex," I said. "Let's think horses, remember? Not zebras."

Dex looked like he was going to argue for a second, but then changed his mind. "Okay. So where do we find the horses? Or . . . the facts? I'm kind of losing hold of your metaphor here."

"The horses are the truth," I said, taking the phone from

Dex's hand and scanning over the email again. "And I have no idea how to find them. I have no idea what's going on, or where my dad really is." I looked up and caught Dex's eye. "But I bet you a million Canadian dollars he's not in Saskatchewan."

I twisted the dial of the lock for the fortieth time, listening to the *click-click-click* noise it made under my hand. My dad's safe was about half my size and pushed into the corner of his tiny office.

Dex riffled through my dad's desk, which was covered in folders, old copies of *Strange World*, case notes, and bills. They were mixed in with snapshots of me at various ages, which had been handled with various degrees of care.

"Anything?" I asked.

"No. Not yet," Dex said.

I leaned my head against the cool metal of the safe and sighed. "There's got to be something in here. Something worth locking up, at least. But I have no idea what the combination is. It's not my dad's birthday, or my birthday, or either of my grandparents' birthdays."

Dex bit his lip, staring at the combination lock. "Let me try something."

He came over the safe, and I made space for him. He crouched down low and used his long fingers to spin the combination lock this way, then that. He pulled on the lock, but nothing happened.

"What did you try?"

Dex shook his head. "Doesn't matter. It was a long shot, anyway. Do you think your dad wrote the combination down somewhere?"

"Hard to say. Maybe? I mean, did my dad ever mention being paranoid about his work, or thinking someone was after it?"

Dex shook his head. "No. He mostly thought no one believed him. Even his editor was a skeptic when it came to Ike's investigation into the Visitors."

I sighed, and my eyes skimmed upward to my dad's corkboard. The top right corner was devoted to pictures of aliens and UFO landings. In one faded photo, a white creature with a bulbous head and round, coal-black eyes stared blankly into the middle distance. The photo had been there for as long as I could remember, longer than almost anything else in the room.

Was it possible my dad really *did* believe in the Visitors? Even if he didn't actually believe in any of the other stuff he sold to *Strange World* for a little bit of cash . . . aliens were the one thing he kept coming back to, again and again.

For the hundredth time that morning, my mind drifted to what I'd seen in the woods the night before. The remains of Bryan and Cassidy, twisted and charred. But the ground beneath them had been untouched. There were no other signs of a fire. . . . What could have done something like that?

I stood up quickly. "I'm going to check his bedroom, see if maybe he wrote the combination down on something in there."

Dex nodded absently from his position at the desk chair.

My dad's room looked exactly as it had the last time I'd checked in on it. I stepped in carefully and looked around at his half-opened closet, the socks spilling out of one drawer, the dirty plate on the nightstand. I felt like I was trespassing, like at any second, my dad would come in and ask me what I was doing in there.

But I just took a deep breath, walked over to the nightstand, and opened the top drawer. I moved through some of the items inside—a crossword puzzle book, various pens, an old glasses case, movie ticket stubs. I moved aside a packet of Kleenex and underneath found—

Condoms.

I slammed the drawer shut quickly, catching my pinkie finger in the process. Without thinking, I yelled out.

"You okay?" Dex came running into the room to find me standing by the nightstand, my pinkie finger half in my mouth.

"No. I mean, yeah. I just slammed my finger in the drawer, that's all."

"Anything good in there?" Dex moved toward the nightstand.

"No!"

Dex stopped abruptly and gave me an odd look before reaching for my hand. "Let me see."

He took my hand before I could do or say anything and turned it over carefully. He ran one of his fingers gently over the newly reddish skin on my pinkie, examining it. As his skin moved slowly against mine, the hairs on my arm began to rise.

"Just a bruise, I think," he said.

"Thanks," I said, pulling my hand back quickly. Dex blinked, and for a moment he looked like I'd just thrown cold water on his face. Then he shoved his hands into his pockets.

"I'm sure it'll be fine," I said. "I don't think we're going to find anything in here, though."

"Yeah, it's weird," Dex said, taking one hand out of his pocket and running it through his hair so it stood up on end. "Your dad kept files on every story he was working on, but I can't find many for this latest one. They *have* to be in that safe."

"Well, unless you're an expert at safecracking . . ."

Dex shook his head.

"Yeah, me neither. But we don't just stop because we hit one dead end. If you're trying to uncover a story and one path turns up nothing, you just start again with another."

Dex leaned up against the doorjamb, watching intently as I started to pace around the room, thinking.

"So what's the other path?" he asked.

"We ask for help."

Dex raised an eyebrow, and I sighed. "I can't think of any other option right now. We know that my dad's out there somewhere, and that he *didn't* send me that email. Which means he could be in trouble. But since we have no idea where to start looking for him, and just the two of us could never comb the whole woods alone . . . we need to get the help of someone who can."

"Someone like . . ."

"The sheriff."

Dex screwed his mouth up to the side. "You think he'll believe you? About the email?"

"I think I have to make him."

FIFTEEN

AS SOON AS we rounded the corner onto Main Street in Dex's car, I heard insistent honking and the jumbled voices of a crowd, two things that were completely out of place on an early summer afternoon in Bone Lake.

Once we parked, the source of the commotion became clear. Three large vans bearing the logos of various news stations were parked along the sides of the street, in one case blocking off access to the community bank. A crowd was gathered in front of the police station. I recognized a few of them as the parents of kids I'd gone to school with: Mrs. Chidester, who used to babysit me, and Mr. Harlan, who owned the shooting range. Hector was there, and Mrs. Anderson. Some people I recognized from the bonfire a few nights before were there too, though I didn't see Micah anywhere. I felt a small pang as I imagined what he must be feeling right now. I hoped he wasn't alone.

I stood up on my toes to try to see above the heads in the crowd, on the lookout for the sheriff. Instead, my eyes were drawn to a middle-aged woman being propped up by a tall, stoic-looking man. The couple stood near the post office, a bit away from the fray in front of the police station. The woman's face was distorted, her mouth open wide as if she were wailing, though she was making no sound. Her hands clutched at the shirt of the man next to her, then fell to her sides, useless. It took me a moment to recognize them.

Cassidy Jones's parents.

Dex was also looking at the couple, his mouth drawn into a thin line. I tried to think of something to say, but came up with nothing.

"Let's go around," Dex finally said.

But I couldn't look away from Mrs. Jones, who had the same freckles as her daughter. I barely knew her, but Cassidy had had a life. Family, school, boyfriend. A favorite TV show, drama with her friends, unopened snaps on her phone.

Plans for the future.

And now all that was gone, wiped out forever. I pulled my eyes away and followed Dex to the alley next to the police station. We didn't get more than a few feet before a shrill voice yelled, "She's here! That's who found them!"

I turned to see Emily Jennings standing on the sidewalk, her brown bob shining in the sunlight, one long arm outstretched and pointing straight at me. So many heads swiveled in my direction, all at once.

A woman in a lime-green blouse with a microphone clenched in her fist reached me first. Her expression was one of concern but also of interest, and as she raised the microphone up to her mouth I realized I was looking into the face of the woman I wanted to be someday.

So I only minded a little when her first words were, "Is it true? Did you find the bodies?"

Dex reached out and pulled on my sleeve, looking a bit shell-shocked as the cameras surrounded us, pinning us in place. But they were just doing a job. As hard and uncomfortable as it might be, they just wanted to get to the truth. And I could help them with that.

I straightened my shoulders. "Yes. It's true."

"What's your name?" The woman asked. The microphone in her hand read WKBM News.

"Penny Hardjoy."

I heard a snicker from my right, and looked up to see Reese standing by Emily. Her eyes narrowed when she saw me watching her, and she mouthed, *attention whore.*

I turned back to the woman in the lime-green shirt, swallowing hard.

"Can you tell us a little bit about what you found? Were the bodies recognizable?"

"That's enough," a voice cut through the crowd. I looked up

to see the sheriff pushing his way over to me. "This girl's a witness in an ongoing investigation. And a minor."

He didn't wait for the journalist to respond, instead putting one hand on my shoulder and leading me through the crowd, away from the cameras.

"You should get on home, Penny," he said, low and into my ear.

"I came to talk to you, Sheriff. It's important."

He gave a terse nod. "Go on and wait inside. I'll just be a moment." Then he walked to the front of the station, facing the entire crowd. The camera lenses followed him like moths following a light.

Instead of going inside the building, I moved a bit into the shadows near the side door, where I could hear whatever the sheriff was going to say. Dex silently moved to stand next to me.

The sheriff cleared his throat. "Good morning. The Charlevoix County Sheriff's Office, along with the Bone Lake PD, is prepared to issue a statement on the two bodies found last night near North Lake. We have identified the remains as those belonging to seventeen-year-old Bryan Ryder and sixteen-year-old Cassidy Jones."

A murmur ran through the crowd, even though it didn't seem like this could be a surprise to anyone at this point.

"Do you know how they died?" the woman in the lime-green blouse asked, pushing her microphone forward.

"How long have they been dead?" a man next to her asked.

"I will not be answering questions at this time," the sheriff continued. "But I will conclude my statement by saying foul play is suspected. We also suspect that these two deaths might be connected to that of John Forrest, the hiker who was found near Raskers' Field in February. While we have no main suspect at this time, we are searching for a person of interest named Ike Hardjoy, a Bone Lake native who disappeared shortly after Bryan and Cassidy went missing. If you have any leads on Hardjoy's whereabouts, please direct them to the sheriff's office. Thank you."

The sheriff moved quickly away from the crowd of reporters, back toward the front door of the station. My own feet felt like lead.

"Person of interest?" Dex asked, his eyebrows furrowed. "That doesn't sound good."

"No, it doesn't," I whispered, my throat going tight. "He thinks my dad's the killer."

"HOW COULD HE possibly think that about Ike?" Dex asked, one step behind me as I walked quickly under the fluorescent lights of the sheriff's office. "He's not dangerous—he's the one *in danger* out there!"

"Guess that's not what the cops are thinking right now," I said, pausing just before we got to the front desk to keep our voices out of earshot of the secretary there. "If they really thought my dad was in danger, then they'd have said that. They'd launch a manhunt or something. But 'person of interest'? That's suspect talk."

Dex shook his head. "But the sheriff *knows* your dad. There's no way he'd think Ike could do something like . . . this."

Adultery was a far cry from murder, but I knew Sheriff Harper had no reason to give my dad the benefit of the doubt.

"We just have to talk to him. Convince him my dad's in danger, not a threat."

But even as I spoke the words, I felt a twinge of doubt. I was positive the email I'd been sent wasn't from my dad, but did that necessarily mean he had nothing to do with what was happening in the woods of Bone Lake? All I really had was my gut feeling that my dad, despite his faults, wasn't a killer. And yet . . . my gut had once told me that monsters were real, and that had turned out to be wrong. My gut also once told me that my dad loved my mom and would never hurt her, and that had turned out to be wrong, too.

So maybe my gut couldn't be trusted. Which meant I had to fall back on facts. And right now, I wasn't working with very many of them.

A deputy led Dex and me to the same back hall where I'd sat with Micah the night before. After twenty minutes, the sheriff finally opened his office door and beckoned us inside. Up close and in the harsh yellow lighting of the room, he looked like he hadn't slept in days. He sighed heavily as he took a seat at his desk.

"You have something you need to tell me?"

I sat up straighter and grabbed the folded piece of paper from my pocket; I'd printed the email in Dad's office before leaving the house.

"I got this early this morning. It says it's from my dad, but I know that it's not. It's possible it might be from someone else, someone who knows where he is."

The sheriff raised one eyebrow as he reached for the printout. While he read, my eyes fell on a framed photo on his desk, one of Reese and her mom standing in front of a Christmas tree, their arms around each other. I looked away.

The sheriff peered at me over the top of the printed-out email, then set it down on his desk. "Penny, this sounds like it's your dad—"

"I get how you might say that," I interrupted, eager to explain myself. "But it's not from him. That's not how my dad talks or writes, and he never calls me Penny. Ever."

"It's true," Dex piped up. "I can back that up."

"But this *is* his email address?" the sheriff asked.

"Well . . . yes. But that just means that someone has access to his account. Which I think means that my dad could be in danger. Maybe the person who wrote this is the same person who . . . who killed Bryan and Cassidy."

The sheriff stared again at the piece of paper before slipping it into a folder on his desk. "I want to thank you for bringing this to my attention." He quickly picked up the receiver of his phone, and I saw something flash across his face, something like eagerness.

That's when I knew I had no chance of convincing him the email wasn't from my dad. Maybe I'd never had a chance. Instead, the email was somehow confirming whatever theory the sheriff already had—and I'd handed it right to him.

He put the receiver to his mouth. "Mary, gather everyone in the evidence room for a meeting in ten." He hung up again, and I knew I was just seconds away from being dismissed.

"I'm telling you, my dad didn't write that," I said, knowing full well the sheriff had already stopped listening to anything I had to say.

"I won't rule out any possibility, Penny," the sheriff said, his voice condescending.

"Sheriff, listen. My dad could be out there somewhere, hurt or . . ." I couldn't bring myself to finish the sentence.

"Rest assured, we are doing everything in our power to find your dad. And even if you think this email sounds odd, it's still the best proof we have that Ike is fine. But if you hear from him again, you let me know immediately, okay? We have some questions for him."

I exchanged a quick look with Dex.

"He didn't do this. I know he didn't."

"No one is saying he did," the sheriff said calmly.

I rolled my eyes. "Please. I know what *person of interest* means."

"*Person of interest* means person of interest. That's all."

He clearly wasn't going to tell me anything. Unless . . .

"Just tell me why you think he had something to do with this." I kept my eyes on his, doing my best to channel the confidence of the reporter outside. I lifted my chin. "You want me to keep you in the loop if I hear from him, but I won't accidentally incriminate my dad just because you have an old grudge against him."

The sheriff's eyes narrowed briefly, and his jaw twitched as if he was grinding his teeth together. From the corner of my eye, I saw Dex's head tilt. He was probably confused about this "grudge." But I wouldn't out the secret the sheriff and Julie Harper had kept all these years. Not unless I had to.

"You know I'm the person he's most likely to reach out to. And if you want me to let you know the next time he does," I said, eyeing the folder, "I need to know why he's a person of interest."

The sheriff kept his cool gaze on me, and for a moment I thought he would kick me out of his office. Or maybe arrest me. Instead, he pushed back from his desk and crossed his arms. One second passed, then two.

"Fine. This will be public soon anyway. An item was found at the scene, near Bryan's truck. It belonged to your father."

I could hear blood pounding through my head, thudding through my ears. Next to me, Dex made a scoffing sound, but I could barely hear it. My arms felt like they were filled with iron, weighed down to the sides of the chair.

"What . . . kind of item?" I whispered.

"That's all the information I can give you right now," the sheriff said coolly.

I knew the signs of a brush-off, and my brain struggled to come up with arguments, to get him to say anything more.

"But . . . just because something of Ike's was out in those woods doesn't mean that he . . . I mean, he goes out there all the time!" Dex said, his voice rising. "Maybe he dropped something there before. Or maybe he found the bodies, and then—"

"Didn't come forward?"

I swallowed. "Just because you found something of his out there doesn't prove he did anything wrong."

"No, it just makes him a *person of interest*. It's important that we find him and ask him everything he knows. So you'll tell me, Penny, if he gets in touch with you?"

All I could do was nod.

"Thanks for your cooperation," the sheriff said, rising from his chair.

Dex and I got up, too, letting ourselves be led from the office. The sheriff even put one hand on my shoulder, ushering me from the room and out into the hall. There was no need—I didn't want to be in this place for one second longer. I needed to think over this piece of information and figure out what it meant. What object of my dad's had been found in the woods with Bryan and Cassidy? And what did that mean, if it meant anything at all?

The thoughts swirled too quickly through my head for me to latch on to any one of them. There were too many gaps. . . . I needed to know *more.*

The sheriff continued to lead us down the hall, as if he was afraid we wouldn't actually make it to the exit without his help.

We passed an open doorway on our way out, and two men I'd never seen before were standing in the small office, their heads bent together as they spoke. They both had dark hair, cut close to their heads. Both wore crisp black suits and shiny black shoes that seemed out of place among the worn brown uniforms and paneled walls of the sheriff's office. These men weren't from the group of journalists outside. They were something else altogether.

I slowed my steps, trying to get a better look as we passed. One of the men looked up, catching my eye. Without looking away or changing his expression at all, he took two steps to the door and shut it firmly in my face.

SEVENTEEN

MY PARENTS HADN'T spoken to each other in four years. If the last year of their marriage was rough, their divorce was even rougher. I tried to block out as much of their arguing as I could, but it wasn't like there was anywhere else for me to go. I wasn't friends with Dex anymore, and Reese wasn't talking to me. Sometimes Cindy would let me hang out with her in the kitchen of Sweet Street while she worked on cupcake orders, teaching me how to swirl little pink roses out of frosting. But I spent most of my time up in the house that sat high in an oak tree square in the middle of Dex's yard and mine. Our dads had built it for us as kids, and our names were still carved into the wood boards—*Penelope and Dex, 2009.*

I was hiding up in that house, reading an old paperback mystery, when my parents' marriage finally exploded beyond repair. I heard a slamming noise, one so loud it made me jump. I scooted over to the tree house's tiny window that looked down over my backyard to see my dad storming out of our back door, his arms full of clothes. A pair of jeans hung down from the crook of his elbow, the frayed hem trailing through the dirt. I recognized them immediately as Mom's.

Dad took four giant steps into the yard and tossed the entire armful—colorful blouses, old worn flannels, even my mom's favorite pajama bottoms—out onto the grass. Seconds later, Mom came running out the back door. She took one look at the contents of her closet, now splayed across our yard, and her mouth fell open. Even from my perch in the tree house, I could see her hands shaking. She whirled on Dad.

"Really? This is what you're going to do?"

Dad turned to face her. His movements were incredibly slow, deliberate. His jaw was clenched tight, and a shadow seemed to cross over his eyes. He looked like a stranger to me in that moment, and I unconsciously ducked down lower in the tree house so I wouldn't be seen.

"You're damn right this is what I'm going to do," Dad said. His voice was cold, but there was a fury underneath, like rapids raging beneath a thin layer of ice, ready to crack free at any moment and pull anything in its path into the undertow.

Dad took one step closer to Mom, hovering over her so she had to physically shrink back. "If you don't want to be here, Nora, then *get the fuck out of my house.*"

Before she could reply, before she could react at all, he turned and walked back inside, slamming the door in her face.

Mom already had her teaching job in Chicago lined up, and she and I left not long after that. It was much easier to say goodbye to Bone Lake than I thought it would be. The first time I spoke to Dad on the phone from my new bedroom in Evanston, he sounded bright, cheery almost. And when I visited that next Christmas, he already seemed to be putting everything behind him. He was back to throwing himself into work, staying up all night to write in his office and taking trips across the country to "hunt" various imaginary beings he could fool people into believing were real. He never knew that I was in the tree house that day, that I'd seen and heard everything. But even if he could move on, I couldn't. That memory stayed lodged in the back of my head, the cold anger of his voice, the darkness in his eyes.

Was it possible that wasn't just a one-time occurrence? That there might be a whole other side to my dad I didn't know about? I knew that sometimes he put work and his stories before everything else—even the people he was supposed to love most. And when he'd had his fling with Julie, he certainly hadn't cared about who might get hurt in the process. I'd spent many years being angry with him for that and for everything else. But it was still hard to believe, even for a second, that the sheriff's theory might actually be true.

That he might be a killer.

After getting back from the police station, I told Dex I

wanted to spend some time alone. He dropped me off at my house with a sad smile and a wave and told me he'd be next door if I needed anything.

But there was only one person I needed to talk to.

I walked inside quickly, shutting the door and then all the windows before sitting down in the far corner of the couch, my cell phone in my hand. I felt sick to my stomach. I wanted to believe there was no way my dad could have hurt Bryan and Cassidy—*no way.* Guilt ripped through me for even entertaining the notion. But I couldn't shut it out, either. I had to talk to someone else who knew Dad—and not just the goofy *Strange World* columnist who was alternately ignored or tolerated around Bone Lake. Someone who really *knew* him.

I took out my international calling card and dialed the number where Mom was staying in Spain. She picked up quickly, but her voice sounded sluggish when she answered. "Hello?"

"Hi, Mom. Did I wake you?"

"No!" she said, her voice suddenly bright. "I was just up doing some reading." I knew she was lying, and I pictured her sitting up in bed, reaching for her reading glasses, which were probably resting on a pile of books nearby.

"It's so good to hear your voice! Don't we have a phone date on Sunday?"

"Yeah . . ." My voice wavered, only for a fraction of an instant. But she heard it.

"What's wrong?" She slipped into her calm, authoritative

tone, the one that always solved problems. It made me want to spill my secrets into the phone, lay my problems at her feet so she could handle them and I wouldn't have to worry about them anymore. And yet . . . if I told her everything that was happening in Bone Lake, about Dad being missing, about the dead teens . . . she'd send me to stay with my grandparents in Florida for the summer. Or worse, she'd fly straight here to get me and take me back to Evanston, where I'd be "safe." She'd miss out on the sabbatical that she'd lobbied and fought for two years to get, the one she'd been looking forward to her whole career. If that happened I might never figure out what was going on, and there'd be no one here who was on Dad's side except for Dex.

If *I* was even on Dad's side.

I decided it would be best to be vague, for now at least. "It's about Dad . . ." I started.

There was a pause then, so deep and silent that I wondered if our call had been dropped.

"Okay," she finally said, cautious.

"I know we don't really talk about him much. Or at all. But . . ." I took a deep breath.

"Honey, is everything okay?"

"Yes," I lied. "Of course. It's just . . . do you think Dad is a good person?"

Another pause. I heard some slight shuffling, as though Mom was repositioning herself. "That's a difficult question to answer," she said.

"Because you hate him?"

"No!" The insistence in Mom's voice surprised me a bit. "Gosh, Penny, I don't hate your father. Is that really what you think?"

"Well, yeah. I mean, he . . ." I swallowed hard. "He *cheated* on you, Mom. It's the whole reason you got divorced. The reason we moved away."

"Oh, no . . . no, no, no, Penny, that's . . . It was so much more complicated than that."

"I was there, Mom. I remember—the cheating, the fights after you found out . . ."

"Yes, that's part of it, but it's not . . ." Mom sighed heavily. "I should have talked about this with you sooner. I just didn't want to force you to discuss the divorce if you didn't want to. You were at such a difficult age—old enough to know what was happening, but not old enough to want the details. . . ."

"I want the details now, Mom. It's important." Embarrassingly, I felt a lump rise up in my throat. Something about talking to my mom over the phone, hearing her voice but not seeing her face, seemed to strip away my defenses. It felt like crawling under a blanket. It felt like being ten years old.

"Your dad isn't a bad person, Penny. I don't think things are as simple as that—a good person and a bad," she said, slow and deliberate.

"Sure it is," I said. "The good person doesn't lie. The good person doesn't cheat."

"That's . . . a very black-and-white way to look at things, Penny. Though, knowing you, that doesn't surprise me." Mom made a small sound then, halfway between a sigh and a rueful laugh.

"That's because the truth *is* black and white."

"Not always, hon," she said, then sucked in a breath. "I was very angry with your father for what he did. Not just that it happened, but that you saw it. I'm *still* angry about that, honestly. It's a hard thing to let go of. But, Penny, Julie Harper did not cause our marriage to fall apart. It was dead in the water long before your dad cheated. It's probably *why* he cheated."

The lump in my throat grew as I tried to reconcile these words with the memories of that year I had in my mind. The memories I'd gone over again and again, until they'd crystallized into unmovable, unchangeable shards that hurt every time I touched them.

I shook my head, even though I knew my mom couldn't see. "I know you were fighting some that year—"

"Not just some. And not just that year. Neither of us had the courage to just be honest and end things, so your dad . . . took a more drastic course of action."

I thought about the photos I'd found in Dad's living room, the ones dating back to when he and Mom first met. Their happy smiles had faded out long before the year everything fell apart. Exactly when did it all go wrong?

"What happened? Please, Mom. I need to know."

A silence again. I pictured Mom pursing her lips, winding a piece of long, dark hair around her finger, like she did when she was thinking.

"Okay, Penny. Okay." Mom cleared her throat. "When I met your dad, he was just . . . different from anyone I knew. He had a way of looking at me that made me feel like I was the most important thing in the world."

"And then he changed?"

"No, honey. *I* did. I was twenty years old when I started dating your dad. I was saving up money to go to college, but then I fell for Ike, and then . . ."

"Then there was me."

"Yes. But listen, Penny," Mom said, her voice growing forceful. "You're the best thing that ever happened to me, then and now. I don't regret for a second the decision I made to stay in Michigan and have you. Not ever. Do you understand?"

The lump in my throat expanded, and it took all my effort to choke out, "Yes."

"Good," Mom said, and let out a big breath. "I really did love your dad, and we thought we could make it work. But with every year that passed, I started to feel it more and more, how small Bone Lake was, how it felt like it was getting smaller. I felt . . . trapped."

As Mom talked, I pushed myself back farther against the couch cushions, fighting the sudden feeling that I might fall over the edge. Mom had never spoken to me like this, not really. She'd talked to me about my life, about my problems, my school, my dreams. But she'd never really talked about herself in this open kind of way. It felt strange to hear her speak about feeling stuck in Bone Lake. It was like reading the scribbled, confused, and unspeakable things I wrote in my own diary.

It was terrifying.

To imagine that my mom could feel just as lost and stuck as me . . . it was like trying to lean back on a solid, familiar wall and finding it had moved a few feet when you weren't looking.

"Penny, are you still there?" My mom's voice sounded small on the other side of the phone, and I wondered if it was just as hard for her to say these things as it was for me to hear them.

"I'm here," I replied. "So you were unhappy, and then you and Dad . . . fell out of love."

"Well . . . I did."

I shook my head, again forgetting that my mom couldn't see. "What do you mean? Dad was the one who fell for someone else."

A heavy sigh then. "I think you're fixating on that one thing. Which is understandable. But your dad tried to hold on to me for a long, long time after I'd let go, after I was already planning a future away from Bone Lake. Because I knew I had to leave, and I knew he'd never go with me. So I pushed him away. Your dad was so hurt, and I didn't know how to make it better. And then he found his own way."

"With my best friend's mom."

"I'm not saying it was a *good* way." Mom paused. "And I know he regretted it, too. Especially since it cost him custody in the end."

"Wait—what?"

Mom took another deep breath. "When I told him I was leaving for Chicago and taking you with me, your dad . . . didn't take it well."

"I remember."

"He told me he'd fight for you, and then he did."

I gripped the phone tighter in my hand. "What? But . . . I don't remember that."

"Well, we tried to keep you away from the legal stuff as much as we could. Your dad fought to keep you in Bone Lake. But with my increased salary in Chicago, your dad making less and less on his column, then his affair with Julie, and how you were the one to catch them . . . the judge said he was lucky to get holidays and three weeks every summer."

The lump in my throat had turned sharp and jagged. I barely recognized my voice when I spoke. "I didn't know he fought for me. I didn't know."

"Of course he fought for you," Mom said, her voice gentle. "Honey, I don't know what's going on between you two right now, and Lord knows your dad's not perfect . . . but he loves you more than anything in this entire world. You do know that, right?"

I pulled the phone away so my mom couldn't hear the quiet

sob I was forcing back down my throat. But she knew anyway. I knew she knew.

"I should have told you all this a long time ago," she said, and I could tell she'd started to cry, too.

"It's just . . ." I said, taking a shaky breath, "When I was a kid, I thought I knew Dad better than anyone. He was, like . . . this perfect person. And then all that changed. And for the past few years, I thought I finally knew the real truth about him, and I've been so . . . so . . . *angry*. . . ."

"Oh, sweetie," Mom whispered.

"And now I just don't know what to think. About anything. If Dad's not who I thought he was—*again*—then who is he?"

"Well," Mom said, sniffing and slipping back into her calm, reasonable tone. "You have all summer to start figuring that out."

I didn't know how to tell her that it might be too late.

"Yeah." I sniffed.

"And you're sure there's nothing else going on? I haven't heard you this upset in a while."

"No, it's . . . I'm fine. Just trying to figure stuff out, with Dad." I swallowed, hating my half lie. "Plus, I think I miss you a little."

She laughed a tiny bit at that. "Well, I miss you a lot," she said.

After hanging up the phone, I sat on the couch, staring off into nothing. I wanted new information, and now I had it. But instead of answering questions, it left me with a million more.

Just who *was* Ike Hardjoy? All of my memories of him were one swirling, untidy mess in my mind. And maybe I'd never seen those memories from a wide enough angle in the first place. Behind every truth was another perspective, and another. And I was no closer to knowing how Dad was connected to everything that was going on in Bone Lake—

Except . . .

I jumped off the couch, the phone almost flying from my hand. Feeling almost like I'd received an electric shock, I ran quickly to Dad's office. I threw open the door and sank down in front of his locked safe. By the time my hand reached for the combination lock, my fingers were shaking. This was a long shot, but if what my mom had told me was true . . .

I entered six digits into the keypad. 10-13-01. My parents' wedding anniversary.

The lock beeped, and the door to the safe popped open with a soft *click*. So this was one of my dad's secrets, then: that after all these years, the date he married my mom was still important enough for him to remember. Important enough to guard all his other secrets. I put my fingers around the edge of the door and pulled, ready to see what was waiting inside.

EIGHTEEN

DEX CAME RUSHING into the room so fast his tennis shoes skidded across the wooden floor.

"You got it open?"

I gestured to the piles of paper that were gathered around me on the office floor. "Yep."

"And?"

I sighed, pulling at the ends of my hair. "And nothing. There's nothing in here about the hiker in the woods, or about Bryan and Cassidy, or where my dad might have gone. All of these papers are at least a decade old. Most of them seem like 'research' for his first story on the Visitors." I held my fingers up, making air quotes at the word *research*.

"Let me see," Dex said. He dropped ungracefully to the floor across from me, one of his knees pushing up against mine. He didn't seem to notice, reaching instead for the piece of paper nearest to him.

It was an article from a local paper, already faded and yellow, that documented how scientists had flooded into Bone Lake after the meteorite fell. The meteorite itself had been larger than most, the size of a love seat. The crater it created in the woods outside town was more than fifteen feet across. I'd already known that, but what I hadn't known about was what drew the majority of scientists—and national attention—to our town. It wasn't the meteorite's size that caused a stir; it was its composition.

I watched Dex's eyes go back and forth as they scanned over what I had just read. The Bone Lake Meteorite contained not just silicate minerals, but a substantial amount of amino acids and other organic material. That in itself was relatively rare for a meteorite, but it also contained a streak of a gold-colored unknown metal running through its middle. That's what really caused all the fuss. People speculated on what the new kind of metal could be, but after testing it was found to be just another, previously unseen kind of iron-nickel alloy. After all that, the whole meteorite crash was really nothing to write home about.

Unless you had the kind of imagination and nose for opportunity that Ike Hardjoy did.

Scattered across the various papers and articles were notes handwritten by my dad. Next to a scientific article detailing the unusually large amount of amino acids in the meteorite, Dad had scrawled, *enough to sustain life?* Next to an image of scientists in giant yellow hazmat suits lifting the meteorite out of the ground, Dad had written, *radiation?!?* If you didn't know my dad, you might look at these notes and think he was some kind of crackpot conspiracy theorist, but I saw what his scribbles really were. They were notes on a story, and my dad had been pumping it for as many exciting details as he could.

"Look at all this stuff," Dex said, awe in his voice. "Ike was really on to something."

"Mm-hmm, the short list for the Pulitzer in bullshitting."

I smiled, but Dex wasn't having it. The bottom corners of his lower lip tightened, and his dark eyebrows pulled together. It almost made him look older, if you ignored the way his messy hair fell over the tips of his ears or how there was what looked like a small mustard stain near the collar of his shirt.

"It's easy to be a skeptic, but there are things in this world that go beyond simple explanation," Dex muttered. "Even *you* have to admit what's happening in town is weird. Burned bodies. Missing people."

Not to mention the sleek black car that had been popping up and the email from "Dad." But there wasn't any point in bringing that up and giving Dex more fodder for his overactive imagination.

"Weird, yes. But not unexplainable. It's true we don't know exactly what's going on yet. But I do know with a hundred percent certainty that it's not 'alien landings.'"

Dex looked up then, his eyes going sharp. "You *can't* say that with a hundred percent certainty. No one can. At least your dad was smart enough to realize there were things out there he didn't know. You *think* you know everything, and you don't."

I opened my mouth to reply, but then closed it again. The conversation I'd had with my mom was still playing on loop in the background of my mind. I'd thought I'd known certain things about my dad to be absolutely true, and it turned out I'd been wrong.

The truth is *black and white.*

Not always, hon.

I bit my lip and went back to sorting through my dad's notes.

"Sorry," Dex said, looking chagrined. "I didn't mean for that to come out so harsh."

"It's okay," I said, but I still didn't risk looking up and letting Dex see how much his words had affected me. I'd been clinging so hard to facts, thinking they'd lead me from point A to point B to a firm explanation. But every time I grabbed hold of new information about my dad, it erased something I already knew. The truth kept mutating, and my grip on facts was slipping.

And that was frightening in about fifty different ways. None of which I was ready to share with Dex—or anyone.

We both went back to silently going through the papers.

Dex held up the local article again. "Hey, did you see this part? About when the meteorite was discovered?"

I looked back over the yellowing front page of the article.

There was a one-paragraph mention of Tommy Cray, a Bone Lake resident who was the first to find where the meteorite landed after it fell from the sky. The paragraph had been circled four times in dark red ink.

"What do you think that's all about? Why would your dad circle this section?"

I shrugged.

"It doesn't make any sense," Dex said, after a few moments. "These papers are all old, but I know Ike keeps notes from his most recent stories in his safe. So maybe he was working on this story again, and some of these notations are newer. Ike *did* think that what happened to the hiker was connected to the Visitors. Maybe he went back over his old notes for that story, trying to find a new angle."

Dex peered at a bit of my dad's handwriting that was scrawled on what looked like a printed-out AP News brief. It covered how government scientists had closed off the meteorite crash site to journalists and the public while they were figuring out how to test the area. In the upper corner, Dad had written *Cover-up?* with a blue pen. Underneath that, in black ink, was the question *Government agency—why?*

"Wait, look at this," Dex said. He was holding another old article in his hands, this one from the *Traverse City Record-Eagle*. "It's not about the meteorite at all. It's from a few years later. Maybe it can help you with that story you're working on for college?"

I straightened, reaching automatically for the piece of paper. I hadn't given my Northwestern article much thought since the moment I tripped over what was left of Bryan and Cassidy in the woods.

Residents of Bone Lake Resilient in the Face of Plant Closure. The article quickly covered the accident, Mr. Jameson's responsibility, the lost military contract, and the subsequent permanent closing of the factory. The mayor had submitted a vague, PR-ready answer about how Bone Lake was a robust community that would survive this setback, and the few residents interviewed gave answers that were even more vague, if that was possible.

> *"One guy screws up and it all goes away," said Wally Watting, who lost his job as a quality inspector at the plant after working there for seven years. When asked about the specifics of the accident that led to the plant closing, Watting had no further details to provide other than those that were already delivered in the official report. "It was just gross human error, not the plant's fault at all, but that doesn't matter, apparently," Watting said. "I guess now it's just time to move on. Best not to think too much about it."*

I sucked in a breath.

"Something wrong?" Dex asked.

"I don't know," I said. "I've seen these words before. Or

heard them, actually. Whenever I ask someone in town about the plant closing, they give this line—'best not to think too much about it.'"

Dex tilted his head to look down at the paper in my hand. His eyebrows knitted together again. "They say that exact line?"

"There's got to be an explanation," I said. And then I tried to think of what that explanation might be. Maybe everyone in town had read this article and started unconsciously quoting Wally Watting?

I shook my head. I'd come back to the weird line later. Right now was about finding Dad.

"Why did my dad have a copy of this locked up with his research anyway?" I asked. "The plant had nothing to do with the meteorite . . . right?"

Dex shrugged. He pointed to the last page of the article, which had one of Dad's business cards attached to it by a paper clip. Across the top edge of the card, Dad had scribbled, also in red ink, *X10-88*.

"X10-88 . . . What's that?"

Dex moved even closer to get a better look at the card, his shoulder bumping against mine. His hair smelled like maple and sugar, like he'd just been in Cindy's kitchen.

"I've never heard of it," he said. "But look, Penny . . ." He pointed to the lettering on my dad's business card with one long finger. There was Dad's name, and his "job title" of *Reporter*, and his phone number and email. "This is a new card. Look at his email."

"You're right," I murmured. My dad had used the same old Hotmail account for years before *Strange World* finally forced him to get a business email—last summer.

"That means I was right! This note he made in red pen is new," Dex said. "Hold on." He pulled his phone out of his pocket and typed *X10-88* into Google. "Nothing's really coming up. . . . Looks like it's the designation for some sheet metal products. . . ."

"I'll do some more research," I said, stretching my back. "It might mean nothing at all—"

I was interrupted by a loud banging noise. Dex jumped a little, and it took me a second to realize someone was knocking on the front door.

I opened the door to see two men standing on my front porch. They were both of average height and build, both with pale skin and dark, brownish hair. The man on the right had a squarish jaw, and the other wore a bright yellow tie with a gray chevron pattern. Other than that, they were practically identical, down to the dark suits with crisp white shirts and shiny, shiny shoes.

They looked like the men I'd seen at the sheriff's office earlier that day, but I couldn't be 100 percent sure. Their faces were incredibly generic; they'd be a sketch artist's worst nightmare.

"Miss Hardjoy?" the man on the right asked. He took off a pair of sunglasses, revealing small blue eyes. The man with the yellow tie kept his sunglasses on.

"Uh, yes," I stammered. "That's me."

The man on the right held up a white card with writing on it. "My name is Agent Rickard, and this is Agent Shanahan. We're with the Federal Bureau of Investigation."

"The . . . FBI?" It was a dumb question to ask, but my head was still adjusting to the fact that two federal agents were standing on my front porch. That they'd asked for me by name.

"We're investigating the recent murders in Bone Lake. You were present at the discovery of the last two bodies, yes?"

It was a question, but Agent Rickard said it like a statement. Next to him, Agent Shanahan remained immobile, his eyes completely unreadable behind his dark sunglasses.

"I . . . yes. But I thought the sheriff was investigating . . . ?"

"The first victim was a resident of Wisconsin, and the second two are residents of Michigan, killed in the same way. That makes this a multistate investigation. We were called in to assist."

His words bounced around in my head. Something about what he was saying didn't add up, but before I could really catch hold of that thought, he went on.

"We have a warrant to search the premises of one Mr. Ike Hardjoy. This is his primary residence, yes?"

Again, that question felt like it was really a statement. My heart sped up at the word *warrant.* I was still standing in the doorway, blocking the two agents from the inside of the house. But I knew I couldn't keep them out if they had a warrant. I wondered if Dex was standing somewhere behind me, or if he was in Dad's office still, surrounded by all his creepy notes on aliens. What would the agents think if they searched Dad's office? Would everything in there help build a case against him? Could it possibly paint him into looking like an unhinged killer?

I stalled, my hand gripping the edge of the doorway.

"Miss," the second agent spoke up, "the paperwork's in order. We're going to need you to move."

Agent Rickard took one step forward, and I couldn't do anything but step back, letting them in. They both immediately headed toward Dad's office, as if they knew exactly where to start looking.

"My dad didn't do anything wrong," I said, finally finding my voice as I followed them back through the hallway. "He's missing. He might be in trouble."

They didn't answer me.

I was just two steps behind the agents by the time they walked through my dad's office door. Some of his papers from the open safe were still strewn about on the floor, but I noticed many of the piles were noticeably smaller, with some papers missing. Dex was missing, too. And the office window was wide-open, letting in the breeze from the backyard. I stifled my sigh of relief.

"We'll start in here, miss," Agent Rickard said, pulling a pair of latex gloves from his pocket. "Please wait in the front area until we are done."

It was stated like a request, but I knew it wasn't one.

I walked back into the living room and perched on the edge of the couch, unsure what to do with myself. Should I offer the agents water? Should I turn on the TV or check my phone? Nothing seemed right. Instead, I stared out the front window, at the agents' black car, which sat parked in front of our yard.

The shiny, new-looking black car.

I nearly jumped off the couch. The wayward thought that had been bouncing around the back of my mind suddenly thudded into place. These agents had said they were called in to investigate the murders after Bryan and Cassidy had turned up in the woods, because they were killed in the same way as the out-of-state hiker.

But I'd seen that car before. I'd seen it driving around Mrs. Anderson's street. I'd seen it moving slowly past my own house.

Two whole days *before* Bryan and Cassidy's bodies had even been found.

NINETEEN

OVER THE NEXT few hours, the agents ended up removing every book, file, and scrap of paper from my dad's office, packing them up into plastic tubs and loading them up in their sleek black car. They took some papers from his bedroom, too, and all of the spare notes that had collected over the years in the junk drawer of the kitchen. They snapped photos of every inch of the house, opening every drawer and cupboard. They even searched my room, not that there was anything to find except for bags of old homework and bottles of dried-up nail polish.

The agents had only taken seven boxes total, but now that they were gone the house felt emptier. Like it was missing something vital.

I was still sitting on the couch, wondering what to do next. My laptop was open and stretched across my thighs, but I was struggling to concentrate. My eyes skipped over my folder full of notes for my Northwestern article. Instead, I clicked to open a new folder and paused before naming it, finally settling on one simple word—*DAD*.

I spent the next few hours typing up everything I knew about Dad and the bodies in the woods. It was early evening when my phone rang, Micah's name flashing across the screen. I paused briefly before picking up, unsure what to expect.

"Hey, Micah."

"Penny, some FBI agents just left my house," Micah said, with no preamble. He sounded agitated, even a little panicked, which was at least better than the zombielike trance he'd been in the night before.

"Yeah, they came here, too," I said. "What did they want from you?"

"They asked me some questions about last night, but . . . mostly they wanted to know about you. And your dad."

My heart stuttered.

"I told them I didn't know anything about your dad, but they kept asking questions. They really freaked out my mom. I haven't seen her this bad in a while."

"Are you okay? I can come over." The words tumbled out of my mouth before I had time to think about them.

There was a pause on the phone, and I wondered if I was overstepping. Micah had just lost two friends, and now federal agents had upset his mom—because of Micah's tenuous connection to me—and, therefore, my dad. What if I was the *last* person he wanted to see?

But to my surprise, Micah breathed out a relieved-sounding sigh. "Yeah," he said. "That would be great."

It took roughly twenty-five minutes to pedal over to Micah's house. He lived off a country road, about a mile from Millers' barn. The small ranch house looked like it was fighting a battle with the Michigan elements and slowly losing. The front yard was meticulously mowed, but the porch steps were broken in a few places. The windows were spotless, but the roof was sagging after one too many winters with heavy snow. It was getting dark as I walked toward the front door, and only one room in the house appeared to be lit.

When Micah answered the door, he looked terrible. His eyes were hooded, his hair unwashed. He clearly hadn't shaved, so there was a fine line of stubble along his jaw.

"Thanks for coming," he said, his voice subdued. He moved aside to let me in.

I took three steps into the house before stopping in my tracks. The living room was clean, bright . . . and a veritable shrine. The walls and shelves were covered from top to bottom in framed photographs, trophies, and ribbons. Pictures of Micah in his football uniform, one for every year since peewee league. Framed photos of his teammates from every year as well. Micah in an elementary school graduation photo, Micah holding a fish, Micah with his first buck, Micah in a homecoming crown.

"My mom likes to frame stuff." He smiled, a bit sheepish and embarrassed, which was at least better than the grief and worry that had been coming off him in waves just moments before.

"I can see that," I said, trying to smile back.

"She says it helps her remember the good things," he added.

In the middle of the mantelpiece was a giant, framed photo of Micah's dad. I recognized Mr. Jameson from the dozens of newspaper articles I'd read about the plant closing. In the picture, Mr. Jameson was thin, with hair that curled over his forehead. I thought about the file I had on him that was sitting on my laptop and felt guilty again for keeping it from Micah . . . but now definitely didn't seem like the time to bring it up.

"Where is your mom, by the way?"

Micah gestured down a dark side hallway. "Resting. This has all been kind of hard on her. It's been hard on everyone in town, I guess."

I thought again of Cassidy's parents, how they'd looked standing in front of the police station, like the whole world around them might crash to pieces at any second. Like maybe it already had.

"Yeah," I replied softly.

Micah sat down on the cushion of a pink love seat, and I

hesitated for a moment before perching on an armchair nearby. He looked over at me and rubbed one hand nervously over his knee before clearing his throat.

"I never got the chance to apologize to you," he said.

"What?" I asked, surprised.

"For last night, before . . . well, during our date—I really didn't know that Kevin and those guys were going to show up."

"Oh. Right." So much had happened in the past twenty-four hours that I'd almost forgotten how I'd come to find Bryan and Cassidy's bodies in the first place. How Micah had laughed instead of defending me.

"I mean, I told them where we were going, but I didn't know they'd come out. And when they showed up, I just . . . I didn't handle it well. Sometimes it feels like I do that stuff without thinking, you know? Kevin makes a joke and I laugh, I go along with it. It's just second nature to not . . . rock the boat, I guess."

"Hmm," I said, not sure how else to respond. It was kind of a lame apology. But in that moment, Micah looked so empty that it seemed cruel to hold that against him. "It's okay. I really haven't given it much thought since everything that happened. But, um, thank you, for apologizing."

The corners of his mouth lifted, just a little.

"So you said the FBI came here, too?" I asked, leaning forward.

Micah looked grateful to have the conversation move on. "Yeah. At first I told them the exact same things I told the cops—how we found the bodies, how it was Bryan's truck . . . but they didn't really seem to care about that stuff."

"You said they asked about me? And my dad?"

"They wanted to know what you and I were doing out in the woods, how well we knew each other. They asked me if you were close to your dad or if you knew anything about his work. They thought you might have been lying about not knowing where he is."

"They actually said that?" I asked.

"Well, not outright. It was just clear they didn't think you were telling them everything, and they thought you might have told me more. Because we were, you know, out there together . . ."

"What did you tell them?"

Micah shrugged. "I mean, nothing really. I told them we went out looking for your dad in the woods, but we didn't find anything. I told them you didn't seem to know where he was, and you hadn't heard from him since you got to town. I mean, that's true, right?"

I thought of the email and shifted my eyes away from his gaze.

Micah's own eyes widened. "Oh, crap, is it *not* true? Did I just lie to the FBI? Or not lie, exactly, but, like, mislead—"

"No," I interrupted, putting out my hands. "You didn't lie. Or mislead. I honestly have no clue where my dad is right now."

And that much *was* true. There was no need to bring up

the email. Micah probably wouldn't believe me if I told him it had been written by someone else, but sent through my dad's account. After all, if the sheriff hadn't believed me, why should he?

Dex did, answered a small, defiant voice in my head.

But I pushed that thought away. *Dex also believes aliens built the pyramids.*

I focused my attention back on Micah, who was looking at me intently. "And that's all the FBI wanted to know about?" I asked.

"Yeah, basically. They kept pushing the issue, and that's when my mom started to get upset. She can be . . . pretty protective."

Glancing quickly around the living room again, I thought that might've been a bit of an understatement.

"Penny, sorry for asking this, but I . . ." This time it was Micah who shifted his eyes away from mine, looking uncomfortable. "I mean, do you think . . . is it possible your dad . . . might have something to do with all this?"

And there it was, the question I'd been struggling with for hours. The question I was no closer to solving. But somehow, hearing it come out of Micah's mouth felt like an affront. Him asking that question was different than me asking it, or Dex asking it. I felt my defenses rise as I quickly straightened my back.

"No," I said, my voice sharper than I meant it to be. "My

dad is out there somewhere, missing. There's no way he hurt Bryan or Cassidy," I said, sounding confident. "Or that he's involved in this." I was less confident about his general involvement. But I didn't want Micah to know that.

"Okay," Micah said, giving a quick nod. "Okay."

But he didn't fully believe me, I could tell. I sat taller.

"The more time the FBI spends focusing on my dad, the less time they'll put toward looking for the real killer."

"But if he's hiding from them . . ."

"He's not hiding from them. He's . . . well, I don't know what he's doing. But I'm going to find out. I'll find him, Micah, if I have to search every inch of the woods to do it."

I said the words so forcefully that I almost believed them.

But Micah looked taken aback. His eyes widened, and he lurched forward and grabbed my hand tightly. "Penny, no, you can't do that," he said.

I looked down to where Micah's fingers gripped mine. They were long, calloused from football, cool to the touch. I was reminded of the night before, just before everything went wrong. When he'd leaned forward, ready to kiss me . . . so much had happened since then, but I still felt something when his hands wrapped around mine. Something that was hard to shake. Something I wasn't sure I *wanted* to shake.

"Please, Penny," Micah said.

I tried to focus and ignore his hands on mine.

"What do you mean, I can't? He's my dad. I have to find

him. You were helping me just yesterday. . . ."

"But it's not safe now. People are winding up dead in those woods, people I *know*, and . . . and I don't want you to be next."

"I'm not planning on dying, Micah."

Micah looked like he wanted to say something, but then stopped. He pursed his lips together instead and looked down at our hands, still entwined. He ran one of his thumbs over the tops of my knuckles. For a second, I let myself enjoy how that movement sent a shiver from the base of my neck down my spine.

"Okay, but, please . . . just don't do anything stupid," Micah said. "I know you think your dad's not involved, but, I mean, you're his daughter. Don't you think that could make you just a bit biased—"

I pulled my hand back quickly. "No. I don't think I'm biased. I know how to examine facts, Micah. No matter what they are." My voice wobbled a bit.

"I didn't mean . . . I just . . . I don't want you to go chasing after a murderer and getting hurt. Is that so bad?"

I shook my head and stood up, suddenly tired. "My dad is *not* a murderer. And yes, there's a killer out there, but like I told you before, I'm pretty good at taking care of myself. You can trust my judgment or not, but you can't ask me to just leave my dad to the wolves. Or worse."

Micah blinked once, twice. Eventually, he nodded. "Okay. I get it. And I do trust you."

"Good," I said.

I felt a twinge of guilt. Was it such a crime for him to be worried? And to suspect my dad? I couldn't blame Micah for not trusting in Ike Hardjoy as blindly as Dex did. As blindly as I once had.

When I was still full of so much doubt as to who my dad really was, I couldn't really hold Micah at fault for his suspicions.

But still.

I wondered if it would be possible to recapture where we'd been just a few moments before. I could sit back down, reach out, move forward. But exhaustion was settling over my shoulders, and my feet were moving toward the door instead of toward Micah.

He stood up and smiled, as if he was looking for a way to smooth things over, too. "I'm glad you came over, Penny. I wish things weren't so screwed up right now."

"Me too."

"I can't imagine a first date going worse than ours did." Micah laughed, but there was a hollow sound to his words.

"It was pretty epically bad," I agreed. "I don't think a first date's supposed to give you PTSD."

"Probably not. And I broke out the homemade pie and everything," Micah said with a smile. "I think we still have leftovers, actually. Do you want some?"

"Thanks, but . . . I should get back home, actually. I'm

staying with Cindy, and I don't want her to worry."

"That's nice that she looks out for you like that." Micah walked me to the door. "I'll see you soon, I hope," he said.

"Yeah, me too."

Micah smiled one more time and shut the door behind me gently, and I walked out into the warm air of an early summer evening. The humidity was just starting to pick up, and I saw a swarm of mosquitos hovering near a streetlight at the end of Micah's driveway.

As I crossed the grass to my bike, I felt the strangest sensation shoot down my back—like I was being watched. I looked back at Micah's house without breaking step, half expecting to see his form at the window, checking to make sure I made it on my way okay. But he wasn't there. I turned back around and picked up the pace, ignoring the goose bumps that rose over my neck and arms. I was halfway to my bike when I heard it—a soft rustling sound. Like someone moving slowly through a pile of leaves.

My limbs froze as I looked over to the source of the noise. The tree line at the side of Micah's house was thick, with large and small trunks alike packed together densely. The leaves of the trees were still full, blocking any sight of what might be hiding underneath them. I peered in the direction of the noise, trying to train my eyes to see through the impenetrable darkness. I barely realized that I was holding my breath.

I heard the noise again, the soft rustling, a *shh-shh* sound.

It was at the edge of the tree line, and it was moving toward me. Something darker than the shadows was stirring, pushing through the blackness, coming closer.

Years and years of my dad's stories flowed through my head, one after another. I knew, I *knew* that they were all lies. The Bigfoot in the woods; the lake monster under the waves; the long-fingered, long-toothed sprites that prowled the trees, hunting for bad children. But all that knowledge meant nothing. It was like the last seven years hadn't happened, like I was ten years old again, terrified to go out in the dark in case the monsters got me.

Something was out there. And it was coming.

I heard a sharp cracking noise, like a twig snapping, and it pulled me back into myself. I forced my arms and legs into motion, twirling to run—to sprint—to my bike. But the second I turned, I nearly crashed into a figure standing in my path.

I screamed.

The figure didn't even flinch, and barely seemed to register I was there. It was a woman, standing eerily still in the middle of the grass, blocking the way to the street. She was about my height, with long, dark hair that fell down from her head in tangles. She wore a loose white shirt and white pants over bone-thin bare feet, and her arms hung limp at her sides. She lifted her head slowly, jerkily, and her eyes were a bright, unnatural blue. They looked empty, and for a second I was struck by the thought that there was nothing *inside* this woman at all.

Then her eyes locked on mine, and suddenly they were no longer empty. They began to fill with anger.

"Who are you?" the woman asked, taking one quick step in my direction. I stumbled back, a second scream building up in my throat.

"What are you doing here? *Who sent you?*"

The woman came even closer, driving me back toward the house. I opened my mouth to speak, but my voice wasn't there. She didn't give me time to answer, anyway.

"What do you want? What do you want? What do you want?"

"Mom!"

I turned around to see Micah racing out of his front door and across the yard, a look of panic on his face. He rushed right past me, up to the woman in white, and put one large hand on her shoulder.

"What are you doing out here, Mom?"

The woman blinked once, then again. Hearing Micah's voice seemed to wake her up in a way, and I watched as the anger faded from her eyes. She tilted her head a bit, leaning into Micah's shoulder the way a toddler might lean into a parent.

"They won't leave us alone," she moaned, putting one hand over her face. "Why don't they leave us alone?"

"Shh, it's okay," Micah said, slowly patting her back. "Let's go back inside."

As he started to gently lead her away, I noticed that Mrs.

Jameson's fingernails were lined with dirt, as though she'd been digging in the ground. I also saw that her clothes, which had appeared spooky and ghostly only moments before, were really a tattered T-shirt and sweatpants.

Micah looked up at me as he led his mom away. "I'm sorry, Penny. I—I'll talk to you tomorrow, okay?"

I nodded, unable to think of anything else to say.

As soon as Micah and his mom were safely inside the house, I ran to my bike and jumped on so hard I knew I'd have a bruise on my thigh the next day. I pedaled fast through the darkness, not stopping once—not even to look behind me—until I was in sight of Dex's front door.

THAT NIGHT, I didn't get to sleep until pale blue light filtered in through the curtains in Cindy's living room (I'd insisted on taking the couch this time). I startled at every creak and groan in the house and silently debated with myself on whether I should get up and ask Cindy if she had a night-light. I eventually decided against it, but only barely.

I woke up when I heard Cindy start moving around in the kitchen, and I crept up off the couch and made my way to Dex's room. I knocked on his door lightly before opening it. He shot straight up in bed. His dark hair stuck out from his face in about twenty different directions.

"P-Penny? What are you—"

"I have an idea, and I need your help. But first I need to see the papers you took from my dad's office."

Dex yawned, then swung his legs over the bed. "'Kay, come in."

I shut the door quietly behind me as Dex pulled a packet of papers out from under his bed.

"It was smart of you to take these when the agents showed up," I said, sitting down on the edge of his bed.

Dex shrugged, but I could tell he was pleased. He scooted a bit away from me, and I realized he was wearing just a T-shirt and boxers. I looked away and kept talking. "See this article about the plant closing? It has the more recent business card clipped to it, the one where Dad scribbled *X10-88*. The note's written in the same color ink as this. . . ."

I flipped through the papers until I found the article about the meteorite site, where Dad had circled a whole paragraph—also in red pen.

"You think it's important?" Dex asked.

"I think you were right—my dad was going through old research for this new story. And if he circled this paragraph recently, maybe that gives us a place to start retracing his steps."

Dex put his finger on the name inside the red circle—Tommy Cray.

"Tommy Cray found the meteorite site. Maybe Dad went to interview him. Maybe Tommy has some clue as to where Dad might have gone next."

Dex looked unsure.

"It's kind of a long shot, I know," I said. "But our only other lead is X10-88—and I have no idea what that means or how to find out. Just that it's connected to the plant, somehow. We can go there, too. . . ."

"We should probably start with Tommy," Dex said quickly. I was relieved. The thought of walking through the abandoned plant gave me the creeps. If the Tommy clue panned out, maybe we wouldn't have to go there at all.

"Awesome. Let's go."

"What, like—now?"

"No, next Tuesday. Of *course* now."

I thought about what Micah said, about how I could get hurt if I went looking for my dad when there was a killer out there somewhere. But Dex didn't even hesitate.

"Right, of course," he said, standing up. "But I should probably put on some pants first."

I'd never heard of Tommy Cray before, and neither had Dex. We looked him up in Cindy's phone book, and it turned out he lived on the west edge of Bone Lake, a couple of miles from the Pineview trailer park. We drove out past Main Street, stopping at the last red light in town. On our right was the Quik Stop, its parking lot half-full of people standing around cars and bikes, drinking twenty-ounce bottles of pop and smoking cigarettes.

Reese and Emily were perched on the hood of a green car, their faces turned toward the sun, pretending to ignore the group of guys in the truck parked across the lot. But then Reese looked over at us, her eyes skimming over Dex's car and landing on me. Her expression hardened, and she stared me down until the light turned green and Dex pulled away.

"She still hates you, huh?" Dex asked.

"More and more every day, it seems."

"What ever happened between you guys, anyway?"

"It's kind of a long story," I said, not wanting to get into the personal Dad-and-Julie details.

Dex didn't press. Instead, he asked me a question I didn't expect.

"Remember when she used to be cool?"

"I'm pretty sure she still thinks of herself as cool."

"No, like . . . cool to be around." Dex's voice lowered. "Remember third grade? Ms. Amie's class?"

I did remember.

In third grade, Dex was my closest friend, and Reese was just a girl who sat at our table in class. One day our teacher, Ms. Amie, passed us out copies of *Little House on the Prairie* for us to read to one another in groups. I don't remember much about the book except for one line, one that jumped up off the page and burned into my eight-year-old brain: "The only good Indian is a dead Indian." When we got to that line, Dex was reading. He stumbled over the words, then stopped. His face turned red and his lips pressed together; he made the face he usually made when we were playing a rough game of Red Rover and he was trying not to cry.

Seeing his face, I wanted to cry, too. I thought of Cindy, and I thought of her parents who came to visit a few times a year and always brought candy and homemade toys for the neighborhood kids. I thought of Dex. *The only good Indian is a dead Indian.*

Ms. Amie came over to see why we'd stopped reading. Dex pointed out the line and told her, in a halting voice, that it was wrong. She looked a little panicked at first, and then she tried to explain to us that it was just a story, and the author wrote it a long time ago. Neither of those explanations made sense to me. They must not have made sense to Dex, either, because his whole expression transformed—from pained to something else, something I'd never seen on him before. His shoulders straightened and his lips pressed together in a firm, determined line as he stood up with his copy of the book, walked slowly to the front of the classroom, and dropped it in the trash.

The whole class went silent. I had no idea what to do. But Reese did. She got up with her book, marched to the front of the room, and dropped it into the trash on top of Dex's copy. Then I did the same. When I got to the front of the classroom, Dex looked nervous.

"Maybe I'm making too big a deal. . . ." he whispered.

Reese's chin jutted out, and her eyes were hard and glittering. "No, you're not."

And she was right. I only wished I'd been as brave as Dex, to get up first. Or even as brave as Reese, who was the first to follow him. Later that night, Dex told Cindy the whole story. She was even angrier than we were, and she petitioned the school board to remove the book from the curriculum (and won).

After that day, Reese, Dex, and I were a trio. For a little while, anyway, before we hit middle school and splintered apart.

"That was a long time ago," I said. A lot had changed since then, it was true. Reese still had that same righteous anger, but now it was directed pretty much solely at me.

"Yeah," Dex said, and his voice sounded sad.

"I'm sorry I wasn't a good friend to you," I said. "In middle school, when . . ." I was about to say *when your dad left* but stopped. "When you needed me."

"It's okay." Dex shrugged, keeping his eyes on the road. "It's nice to have you back," he added, his voice only barely loud enough to hear over the sound of the car driving over the rough pavement. I felt a warmth spreading through my chest but didn't know how to respond.

Before long, we were turning down the dirt road that led to Tommy Cray's house. He lived in a one-story ranch set back near the woods. His front lot was covered in junk: two old cars up on cinder blocks, a stack of tires, piles of wood and bundles covered in tarps, a rusted weather vane that blew in the wind.

The man who answered the front door was older, with a grizzled white beard and thick glasses that magnified his eyes.

"Tommy Cray?" I ventured.

"Who wants to know?"

"I'm Penny Hardjoy, and this is—"

"Hardjoy? You Ike's kid, then?"

"Yeah," I said, encouraged. "And this is my friend Dex. We're looking for my dad."

"Well, you should try his house," Tommy said, and I couldn't tell whether or not he was being sarcastic.

"Um . . . we looked there. But my dad's been gone a few days, and I think he might have come to talk to you recently?"

Tommy Cray leaned against his doorjamb, where the painted surface was peeling off in curling chips. "He came by."

"Really?" Dex asked, his voice rising in excitement. "Did he say where he might have gone?"

"Nope," Tommy Cray answered, blinking slowly behind his giant lenses. "But I imagine he headed out to the woods. To the crash site."

My heart beat faster. "What makes you say that?"

"'Cause your dad's an idiot, and that's the kind of thing an idiot would do."

Again, Dex and I looked at each other, at a loss. "Did he mention the crash site specifically . . . ?" I finally managed to ask.

"Course. That's what he always talks about when he comes out here. Always asks me the same question, and I always give him the same answer. He wants to know what I remember about finding that meteor. And I tell him: nothing."

Dex looked confused, his eyebrows drawing together. "Nothing?"

"*Nothing*," Tommy Cray said louder, as if Dex was hard of hearing.

"But . . . you did find the meteorite, right? That's what the paper said."

"Yeah, that's what the paper said," Tommy Cray replied. "That's what they tell me, too. But I got no memory of it. I remember seeing the flash as something fell through the sky. I remember heading out to find it. Then I remember waking up in my bed, watching the sun rise. That's it. Ike keeps coming back here, hoping I'll remember more, but I don't. I told him not to go out there, not to mess with that godforsaken place. But he wouldn't listen. 'Cause he's an idiot."

Dex's eyes went wide, and I guessed he was already spinning alien-related theories in his head. But I looked past Tommy Cray into his darkened living room, where newspapers and grocery bags were strewn about old furniture. Empty bottles, some dark, some clear, were scattered over the rug or lined up against the walls next to dying houseplants.

"Do you . . . forget things a lot?" I asked.

Tommy Cray looked affronted. "The hell are you implying?"

"Nothing," Dex said quickly. "She's not implying anything."

"I think you should go."

"We will," I said. "Thank you for your time."

Tommy Cray nodded slowly. "If you find your dad, remind him he owes me thirty bucks," he said before closing the door on us.

Dex turned to me, color high on his cheeks. I put up a hand to stop him from speaking. "Don't jump to conclusions."

"But the guy who found the meteorite *doesn't remember* finding it! Don't you think that's something worth investigating?"

"The only thing I want to investigate right now is where my dad went."

Dex's expression turned eager. "Then I think you know where we have to go next."

"Yeah." I took a deep breath and turned toward the massive pines that surrounded Tommy Cray's yard. "Into the woods we go."

THE SITE WHERE the meteorite had landed was across town, in the middle of what had once been state-owned land but was now private property. Even though it was miles away from the lake where we'd discovered Bryan's and Cassidy's bodies, I still felt spooked as Dex and I walked through the quiet woods. I half expected to take a turn around a tree trunk or climb over a fallen log just to stumble across a burned limb sticking out of the dirt.

As if sensing my unease, Dex stuck close by me as we walked along the main path that had been widened by gawkers over the years. I stepped around a bright green, pointy-leafed plant that looked suspiciously like poison ivy, nearly crashing into Dex as I did so. He seemed to take it as another sign of my jumpiness and started talking in an overly loud voice.

"Hey, remember that Halloween when your dad brought us out here and scared the crap out of us?"

"Yeah, I remember."

"That was classic. I think Reese almost peed her pants."

I smiled; I hadn't thought about that night in ages. One Halloween, my dad loaded me and my friends in a big wooden wagon and hooked it to the back of his four-wheeler, then drove us through the streets of Bone Lake. We moved fast like we were in a car, but there were no seat belts, no windows. Just us sitting on a rickety wagon floor, eating bite-size candy and laughing as the wind whipped past our faces. It felt dangerous, but in a fun way. Probably it was illegal.

Not that Dad cared. Every time he hit a bump or took a curve, sending us flying into each other and shrieking in glee, he'd laugh loudly, the sound of it carrying on the wind. We got to the path leading into the woods to the meteorite site, and Dad turned to take it. He moved slowly down the path, and my friends grew quieter. They chatted nervously and made dumb jokes as we wound farther and farther into the darkness.

Eventually, Dad stopped the four-wheeler and cut the engine. He came to sit in the back of the wagon with us, and then he asked us what we knew about a murderer with a hook for a hand who'd escaped into those same woods that morning. Some of the kids laughed, thinking Dad was joking, but he had this way of telling a scary story so that it seemed real. The killer's name was Hook Hand Pete, he said. He'd lost his hand working at an evil candy factory, and he'd had it replaced with a sharp-ended hook. Now he roamed the woods, vowing to get his revenge on any little kid he saw eating candy.

"Like, *all* candy?" Emily Jennings had squeaked, pushing away her pillowcase full of Halloween candy.

Dad had looked at her like it was the smartest question in the world. Before he could answer, though, he turned his head sharply to the right. "Did you hear that?"

More squeaks. A chorus of "What, *what?*"

"That . . . creaking noise. It sounds almost like . . . *footsteps.*"

Emily moaned. Dex giggled, but I could tell it was a fear-giggle. Reese gripped my arm so tight, her fingertips left bruises I only saw the next morning. But I smiled. Everyone stared at my dad, rapt, and I felt something warm spread deep in my stomach. Pride. Most of my friends' parents worked boring jobs or watched boring TV or played boring card games, but my dad was different. With a single story, he could command the attention of everyone around. And he was *mine.*

"What was that?" my dad asked, whipping his head toward the woods again. The kids all followed his lead, staring off into the trees. Dad took that moment to look at me briefly and wink. I grinned. This was all a game, and he and I were in on it together.

A couple of years later, after the Bigfoot incident—and the divorce—my memory of that night became tainted by everything that happened after. I thought it had been me and Dad against the world, playing a joke on my friends. But once I discovered that nothing else Dad "believed" in was real—not yetis, not the Loch Ness Monster, not even the Visitors—I realized that my dad had been playing one giant joke on everyone. Including me.

"Hook Hand Pete." Dex chuckled, pulling me back into the woods of the present. "Man, that was fun."

I bristled. "I remember it differently. Anyway, *your* dad was the truly scary one that night, remember?" I thought back to what had happened after my dad had told us the story of Hook Hand Pete. Someone *had* been out in the woods that night, just waiting for his cue to sneak up on us. "When your dad came busting out of the trees with that hook on his hand—"

"You mean the coat hanger—"

"Right, and he starts going, 'Who's eating candy? I smell CANDY. . . .'" I laughed. "I really thought Reese was going to scream herself to death."

"Or scream *me* to death," Dex added. "I couldn't hear out of my left ear for a week."

Our laughter trailed off as we continued walking through the quiet woods. Dex's smile faded.

"That was one of the last times I remember my dad laughing," he said.

I pursed my lips, feeling like an idiot. Why had I brought up the part of the story with Dex's dad, just to avoid talking about my own?

"I'm sorry, Dex," I said, but it sounded inadequate.

He shrugged, and I waited for him to make an off-the-cuff remark, or to change the subject. But his face remained uncharacteristically stony.

"Have you . . . heard from him lately?"

Dex kept going down the path, moving a little ahead of me so I could no longer see his face. "We heard from him a lot right after he left, but not much recently."

"Oh."

"Not for, like, a year, actually." Dex's shoulders rose in a shrug again, but I couldn't see his face. "Last we heard, he finally found work in Tampa, and then . . . nothing."

"That really sucks."

"Yeah," Dex said, his voice going lower. "But I've been wondering lately if there's not, like, some *other* reason—"

I heard my phone chime, and I got it out to see a text message. From Micah.

I'm so sorry about last night.

I stared down at the words, stumbling a bit in my tracks. Dex looked over, curious.

"Sorry, what were you saying?" I asked.

He shook his head. "Nothing."

I wrote back to Micah—It's okay.

A quick response—It's not. I swear my mom's not always like that. It was just a bad day. She feels bad about scaring you.

Tell her it's fine, honest.

I watched the dot-dot-dot on the screen, the sign that Micah was typing back. One minute passed, then two. But when the text finally came through, it was only: I hope we can hang out again soon.

Definitely, I responded. I put my phone away.

"That Mr. Perfect?" Dex asked. He was looking away from me, his eyes straight ahead on the trail. He kicked a rock out of the path and watched it bounce off into the underbrush.

"Micah's not *perfect*," I said. "But he is a good guy."

Dex snorted.

"You could have a bit of empathy for him, you know. He's been through a lot. He lost his dad, too."

"Yeah," Dex said, looking a bit sorry. "I guess this isn't a great town for keeping those around."

Dex suddenly picked up his step, pointing ahead of us. "We're here."

I followed him to the end of the trail, which widened into a small clearing. The crater opened up just inches from our feet, stretching out in an irregular circle. Some of the trees on the outside of the wide hole were bending away from it, as if they were still trying to crawl themselves out of the blast zone. Right after the meteorite fell, this place had been roped off and covered in warning signs. Now that was all gone; a single, rusted *OFF-LIMITS* sign remained, stuck into the side of the crater at an odd angle, one of its metal points digging into the dirt.

Dex looked at me, expectant. "Well? Now what?"

I stayed still and looked around the area. It wasn't like I'd expected to find my dad just standing here, waiting for me. So what *had* I hoped to find?

I looked around the edge of the crater for footprints. But all I saw was grass and rocks and sticks. There weren't even any pieces of meteorite left; every scrap had been hauled away years before.

I took out my phone and started taking pictures of the crater to add to my file once I got home. Dex took out his phone, too.

"Crap," he said. "Text from my mom. I totally forgot she wants my help on a catering gig tonight."

I nodded, still taking pictures, as Dex walked around the side of the crater, touching the trunks of the bent birch trees. "So, what are the odds that Ike left a note? Maybe with an arrow pointing in the direction he went, like, *This way, kids!*"

I rolled my eyes. "Since when are *you* the cynical one?"

Dex smiled. "Just keeping you on your toes—"

Click.

"Stop. Did you hear that?"

"What?"

"That clicking noise. It was soft, almost like . . ."

I looked up in the direction of the sound. It had definitely come from above me. I walked over to the trunks of the nearest trees, craning my head upward. And that's when I saw it—a small, shiny camera. It was fixed to a tree branch with zip ties and facing down at the crater site.

Dex came over to me and looked up, his eyes going wide. "That's one of Ike's!"

"Help me up, would you?"

Dex joined his hands together to form a step, and I put one foot inside. I rested my hand on his shoulder, propelling myself up. I got just high enough to unhook the camera from its fastening and pull it down. It was identical to the camera I'd found on our coffee table, the one that had nothing but pictures of trees on it.

"He *did* come here," Dex said, sounding excited.

The camera had gone back into sleep mode, and I clicked it on with my thumb. The first picture was of the back of my head, looking at Dex across the expanse of the crater. I felt a small shiver run down my spine, thinking that something had been recording me, *watching* me, without my knowledge. I clicked to the next picture. It was taken from the same position, but it was just trees, grass, the crater. There was a time stamp on the image.

"This one was taken ten minutes ago," I said.

I clicked back to the previous picture. It had been taken ten minutes before. The next one, ten minutes before that.

"Ike must have set the camera up to wake up and go off

every ten minutes," Dex said. "But why? What exactly was he hoping to see here?"

I clicked through another photo, then another, going back through the images faster and faster. It was the same scene. The light in the images grew darker and darker, until they were just shadows. Then they lightened.

I pushed on the button to see smaller thumbnails of the pictures.

"There're thousands," I murmured, scrolling quickly through them. "Days' and days' worth."

"Stop!" Dex said. "Go back."

He clicked on one of the thumbnails. It showed the same crater area, in the middle of the day. Only there was a man standing off to the right, showing his profile to the camera. He was wearing a brown uniform.

"Is that . . . ?" Dex started.

"The sheriff."

In the image, Sheriff Harper was staring straight ahead and slightly down, as if he was looking at something on the far end of the crater, near the ground. I clicked over to the next image. For a second, I thought something was wrong—the second image was exactly the same. Sheriff Harper was standing in the exact same position. His arms loose at his sides, his feet slightly apart. His head angled in the exact same way.

The next image was identical, and the next, and the next. Only the time stamps showed that the images were in fact taken at different times, each ten minutes apart.

"How long did he just . . . stand there, staring, like that?" Dex asked, his voice soft.

I clicked through ten images, then ten more. "Three hours? Maybe four?"

"He's the same in every picture," Dex said. "Like he didn't move . . . at all."

The shivers again, down my spine.

All I could do was slowly shake my head, keep clicking through images. Finally, we landed on one that was different. The sheriff was still in it, but he was standing a few feet away. He was looking at a different point of the crater, and he was gesturing. His mouth was open, and it looked like he was talking to someone standing just offscreen. He looked angry.

In the next image, he was gone.

I breathed out slowly.

"What the hell was that?"

I shook my head. "I don't know."

And I didn't. I didn't have any clue. The sheriff clearly didn't know this camera was here, and I was no closer to understanding why my dad had put it up in the first place, or where he might have gone next. What would happen if I showed this to the sheriff? What kind of stuff was he hiding from us? And did this weirdness even have anything to do with the killer in the woods?

None of the pieces were adding up; nothing was making

sense. Instead of leading us to a logical explanation, all of these bits of information were adding up to something outlandish and confusing, like something you'd read about in the *National Enquirer* or *Strange News*.

Like we'd landed in the middle of one of my dad's own stories.

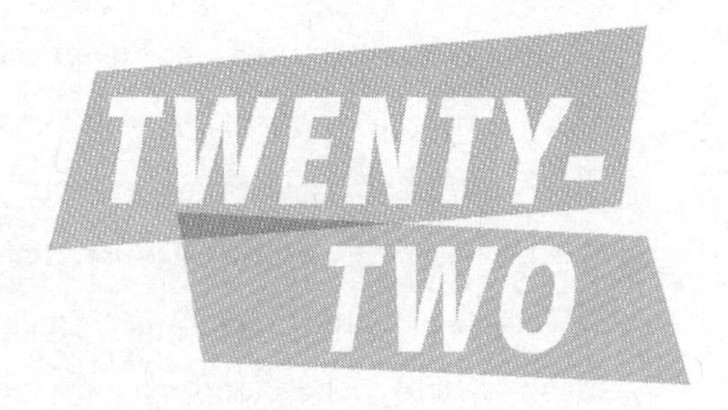

THE BLACK CHERRY ice cream was frozen solid. A thick layer of white frost circled the edge of the bin, making it impossible to get through to the pinkish ice cream underneath. I hacked away at the frost with a metal ice-cream scoop, but I knew I wasn't getting anywhere. The lack of sleep the night before was catching up to me, and my limbs felt heavy and useless. As I worked, my knuckles turned blue with cold, and jagged pieces of frost flew up against my apron with every fresh blow.

"Hey, what'd that bin ever do to you?" Cindy's warm voice floated across the store. I turned to see her standing in the door to the kitchen, a spatula in one hand and a grocery bag in the other. She looked at me with a bemused expression, but there was concern there, too.

"Picked a bad day to mess with me," I joked weakly, once

again plunging the metal scoop down to the rock-hard surface of the ice cream.

"Well maybe go easy on it, hmm? Every day's a bad day to be black cherry ice cream." She wrinkled her nose.

I backed reluctantly away from the case, running the scoop under a stream of warm water in the sink. The truth was, it felt good to hack away at the frozen bin, to do something physical and repetitive. Even if I was incredibly tired.

I couldn't stop seeing the image of the sheriff, staring vacantly across the crater at something invisible on the other side. In my mind, the image kept getting conflated with my memories of the night before, and how *not there* Mrs. Jameson had looked, standing stock-still at the edge of her yard.

And then there was Dad. Let alone what the sheriff and FBI thought of his connection to the murders, the longer he was out there, the less chance he had of coming home alive. The meteorite site hadn't turned up any more clues as to where he might have gone, but there was always the plant, and the mysterious *X10-88* note in his files.

The urge to go to the plant right now, to *do something* right now, was even stronger than the urge to go home and take a nap. Repeatedly smashing a metal ice-cream scooper into a bin full of frozen black cherry was a barely acceptable compromise, but I'd promised to work while Cindy and Dex left on their catering gig.

I didn't notice that Cindy had come up behind me until she

put one hand on my shoulder. I jumped a bit, startled.

"Honey, I've been thinking maybe it's time we called your mom and told her what's going on."

I whirled to face her. "No, it's okay. I'm okay. Honest."

"What you found in the woods . . . It's a lot. I know you haven't been sleeping well, and your dad's been gone almost a week now—"

"I promise, I'm fine. Really. Mom will just get worried and come back here, and she's worked so hard to get to Spain. It means so much to her. Plus, if she comes here she'll be angry with my dad, and she'll take me away before he gets back, and I just . . ."

I trailed off. I wasn't sure if what I'd just said was true—if Mom would take me from Dad because she was angry. After our phone call, a lot of assumptions I'd made about my parents seemed to be false. But I did know Mom would be worried. And that, alone, would be enough reason for her to take me back to Chicago before I could find the truth. Before I could find Dad.

Cindy pursed her lips. "I still think it's her decision to make."

Her voice was gentle, but she was a mom first, and my friend second. I knew she'd call my mom in a heartbeat if I didn't.

I took a deep breath and nodded. "You're right. I'll call her."

"Good," Cindy said, giving a small, relieved smile. I felt guilty for misleading her, but *technically* I hadn't lied. I *was* going to call Mom and tell her everything—just not until I figured out what was going on.

"Dex and I won't get back till after dinner probably. But there's a lot of chicken casserole in the fridge, and stuff for a salad."

"Thanks, Cindy," I said.

"And you really can take Dex's bed for as long as you need. I could tell you didn't get much sleep on the couch last night. And Dex, well, that boy can lay his head down just about anywhere and pass out within a minute."

Cindy grinned. But despite the chilly air behind the ice-cream bins, I felt my face heat up. For some reason, the thought of spending another night in Dex's bed, lying on his pillow and under his sheets, made my stomach drop in a way I couldn't explain.

"I can take the couch again," I said, a bit more forcefully than was necessary. "I really don't mind."

Cindy eyed me for just a second before nodding. "Okay, hon, whatever you want."

A half hour later, she and Dex had loaded up the van with cupcakes and were on their way to a fiftieth anniversary party in Kalkaska. Manning the shop on my own turned out to be a lot easier—and more boring—than I had anticipated. Bone Lake wasn't the most bustling of towns in the best of circumstances. But in the wake of finding Bryan's and Cassidy's bodies, it seemed few people were in the mood to go out and get a cone full of crunchy caramel swirl.

Which left me plenty of alone time to stew over what Dex and I had found. For the third time, I went over to my purse and took out the camera Dad had placed in the woods, searching for more odd pictures like those of the sheriff. But there weren't any. The only other photograph that had anyone in it was the very first one, which was a close-up of my dad's face. It must have snapped as he was strapping the camera into the tree. I got the disconcerting feeling that he was looking out of the camera screen and at *me*, as if he knew I would be the one to find this image.

I clicked the camera off and slid it back into my purse. By the time I looked up, someone was pulling open the door of Sweet Street and sauntering inside.

Reese.

She was wearing a black sundress with tiny white dots on it, and her hair was coiled up in braids around the top of her head, like a milkmaid. She walked right toward me, purposeful, her arms crossed loosely over her chest.

"Can I help you?" I asked.

"It's really rich, you working here," she said. Her voice was calm, her words deliberate.

"I have no idea what you're talking about," I said, then instantly regretted it. Reese's lips curved up in a slight, sharp smile, and I knew I was playing right into whatever script she'd written for this moment.

"Don't you? You say you came back here to visit your dad

and work for Cindy, but that's not the real reason, is it?"

"What?" I asked, genuinely confused.

"I had a nice chat with Hector. You know Hector, at the hardware store?"

I felt a quick thump of anxiety in my stomach, but forced my face to stay still. "Yeah, Reese. I know Hector."

"He was at church this morning. Everyone was there, preparing for the memorial service. Well, everyone who actually *cares* about Bryan and Cassidy. So I'm talking to Hector and he brings up this interesting story. About why you're really in Bone Lake this summer. Doing a little investigating, huh?"

I took a deep breath. "I'm just writing an article for college admissions. It's not a big deal."

"Making Bone Lake look bad isn't a big deal? *Using* us just so you can get into some snotty school?"

"I'm not using anyone. And Bone Lake isn't just your town. It's mine, too."

"Please," Reese said, rolling her eyes. "You might come slum it here a couple of weeks a year, but you don't belong here. You've always thought you were better than us."

"That's not true," I said.

"There you go, lying again," Reese trilled. She took a step closer to the counter, so close I could smell the red candy scent on her lips. But if she expected me to take a step back, she was mistaken. I held my ground.

"I'm not a liar," I said, meeting her glare with my own.

"Really," Reese said, smirking. "Then why doesn't everyone know about your little story? Micah, for one, seemed really surprised to hear about it."

And there it was: the bomb Reese had come all the way here to drop in person. The anxiety that had been building up inside me ballooned into panic.

"Right after I talked to Hector, I called Micah. I knew he was just being nice by hanging out with you, but I figured he had a right to know why *you* were hanging out with *him*. He seemed pretty shocked to learn the truth."

"Why would you do that?" I shook my head, genuinely taken aback, though a part of my brain was screaming at me that I should have been honest with Micah from the start.

Reese's eyes were like tiny blue stones, hard and cold. "Like I just said, he had the right to know. He said you made it seem like you liked him, got him to open up to you . . . and it was all for some horrible article about his dad. It's sick, honestly. *I* knew what you were capable of, but Micah's never hurt anyone in his life. How could you just use him like that?"

"That's not . . . I didn't . . ." I sputtered.

"Typical Penny. Telling lies and doing whatever you want. Not caring who gets hurt in the process," Reese said. Her mouth pursed, and she spit out her next words like they tasted bad. "Just like your dad."

For just the briefest of moments, my heart felt like it stopped.

But Reese didn't notice. She just kept looking at me like I was something she'd scraped off the bottom of her shoe. Which was just about what I felt like.

Reese flipped open her purse and pulled out a dollar bill, which she dropped on the counter. Then she plunged her hand into one of the candy bins sitting on a shelf next to the counter, taking out a fistful of individually wrapped Ring Pops. Without giving me a second look, she spun on her heel and walked out the door.

I felt frozen in place until the glass door closed behind Reese and she disappeared from sight. I pulled out my phone and texted Micah—

Did you talk to Reese? I can explain everything, I promise.

But would that matter? If I explained? I waited another minute, then added—

I'm so sorry.

I was jittery for the rest of my shift, but thankfully, no one came in. I closed up the shop early and hopped on my bike. But instead of riding home, to Cindy's, I went in the opposite direction. To Micah's.

But what would I say once I got there? If he really believed what Reese said, that I'd only shown interest in him for the article, that I'd purposefully tricked him into opening up and being vulnerable . . . I remembered the night he told me about his mom, and how he said he never talked about it to anyone.

Shame burned through me. I wanted to explain that I hadn't used him. Not intentionally. That Reese had it all wrong. Because she did. She *did*.

Right?

I rode hard past the rest of the buildings on Main Street, the lone gas station on the corner, the last stoplight in town. The wooden houses on either side of the street got more and more spaced out as I pedaled, until eventually I hit the two-lane county roads. Reese had said that Bone Lake wasn't my town anymore, but very single inch of this town was still familiar to me. I could probably find my way to Micah's street with my eyes closed. It was true that I'd wanted to get out of Bone Lake after the divorce—and after I'd lost Reese as a friend—but that didn't mean I thought I was *better* than my hometown.

Did it?

I tried to parse out the facts, look at things in black and white. I didn't like coming back to Bone Lake in the summers, it was true. Partly because I was angry at Dad, and partly because I had no friends here. But it wasn't just that, was it? Mom's words came back to me suddenly, the way she'd described feeling stuck in her hometown and believing there was something out there for her, something *more*. I'd believed it for myself, too. But did claiming Chicago and a future at Northwestern mean giving up my claim to Bone Lake? Maybe Reese was right, and I didn't belong here anymore. Maybe Bone Lake's story was no longer mine to tell.

My head began to ache as I rode harder and harder, moving through the humid summer air. I hadn't meant to hurt Micah, but maybe what I'd *meant* to do didn't matter.

Telling lies and doing whatever you want. Not caring who gets hurt in the process.

Just like your dad.

I was out of breath as I neared Micah's driveway. I steeled myself, urging my heart to stop racing.

I walked slowly up to the front door, took a deep breath, and knocked.

No one answered.

I waited one minute, then three, then five, before I turned around and walked back to my bike. The energy that had been building up in me during the ride over was still all pent-up in my limbs; I could feel it scratching to get out. When I got back on the bike, I didn't turn toward home. I kept going, past Micah's house and toward the woods.

Just like your dad.

But I wasn't like Dad, was I? He falsely represented the truth, twisting it and bending it to make it into something different. Turning bears into monsters, scaring people for profit. He'd exploited Bone Lake after the meteorite crash, not to get to the bottom of things or to expose any great secret, but to make money. I might have misled Micah, sure, but it wasn't in service of a lie. I wanted to get to the truth.

I nodded along as these thoughts raced through my mind.

But no matter how hard I fought against Reese's words, I couldn't shake the feeling that she had a point. Because "misleading" Micah was the same as lying to him, and I was doing it all for my own gain, my own end goal—Northwestern. Was my reason any better than Dad's?

I didn't slow my bike until I reached the main driveway of the abandoned plant. Its driveway was cracked, and green weeds pushed up through the asphalt. There was a thin trench in the ground where a large sign bearing the plant's name used to be. Beyond that, the long, gray building hunched low to the ground, some parts of it hard to see beyond the green saplings that had sprung up around it in the past decade.

The crumbling parking lot was empty, as it had been for years. There was no proof that Dad had come here recently, or even at all. The only reason I had to be here was the single article found in his safe. But it was the only clue I had. And I couldn't turn back around, pedal back to Dex's, and wait.

I had to know. I *had* to. Not just what was going on in Bone Lake, not just what happened to Bryan and Cassidy and that hiker, not just why the FBI were in town and why the sheriff was acting so strange. I had to know why Dad was looking into this story. Why he'd been obsessed with the Visitors in the first place. Why he did the things he did at all.

If we were, at our core, the same.

I had to know.

I texted Dex to tell him I was checking out the plant on my

own. I couldn't wait until tomorrow. This whole thing might lead to nothing, but I walked toward the gray building with purpose, as if I were sure of what I was doing. As if I knew my dad—and all the answers I wanted—were somewhere inside.

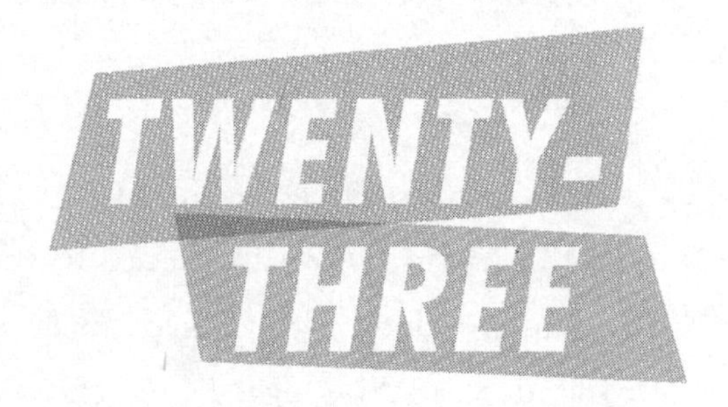

AFTER SEARCHING EVERY other entrance to the plant, I found a small side door that wasn't padlocked. I reached for the handle and prepared to pull with all my might but was surprised to find the door swung open easily.

The door led right onto the factory floor, a cavernous space that stretched into shadowy corners too dark for me to see. The vast emptiness of the room threw me off for a moment, though of course the plant's owners would have sold off any valuable equipment before closing the doors on this place. As I walked slowly across the dusty cement floor, I saw only a few shapes strewn about: some rusted tracks that might have once held a machine in place, corrugated bars of metal lying haphazardly under a window, a rusted beam that looked like it had fallen from the ceiling.

I walked quickly across the large space, moving toward the darkened offices on the other side of the room. Large interior windows opened up into these smaller office areas. I imagined that managers and supervisors used to stand behind those windows, overseeing the giant metal machinery at work on the other side.

I passed through the entrance to a hallway, which had doors on either side providing access to the small offices. I pushed open one door and walked directly into a huge spiderweb, filaments sticking against my cheeks and hair. Shuddering, I backed away.

I only took two more steps down the hallway before I heard it: a small scratching noise, coming from somewhere in front of me. I stood still and held my breath, waiting to hear the noise again. I took out my phone and turned on my flashlight app, swinging it up and around the walls of the hallway, but I couldn't see anything that might have made any sort of noise. I knew I hadn't imagined it, though.

After another moment, I heard the scratching noise again. It was definitely coming from the end of the hall. I slowly made my way farther into the darkness, keeping my right shoulder close to the wall and continually looking behind to make sure nothing could sneak up on me.

It's nothing, I thought.

A small voice in my head responded, *or it's something.* The voice sounded something like Dex's.

Knock it off.

I imagined Dex's response—*Anyone could be hiding in this building. . . . It's abandoned, the perfect place for someone—or some*thing—*to hide.*

My heart pounded as I neared the end of the hall, which turned left into another smaller corridor. I swung my phone in that direction in time to see a dark shape shoot across the floor.

I jumped and let out a little yelp, and my phone slipped from my hand, hitting the ground before I could catch it. I quickly snatched it up, holding it out toward the second corridor, where the light flashed a glare into a pair of yellow eyes that were fixed in my direction. I almost screamed again before the eyes blinked, then darted quickly away. I saw a brown-and-black striped tail swish twice and then scurry into darkness.

A raccoon.

"See, I was right," I said, letting out a relieved sigh. Then I remembered that I hadn't *actually* been talking to anyone, and I felt stupid. It was irritating, hearing Dex's voice in my head. Knowing what he'd say if he were here. But at the same time I suddenly and annoyingly wished for him to be by my side. Arguing with him in real life was much better than arguing with the Dex in my head.

And it would take my mind off my fear.

I walked quickly down the second corridor, flashing my light up all around me. A paper poster was still fixed to the cinder-block walls. On it, stick-figure men carried out proper safety procedures. Those who did it wrong were covered in large red Xs. Eventually, the corridor dead-ended in a metal door. It had no window, just simple blocked words that hadn't faded even after all this time: *AUTHORIZED PERSONNEL ONLY.*

The lock on the door was broken, and it was slightly ajar.

A familiar feeling rose up in me then—the rush of adrenaline that told me I might be on to something good, a break in the story. Maybe all these open doors were a sign that my dad had already been here. The door opened up onto a metal stairway that was basement-level dark, the kind that prevented you from seeing your own hand in front of your face. Even with my flashlight app, I could only see ten feet in front of me as I moved quickly down the stairs, each step creaking heavily under my feet.

The stairs opened up into another hallway. This one was entirely different from the cinder-block hall upstairs. It didn't look like it belonged in a plant at all, but maybe in some kind of hospital or sterile facility. The walls of the hallway were smooth and white, and painted black doors were set in them every twenty feet or so. The first door had writing on it—*X01.* The next door was labeled *X02.* Without even stopping to look in these rooms, I continued walking until I reached a door on my left—*X10.*

X10-88. The first part of the number that had been scrawled on Dad's business card matched the number on this door. That couldn't be a coincidence. But what did it mean? Had my dad's notes been referring to this specific room?

I heard a light thumping noise, then, and I turned around, aiming my flashlight at the opposite door, the one labeled *X09*. The door was closed, and though I waited several seconds, I didn't hear the noise again. Probably another animal.

Instead, I reached out and pushed open the door of room X10. I put my hand with the flashlight inside first, scanning it around the room, heart tripping in my chest. First one corner, then another, then another—

Nothing.

Or not *nothing*, but certainly nothing earth-shattering. The windowless room was almost completely empty, except for a small metal table set up against one wall. The wall had blackened scorch marks in places, as if pieces of it had been set on fire. The table pushed against it was about six feet long, and it reminded me almost of the type of examination table you'd see at a doctor's office . . .

. . . or a morgue.

But that couldn't be right. . . . What would an examination table be doing at a plastics plant?

I took one step farther into the room, and that's when I felt it—a rush of air, not quite a breeze, but a movement. Like someone was coming up fast behind me—

And then my phone fell, its light blinking out, and then—

Then—

Then . . .

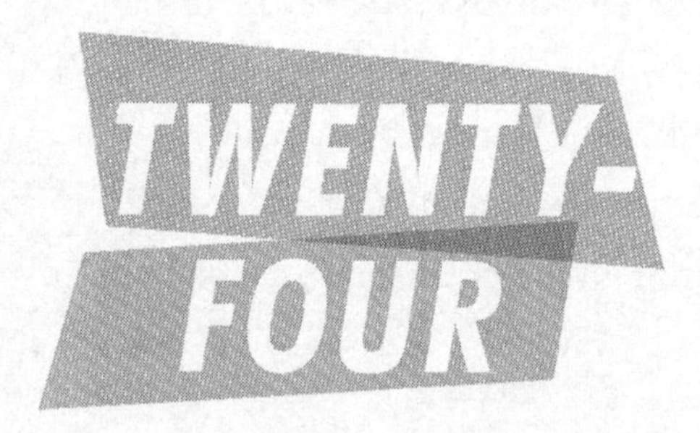

SUNLIGHT BEAMED THROUGH the slits of my half-opened eyes. I blinked, then blinked again. Above me I saw green leaves, an interconnected web of them moving toward and then away from one another in the breeze. I was lying on something hard and cold, and from the dull pain in my neck and shoulders I knew I'd been there for a while. I sat up quickly.

I was on my back porch.

My brain struggled to piece this together. How had I gotten onto the porch? How was it morning already? I searched my mind for the last thing I could remember—going into the plant, finding the door labeled *X10*, seeing the scorched wall, hearing a noise, and then . . . nothing. Not even any dreams. Just an absence, as if I'd closed my eyes one moment and the next been transported to another place and time entirely. I could still feel the chill of the factory basement on my skin, the remnants of spiderwebs in my hair.

I reached for my phone and saw I had five voice mails and sixteen texts. The texts were all from Dex and Cindy, asking where I was and if I was okay. They got increasingly panicky-sounding as they went on. Three of the voice mails were from Dex, too. One was from my mom. But the last one . . .

The last one was from my dad's cell.

For a full ten seconds, I just stared at his name on my screen. He'd called just an hour earlier and left a fifteen-second message. With shaking fingers, I held my phone gingerly up to my ear.

"Penelope, it's Dad."

My heart thumped so hard it hurt. That was him. It was definitely him. That was his gruff, deep, slightly rushed voice. That was the way he always greeted me when I answered the phone. *Penelope, it's Dad*, he always said, as if I wouldn't have seen his name come up on my screen, as if I wouldn't know his voice by heart.

A quick sigh, and then the message continued, "I know you've been looking for me, and I'm telling you now to stop. Not asking, telling. I'm on a big story, kiddo, but it's really dangerous. More dangerous than—" His voice broke up a bit, as if he pulled the phone away from his mouth. Then he went on, "So I mean it when I say I want you to stay out of this. Just . . . listen to me for once, Pen. Stay safe."

I listened to the voice mail again. And again. His last lines rang in my ear.

Stay safe.

Just listen to me for once, Pen.

But already, I knew I wasn't going to.

Somehow, my bike had been left in my front yard. It was set upright, the kickstand resting gently on the grass near the front porch. I walked over to Dex and Cindy's first, but no one was home. Then I pedaled like mad for Main Street, trying to ignore the lead ball that was sitting at the base of my stomach. Questions swirled through my head.

What had Dad gotten himself into? I had no idea.

Was he in danger? Probably.

And, the million-dollar question—*What the hell happened last night?* But in answer, there was just a blank space in my mind, like a file deleted.

Sweet Street's door was unlocked, but only half the lights in front were turned on. Through the window, I saw Dex standing behind the counter. He glanced up as I pulled open the door, and I could literally see the relief flooding through his facial muscles, erasing the strain in his eyes and mouth.

He didn't even go around the counter, but jumped over it, rushing over to pull me into a hug. My face was crushed up against his shoulder, and his arms were pushing mine against the sides of my body, but it felt good to be hugged so tightly like that. We stayed like that for a few seconds, Dex squeezing me tight and both of us breathing hard, until self-consciousness kicked in and he released me suddenly, stepping back.

"Penny, where have you been? I've been texting and calling—"

"I know—"

"I got the text that you were at the plant, but when I went I couldn't find you—"

"You went to the pla—"

"And then I had to tell Mom, and she had to call the sheriff—"

"Whoa, whoa, Dex, stop. Let me explain."

Dex's mouth snapped shut. But his eyes stayed fixed to my face, as if he was afraid I'd disappear if he so much as blinked. I filled him in on what I remembered—going to the plant, finding the strange underground area, and then the door labeled *X10* and the room beyond.

"And then . . ." Dex prompted.

"And then that's it. I don't remember anything else. I woke up on my back porch just now and saw all your texts."

"Your porch? We checked your whole house last night, and you weren't there. I looked again this morning but didn't think to check the back porch—"

"I woke up there like a half hour ago. That's all I know."

"Whoa," Dex said, running a hand through his unruly hair, "so you remember . . . nothing? Just like—"

"Don't say it."

"Tommy Cray."

"Dex . . ."

"Come on, Penny. This isn't normal!"

"I know," I said, letting out a ragged sigh. I walked over to a white wrought-iron chair by the window, and Dex took the one next to me. He still had his phone in his hand, and he sent a quick text to Cindy before looking back up at me. His mouth moved slightly, like it was threatening to spill over with questions, but instead he watched me, waiting.

"And there's more," I said. I got out my own phone and played Dad's voice mail on speaker.

"Whoa," Dex said, eyes wide. "Whoa, whoa."

"You said that already."

"I mean, that was definitely him. That was Ike."

"I know. And I think this proves that the email I got before was Dad trying to throw me off the trail. I have no idea why he didn't sound like himself in that email, but . . . this voice mail was *definitely* him. And there's no way he's in Canada. I think he's here. He's close."

Dex smiled. "And he's alive."

"Yeah," I said, smiling, too. "He's alive."

"But wait, how does your dad know you were looking into any of this? Do you think he knew you were at the plant last night?"

"I have no idea."

"And Penny . . . what *were* you doing at the plant last night? Weren't we going to go together? It would have been safer that way. . . ."

"I know," I murmured. Dex was right, of course. And maybe if I'd waited for him, I wouldn't be missing the last sixteen hours of my life. But aside from the irritation of me screwing up, there was something else in Dex's expression. He was hurt that I'd left him behind.

The shameful energy that had coursed through my whole body as I pedaled to the plant the day before was all gone, but the lingering feeling remained. In trying to find answers and prove I wasn't like my dad—hurting whoever I wanted to get what I wanted—I had, again, hurt someone. Dex.

I searched for the words to explain what had compelled me to do something so stupid, but I couldn't think of anything that would excuse my actions. All I had were excuses, and what good were they now?

A memory flashed, suddenly and unwelcome, into my mind. Dad and Julie in the back room of Vinny's Bar, arms wrapped around each other, faces flushed. Dad had turned to me, caught red-handed, and instead of offering an explanation—or an excuse—he'd asked me what I was doing there.

Maybe his response hadn't been callousness, I thought now. Maybe the reason Dad never gave me an explanation about that night was because he didn't *have* one, or at least not a good one. Maybe he knew explanations and excuses weren't enough, no matter how badly I thought I wanted them. . . .

Dex was still looking at me expectantly, waiting for my own explanation. But I was saved by the jangling bell above the door of Sweet Street. Cindy ran into the store, followed by an irritated-looking Sheriff Harper.

"Oh, Penny!" Cindy exclaimed. She wrapped me up in a hug, just as fierce as Dex's. "Where have you been? We looked everywhere, we were so worried—"

"I know. I'm so sorry," I said. I looked up at the sheriff's stern face and knew there was no point in delaying the truth. "I went to see if my dad might be hiding out in the old plant."

"What made you think he might be there?" the sheriff asked. His pale eyes peered into mine, not blinking. I thought about the pictures Dex and I had found of the sheriff at the crater site, and all the questions they raised. I had no idea how wrapped up he was in all of this; all I knew was he wanted to pin Bryan's and Cassidy's murders on my dad.

"I had a hunch," I replied, avoiding looking over at Dex. It occurred to me that Dex might have told the sheriff everything in the hours I'd been gone—though he might not have, so it was probably best to keep my answers vague.

The sheriff's eyes narrowed. "We searched the plant for you and found nothing. Where did you go after that?"

"I don't know. I don't remember." I lowered my eyes, hoping the sheriff would think I was traumatized, not being evasive. "I don't remember anything." I put my hands over my eyes and shook my shoulders a little bit for emphasis. Acting was definitely not in my skill set, but it helped that, technically, I was telling the truth.

As I rocked back and forth a little, Cindy quickly pulled me into another hug.

The sheriff wasn't so sympathetic. "Nothing at all?"

I shook my head, thankful that Cindy's hair now hid the better part of my face. "No."

"Well, that's convenient," the sheriff said.

Cindy flew back from me then, rounding on the sheriff with fire in her eyes. "Bud, the poor girl is clearly shook up. We're lucky that she's back, that she's *safe*."

Sheriff Harper wasn't at all fazed by Cindy's anger. He crossed his arms. "You're right, Cindy, we're all lucky she's safe. And that's what she is, too—lucky." He turned to look at me. "We have a killer out there—a killer of *teenagers*, you'll recall—and you're running around all night on your own? You're lucky you're not dead. You're also lucky I don't arrest you right now for impeding an investigation. It's not your job to follow *hunches*. Your only job is to stay out of our way and let us know immediately if you hear from Ike."

Again, I carefully avoided looking in Dex's direction. There was no way I was turning Dad's voice mail over to the sheriff.

"Do. You. Understand. Me?" the sheriff asked, eyes boring into mine.

"Yes," I replied, my voice clear as a bell. "I understand."

The sheriff stared at me a few moments longer before turning to Cindy. "Cindy, if you'll come back to the station with me, I have a few more things to go over with you."

Cindy nodded, and I could tell that after the sheriff's stern talking-to, her concern for me was also cooling into something like anger.

"Both of you go back home and wait for me there," she said.

"But, Mom, the store's still open—"

"Now, Dex." And without turning back, Cindy followed the sheriff from the store.

"Man," Dex said as soon as they were gone, "that was tense."

"Yeah."

"Nice bit of acting, by the way. I almost thought you were going to cry. But Mom totally bought it, at least." He drew in a big breath, running his hands over his eyes as if he'd been up all night. It occurred to me that maybe he had been. "So," he said, "I take it we're ignoring Harper—and your dad? We're going to keep looking into this?"

I looked down at my phone, still warm in my hands. How could I do nothing? It was *my* dad out there. And it was the last sixteen hours of *my* life that were missing. It was possible, I thought, that the "right" and the "wrong" thing to do from here weren't superclear, and that I wouldn't know until after the fact whether I was saving the day—or screwing everything up.

I looked up at Dex. "Oh, we're definitely going to keep looking into this."

As the words came out of my mouth, I'd never felt more like my father's daughter.

OF COURSE, DECIDING to get to the bottom of a mystery no matter the risks was entirely different from figuring out *how* to do it. A half hour later, Dex and I sat on opposite chairs in Dex's living room, running through possibilities and getting ourselves nowhere. Going back to the plant seemed too risky, but we'd already run through the list of exactly two clues Dad had left behind in his safe notes.

We hadn't gotten any closer to figuring out our next move when Cindy came bursting through the front door.

"All right, you two," she said, standing before us and crossing her arms. "I've just had a good long talk with the sheriff—which was *not* pleasant, by the way—and I think you both owe me a lot of answers."

Dex and I exchanged a quick look.

"No, no, no," Cindy said, holding out one finger. "Don't look at each other. Look at me."

We did look at her, but it soon became clear that wasn't going to be enough. Cindy's glare bounced between us, as if not sure where to start, but then settled on Dex.

"Dexter, I want you to tell me, honestly, what's been going on here."

Dex held strong under his mom's gaze for about three seconds before caving. "We've been looking for Ike."

Cindy's shoulders dropped an inch. "Yes, I've put that together. You two aren't as clever as you think you are, you know. But it's one thing to tell the sheriff when you get an email from Ike—it's another to go out on your own to an old factory that's been abandoned for years."

Neither of us said a word, and Cindy finally took a seat on the ottoman between us, running her hand through her dark hair in a way that reminded me so much of Dex's signature move that I almost smiled.

"Anything could have happened to you there, Penny. A beam could have fallen, you could have stepped on a rusty nail—"

"I could have lost entire hours of my memory?"

I gave a hopeful smile, but Cindy was not amused.

"Is that a joke? I have half a mind to take you to the hospital—"

"No, I'm okay, really," I said. "I feel fine."

Cindy studied me, lines of tension pulling her mouth

straight. She closed her eyes as if drawing patience down from some hidden source.

"I just don't understand *why*," she said. "Why would you put yourself in danger? Why not leave it to the police?"

"The police think my dad is the killer. But you know my dad," I said. "At least better than most people in town. Do you really think he could have killed two kids? Or that hiker?"

"Of course not."

"The police want to blame Ike," Dex added. "But we're the only ones trying to *help* him. Something weird is going on here, Mom."

"It's not weird, Dex, it's *dangerous*."

"It *is* weird!" Dex yelled back, surprising me and Cindy both.

"There's no need to raise your voice."

"There's *every* reason to raise my voice," Dex continued. I widened my eyes at him, trying to get him to be cool, but he wasn't paying attention to me. His whole focus was on his mom.

"Weird things have been happening in this town for years, and no one's done anything about it, except for Ike. Now he goes missing, and we're just supposed to let it go? Hope that idiot Harper and a couple of FBI agents will know what the hell they're doing?"

Cindy shook her head, confused. I was tempted to do the same.

"No matter how competent our sheriff might be, it's his *job* to solve murders, Dex," Cindy said. "And I'm not sure what you mean about 'weird stuff.' But I do think you need to take a breath, calm down—"

"I don't need to calm down! You can't always just tell me to calm down, to forget about it. Maybe you're the one who needs to *wake up*."

"Dex, you can't just talk to me like that. . . ." Cindy started, her voice almost a whisper.

"Someone has to! Look at what's happening in this town, Mom. After the plant closed, it's been dying. People have been leaving, disappearing. . . . We have to *find them*."

Dex's final word—*them*—hung in the air.

Cindy seemed to realize a second before me who Dex was really talking about. Her lips pursed together, and she looked like she was trying not to cry.

"Them?" she asked. "Dex, you don't mean . . . you don't think. . . ."

Dex breathed out heavily, and for a moment he looked angry at himself for his outburst. As if he'd been keeping something inside for a long time, and he hadn't been quite ready to let it out yet. But it was out, and there was no putting it back in. He looked up at Cindy with plaintive eyes.

"We haven't heard from him in over a year, Mom. A *year*. I've thought about it over and over again, and it just doesn't add up. Dad wouldn't just leave us in the lurch like that."

"Dex . . ." Cindy said, her voice heavy with surprise, and also sadness.

"He wouldn't leave *me* like that. Something must have happened."

Dex's face was open and raw, the secret belief he'd been hiding finally out in the open. I realized that I should have known, should have figured it out for myself. The clues were all there—Dex's weird comment about dads going missing in Bone Lake, his insistence that something supernatural was at work. It wasn't just *my* dad he was looking for. He really believed that somehow, through all of this, he was going to find his own.

Cindy shook her head. "No, Dex—"

"Just *listen* to me," Dex said, his voice rising again. "No one ever listens. No one except Ike. I was reading online about all these people who went missing for, like, years. All over the country, this was happening. People who left without taking their things or saying goodbye, just completely out-of-character stuff. And there were all these weird circumstances around their disappearances. Weather anomalies, strange lights in the sky—"

"Dex," Cindy repeated, her voice gentle, her eyes full of pain.

"It could have happened to Dad. It could have happened, Mom, it could have . . ."

But one look at Cindy's expression, and I knew Dex was wrong. I knew she was going to say something to shatter the illusion he'd built for himself. I suddenly wanted to be somewhere else, somewhere I wouldn't have to see the hope wiped off Dex's face.

Finally, Cindy took a deep breath. She leaned forward, covering Dex's hand with her own. He flinched but didn't move.

"It couldn't have happened to him because your dad isn't missing, Dex."

"Then where is he? Why wouldn't we have heard from him in a whole year?"

"I have heard from him," Cindy said gently. She gripped his hand tighter, but this time he pulled it away.

"What are you talking about?"

"Your dad's still in Tampa, honey."

Dex shook his head as if he couldn't believe what he was hearing. "But . . . they have phones in Tampa."

Cindy paused a moment. When she spoke, she seemed to be picking each word carefully. "Your dad went through some . . . rough times about a year ago. We decided together to keep you out of it—"

"*You* decided? You can't just decide like that! He's my dad! I have a right to know."

"I only wanted to do what was best for you," Cindy said, looking pained. "After he lost his job, your dad got into a little bit of debt trouble. He tried and tried, but he just couldn't get out of it. . . . He was arrested for writing bad checks. They sentenced him to two years. He didn't want you to know . . . didn't want you to think of him any differently. He was always going to come see you when he got out . . . when things started looking up again."

"Always?" Dex said, anger flashing over his features. "So you've talked to him recently, then. You've been talking to him this whole time?"

Cindy didn't flinch away from the sharpness in his voice. "Yes," she said.

"I can't believe this," Dex said. And then he was shooting up, out of his chair. He paced forward a few steps, then stopped. "How could you both just make that decision? How could you think it was better not to talk to me at all, to let me know what happened? To let me think . . . ?"

He trailed off, clearly too angry or embarrassed to explain what he had thought. And what he'd thought didn't even matter anymore, because every fantasy scenario he might have had to explain his dad's extended absence from his life had just been snuffed out by one simple truth. His dad hadn't been abducted. He didn't need to be saved. He was just a regular man who'd made some mistakes and didn't have the courage to tell his son.

Without saying another word, Dex stomped out of the room, slamming the front door behind him.

When he was gone, Cindy immediately crumpled.

"I really thought I was doing the right thing," she said, almost too softly for me to hear.

I nodded, not sure what there was to say.

After a few moments, Cindy looked up at me, wiping tears from her eyes. "You should know I called your mom."

"I . . ." My mouth stayed open, but I couldn't figure out a

way to end that sentence. Of course Cindy had called my mom.

"When we couldn't find you, I thought maybe . . . but she told me she hadn't heard from you."

This time I was the one to hang my head, guilty. "I was going to call her," I mumbled. "I just wanted to try to fix everything first."

Cindy gave a small pained laugh, then looked to the door Dex had run through. "Don't we all."

She shook her head and stood up. "Your mom was real worried for you. She told me she was looking into flights. I called her from the sheriff's office as soon as you were found, but I think she's still planning on coming back. You really do need to call her."

I nodded, keeping my eyes on the ground. Maybe it was the mention of my mom, or the idea that she'd come here and pluck me out of Bone Lake before I got a chance to find Dad, but suddenly I felt like crying.

"Maybe it wouldn't be the worst thing," Cindy said gently, "for your mom to take you home."

I kept my eyes trained on the carpet. "This used to *be* my home."

I realized in that moment what I'd tried so long to deny—how badly a part of me missed Bone Lake. Not just the town, but the Bone Lake I remembered—me and Mom and Dad, together. When everything had fallen apart, I'd pretended I didn't need this place anymore. But things weren't that simple.

"Oh, Penny, this place will always be your home," Cindy said. She leaned toward me. "I know how hard it is when you feel like maybe you don't belong in a place anymore."

Cindy's eyes went to a framed photo behind the couch, a picture of her and Dex with her parents. Sometimes I forgot that Cindy, unlike most of the people in Bone Lake, hadn't been born here. She'd grown up a few hours away in Mount Pleasant and met Dex's dad when he went to school nearby. She'd left her entire extended family behind to move with him to his mostly white hometown. And then he'd left her here, too, not just Dex.

"But your home doesn't have to be just one place. And, honey, no matter where you go, you will *always* belong here."

Cindy patted my hand. I sucked in a shaky breath, already feeling better.

"Now, I think I have another person to go cheer up," she said.

"Mind if I try?"

"Of course not. You probably have a better chance of making him smile than I do at the moment."

I got up and went after Dex. I hadn't seen which direction he'd gone, but I knew exactly where he'd be.

The ladder leading up to our tree house wasn't actually a ladder, but instead some pieces of wood nailed to the trunk of the tree in erratic intervals. Some of the pieces of wood held steady as I climbed, while others creaked under my weight. Eventually,

I pulled myself up through the house's "door," which was really just a rough opening in the graying slabs of wood.

Sitting there, on the far side of the house, was Dex. His legs were splayed out, taking up nearly all of the floor space, and he was slumped against the wall. Soft light shone in through the slats in the wood, so I could make out his movements as he shoved something beige-looking into his mouth.

"Please tell me that's not what I think it is," I said, crossing my legs and sitting down in the little bit of space not taken up by Dex.

In response, Dex tossed something light in my direction. I picked it up, and sure enough, it was a Twinkie wrapper. I remembered the day we'd taken a small box full of Twinkies and Ho Hos from Cindy's pantry and stashed them in the tree house in case of a zombie apocalypse. Now, the small shoe box full of snacks was opened, its cobweb-covered top sitting near the house's door. Dex reached his hand in for another snack.

"Dex, those are, like, six years old," I said, reaching to grab the Ho Ho from his hand.

He pulled away from me, opening the plastic package and shoving the chocolate into his mouth.

"This stuff lasts forever," he said around a bite.

"Uh, I don't know if that's actually true."

Dex's shoulders slumped as he swallowed. "Too bad we weren't smart enough to store liquor in here."

I raised my eyebrows. "Have you ever *had* liquor?"

"No," Dex mumbled. "But it seems like a good day to try it."

I sighed, scooting to sit next to Dex while surreptitiously edging the box of old snacks away from him.

"I'm so sorry, Dex."

He gave a small, humorless laugh. "I should be relieved, right? I mean, going to prison is way better than being abducted by aliens. Probably." Before I could respond, Dex smacked his forehead. "I'm such an idiot."

"No. You're not."

"I am. You were right to Scully me. You were right the whole time."

I sighed. "After everything that's happened in the past few days, I'm not so sure about that. I think *I* could use a little Mulder-ing."

Dex gave a small smile then, and seeing it made me feel oddly warm for a moment. But then the smile faded.

"This whole thing with my dad . . . it's why I started hanging around Ike in the first place," Dex said. He drew his legs up closer to him and wrapped his long arms loosely around his knees. "I know it's dumb, but I really thought your dad might have known something about where mine went. I thought if I helped him, showed him I was trustworthy, that I was old enough to know the truth . . ." He shook his head. "I was such a moron. The real truth was right there the whole time.

"And I think a part of me knew it. I told myself I didn't want to let my mom in on my suspicions because I didn't want her to worry about me, but maybe I knew, deep down, that as soon as I asked her to tell me the truth, it would all be over."

Dex went quiet then, looking down at the old floorboards. In the dim light of the tree house, his long eyelashes cast triangular shadows down his face.

"I know it sucks, but I think it's better to know the truth," I said tentatively. "Even if the truth is . . . not what you were expecting or hoping. It's always better to know."

Dex gave another rueful smile. "I knew you were going to say that."

"Can I ask you something?"

Dex nodded.

"When you were trying to open my dad's safe, you put in a number. . . ."

Dex leaned back, his head knocking lightly against the age-softened wood. "The day my dad left. That's the date I put in."

I nodded once, a puzzle piece clicking into place.

"Like I said." Dex sighed. "Idiot."

"Would you stop that? You're not an idiot for believing in something you wanted to be true."

As soon as the words were out of my mouth, I thought of my childhood self, holding on to stories about the supernatural. I'd felt so ashamed for so long, that I'd let myself believe in such enormous lies. I'd believed in them because my dad said it was all true, but I'd also believed because I wanted to. I'd *wanted* the fantastic things to be real.

For the first time in a long time, I wasn't just angry at how naïve I'd been as a kid. I was also a little nostalgic for the girl who'd believed so hard in werewolves and sea monsters and fairies. For the girl who could believe in anything, blindly. I understood why Dex would want to do the same.

He still sat dejectedly, his mouth turned slightly down in a frown, his dark hair hanging over the tips of his ears and curling at the nape of his neck. He looked like the boy I'd always known and like someone different, all at once. There were parts of him that were as familiar to me as my own thoughts, and parts that felt as unreadable as a secret. I felt a sudden urge to uncover that secret, to see the parts of him I didn't know.

Feeling uncomfortable, I pushed the thought down and tore my eyes away from him. This was just Dex, after all. Dex wasn't unreadable; he was *Dex*.

And yet.

I looked up suddenly to see him staring at me, a bemused half smile on his face.

"What?" I asked.

"Do you remember the last time we were up here together?" His question was straying weirdly close to my own thoughts, but it was so nice to see him smiling that I decided to just go with it.

"Of course I do," I said, keeping my voice light. "A girl doesn't forget her first kiss."

Dex gave a small sigh-laugh. "My first kiss, too."

"Sorry it had to be with me," I said, playfully kicking his foot with my own.

But instead of laughing, Dex looked confused.

"I know you were really into Reese," I continued.

"What?"

The shock in Dex's voice threw me off guard.

"What would make you think that?" he asked, looking genuinely confused.

"What do you mean? You were into Reese for years. Everyone knew it."

"Uh, *I* didn't know it. Because it wasn't true. Wait, everyone thought I was into *Reese*?"

"Well, yeah. She said—" The stupidity of the statement stopped me before I could even finish it. It had been Reese who told me Dex was into her. I hadn't even thought to argue. Why would Reese say something like that if it wasn't true?

Ha.

"Wow. Now *I'm* the idiot," I said, shaking my head.

Dex's hands were over his face. "Is it possible to die of retroactive embarrassment? I never *liked* Reese like that. Actually, she was the only one who knew that I liked . . ." Dex froze, his hands still over his face.

"Liked who?" I asked, and felt my own insides go still.

Dex slipped his hands, inch by inch, down his face. He shrugged and smiled then. But it was a jerky smile, shot full of false confidence. "I thought you knew. I always had a crush on you," he said, quickly adding, "when we were kids."

I couldn't help shaking my head in amazement. "You did?"

"You really didn't know? Reese used to tease me about it all the time. I think that's why she dared me to kiss you. She wanted to embarrass me."

"Because she was jealous," I realized.

Dex's eyebrows shot up. "Reese was into *me*?"

I laughed, then felt bad and cut myself off. "I don't think so . . . but I don't think she would have liked you being into me. She hated not being the center of things."

"Ugh . . . *Reese*," Dex said, wrinkling his nose. Then he cocked his head. "Still, she might have been a *little* into me."

"Sure. Totally." I laughed. "You were a ten-year-old catch."

Dex laughed, then bumped his shoulder against mine. The movement caught me by surprise, knocking me over a little bit. When I pushed myself upright again, I was closer to Dex, just a few moldy floorboards between us.

"I mean it," I said, grinning. "All four feet, eight inches of you."

"Hey, I grew into myself eventually."

"I can see that," I said, reaching out and gently pulling on the cuff of his jeans, which were starting to ride a little high up his ankle. "Nice Batman socks, by the way."

"Thanks," he said. "I'm gonna pretend you meant that as a genuine compliment."

"Oh, it was totally genuine. These Batman socks are a huge

step up from the Curious George ones you used to wear. More mature."

"Batman has very adult themes."

"Exactly."

"And Bruce Wayne is classy. He has a whole manor. And a butler. These are very grown-up socks, is what I'm saying."

I laughed, leaning my head back against the flimsy wood wall. "Man, Dex. I know so far this summer has been . . . messed up. But I'm glad we're hanging out again, at least." And it was true. Dex could irritate me like no one I knew, but I was suddenly glad it had been him by my side all week. And glad it was him sitting by me now.

"Me too."

I felt a surprisingly strong flutter rise up in my stomach as he looked at me—and didn't look away.

"After you picked me up from the airport, you said I've changed," I said. "But I'm not the only one. You've changed, too."

Dex shifted his body weight to rest on the arm nearer to me, bringing him closer.

"Yeah?" he asked, his voice low and throaty.

The flutters in my stomach increased, spreading outward through my whole body—my hands, my toes, the back of my neck. It was incredibly strange to be feeling this way—while sitting next to *Dex*, of all people. Dex, with his ridiculous theories on everything. Dex, who I'd started arguing with in my head.

Who I was starting to miss when he wasn't around.

As Dex's dark brown eyes stayed fixed on mine, Cindy's words flitted through my head.

You will always belong here.

The flutters in my stomach continued. I was afraid that if I moved they would go away.

Or get stronger.

"I've changed . . . in a good way?" Dex asked. The fingers of his hand were splayed out on the wood, an inch or less away from my own.

"Yes," I managed. "In a good way."

I was about to make another crack about Batman socks, but the words fell apart in my mouth. Dex moved nearer to me, and I knew that this moment in the tree house had taken a turn, one I wasn't sure I had a handle on yet. The eyelash shadows on Dex's face lengthened as his lids dropped down, and his mouth opened slightly as he leaned forward. I realized belatedly that my body was leaning toward him, too.

His features became indistinct, and it suddenly reminded me of Micah, how he'd almost kissed me on the back of his pickup truck in the woods. My stomach twisted as I thought about him for the first time in hours. Micah, who was probably still pissed at me, and had every reason to be. I hadn't even gotten close to fixing that situation, and now here I was, on my way to potentially ruining another one.

What if I regretted this?

What if, once again, I hurt Dex? And what if this time, it was really bad? Like the kind of hurt it's hard to recover from. The kind of hurt that pushes people away forever.

Just like your dad. Not caring who gets hurt.

I pulled back from Dex with a violent start. His whole body half shook in confusion, as if I'd just poured a bucket of water over him.

"I'm sorry . . ." I said, shaking my head lamely. "I . . . um . . ."

Dex still stared at me, his face transforming from confusion into something worse, something that twisted me up inside just to look at it. I quickly turned my head.

"I'm just . . . sorry."

I headed for the tree house's makeshift door, barely looking back at him as I set my shaking feet on the rungs, one by one, heading back down to Earth.

THAT NIGHT, I had trouble sleeping. Again. Though technically, I was still in the dark about the sleep—or lack thereof—I might have had the night before. The unease of having those missing hours just added to the ever-growing list of problems and mysteries that were currently keeping me up.

Thinking about Dex made me feel prickly hot and guilty, and thinking about Micah just did the same. And I was trying to avoid thinking about Mom all together. I'd sent her a quick text letting her know I was okay, and then didn't pick up when she tried calling immediately after. I just didn't know how much I'd be able to tell her over the phone without worrying her more. She'd already left a voice mail that she'd put her sabbatical on hold, booked a flight from Spain to Detroit that left in three days, and was trying to get on an even earlier one.

I knew there was no stopping her, and she was going to learn everything eventually, anyway.

I pushed the old quilt off me, stamping it down to the far end of Cindy's couch with my feet. Dex had gone straight to his bedroom after coming down from the tree house, and I hadn't heard a peep from his room since.

When I finally made it through to morning, I felt groggy and heavy. Cindy lightly shook me awake early, telling me it was time to go to Bryan's and Cassidy's memorial service. I hadn't packed anything appropriate for such a horrible occasion, so Cindy let me borrow something of hers, a navy-blue maxidress that billowed up around me every time I moved. It felt weirdly appropriate, since the lack of sleep had put me in a dreamy state that made me feel disconnected and floaty.

Dex pretty much ignored me all morning. I couldn't get a read on whether he was more confused, angry, or embarrassed about our near kiss and my abrupt departure the day before. His feelings toward Cindy were much clearer, though. It was obvious he still hadn't forgiven her. The tension in the car was thick as the three of us rode in silence into the heart of town.

The Methodist church was a sturdy, one-story building made of light yellow brick. People were already filing inside; instead of their usual Sunday dresses and short-sleeved, button-down shirts in summer colors, they wore somber outfits that looked too heavy for the time of year.

Cindy, Dex, and I sat silently in a pew near the back of the boxy room, which smelled like thirty-year-old carpet and fresh hydrangeas. The sheriff, in a stiff black suit rather than his uniform, sat iron-backed on a pew near Julie and Reese. Emily Jennings and Kevin Abnair were there with their families, heads down. Hector from the hardware store was passing out pale pink programs with somber nods of his head to everyone who came in.

And Micah was there, white-faced, sitting near the front with a group of football players. My body stiffened when I saw him, and I looked away quickly. My eyes landed on a pair of men standing against the far back wall—the two FBI agents, Rickard and Shanahan. In their dark suits, they should have blended in with the crowd, but if anything, they looked even more incongruous standing there with their blank expressions and identical postures, hands clasped neatly in front of them. The agent on the right wore a bright yellow tie with polka dots, the only thing that distinguished him from his partner.

After the service, Cindy, Dex, and I walked out of the church, blinking furiously in the sunlight. We headed toward the parking lot, but I caught a glimpse of a figure walking alone across the lawn. It was Micah, moving slowly with slumped shoulders. I mumbled to Cindy that I wanted some air and would walk home, and took off after Micah before she could respond.

I caught up to him just as he reached the road.

"Micah," I said as I slowed, already a little breathless.

When he turned to me I expected him to look angry, but instead he just looked hollowed out.

"Are . . . are you okay?" I stammered.

"Not really," he said, motioning with his head toward the emptying church. "That was pretty rough. I mean, I knew it would be, but . . ." He trailed off, shaking his head.

"Yeah," I replied in a small voice.

For a few awkward seconds I had no idea what to say next, even though I'd been the one to chase him down. Now that he was in front of me I realized he probably needed more than an apology right now. My mind searched for the right thing to say, but Micah startled me by talking first.

"You going somewhere right now?"

"Oh, uh . . ." I stammered, looking beyond Micah in the direction he'd been walking. The street would lead us to Main, which would take me back to Cindy's. "Just home, I guess."

"I can walk you, if you want," he said.

I took that as a good sign.

"Yeah. That would be great." I sucked in a breath. "I'm so sorry, by the way. I know Reese talked to you about the article I was writing, and I should have been up front with you about that all along."

Micah was silent for a moment. "Well, yeah," he said finally. "It was kind of weird to hear. For a second there I thought you were really into me."

"I was! Or, I am. I mean . . ." As soon as the words were out of my mouth, I thought of Dex, and how I'd felt around him the night before. *Was* I still into Micah? Even with all those old-crush feelings buzzing in my stomach, being near him was easy. *He* was easy. Dex was . . . not. He was always questioning me, always challenging me.

But he was also the one who lived in my head.

Did that mean I liked Micah any less? I wasn't sure. I was getting less and less sure of everything these days.

"I just . . . I'm so sorry. I know you don't really have a reason to believe me, but I didn't just go out with you to ask you questions about your dad . . . I wanted to go out with you *and* ask questions about your dad."

Micah raised his eyebrows, and I winced.

"Yeah, that doesn't make it right. I know. I get it if you don't want anything to do with me anymore. I just . . . I wanted to apologize."

Micah paused again, and for a second I thought he wasn't going to respond at all. But then he gave a small shrug of his shoulders.

"Okay."

"Okay?" I asked, hopeful.

"Well, it's not *okay*. I'm not really sure how I feel about it, you writing an article about my dad. That stuff's private, you know? But after today, after that service . . . it just feels like there's bigger stuff going on."

"Yeah," I squeaked out. The guilt felt like a vise around my throat. I didn't feel like I deserved for Micah to let me off the hook so easily. But I wasn't surprised that he did.

We walked in silence for a few more minutes. Everything we passed—the Sunday-school building, the adjacent playground, a small textiles store—was emptied or closed. It was like the whole town had shut down to go to the service.

When we were nearly halfway to Cindy's house, Micah cleared his throat. "Any news on your dad yet?"

"Oh, um . . . sort of," I said, thinking of his voice mail.

Micah looked confused. "Sort of?"

I bit my lip, wondering how much I should share with Micah. But there was no good reason to keep the past couple of days a secret from him. I remembered how he'd gotten scared at the thought that I might get hurt out in the woods, looking for Dad. I was annoyed at the time, but he'd been right. Something *did* happen to me at the plant. And now he had a right to know that things in Bone Lake were even stranger—and possibly more dangerous—than they seemed.

"There's kind of . . . some stuff I have to tell you," I started. Then I launched into the whole story of the past few days, explaining about dad's email, his voice mail, the sheriff's suspicions, and my lost time after visiting the plant. I left out the more personal details—my run-ins with Reese and Julie. My call with mom. Dex.

Micah was quiet as he listened to me.

"I know it all sounds kind of . . . unbelievable," I went on. "And I don't have a ton of *actual* proof yet, so I get if you think I'm losing it."

"I don't think you're losing it," Micah said in a low voice. "But some of the stuff you said . . . it reminded me of my mom. And I've been trying to pretend *she's* not losing it for years, so . . ."

"What reminds you of your mom?" I asked, confused.

Micah drew in a deep breath. "Well, that room number you talked about in the plant, X10? I've heard of it before. From my mom."

"When?" I asked, trying not to sound too eager.

"It's kind of a long story."

"Oh, don't worry, I like those."

Micah's face finally broke into a small smile, but only for half a moment. "Okay. Well, this is all according to my mom, okay? So who knows how much of it is . . . anyway . . . Apparently, before Dad died, the plant got this new kind of hush-hush contract. All of a sudden, certain parts of the building were closed off to regular employees. They just weren't allowed in. But I guess Dad went to part of the restricted area anyway. Room X10."

Room X10. With its single medical table. The scorch marks on the wall.

"What was it?" I asked, unable to help myself.

Micah shrugged. "I don't know. Mom just told me that Dad

came home from work all freaked out one day 'cause he'd been inside X10 and seen something he wasn't supposed to see. My mom told him to calm down, that he was probably making a big deal out of nothing. She asked him to take the next day off work, but he didn't. He went back in. And that's the day he had his accident."

"The . . . very next day?"

"Yep. That's what really sent my mom over, I think. It wasn't just that she lost my dad, it was that she hadn't believed him and then he was just . . . gone. She started to obsess about what Dad might have seen in that room, thinking there was a conspiracy or something behind his death." Micah got quiet again. "Every year, she gets a little worse."

"Do you believe her?"

"I never really did," Micah said, squinting his eyes a little against the sun. "I mean, I missed my dad. I didn't understand why he was gone, either. But eventually I accepted that he was dead, and he wasn't coming back. I think a part of my mom never really did, though. I kind of resented her for that, for living in a fantasy world and letting her obsession take control when she *should* have been taking care of me. . . ."

Micah trailed off, his cheeks turning red. "Sorry," he muttered.

"You don't have to apologize."

"I just . . . I hate talking about it. And people mostly let me get away with not talking about it . . . I mean, so long as I could throw a ball forty yards and always pick up the keg for parties."

"That really sucks, Micah. I didn't know. About your mom, I mean. Not until—"

"You saw it for yourself? Yeah, there's a reason I don't ask a lot of people over to the house. I never wanted people to see how bad it got, or to think . . . I don't know, that I could wind up like her. Like my mom. I know that's shitty—"

"No," I interrupted. "It's not."

Micah cleared his throat, still looking embarrassed. "Anyway, that's the reason why I didn't tell you this next part sooner."

"There's more?"

"It's about the agents—the ones who came to my house? Part of why I called you after was because I was so freaked out. Not just that federal agents were asking me questions, but because . . . because my mom *recognized* them. After my dad died, I remember these two men in black suits coming over to talk to my mom. They said they were with the plant's insurance company and asked her all these questions, got her really upset. And then they just left. We didn't see them again."

Micah paused, slightly biting his lip.

"Then the other day, when those two agents showed up, asking about your dad . . . Mom thought they were the same agents as the insurance ones who came before. She flipped, told them to get out of the house and not come back again. And . . . I kind of believe her."

I did my best to try to keep my eyebrows from shooting up. I didn't want Micah to think I doubted his story.

"I know what it sounds like. I was so young when those insurance guys came to the house, but one thing I do remember, so clearly it's like, burned into my brain, is that one of them had on this bright orange tie—"

"A tie?" I asked, my head already spinning.

"Yeah. And when those FBI agents came to the house a couple of days ago, one of them wore another bright tie, only it was yellow."

"Hmm."

"I know, it's not a very big thing. And it's not like I could remember the insurance agents' faces at all. But my mom was so *sure*. Between her *and* the tie . . ."

"If you're right," I started carefully, "if the men who came to your house are the same ones from all those years ago . . . what does that mean? Why would the people who investigated your dad's accident come back years later to look into a series of murders in the same town?"

"That," Micah said, "is a really good question. And it's been keeping me up nights, you know? Not only are Bryan and Cassidy dead, but they died just like my dad."

"Wait . . . what do you mean?"

"The accident that killed my dad, it was a fire."

I thought of the scorch marks I'd seen on the wall in room X10 and shivered.

"I've read through all of the newspaper accounts about the accident and the plant shutdown. None of them mention a fire," I said.

Micah shrugged. "I don't know why that would be. But I saw my dad's body before we buried him. It was burned."

I swallowed hard, my mind racing.

"It's possible it might be a coincidence," I hedged. "But . . . if the manner of death is the same, and those *are* the same agents . . ."

"Then something pretty screwed up is going on."

"Yeah," I said. "If only I could get closer to the agents, ask them some questions . . ." My heart raced again as thoughts and plans whirred though my mind. Here, finally, was another lead.

"You're just going to go up to some federal agents and ask some questions?" Micah asked, one eyebrow raised. "Even for you, that seems pretty bold. I mean, who even knows where they're staying, for starters—"

"Where they're staying . . ." I repeated, cutting Micah off. "Micah, you're a genius."

"Huh?"

I bit my lip, letting a plan slowly form in my mind. "I'm not quite sure how yet, but if we can figure out where the FBI guys took the info from my dad's office, we can see what other information they're hiding. . . ."

Micah's eyes went wide. "Isn't that kinda dangerous?"

I smiled. "Not if I don't get caught."

"How are you going to manage that?"

"I don't know yet. I still have to figure it out. And maybe it won't come to anything, but . . . I have to see for sure." I felt myself fighting a grin, actually hopeful for the first time since I'd woken up on my porch, missing a full night of memories.

"Man, there's just no stopping you, is there?" Micah turned to me with an expression on his face that was almost like . . . awe. And he was smiling—a full, big-toothed smile this time—which I took as a good sign. "Do me a favor?" Micah said. "If you do find something out about the agents, let me know? Even if it's that I'm wrong, and these FBI guys have never been here before and have nothing to do with my dad. Just . . . knowing for sure would help. A lot."

"Of course," I said, without hesitating. "And Micah, I'm sorry again. For not being more up front about why I wanted to hear about your dad."

"Yeah," Micah said, slowing his pace. We were almost at my house. "If you'd just asked, I probably would have said all that from the start."

I looked down, feeling ashamed all over again.

"Then again, maybe not. I haven't always wanted to talk about this stuff. You're like, the first person I've told this to. Ever."

"I'm flattered. Really," I said. And I was. "Thanks for trusting me."

Micah shrugged, like it wasn't a big deal. And then he did

something kind of unexpected. Just as we reached my house, he reached out and pulled me into a hug. As he gripped me tight I was tense for a few moments, but then relaxed.

"Sorry about before," Micah said against my ear, surprising me even more. "At my house, when I thought your dad might be . . . you know. A murderer or whatever. I was just all messed up over Bryan and Cassidy, and freaked out about the agents—"

"It's okay. I get it."

Micah pulled away gently and looked me straight in the eyes, pulling me back to this moment.

"Let me know what you find?"

"I will. I promise."

Micah smiled and turned away, walking slowly back down my road. It looked, from my perspective, like his shoulders were maybe a little less slumped than they had been when I'd first caught up to him outside the church.

Then I turned around myself, going past my driveway toward Cindy's house. I took a few steps before stopping in my tracks.

Dex was sitting on the edge of his porch, his elbows propped up on his knees. For a second I thought his eyes were on me, but then I realized he was watching Micah slowly walk down the street. He looked up at me as I made my way up his front walk, stopping a few feet from him. His long legs stretched away from the porch steps, his too-short suit pants riding up his ankles. He straightened as I got closer, and I could tell he was trying to reorganize his facial expression into something neutral.

"Hey," I croaked out.

"Hey," he said. Dex's cheeks flushed red, his telltale sign for embarrassment. It was almost worse than the tense silence of the morning.

Dex's eyes wandered again to Micah's retreating form, and his mouth opened as if he wanted to ask a question. But then it snapped shut again.

"I was just sitting out here," he stammered. "I wasn't, like, waiting for you or anything."

"No, I know. I didn't think you were."

"Okay. Glad that's . . . clear."

I wondered if it was possible for this conversation to be more excruciating.

"I should probably go help out at the store," Dex said, rising.

"I thought Cindy closed it for the day?"

"Oh . . . right."

As Dex struggled for some other excuse to get away from me, I realized that yes, things could get a *lot* more excruciating.

Ordinarily, I would have launched right into the new possible lead I'd learned from Micah, telling Dex everything, but now . . . now last night hung between us, a giant, awkward ball of tension that there was no pushing past or going around. I didn't want to talk about it, and I could tell Dex didn't, either.

But I also didn't want to just walk past him and let our relationship to go back to the occasional polite, somewhat awkward pleasantries we'd exchanged for the past few summers.

And I didn't want to do this alone. My mind caught on the only possible thing I could say to get us both out of this conversation before things between us became irreparable.

"So . . . want to go stake out the FBI with me?"

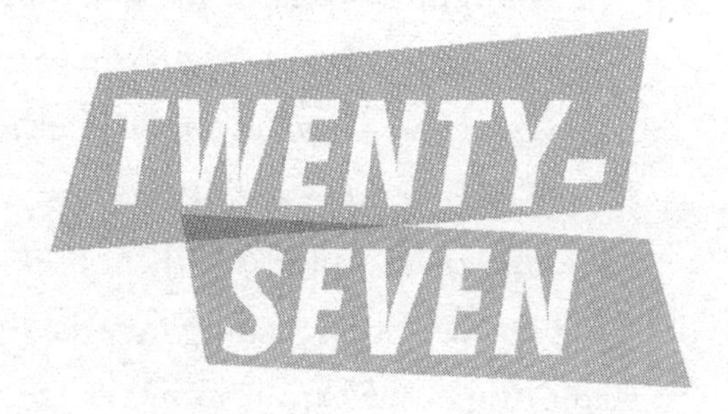

THE ONLY PROBLEM was that neither of us actually knew *how* to stake out FBI agents. I figured in a town like Bone Lake, two strangers in shiny black suits would stick out like a couple of yetis in a swimming pool, but that day everyone in town was wearing suits. I called both the Harper Creek Bed & Breakfast near the church and the Motel 6 on the edge of the highway, but neither would tell me whether two men driving a black car were staying with them. Dex and I drove by both locations, but we didn't see any black cars in the parking lots or men in dark sunglasses standing around.

So we settled on what seemed like the next best thing—driving around town until we spotted the car, and then following it.

"What happens if we actually find them?" Dex asked, in

between bites of a burrito we'd picked up at Gary's Tacos.

"I don't exactly know," I admitted, wiping taco remnants from my own hands with a napkin.

"I mean, are you just going to walk up to them and say, *Hey, quick question, but are you FBI agents in town for any shady reasons, and if so, would you mind sharing?*"

"I wouldn't put it quite that way. The best-case scenario is we find them and follow them back to wherever they're keeping Dad's files. Hopefully they have something else there, too, something that explains why they're really here."

"So you do believe Micah's story? That these agents might be connected to the accident at the plant somehow?"

"I don't know. I believe it enough to check it out, at least."

Dex's mouth quirked up into a smile. "Who's the Mulder now?"

I frowned. "Let's not get carried away. First things first." I wanted to brush off Dex's comment, but inside I was fighting back a small wave of doubt. *Was* I taking a huge risk on a wild theory? Was I turning a perfectly ordinary bear into a Bigfoot? I tried taking a calming breath.

"So . . . if we find where these agents are staying, you're going to, what, sneak in?" Dex asked. "Like bust open a lock with a hairpin and start going through their files by flashlight—"

"A hairpin?"

"Yeah. And also you should be wearing a trench coat—"

"Dex," I said.

"And a fedora."

"*Dex.* Stop." I tried to sound irritated, but honestly, I was glad. It was nice to know that Dex was still Dex—still getting excited about the most ridiculous scenario. That meant I could go straight back into the role of realist. Where I was most comfortable.

"This isn't some story," I said. I felt calmer just saying the words. "Once we find where they're staying, we'll make a real plan."

"A 'real' plan can still have a trench coat," Dex muttered.

We continued to discuss—and argue about—different possibilities as we drove around and around town, circling the main roads, cruising through streets lined with old wooden and brick houses, going down country lanes bordered by a dark line of woods on either side. We talked about the plant, Micah's dad, my missing hours. It was on our seventh trip back up Main Street, around 3:00 p.m., that we finally saw the black car. It was pulled up outside the hardware store. The side and back windows were darkened, but I could see through the windshield that the car was empty.

"Duck!" Dex said, dropping down low in the driver's seat.

"Dex! You're still driving!"

Dex's car slowed to a near stop right in the middle of Main Street.

"Right, right," he said, straightening up enough to pull his car over to the side of the road, right across the street from the hardware store. Then he immediately slid back down again.

"Genius," I said. "Now if anyone looks over at us, they'll think your car just parked itself."

Dex didn't laugh. I sighed and slid down in the passenger seat until I could just make out the windows of the hardware store if I tilted my head up. It was a few minutes before we saw one of the FBI agents—Shanahan, still in the yellow tie—walking out of the store. A white plastic bag, weighed down by something small and heavy, swung from his hand. Dex and I watched as he smoothly lowered himself into the black car, started it, and did a three-point turn heading back up Main Street and out of town.

"Follow him?" Dex whispered, already shifting his car from park to drive.

I nodded silently, but Dex was already easing down the road, staying a few car lengths behind the agent. We didn't speak, and the car was filled only with the heavy sounds of our breathing. Dex's hand shook as he moved the wheel to follow the black car off Main Street and onto Morning Glory Drive, then over to County Road 7. We were headed out of town. The car ahead of us made smooth turns, staying a consistent three miles above the speed limit. As we drove down the country road, I was struck by how empty it was; few cars came from the other direction, and none were behind us.

The black car pulled ahead, almost imperceptibly, as if the driver had tapped lightly on the gas. Dex did the same. A pair of sunglasses filled the frame of the black car's side-view mirror. He was watching us.

"Wait," I hissed. "Turn here. Slowly."

I motioned to a small dirt road that cut through a neighboring field.

"What?" Dex asked in a whisper, even though there was no way the agent in the other car could hear us.

"It's too isolated out here. He'll know we're following him, if he doesn't already. *Turn.*"

Dex tightened his grip on the wheel and breathed in heavily through his nostrils, as if his very body was fighting what he was about to do. But he did it anyway—he turned onto the dirt road, sending a small brown cloud up and over the tall grasses of the field.

"Now we'll never find him," Dex said as the car jerked over the bumpy road.

"You honestly think I don't have a backup plan?" I smiled. "Keep driving."

The smell of maple sugar was overwhelming. The day was getting so hot that just on the two-minute walk from Sweet Street to the hardware store, the candies were already starting to slowly melt and clump together.

I tossed a quick nod at Dex, who was once again waiting in the car across the street, before I walked into Hector's store with the bag of maple candy held before me like an offering.

"PENNY!" Hector boomed. He was standing in his regular spot behind the counter, though instead of his usual U of M T-shirt he was wearing a button-down shirt with light sweat marks around the armpits—the same one he'd worn to the memorial.

I forced myself to smile in a way I hoped looked innocent and casual.

"Hey, Hector. I remembered you saying how much you liked Cindy's maple candy. I couldn't find the recipe, but I figured, next best thing. . . ."

His eyes grew comically large as I placed the bag in front of him on the counter. "Well, isn't that just the nicest . . ." Hector shook his head as if he couldn't believe the bag of candy on the counter was actually for him. For a moment, I felt a twist of guilt in my gut—something that was becoming distressingly familiar—but in the next moment Hector sniffed loudly and reached for the bag with a grin.

"Thanks, Penny."

I shrugged. "It was nothing. Especially on a day like today."

Hector's smile melted off his face. He looked down, and for a moment I wondered if I miscalculated, if there were some things that were just too hard for *anyone* to gossip about. But then Hector sighed a familiar, put-upon sigh and leaned forward, elbows on the counter.

"I tell you, little Hardjoy, I've never seen anything like that."

"I know what you mean."

"No, I'm telling you. I've lived in this town my whole life, and that . . . that was the saddest fucking—sorry, excuse my language—the saddest goddamn thing I've ever seen. Those poor parents. Just can't imagine, can't imagine . . ."

"At least they knew everyone in town was there, showing support."

"Of course," Hector boomed. "It affects the whole town, you know, something like that. Lot of businesses even closed down today, out of respect. I was closed this morning, and I even considered staying closed, because, you know, it seemed like the right thing to do. But then I was telling Jimmy . . ."

I nodded like I knew who Jimmy was.

". . . I told him, I got orders to fill this afternoon. And it's not like I'm *disrespecting* those poor kids. I mean, I used to go to every single one of Bryan's home games. And some away games, too, if it wasn't raining. And I paid him fifteen cents more than minimum wage. So I don't think he'd mind much that I opened the store this afternoon."

"Of course he wouldn't."

For all his bluster, Hector looked relieved that I agreed with him.

"I think it makes sense to open the store," I continued, "especially with the town so crowded right now."

"Oh, you're telling me," Hector said, setting off on this new conversational track with as much zeal as if he'd been the one to bring it up. "Town hasn't been this busy in years, not since . . . well, they always seem to come when there's bad news, is all. . . ."

Hector trailed off and popped a piece of maple candy in his mouth. He pushed the bag over to me.

"Yeah," I said, trying to sound casual and taking one of the candies for myself. "I saw some of those journalists were even at the memorial service today."

"Vultures," Hector mumbled. A small bit of candy shot from his mouth and over the counter, landing on my shoe. I pretended not to notice.

"Even those FBI guys were there."

"I saw 'em. They've been all around. One of 'em even came in here just today."

"Really?"

"Oh yeah. Just now. Weird guy, he was. Barely spoke two words. I asked him how he was liking Bone Lake, and he says, 'It's hot.' Just 'It's hot.' I ask him where he's from that it's any cooler, and he doesn't say. Weird guy, I'm telling you."

"I wonder where they're all even staying? Not like there're a lot of hotels nearby."

Hector shrugged, reached for another candy. "Don't know about that. But I bet they're using some kind of storage unit near here."

"Really?"

"Oh yeah. So the weird guy comes in, and all he buys is an industrial lock. He says he wants the biggest kind I got, so I tell him the biggest one I got is a Master padlock, like for a storage facility door, and he goes, 'That's just what I need.' He talks just like that, only using a few words at a time. Real odd, I'm telling you. Don't know what he needs a Master padlock for, but I can't imagine it's for a dinky closet safe at the Motel 6, you know?"

"Weird," I said, shaking my head.

"*Weird*'s the word for it. But business is business. That's what I'm always saying. Even on a day like today, business is business."

"Yeah," I said, sensing the conversation was about to detour once again. "Well, I better get going before I eat *all* your maple candy."

Hector waved his hand like there was nothing to be worried about. "Thanks again, Penny. And stay safe out there, okay? Scary times."

"Yeah," I said, "you're right about that."

It was hard to sit still as Dex drove to the only storage facility in a twenty-mile radius: the Store-4-U off of M-66. My fingertips tapped out a quick pattern against my knee, and I couldn't keep my feet from bouncing against the floorboards. A rush of adrenaline still pumped through me even twenty minutes after I'd gotten the info out of Hector. *This* was what journalism was about, when it was done right—when you asked just the right question at just the right time and got the answer someone else might not have been able to get. This, I loved.

"You need me to pull over or something?" Dex asked, motioning to my bouncing knee.

I forced my limbs to be still. "I'm fine. Just hope we're actually right about this."

"Why else would someone buy a giant storage-unit padlock if not to use it?"

I pressed my lips together, considering. "Maybe the lock's for his own personal use. Or maybe he's going to put it on a shed, or a garage, or something."

"What, like they rented a house? You think the FBI uses Airbnb?"

I shrugged. "You never know."

Dex laughed.

"What?" I asked.

"Nothing, just . . . You're so used to arguing with me I think you forgot this whole storage locker thing was *your* idea."

I bristled. "I'm just testing for holes in the theory."

"Sure, sure. What good's a theory without some holes?" Dex smiled. "Anyway, there's no harm in at least checking it out, right?"

"Right."

A long, tan building rose up into view as we crested a hill, and I could just barely make out the Store-4-U sign sitting on two metal posts at the edge of a parking lot. As Dex slowed the car, my pulse sped up.

The storage facility was large, but the bulk of it faced the roadway. Hundreds of white doors were set into the low building, which backed up into the woods. Dex brought the car down to twenty miles per hour as we passed by the building. I scanned the parking lot for any sign of a sleek, black car. I saw dusty pickups, small hatchbacks, and even a few minivans parked outside of the various doors, but nothing that looked like what the FBI agents drove.

I sighed in disappointment, just about to lean my head against the passenger seat and tell Dex to turn around, when I saw a flash of red tucked inside the large opening of the last storage unit. I gripped the edge of my seat, twisting all the way around to try to get a better view as we went past the unit, no longer caring who might see me.

"What is it?" Dex asked, scanning the building in the rear-view mirror. He swerved a bit on the road, then tightened his grip on the wheel and kept his eyes forward.

"Be cool," I said, my voice low. "Drive normal."

I turned back around in my seat, willing my heart to stop jackhammering inside my chest.

"I was *trying* to drive normal."

"Okay, see that stand of trees off the road up there?"

"Yeah."

"Pull off the road and park behind them. Pull as far off the road as you can."

"How is *that* normal?"

"Dex—"

"Okay, okay, got it."

Dex checked to make sure no one was behind him, then pumped the brakes and pulled his car off the right-hand side of the road, behind a thick stand of pine trees. As soon as he turned the engine off, he turned to look at me, expectant.

"Well? What are we doing? Did you see something back there?"

"Yeah," I answered, taking a breath as I tried to figure out what to do next. "I saw something in the big unit at the end."

"Well? What was it?" Dex's whole body twisted in his seat to face me.

"My dad's truck."

STEALTH DIDN'T EXACTLY come naturally to Dex.

As we crossed the road and moved through the thick patch of trees leading up to the storage facility, Dex's long body managed to crash into every branch he passed.

"Ow," he said, after he pushed a pine bough roughly out of the way only for it to double back and smack him in the face.

"Shh," I responded. I'd never snuck up on a government official before, and I certainly didn't want to get caught doing it now—at least, not before I got a good look at my dad's truck.

"Sorry," Dex loudly whispered back, picking his way over a long-dead log that stretched across our makeshift path. "But are you sure this is the best idea?"

"No," I whispered back.

Eventually, I saw glimpses of the storage facility through the trees. The biggest units were on the far ends. They were square in shape, stretching out past the other, smaller storage units so the whole building looked like a U that faced the woods. The biggest units had larger doors and even small windows set into their sides. As Dex and I moved closer, I got lower and lower to the ground. I'd changed into a dark T-shirt and jeans after the memorial, and I was hoping my clothes wouldn't stand out behind the shrubs.

"Well?" Dex asked as we finally neared the front of the building. "Where is it?"

I shook my head. Every single door on every single storage container was shut. The largest unit, nearest to us, was locked up tight with an industrial-size padlock. I could see the Master Lock logo from my spot near the trees.

"That unit was open a few minutes ago. I saw the truck in there; I know I did. Let's get closer."

Dex swallowed. "Are you sure that's a good idea—"

"Stop saying that," I replied. "And yes, I'm sure. If the storage unit was open, that means someone *was* here, and they just left. Which means it's the best time for us to check it out before anyone comes back."

"Okay, but . . . how?"

"There." I pointed up to the tiny, rectangular window in the side of the unit I was sure housed my dad's truck.

"You can't be serious," Dex said. "How would we even get up there?"

Ten minutes later, we'd hauled the fallen log out of the woods and propped it up against the side of the storage unit. The log was clearly rotted through, the damp wood falling off in chunks where it met the corrugated metal side of the building. Dark pieces of bark stuck to my hands even after I tried to brush them off on my jeans.

"Okay, now I *know* this isn't a good idea," Dex said. He had his hands on his hips, elbows out, and he stared up at the top of the log with his eyebrows raised. Looking at him in that stance, I was struck again by how he looked both familiar and not at the same time. With his knobby elbows sticking out like that, I was reminded of the neighbor kid who used to flap his arms when he ran during tag. But those elbows were also connected to long arms with outlines of muscle just under the skin that seemed entirely foreign, but oddly hard to tear my eyes from. . . .

I shook my head back and forth once, quickly. "Just think of it like the ladder to the tree house," I said, keeping my eyes on the log and off Dex.

"Right, sure. Just like a ladder. That has no rungs. And is full of worms."

"Exactly."

Dex took one last deep breath and lifted his leg, putting his foot tentatively on the bottom slope of the log. He leaned against it, and the log held. For two seconds. Then it bent under his weight, and I lunged forward to catch him. But the bending stopped, and Dex was still there, one foot off the ground. He exhaled and started slowly climbing. When he got to the bottom of the window, he stopped and peered inside.

I could tell right away, just by how his shoulders stiffened, that I was right.

"It's in there, Penny," he whispered. "Ike's truck."

"We have to get inside."

Dex pushed and pressed against the window, but it held firm.

"Hold on," I said, searching the ground near my feet. Grass, weeds, pebbles—*there*. A brown rock the size of a cantaloupe, half-buried in the ground. I pulled against it with my fingers. Behind me, I heard the muted groan of rotted wood collapsing in on itself.

"I don't think it's gonna hold much longer. . . ." Dex called out.

I finally wrenched the rock free, glad to feel the solid weight of it in my hands.

"Move your head to the right," I said.

"What?" Dex looked at the rock in my hands, and immediately turned white. "Oh God." But he still ducked right, freeing one arm to protect the back of his neck. The log creaked again.

I pulled my arm back and threw as hard as I could. The rock didn't hit the center of the window like I'd hoped, but it did catch the lower left corner. Instead of shattering the whole square of glass, it had gone almost cleanly through, leaving a cantaloupe-size hole framed with jagged edges that shone in the sunlight.

"Can you unlock it?" I asked.

Dex adjusted himself on the log and stuck his arm carefully through the hole. His skin hit one of the jagged edges of glass, and he flinched but kept going. After a few moments, he was able to slide the window to the right, leaving a hole just big enough to crawl into.

"I feel like I already know the answer to this," Dex said with a heavy sigh, "but you want me to keep going, don't you?"

I smiled. "I'll be right behind you."

Dex angled his body into the window without losing his balance on the log and then dropped down to the other side. Then it was my turn. The log held more easily for me, and I was able to shimmy into the window hole more easily, too. But the drop down to cement was jarring, and I landed hard on my ankles and kept on going until my hands hit the ground, too.

The storage unit was large, maybe forty feet by forty feet. And it was almost entirely empty. My dad's truck sat alone on a stretch of cement under a single, unlit bulb hanging from the metal ceiling above. The walls and four corners of the room were completely empty. Standing on its own, just a few feet away from my dad's truck, were a few large plastic containers filled with papers. After just a glance, I recognized them as coming from my dad's office.

"This is it?" Dex asked. "This is their whole investigation?"

"My *dad* is their whole investigation," I murmured. "But there has to be more, something they're hiding."

I moved slowly toward the red truck, passing a pile of my dad's camping equipment that looked like it had been tossed haphazardly into the open bed. I opened the door to the familiar smell of fading pine-scented air freshener and Old Spice aftershave, and had to blink hard as I climbed into the front seat of the truck, sliding over to make room for Dex. I felt the crunch of old CD cases beneath my feet, and I kicked them out of the way.

"What are we looking for?" Dex asked, gently closing the truck door behind him as he slid behind the wheel on the driver's side.

"I don't know. There must be a reason the FBI agents brought this here. If only we knew where they found it, we could go there and look for him. . . ."

"They've probably done that already, Penny."

"Yeah, but they don't know him like I do," I said, then looked up and met Dex's eyes. "Like we do."

Dex held my gaze for a beat. He opened his mouth to say something, but at that moment we both heard it—a light, scraping noise. Our heads both swiveled automatically toward the main door of the unit, which was clearly visible through the truck's windshield.

Another metallic scraping noise, and then a small, unmistakable *click*.

"They're back," Dex whispered. "Why are they back already?"

"I don't know, I don't know," I said, fighting back against panic. There was no way we'd get up to the window and back out in time.

The whole front door of the unit started to slide upward like a garage door, revealing a crack of sunlight that grew bigger and bigger.

"Duck!"

I threw myself to the floor of the truck's cab, and Dex followed. He landed hard nearly right on top of me, then adjusted quickly so we were face-to-face, the gear stick above us and the truck floor below. All day I'd been trying to stay a careful, friends-only distance from him, and now the lengths of our bodies were pressed together, his knee just above my shin, his shoulders arched a few inches over mine.

For a moment it was just the two of us, awkwardly close. I intentionally averted my eyes, looking instead in the only direction I could, toward the ripped driver's-side floor mat coated in years of dirt and dust. I held in a sudden sneeze, my whole body rippling. Dex tensed above me, and I didn't dare look at his face.

And then—footsteps. Followed by low voices. I strained to make them out over the sound of our comingled breaths and my own racing heart.

". . . telling you, it's worth it," said one male voice. It sounded like one of the agents, but I didn't dare try to lift my head up to make sure. "Best in the whole state. Whole country, really," the voice continued.

Another, deeper voice scoffed. "I don't care if it's the best in the whole damn galaxy. You tell me we're meeting here at two, I expect you at two." I moved my head up a little, as if getting closer could help me distinguish the voices better. I really thought the gruff voice sounded familiar, maybe like the slightly taller agent, the one named Rickard. . . .

"Just try some before you snap at me," said the other agent, the one we'd seen come out of the hardware store in a yellow tie. Shanahan.

A rustling noise, almost like paper. Then a grunt from the gruff voice. A pause, then a sigh. "Damn. That *is* good."

"I'm telling you, it's the cherry filling. I remember it from last time."

"Mmm," Rickard said around what sounded like a mouthful of food.

"And I *was* here before two," Shanahan said. "Brought the new lock and parked around back. But then I remembered that diner down the highway, and we *did* skip lunch today—"

"We'll have to skip dinner, too," said Rickard, "if we don't make headway on this soon."

"I'm telling you, we need a new approach. Following Hardjoy's leads has gotten us nowhere. He's probably a dead end. Just another body out there waiting to be found."

My throat tightened, and I instinctively clutched at the closest thing to my hand—which happened to be Dex's upper arm. He stiffened a bit, and I looked up at him, our eyes meeting. I saw everything I was feeling there—the worry, the confusion. Neither of us could say a word without risking getting caught, but he moved his head a fraction, a small, barely there nod that brushed the top of his forehead against mine, and I knew immediately what he wanted to say.

He's still alive. Of course he is.

"Or he's the one doing this," Rickard said. "Just another backwoods serial killer. Granted, a weird one." Then I heard a *thump*, and the sound of something scooting across the floor. My dad's files? "A weird one who might know more than he should."

"Still doesn't explain the infected," Shanahan said.

Infected?

Dex's eyes widened, inches from my own.

A long sigh, from Rickard, I thought. "Don't go down that road, Jim. Not until we have to. Honestly, sometimes I think you *want* to be fired."

"I'm telling you, I've had a bad feeling about this from the start," Shanahan replied. "You think we'd get lucky enough for this to all be some pyro wack job or a conspiracy nut trying to get our attention? Even if the bodies were too burned to tell, they *had* to be infected. I just know this is all because of that damned site somehow. Come back to haunt us."

"You gotta get off that idea. Whole place was wiped clean."

"Maybe not clean enough. If we'd just razed the whole town after the plant fiasco like I suggested, we probably wouldn't have had to come back here at all—"

"Yeah, well, we didn't. And we're here again. Deal with it. At least you got your precious cherry filling."

Shanahan mumbled something I couldn't hear in response.

"You wanna say that a little louder?" Rickard asked, angry.

There was a silence.

"That's what I thought. You need to spend less time sampling the local snacks and more time focusing on this case."

"I *am* focused," Shanahan said, snippy. "And I'm telling you, the more time we waste in here on Hardjoy's file box of crazy, the more people out there are gonna die gruesome. And this time when the company comes to do cleanup, they'll start with us."

"God, you're dramatic. Wait . . . what is that . . . ?" Rickard said. But then there was a pause, one that stretched out so long, I wondered if the agents had moved away from the truck. And then I remembered the window, the one we'd slid open to sneak inside. I'd closed it most of the way shut behind me, but there was still a hole in one corner of it, and probably glass on the floor, too. I sucked in an involuntary breath and went rigid. Above me, Dex looked confused.

I stayed completely still for one second.

Two.

Three.

Just when I thought we were going to be caught for sure, I heard Rickard speak again, this time around the sound of chewing.

"Is that . . . custard? Right in the middle of a cherry turnover?"

"Yeah, so?"

"So it's an abomination, is what it is."

I heard another soft sound, like a *splat*.

"Oh, now, that's just wasteful," Shanahan said.

Another big sigh from Rickard. "All right. So we widen the search from Hardjoy."

"Really?"

"I'm not saying you're right about the infection, but we might as well rule that out. So we start at the ground floor, see if anyone else is acting strange—"

"Strange? You have *seen* this town, right?" Shanahan scoffed.

"Hey, this is *your* theory we're testing. Do you want to get to work on it or not?"

Shanahan again mumbled something I couldn't make out.

"So we divide up tonight," Rickard continued, as if he hadn't spoken. "You go search the crash site. I'll canvass the area for signs of any infected."

There was a silence. Shanahan must have nodded or given some sign of assent, because the next thing I heard were footsteps leading away, the storage unit door slowly sliding up again.

The two agents began bickering again as they locked the door back up. Then the faint slams of two car doors, two engines revving up and fading away.

I let out a long exhale, and Dex's body moved to fill the space just above my rib cage. My limbs felt cramped, one elbow lodged in the small space between the truck seat and the floor, my feet jammed against the bottom of the passenger-side door. I knew it was time to get up, to *think*, but all I could focus on was the roaring in my ears, and the heat coming through Dex's T-shirt, the skin of his arm against mine.

"Dex—"

He jumped up quickly, as if I'd held something hot against him, moving so fast that his head knocked against the underside of the steering wheel. He kept going, pulling himself up onto the seat. With jerky movements I followed, careful to sit next to him without touching him. Both of us faced the front of the storage unit, looking through the windshield to the large, locked door.

I felt shell-shocked.

"What," I started. "The. Hell."

Dex just shook his head, eyes straight forward.

"I mean, Dex, what . . . *what the hell*?" I sputtered, unsure of where to start. "What kind of agents *are* those?"

"I don't know," Dex replied in a strained voice.

"No, I mean . . . when they came to my house, they said they were with the FBI. But now they're talking about infections . . .

that's CDC stuff. But they're definitely not with the CDC. What's going *on* here?"

"They were talking about the meteorite site. . . . How it could infect people?" Dex spoke slowly, as if organizing his own thoughts while talking.

I shook my head. The only thing Bryan, Cassidy, and the dead hiker had in common was being burned to death. What kind of an infection was that?

"Or maybe . . ." Dex continued, "maybe something that came *out* of the meteorite can infect people. . . ."

I shook my head. "No. no, no, no. Don't say it. Don't say—"

"Aliens? I think we *have* to say it. Penny, I know you don't want to go there, but after everything we've seen and heard, can you honestly tell me there's not something beyond the ordinary at work here? Something even unexplainable?"

Dex's words crashed around in my head, mixing together with all of the doubts that had flooded through me the last few days. I didn't believe in make-believe things. I believed in facts. Evidence. But if the evidence was the very thing leading me somewhere make-believe . . .

"Because you heard those agents," Dex continued. "If it's not aliens, then the only other possibility is a human murderer. And the only person in town currently unaccounted for . . . is Ike."

"No. There's no way. Everything can be explained." I paused for a moment. "Even if that explanation is . . . potentially . . . meteorite-*related*," I added.

I looked away before I could see the gloat of triumph spread across his features.

"You mean alien-related?"

"Don't push it." I sighed. "There's too many strange, conflicting pieces of evidence. So let's consider it all. The deaths. The meteorite crash. What those FBI agents are really looking for, and what it has to do with the accident at the plant. Because now we *know* those two things are connected—it's definitely the same agents who came after Mr. Jameson died. Micah was right."

Dex bristled for just a moment before barreling on. "Right. And don't forget about the whole creepy 'infection' thing," Dex added. "That seems pretty crucial."

"Very. Especially because the agents are looking for infected people in town *right now*. I mean, what does the infection look like? How do you get it?"

"Hopefully not by going to the crash site, or we could have it . . . at this very moment. . . ." Dex tried an awkward laugh, but it was tinged with a bit too much actual fear. I softened.

"The agents said they were looking for people acting strange. That was their exact word. And I don't think I've been feeling any stranger than usual. Have you?"

"Um . . ."

The unbearably silent moment stretched and grew. Maybe, to Dex, trying to kiss me *had* been strange. Him yelling at Cindy certainly was. But still, none of that behavior seemed like the kind the agents were looking for. . . .

"Dex, I don't think they meant . . . that," I started awkwardly. "I think they meant 'strange' as in, like, inexplicable behavior—"

"Like losing a whole night of your life?"

My mouth fell open as I realized that Dex hadn't been thinking of his own behavior at all—but of mine. But before I could argue that I was in no *way* infected, Dex straightened and turned to me, his eyes suddenly wide.

"Or like staring straight into nothingness while standing absolutely still for hours on end at the site of a meteorite crash? That kind of behavior?"

"Yes. Exactly like that."

Too many questions were swirling around my head, thoughts and pieces of information like kite strings in a storm, and I couldn't get a grip on any of them. But here, finally, I'd latched on to something with promise.

"We need to find the sheriff."

I TRIED CALLING Micah twice on the ride over to the police station, to make good on my promise to keep him updated on anything I found—after all, it had been his idea to find the "FBI" agents in the first place, and he deserved to know that his mom was right. But both times my call went to voice mail.

The sheriff wasn't at the station, so we decided to try him at home. The sky was almost fully dark by the time Dex parked his car in front of the Harpers' house.

"What are you going to say to him?" Dex asked as he turned off the engine.

I stared up at the Harpers' wraparound porch, once as familiar to me as my own. I hadn't climbed those steps in years.

"I mean, are you just going to go up to the sheriff and ask him nicely if he's been feeling *infected* lately?" Dex continued.

I kept my eyes on the house. "We'll just ask him some questions about the crash site, see how he reacts."

"His reaction could be to arrest us."

"He won't arrest us," I said.

"You know, you sound really confident when you say stuff like that, but sometimes I wonder if you're just making things up."

I rolled my eyes, unwilling to let on how right he was. Instead, I doubled down. "Dex, we just followed some shady, maybe-FBI agents to their secret warehouse and didn't get caught. I think we can handle talking to the sheriff of Charlevoix County."

Dex breathed out slowly and then finally nodded. "All right. Let's do this."

We got out of the car and made our way over the familiar gray-painted boards of the front porch. I looked over to the wicker chairs, where Reese and I used to sit and take quizzes from magazines, her sucking on a Ring Pop and me slowly marking off As, Bs, Cs, and Ds in bubbly circles.

I pushed the memory—and my nerves—far down and knocked on the door. A few moments later, it opened wide, revealing not the sheriff's face or even Reese's, but Julie Harper's.

Her features tensed when she saw me, and then spread into a too-wide smile.

"Hi, Julie," I said quickly. "Is the sheriff in?"

Julie's smile stayed plastered on, but she didn't move away from the door or offer to invite me inside, the way she would have done years ago.

"I'm afraid Bud's out at the moment. Is something the matter?"

I shot a quick glance to Dex as I wondered how to answer. Didn't Julie deserve to know if her husband was possibly "infected" with something? What if she was infected, too? She looked mostly normal standing before me, her hair pulled up into a messy bun and a dish towel hanging loosely from one hand. Mostly normal except for that distracting, too-cheery smile.

"Um, we just have some questions for him," Dex said. "Urgent questions."

Julie stepped forward, her smile transforming into a look of concern. "Urgent? If something's wrong, you two should go on up to the station. Bud'll be back soon."

"It's not *that* urgent," I quickly corrected. "We just need to ask him something."

"Well, like I said, he'll be back soon. He just went up to bust a party at Millers' barn. Shouldn't take him that long."

"A party?"

"I know," Julie said, shaking her head in disappointment. "As if now's a good time to be rolling a keg out into the woods, what with everything going on. I have half a mind to ground Reese till fall."

I thought of Reese and Emily and all the others out there in the woods, just a few miles from the meteorite crash site. And even closer to the plant, where I'd lost an entire night of memory. My feet started to move backward off the porch before I even thought of a good way to wrap up the conversation.

"Uh, okay. We'll just go wait at the station, then. Thanks, Julie!"

I tugged lightly at Dex's sleeve until he followed me down the stairs.

"Well . . . okay," Julie called out after us, her concern now tinged with worry. "Stay safe, kids."

"We will!" I called, trying to keep myself from flat-out running to the car.

When Dex got behind the wheel, he looked at me, his eyes asking what to do.

"Millers' barn," I said.

"You don't think we should just wait for the sheriff at the station?"

I shook my head. "Millers' barn is close to the crash site. If he is infected, we have no idea what he might do."

"I don't think he's really going to *do* anything," Dex said slowly. "I mean, Reese is out there."

He was probably right, but I hated the thought of going to the station and sitting in the waiting room until the sheriff came back. I felt the rush of momentum, pushing me forward. We couldn't stop now; we couldn't let this lead go cold. Dad was out there somewhere, and I couldn't waste any more time.

"Let's just head that way," I said. "It's best if we talk to the sheriff outside the station, anyway. Two-on-one."

This time I wasn't totally sure I'd convinced Dex. But he started the car up anyway.

We drove back through town, quickly leaving the main businesses behind. Eventually, we reached the dark stretches of woods that were broken up here and there by houses, only distinguishable from the dense shadows by the squares of yellow light that showed still pieces of the lives inside—a lampshade here, a table edge there.

I looked at Micah's house as we passed, but there were no lights on inside. I wondered if Micah was at the party, though the last time I'd seen him he hadn't exactly been in a partying mood.

Less than half a mile from Millers' barn, we saw a car pulled up on the side of the road. It was parked haphazardly, facing the wrong direction, two back wheels on the asphalt and two front wheels dipping low into the grass and weeds. The passenger-side door was wide-open.

The side of the car read *SHERIFF*.

Dex pulled over right away, stopping the car a few feet from the sheriff's.

"Why would he stop here?"

I shook my head. Something about the car looked *wrong*. The way it straddled the edge of the road, one door flung open as if someone had spilled out of it. The inside of the car was completely empty.

I climbed out of Dex's car and walked toward the sheriff's, goose bumps rising up my arm and trailing across my neck.

"Penny," Dex said once, his voice low and warning. But I didn't stop, and after a few seconds he got out and followed me.

The world around us was eerily quiet. No rustle of leaves in the still air, no car motors coming in our direction. The headlights of the sheriff's car shone straight forward, casting the trunks of the nearest trees in a yellow glow.

I walked slowly around to the driver's side and looked in. Nothing inside the front of the car looked strange. The driver's seat was ramrod straight, a seat belt dangling from one side. The car was in park, its engine off.

A cracking noise sounded suddenly, from the woods. My head whipped around, but I couldn't see anything beyond the circle of light from the sheriff's headlights. Dex came around the car to stand near me, and we both looked silently into the dense shadows of the trees.

"I don't like this," he said.

I swallowed. "I don't, either."

I heard the cracking noise again. I couldn't tell if it was getting closer or farther away. I tried to keep my breathing shallow so I could hear better, but it was hard given how fast my heart was beating. As if I'd just sprinted a quarter mile instead of slowly stepping out of Dex's car.

After a few moments of silence, I took a step forward, then another.

"Penny, wait." Dex's voice was urgent, and he reached out to grab my arm.

I looked back at him in annoyance, but his eyes were on the ground, at the spot under where I was about to step. I looked down, then took a sharp breath.

Right under my foot was something cherry red and bright, glistening oddly in a clump of dirt and grass.

A Ring Pop.

"Oh God," I whispered. "Reese."

I moved quickly then, my feet taking me into the trees before my brain really registered what I was doing. Dex stayed right beside me, his heavy breaths constant and comforting. Together, we pushed aside branches, stumbled over shrubs.

"Reese," I called out, my voice carrying far in the silent air.

The fear didn't just prick at me, it stabbed. Every time I pushed past a tree trunk, I expected to see them again—the burned bodies, the twisted skin. Except this time it wouldn't be Bryan and Cassidy. It wouldn't be a deer in the woods. It would be Reese. Quick, stubborn, angry Reese, reduced to a pile of burned pieces. Of ash.

No. *No, no, no.*

"Reese!"

Dex yelled, too, his voice deeper and louder than mine, traveling farther. We moved quickly, and I wasn't even sure what direction we were heading in. The trees in this stretch were unfamiliar to me, and I didn't know if I'd be able to find my way back to the road from here.

"REESE!"

"Jesus, *what*?"

I heard her before I saw her, but then a blond head pushed past a small sapling just a few feet away. She flicked at a branch, staring at it as if it had conspired to get in her way and annoy her. She lifted her head and gave me the exact same look.

But I didn't care. Relief flooded through me, washing away the adrenaline that had been building through me all day, pushing aside all my momentum.

"What is your problem?" Reese asked, crossing her arms. "What are you even doing here? I didn't see you at the party."

"We thought that you were . . ." I trailed off, not sure how to answer that sentence.

"We were looking for your dad," Dex said, picking up my slack. "We saw his car on the road and thought something might have happened."

"Nothing happened," Reese said, her voice still dripping with scorn. "Except for my dad being a total freak."

I shot Dex a quick look, and his eyebrows rose.

"A freak how?"

In the darkness of the woods, it was hard to make out Reese's expression. But I could practically hear her roll her eyes as she sighed. "Well, first he breaks up a perfectly tame party at Millers' barn. As if the hypocrite didn't party there when *he* was my age. But he busts in, all weird and yelling at everyone to go home and making me get in the car. He was mental. And then we're driving back and he just whips the car off the road. He said he saw something in the woods, some kind of light or something? He told me to stay inside, but he's been gone for, like, fifteen minutes."

Reese told her story with agitation, but I could hear the worry pulsing at the edges of her words. It didn't seem like normal behavior for the sheriff—pulling over the car so recklessly, leaving his own daughter behind, not coming back to check on her.

But as we stood there, letting the story sink in, Reese sighed and shifted onto her other foot, her expression moving carefully back into bored disdain.

"Whatever. Do either of you have a phone? Mine's not working out here—"

That's when we heard the yell. A man's voice, coming from somewhere behind Reese, somewhere in the woods. The shout was clear, and then it cut off abruptly.

"Dad?" Reese whipped around, all pretense gone. She started running off in the direction of the sound.

"Reese!" I called out.

She didn't turn back, didn't acknowledge me at all. I touched Dex's hand once, on impulse. For guidance, maybe?

Or reassurance. Then I took off after Reese, deeper into the trees, and Dex followed.

It was hard to see where we were going. The tops of the trees filtered out a lot of the moonlight, and I didn't have time to reach for my phone and get out my flashlight app. It was easy to follow the sound of Reese, though, pushing her way through underbrush and snapping against small branches.

I heard Reese stop before I saw her figure outlined underneath a large tree, so close that I almost crashed into her. Just beyond her shoulder I saw the large, hulking shadow of a building—the back side of Millers' barn. But Reese wasn't looking at the barn; she was looking just to her right, where two figures were huddled in the dirt.

"Micah?" Reese asked, confusion and fear making her voice high.

I came to stand by Reese and saw that the crouching figure was Micah. His eyes widened as we approached, and I saw fear in them. At his feet was the sheriff, sprawled out, not moving.

"I just—found him here," Micah stammered. I could see now that he was shaking the sheriff's shoulders, trying to get him to move. Micah's head snapped out in the direction of the woods. "Something's out there."

"What?" Reese asked, moving forward and dropping down by her dad. "What the hell happened? *Dad?*"

"He's unconscious," Micah said.

Dex and I stepped into the small clearing, and Micah's eyes fixed on me. "Penny? What are you doing here? I didn't see you at the party. . . . I don't think I did. . . ." He was rambling, his voice rising and falling. I knelt down next to him.

"Micah, you said something was out there. What is it? What did you see?"

Micah shook his head. "We have to get out of here."

"What happened to my dad?" Reese shrieked.

"Shh! It's out there; it'll hear you."

My brain reeled. There was too much happening, all at once. The darkness around us felt like it was pressing in, and I got the sudden, undeniable sense that someone *was* out there, watching us.

Or some*thing*?

I shook my head. The sheriff. That's who we'd come here for. That's who we'd focus on. I reached one hand out toward the sheriff's still form. His eyes were closed, his face slack, cheek pressed down into some muddied leaves. But he was breathing. I didn't see blood or burn marks anywhere.

"Let's get him out of here," I said, trying to sound as confident as possible.

Dex knelt down next to me, looking for the best angle to help lift the sheriff up.

"Don't hurt him!" Reese yelled. I looked over and saw she was crying, her hair and face both drained of color in the thin light.

"*Shh!*" Micah said again. He swiveled his head to examine the trees around us, left to right and back again.

"Micah, help," Dex whispered. He put his arms underneath one of the sheriff's shoulders, and Micah leaned down to get the other.

I leaned down to help, too, and that's when I saw it. A flicker at first, just out of the corner of my eye. A light. Not the yellow of a headlight or a flashlight, but pure white. Like opening your eyes onto the brightest of mornings. A light so intense it hurt to look at.

We all froze. Me, Micah, Dex, Reese. The boys had the sheriff half-lifted off the ground, their shoulders hunched awkwardly around him. But they stayed glued in place, staring at the light as it moved through the trees.

It was coming straight for us.

"Oh God," Micah said. "We have to get out of here. *Now.*"

"What is it?" I asked.

But of course no one knew. And it was getting closer, growing bigger. Like the purest of fires.

Fire.

"Dex," I said, whipping around to him, even though Micah was closer to me. "The bodies . . . all burned up." The thought was crystallizing in my mind as I spoke it out loud, the words tumbling out of me.

Dex's eyes widened, and I knew he understood. Whatever was coming at us now, *that* was what had killed Bryan and

Cassidy. The hiker. The deer. And it was less than twenty feet away. No way we could run away fast enough, not with the sheriff in tow.

My head scanned around wildly, looking for escape. "The barn."

"No," Micah yelled. "We have to *run*."

"We can't just leave him!" I motioned to the sheriff.

Micah hesitated for a moment, just long enough for Reese to push him away roughly with her shoulder. She took up her dad's arm and looked at me. "Let's go."

Together, the three of us began to haul the sheriff as quickly as we could toward the shadowed outline of the barn. After just a moment, Micah picked up the sheriff's legs and followed. The sheriff's limp form was heavy, dragging us down as if it *wanted* to be back on the solid earth. But I gritted my teeth, adjusting my grasp on his midsection. The metal teeth of his belt caught on the skin just inside my elbow, and I felt it start to tear.

But there was no time to slow down.

I didn't turn back around to see how close the strange light was to catching up with us. I kept my eyes firmly on the back of Dex's brightly illuminated head, following in his steps, concentrating on not dropping the sheriff.

We finally got around to the door of Millers' barn, but it was locked. Dex pulled hard on the handle, but the door didn't budge. He turned around to the tree line of the woods, and the white glare lit up his features, getting brighter and brighter.

"I can feel heat." His eyes were still fixated on the distance. "Even from here . . ."

I felt it, too. A wave of heat, like I was standing less than a foot away from an open oven.

Dex turned back to the door and threw his shoulder against it.

"Wait!" Micah called out. "There's a key around here somewhere."

Micah carefully extracted himself from the sheriff's legs and started looking around at a clump of rocks near the edge of the door.

"How do you know that?" Reese asked, her voice edged with hysteria as she watched Micah. "Oh my God, is *this* where you hooked up with Mandy Colbert?"

"Reese," I said, my voice low.

She turned to me, eyes narrowed, but then her gaze caught on the thing beyond my shoulders, and her lips pressed tight together. Fear rolled in my stomach.

I turned around.

The white light had finally moved into the clearing. It was moving slowly, rhythmically, bobbing a bit up and down. I had to turn away, the light was so blinding, so unnaturally bright—

"Got it!"

I turned back around to see Micah straighten and jam a key into the barn's door. He pushed the door open, and we all moved so fast that we tripped over each other and barely made it inside the darkened space before half laying, half dropping the sheriff on the floor.

Micah slammed the barn door closed behind us.

"How do we know it can't get in?" Reese asked.

I shook my head helplessly, and as I did, my eyes caught a hunched shadow in the corner of the barn. It was so dark in there that it was impossible to see. Struggling to catch my breath, I quickly took out my phone and turned on the flashlight.

"Penelope?"

The voice that crossed the barn to reach me was low and rumbly, familiar in a bone-deep way. My heart stopped.

I swallowed hard, my hands shaking as I slowly moved the phone across the barn, the flashlight catching first on wooden boards, then on some lines of rope and some rusty tools hanging from the wall. And finally, lighting up the far corner of the room, where a man was hunched in a ball, his eyes round circles that stared at me as if they couldn't believe what they were seeing.

I knew the feeling.

"Dad?"

THIRTY

MY BRAIN WAS glitching out—it had to be. The fear and the chase from the woods—it must have gotten to me. There was no way, after all this time, that my dad could be *here*. Here, in Millers' barn, where just a week before I'd drunk keg beer around a fire thirty feet away.

But the evidence was right there, before my eyes. A fact. My dad was here.

"Penelope, what are you doing here?"

Dad's voice was beyond stern, and disappointment crashed through me. Wasn't he glad to see me? I'd found him. *I'd* found him.

"You have to get out of here," Dad continued before I could find my voice to speak. "You have to get help. *Now.*"

"What . . . ?" That's when I noticed the awkward angle of his arms, crossed in front of him. The metal circles around his wrist, the chain that led off into darkness. Was he hurt? Or something worse?

Infected?

Dad didn't seem to notice my hesitation. He continued talking, his voice low and urgent. "He could come here any second, Penny. He—"

His voice cut off abruptly as a warm light lit up the barn. I turned briefly to see that Dex had found and turned on a small, battery-operated lamp, the kind campers use. But Dad wasn't looking at Dex. He was looking just beyond him, his nostrils flaring.

"Dad," I said, trying to regain his attention. "Who are you talking about? Who could come at any second?"

But Dad just kept staring beyond me. I turned around fully to see what he was looking at, fear tickling up my spine. Just outside the circle of light, Micah was standing and facing us, the sheriff lying still at his feet. For a moment, I thought my dad was afraid of the sheriff.

Then I saw the gun in Micah's hand.

"Me," Micah said, his voice low. "He's talking about me."

He held the gun loosely, looking down at it like he wasn't sure how it got there. The sheriff's holster rested against the floor of the barn, its inside a black hole still holding the gun's shape.

"Good idea," Reese said, her voice shaking behind a false bravado. "Go shoot that thing outside before it can come in here."

"No," Micah said. "He won't come in here. He won't hurt me."

A pool of unease started spreading in my stomach.

"Micah? What's going on? Who's out there? *What* is out there?" I asked.

Micah still wouldn't look up. He closed his eyes for one second, two. Finally, he opened them.

"My dad."

Micah's words bounced around the small space, but they wouldn't seem to land in my brain.

"Your dad? But that's not possible—"

"And I have to protect him," Micah said, cutting me off as if I hadn't even spoken. "There's no one else who can do it, no one else who will."

That's when he tightened his grip on the gun and raised his arm.

I took a step back automatically, tripping a little as I did and holding both my hands out in front of me, half reaching toward Micah and half defending myself.

"Whoa, man," Dex said. "Take it easy."

"What the *hell is happening*?" Reese screamed.

Micah just swallowed, shifted from one foot to the other. "It wasn't supposed to go like this. It wasn't. . . ."

The gun waved, the barrel now aiming toward me. I yelped, a small noise, something I couldn't control.

"Micah," my dad said, his voice carrying an unnatural calm given the situation. "Put the gun down, son. You promised not to hurt Penelope. You promised to leave her out of this."

Suddenly, Micah laughed, a strange, high-pitched sound. "As if I didn't try! You know how hard it was to keep her from digging, from trying to find you? *Leave her out of this,*" he said in a low, mocking imitation of my dad. "Have you ever *met* your daughter?"

And somehow, with those words, my fear transformed into something else. *Leave her out of this?* Like my dad thought I was a child, one who deserved to be kept in the dark. Who deserved to be lied to.

He was wrong.

"Micah," I said, lowering my hands to my sides. Fighting against every instinct in my body, I took a step toward him, toward the barrel of the gun. "Micah, it's *me.* You can trust me, remember? You can tell me what's going on."

"No, Pen, you don't understand. . . ." my dad started.

But I ignored him, stepping past Reese, who cowered against the wall on my right, and Dex, who still held up the camp light with one shaking hand on my left.

"I can help you, Micah. I know you're a good person. Let me help you."

"I tried before," Micah said, his voice nearing a whimper. "I tried telling you everything before, and it didn't work. I had to make you forget."

"Make me . . . ?" And then I realized. My missing hours. The blank space of time right after I visited the plant. But how could Micah have caused that?

"I don't know what I did before," I said, forcing my voice to stay level. "But I know what I'll do now. We're going to get out of this together, Micah. But I need to know why my dad is chained up in this barn. And why you think that glowing-light thing out there is your dad."

Micah stayed absolutely still, his eyes on mine. He pursed his lips together, as if he was seriously considering my request. The whole barn was silent. I didn't dare turn back around to look at Dad, afraid that he might disapprove of my tactic, afraid that disapproval would shake my confidence.

"I can trust you?" Micah finally asked, his voice barely more than a small squeak.

"Yes, absolutely. Everything is off the record," I said, forcing my mouth into a smile I hoped was believable.

At my lame joke, Micah's mouth quirked upward on one side, and his shoulders relaxed, just for a moment.

"I didn't mean for any of this to happen. I don't know how it all got so bad. My dad was fine for years, and then . . ." He trailed off.

"Your dad was . . . fine?" I prompted, taking one more careful step forward.

"He didn't really die, Penny. That's the whole thing. The whole secret." Micah sighed then, and I noticed that the gun dropped a fraction as he did. Out of the corner of my eye, I saw Dex move—not much, just an inch or so—in Micah's direction. His eyes never left the gun.

"I don't understand," I said, my voice light and calm.

"It was the meteorite," Micah said. "My dad was right. He knew there was something strange going on at the plant; he *knew* it. Those government scientists didn't move the meteorite out of town to study it, they moved it *to the plant*. Set up a whole secret lair in the basement. You were there."

Another wave of anger crested up inside me as I wondered what exactly Micah had made me *forget*. I fought to keep calm.

"I remember," I said. "The hallway with all the locked doors—"

"I *had* to keep them locked. That's where my dad lived, where he had to live for years after what happened to him. After what *they* did."

"What? What did they do?" Reese asked, her voice squeaking. Micah and I both looked over at her in surprise, and when we did, Dex moved just a little closer to Micah. I wondered briefly if Reese had drawn Micah's attention away on purpose.

"They left him for dead!" Micah yelled. "They studied the stuff from the meteorite down there for months, in secret, making different things out of it in those labs. Dangerous things.

The meteorite stuff—somehow they knew it affected people's memories."

Tommy Cray, I thought with a jolt. He'd discovered the meteorite, but had no memory of it. If the meteorite itself had *caused* his memory to disappear, had affected his brain somehow . . . scientists would want to study that. Maybe they'd want to *use* it.

"But their experiments got out of control. My dad was on to them. He was just a security guard, but he knew something was shady. He went to go gather information, to expose what they were doing right here in *our* town—but something went wrong. He never remembered it, what exactly caused the fire in room X10. But he was inside the room when it happened—trapped inside with their meteorite chemicals."

I nodded, trying to keep up. Micah was on a roll now, the words pouring out of him quickly. He waved his hands around a couple of times during his speech, as if he'd forgotten he was holding the gun.

"Dad was so badly burned they could barely recognize him. Declared him dead right away. But he wasn't actually dead. Just changed." Micah sniffed, his voice thick. "He actually snuck out of his own casket, right before it went into the ground. Can you imagine what that must have been like for him? We knew if we didn't keep him hidden, they'd come after him. Do more experiments. So we kept on pretending he was dead, and we hid him in our basement—for a while. Then the plant closed altogether. They just packed up and went away, leaving their mess behind. Blaming it all on my dad."

The bitterness in Micah's voice was heavy. I tried to focus on what he was saying, on all the pieces slotting into place, one by one.

"But half the town worked at the plant. They would have known about a secret lair, about the fire. . . ."

"No," Micah said, shaking his head. "That's the thing—one of their experiments worked. They actually made something from the meteorite that could affect people's memories in small doses."

"X10-88," I breathed.

"They used it on the entire town."

"*What?*" Dex this time, his voice incredulous.

"That's how the drug works. You give it to someone, and you can make them forget a certain amount of hours, or you can plant suggestions that they think are true, and they become like new memories, pasted over the old ones," Micah said.

Plant suggestions . . . new memories.

That line of dialogue jumped to the front of my brain, the one I'd heard repeated so often in the past week—by Cindy, Hector, even Mrs. Anderson. I'd asked all of them about the accident at the plant, and they'd all answered in a similar way . . . not just similar, but identical.

It's best not to think about it too much.

The goose bumps were back, crawling up my skin. It wasn't

just a common expression, or one they'd read in an article. It had been put into their mouths. Planted into their brains.

"Oh my God," I whispered.

"No one remembered what was going on in that basement or what really happened to my dad. *No one.*" Micah's eyes were wild with anger. His voice got louder. "Do you know what that's like? To have everyone think your dad is some fuckup who lost the town the plant contracts and all their jobs, when really he was a hero just trying to get to the truth? And I couldn't tell anyone. If the agents guessed he was still alive, they would take him away. Or worse. So he *had* to stay secret. He had to stay locked up. The basement was too small, and the house is made of wood, so a few years ago, we moved him to the plant."

"The house is made of wood? What did that have to do with anything . . . ?" I asked, shaking my head in confusion. Micah bit his lip, as if he'd said too much, and then it made sense. "You were afraid he'd burn it. You said your dad . . . changed? After the accident?"

Micah's eyes fell again, and his mouth pulled into a tight line. For a moment, he looked like he might cry.

"Oh, he changed," my dad said. I turned slightly to face him. His expression was grim as he kept his eyes on Micah. "I found a body in the woods a few months ago, a hiker. Something was weird about it, though. No one would believe me. Not that that's anything new. But I thought I could catch the killer. I set up cameras in the woods. . . ."

"I know," I said. "I found one of them."

Dad looked at me then, with a strange expression. "You did?"

I nodded, and a strange look settled into the lines of his face. He looked surprised and almost . . . proud.

"I captured a strange image on one of the cameras. It was almost alien-like. Or at least, I thought so at the time," Dad continued. I pictured the image I'd found on his camera my first night back in Bone Lake. The strange bent branch that looked like an arm. "That was the camera I'd set up in the woods not too far from the Jamesons' place. I went to check it out, and that's when I saw Hal Jameson, in the woods."

"He started going out, wandering in the woods on his own," Micah said, his voice strained, almost desperate. "I told him not to, but he . . . eventually he . . ."

"He killed someone," Dex interrupted.

"He didn't mean to!" Micah yelled, whirling on Dex. "You don't understand. That meteorite stuff they were experimenting on—it changed him. Maybe he got too close to it, or maybe when it mixed with the fire, it . . . I don't know exactly what happened to him in that room. But that stuff they were messing with, it burned itself into his *insides*. It, like . . ."

"Infected him?" Dex asked.

Micah kept going as if Dex hadn't said anything. "For the first few years, he was just sick. He couldn't move, couldn't remember who he was most days. Sometimes he'd complain about being cold all the time, even though his skin was burning up. Then small things started catching fire when he touched them. Then he started getting out of the house at night. . . . That's when we moved him to the empty plant, so he'd be safer. I didn't know he was going to hurt anyone. . . . I didn't know he *could*."

"But you found out," Dad said, his voice still cold. "When I found Hal out in the woods, you knew I'd put it all together. So you sucker punched me and locked me up."

Micah just swallowed, not confirming or denying what he'd done. Dad turned his head to address me. "I woke up in the basement of the plant, and he injected me with gold liquid from a vial—X10-88. But it didn't work."

"It should have!" Micah exploded. "I was going to fix everything. I've seen how X10-88 works before. Before the accident, Dad stole some of the stuff from the plant. Mom was afraid of it at first, but when those agents came to use it on her . . . she recognized it. They still gave it to her, and she forgot *everything*. Everything my dad had uncovered, even the fact that he was still alive. When she saw him in the basement later that day, she nearly had a heart attack. I had to explain everything to her—all over again. What had happened to my dad, why everyone thought he was dead. It was so hard on her, keeping the secret. Keeping Dad in the basement when he was so . . . changed. Burns on ninety percent of his body. He couldn't remember us most days, could barely move on his own for months, could never leave the house. . . ." Micah's voice lowered to just above a whisper. "Mom started taking the stolen drug on her own sometimes. When she *wanted* to forget what our lives had become, even just for a little while. I couldn't blame her, but it was so hard . . . taking care of everything on my own."

Micah was unraveling now, and I felt a wave of pity for him. He hadn't asked for any of this to happen to him—for the meteorite to crash here, for the government to do secret experiments on it in our town, for his dad to get hurt or his mom to lose her mind from grief and maybe something worse. His face was drawn in the dim light, and his shoulders were hunched. He was staring at me, out of everyone else, like he wanted *me* to understand. Like everything rested on me understanding.

But my dad was chained up behind me, and people were dead, and understanding was different from forgiving.

"So you used your dad's stash of drugs on my dad?"

Micah blinked, disappointed. But not ready to give up. "It was going to fix everything. But I didn't know how the whole suggestion thing worked. I couldn't plant a new memory into his head like the agents could. I just had to give him enough of it to make him forget the past few days—forget seeing my dad. He'd wake up at home, and not remember anything. It'd just be like . . . a blank space. But there wasn't enough of the drug left to make him forget more than half a day. I kept trying, but after all these years the stash was running low."

"And you had to use it on other people," I said. "Like me."

"I'm sorry," Micah said, but it was more of a whine than an

apology. He still didn't understand why I wasn't siding with him. "I really wanted to keep you out of it. After we found Bryan and Cassidy, I saw how worried you were about your dad, so I wrote that email from his account so you'd know he was safe. But you *didn't stop looking*. And then you came to the plant, and you almost found your dad in one of the rooms. . . ."

I shook my head. I remembered going down into the basement hallway, opening door X10 . . . and hearing noises in a neighboring room. I'd thought it was a raccoon again, but really . . .

"Dad was there?"

He'd been so close. . . . I'd been *so close* to finding him. . . .

"I saw you in the plant and I followed you. I told you everything," Micah said. "I tried to get you to understand why your dad was in the plant, why you couldn't see him yet. But you were so mad. You said you were going to go to the sheriff, that he was probably already on his way. So I used some of the very last of my stash to make you forget, and then I made your dad leave you that voice mail to help you stay away, and I moved him out here to the barn."

I shook my head, torn between wanting to punch Micah in the face and knowing I had to get all of us out of here in one piece. Another small bit of information clicked forward in my mind.

"I wasn't the only person you used the drugs on, was I?"

Micah shifted on his feet but didn't respond.

"The sheriff. You gave him the drug, too. Was it just because he was at the crash site? Or did he see something else you didn't want him to see?"

Micah pursed his lips. "The sheriff and I were both out in the woods for the same reason—trying to find the rest of Ike's cameras. Reese told me that's what the cops found near Bryan's and Cassidy's bodies: a camera of Ike's."

"I told you that in confidence!" Reese said. She looked slightly abashed at her outburst. "Not that it matters now, I guess."

"If my dad had been captured clearly on any of those cameras, it would be all over," Micah went on. "I had to find them. But my dad must have followed me out into the woods. He was getting harder to control, refusing to stay locked up anymore, no matter how hard I begged him . . . and when I got to the crash site, the sheriff was already there. He saw me—and my dad. I had the drug on me, so I just . . . I only used a little bit, enough to make him forget a few hours. I never found another camera."

"We did," Dex said. "But in the pictures we saw, the sheriff was just standing there, staring . . ."

"That's how it works," Micah said, miserable. "The drug makes you fade out for a bit, and then you forget. Or if you're the *government*, you make people remember things that aren't true. But *I* never did that."

"I'm sure your medal's in the mail," Dex retorted.

"And there's more, isn't there?" I said, slowly realizing. "Mrs. Anderson. We found her in the street one day, and she was dazed and couldn't remember where she'd come from. She kept talking about pie . . . that she'd just brought a pie to someone. It was you, wasn't it?"

Micah's face twisted in chagrin. "She came to our back door. She shouldn't have done it. My dad was confused, wandering in our backyard, and she saw him. I only used a *little* of the drug on her, I promise. And she's fine now! She only lost a few hours, right?"

"We had pie later, on our date. Was it hers? You drugged her and then fed me her pie?"

Micah bit his lip, and I took that as a yes. I felt sick. All that evidence, right there before me, and I hadn't put any of it together.

A loud thumping noise made me look up. Reese had just stamped her shoe on the ground. "Pie? Who the hell cares about pie?" Reese yelled, waving her hands in the air as if trying to get us to see something obvious. All her cowering fear was gone. "Micah, you just admitted that your dad *killed people*. He killed Bryan and Cassidy, didn't he? *Didn't he?*"

Micah looked taken aback by Reese's outburst and put his head down, as if he couldn't face her.

"He didn't mean to," he finally whispered. "He's in so much pain, and he gets so confused, and he can't control it. I didn't even know he could do that to someone until the hiker. And I hoped Bryan and Cassidy had just run off; I really wanted that to be true. . . ."

"But *you* were the one who found their bodies," Reese continued. She waved a loose hand toward me. "Both of you. You knew then what your dad did. You knew what he could do, that we were *all* in danger. And you did nothing."

"I was going to fix everything," Micah said for the third time, like a mantra he couldn't stop repeating. "When I saw those agents were back, I knew they'd have more of the X10-88, or at least know where some was. I just had to get some more of it, enough to make Ike forget everything. And then I was going to take my dad out of town, somewhere far away, where he couldn't hurt anyone else."

"That's why you finally told me about the agents?" I asked. "You set me up to track them down, all so you could get your hands on more X10-88?"

"I didn't want to get you involved, but since you were clearly hell-bent on figuring everything out—even *after* losing your memory at the plant—I figured I might as well use that to help set everything right. Once you found out where the agents were keeping the drug, I could go get more. Then everything would be fine."

"It wouldn't be fine," Reese said, the rage still seething from her. "Nothing would be fine. Look at my dad! Did that . . . *thing* out there do that to him?"

"No," Micah said. "I did."

"What?"

"I had to keep people away from here! When I heard about the party, I called it in to the cops to get them to bust it up before anyone could sneak in here and find Ike. But the sheriff just couldn't leave it alone. He went out looking in the woods, and I had to make sure he wouldn't find my dad again. For both their sakes. I had to knock him out. And then I tried to get all of us to leave, to run, but no, you wouldn't listen to me."

"And that makes it all better?" Reese's voice rose higher. "You knocked out my dad! Bryan and Cassidy are *dead*. And the monster who killed them? He's out there *right now*."

"HE'S NOT A MONSTER!" Micah's face was so twisted up, he looked like a stranger.

I exchanged a look with Dex, who was only a few feet away from Micah now, closer to him than the rest of us. Another wave of fear jolted through me—I could guess what Dex was going to try to do as soon as he got close enough, and I didn't want him to take the risk and get hurt. But I couldn't communicate that without tipping off Micah.

As for Micah, he seemed a little shocked by his own outburst, and certainly unnerved by how scared we all were. He ran one shaking hand through his hair and took a deep breath through his nose. "My dad is not a monster," he said, slowly and more calmly. "He's my family." He looked up at me then, and I saw again that look in his eye—that desperate wish to have me understand him. I kept my eyes trained on Micah as Dex slowly began inching toward him again.

"No dad is perfect," Micah said. He waved a hand—the hand with the gun—toward my dad. "I mean, what about everything you told me about him? About how much he let you down? But you still went looking for him. Because he's family."

I kept stock-still, not wanting to turn around and see my dad's expression. But my eyes darted to him unwillingly. I expected him to look angry, but he just looked confused. Like he was truly surprised by what Micah was saying.

And it occurred to me that for all the years I'd been angry at him, I'd never really gotten up the nerve to tell him why, or to demand a reason for his behavior. And why *hadn't* I ever told my dad how I felt? Why hadn't I told him how angry I was, about finding him with Julie Harper, and losing Reese, and the divorce, and the stupid black bear in the woods? The split between us had seemed so wide, and we'd fallen so far apart, that it hadn't occurred to me to just *talk* to him. To hear his side, to tell him mine.

And if we didn't figure a way out of here, I'd never get that chance.

Micah stared at me, waiting for a response.

"You're right," I managed to say. "We do a lot for family, no matter what. But, Micah, you said yourself your dad hurts people without meaning to. He *burns* them, somehow. And right now, he's out there, and he could come in any second—"

"No," Micah said, with a surety that surprised me. "I was the last one in, and he saw me before I came inside. He saw me, and he went back into the woods. My dad would never hurt me."

"And the rest of us? Would he hurt us if he saw us leave here?"

"You *can't* leave here. Not until I get this figured out!" Micah put his free hand up to his eyes and rubbed them, hard. He was coming apart. He wasn't going to figure anything out—and even if he did, I definitely didn't want to be part of his solution.

But I didn't get a chance to think up a solution of my own. While Micah was rubbing his eyes, Dex made his move.

It happened so fast, I barely had time to register it, let alone try to stop it. Dex had maneuvered himself so he was only a couple of feet away from Micah. As soon as he was in reach, Dex lunged out, his long legs closing the gap between them, his arms wrapping around Micah's upper shoulders to trap him in place. For just a moment, Micah stood frozen, stunned by Dex's sudden move. His gun arm was pinned to his body, the barrel pointed at the ground. But then his jaw hardened in anger. His shoulder muscles bulged up easily. And Dex realized his mistake the same moment the rest of us did—though he had the element of surprise, and even an inch of height on Micah, he was nowhere near as strong as Bone Lake's superstar quarterback.

It took less than three seconds for Micah to break Dex's hold. The momentum sent Dex flying backward. He caught himself before falling, but then Micah spun around on him, the gun aimed squarely at Dex.

A scream tore out of me. I thought Reese might have been screaming, too, but I could barely hear it over the sound of blood rushing through my ears. Everything else in the barn was forgotten—Reese, my dad, the potential killer roaming just outside the flimsy barn walls. My whole world was narrowed to that small, dark gun barrel and the few inches of space between it and Dex's chest.

"You shouldn't have done that," Micah said.

"Don't shoot him, Micah," I begged. "Please, *please* don't."

"I don't *want* to shoot anybody!" Micah said. With his back to me, I couldn't see his face, but his voice sounded pained. "I never wanted to hurt anyone!"

"Micah," my dad's voice called out. "Think about what you're doing. Things have gone too far, son. There's no fixing this. The only thing left to do is let us go."

"I can't!" Micah yelled. "I can't lose him. Don't you understand? I *can't.*" The panic was rising in his voice, and his hand tightened on the handle of the gun.

My dad started to talk again, but I interrupted him, making my own voice louder.

"I know, Micah," I said. "I hear you. Just . . . tell us what we can do. Tell us what you need. Please."

Micah stayed still. One second passed, then two. Finally, his shoulders relaxed a moment.

"I need the drug. The X10-88. Did you find the agents, Penny?"

"Yes," I said. "I did. And I can tell you where they're storing stuff." I didn't remember seeing anything in the storage unit that resembled any sort of drug, but at the moment, Micah didn't need to know that.

"I'll tell you," I continued, "but first you have to put the gun down. Let Dex go."

The barrel of the gun dropped two inches, and Micah quickly jerked his head, indicating Dex could move. Dex's eyes closed in relief, and then he quickly melted away to the side of the building, made his way back to where I was standing. I wanted to reach out and grab him up, to push him behind me and keep him safe, but I didn't want to make any more sudden movements.

Micah slowly turned to face me.

"Thank you," I breathed. "There's a storage facility outside of town, off of M-66. The agents were there."

"Okay," Micah said, nodding his head quickly, thinking. "Okay. Everyone get out your cell phones. Toss them over to me."

"What?" Reese sounded strangely offended, as though *that* were the strangest thing for Micah to ask of us that night.

"Do it!" Micah said, vaguely raising his gun.

Dex, Reese, and I reached for our phones and tossed them to the ground at Micah's feet, where they landed with three distinct clatters.

Micah picked up the phones and put them all in his pocket. Then he backed slowly toward the barn door and opened it, keeping his gun trained on us the whole time.

"You can't seriously just leave us here!" Reese called out.

"I just need to get more of the drug. Then I'll come back, give it to you all, and everything will be fine again. It'll all be fine."

"But what about the monst—sorry, *your murdery dad*—right outside?"

"I told you, he saw me come in here. He wouldn't hurt me," Micah said, keeping one hand steady on the open door. I could see a patch of darkness outside, but nothing beyond that. It was impossible to know if lurking out there, somewhere, was a meteorite-infected man consumed by blinding fire.

"But you're leaving," I said. "What if he comes back for the rest of us?"

Micah paused for a second, his mouth moving quietly. "He won't," he finally said, but his voice lacked any conviction. "Besides, I'll be fast. Just stay here."

"Micah!" I called out, but the door had already shut behind him. I heard a key turning in a lock and realized, stupidly, that he hadn't "found" the key as we were trying to get inside—he'd probably had it on him the whole time.

"Just stay there!" his voice called out from the other side of the wall.

I heard his footsteps moving away through the leaves, and

then nothing. I quickly scanned the barn, but there was no window, no other way out.

We were trapped, alone in the woods, with a killer right outside. A killer who'd been infected by meteorite alloy that had been experimented on by the government.

As soon as the thought passed through my mind, I could feel something bubbling up in my throat, and at first I thought it might be a scream. But what came out was a single burst of laughter. The noise was startling in the small, enclosed space of the barn, even to me.

"Penelope?" Dad asked. "What is it?"

"I just . . ." I gasped, my voice rising as I struggled to speak, "I was just thinking . . . it was a zebra the *whole time.*"

"A zebra?" Reese asked. "What the hell are you talking about?"

"When you hear hoofbeats, think horse, not . . ." I said, then broke into a round of panicked giggles that got stuck in my throat.

A split second passed, and then Dex's face broke into a smile, too. "Zebra."

"It was a zebra!" I felt my voice rising in a fit of panicked laughter, but I couldn't stop it. I just threw my hands up in the air. "And who knows? Maybe aliens *are* real. Bigfoots, too!"

"Are you losing your minds?" Reese asked.

"Maybe!" I said, then turned to see Dad was watching me with concerned, wondering eyes. But he was also smiling.

"How is this funny?" Reese's voice rose higher, its panicked pitch nearly matching my own hysterical one.

But her outburst only made me laugh harder. For just a second, the horror of the evening let up, my chest loosening a fraction.

But before that second could stretch into two, I heard the noise. We all did.

It was low but distinct, like feet dragging slowly through the underbrush. It was coming from outside the barn walls.

And it was getting closer.

EVERYONE INSIDE THE barn went still. We looked at the wall with the barn door as if we could will ourselves to see through it, as if we could somehow *hear* better if we just stared hard enough.

There was the noise again, soft but distinct. And deliberate. Something was cutting a path toward us through the woods.

"Maybe it's Micah? Maybe he changed his mind?" Reese whispered.

Another noise, like a footstep. I peered through the thin cracks in the wall's boards, looking out for any kind of glowing light.

"Penny," Dex said, his voice low and in my ear. With a start, I realized he'd moved to stand right beside me. "Micah said they had to move him from the basement because he kept accidentally setting things on fire. We're surrounded by wood right now."

He was right—the entire barn was made of wood slabs. Even the floor of the building was made out of old, coarse boards. If any single part of the building caught fire, with us trapped inside—

"You have to get out of here," Dad said from the corner. "Get past whatever's left of Hal Jameson and run."

"How?" I asked.

"Over there," Dad said, motioning to a dark, shadowed corner of the barn. "There's something over there, something metal with a handle. I haven't been able to move from this spot since the kid chained me in here, but in the daylight I saw it—a shovel or something."

Dex ran over to the corner and began searching. Something fell to the ground with a clatter, the noise ringing through the barn. For a moment I felt my heart stop. We all froze, held our breaths, waiting to hear if we'd drawn the attention of the thing outside.

"Sorry," Dex whispered. He leaned down and picked the object up off the floor. It was an old pickax, its handle the size of Dex's forearm, the head covered in rust.

"How can we use this to get out?" Dex asked in a rushed whisper. "The lock's on the other side of the door. . . ."

"Look for a weak spot in the wood," Dad answered. "This barn is ancient. There has to be a loose or rotting board somewhere. Knock lightly on the wood. If it's soft, use the axe to knock it down."

"But, you know, quietly," I added.

Dex gulped and then started in on the nearest barn wall. Reese and I took others, making our way around the room while being careful not to step on Dad or the sheriff's still form. I pushed my hand against the wood, wondering the whole time whether Micah's dad was just on the other side, capable of burning me alive with a touch. After running my fingers over one splintered board after another, I finally pushed against wood that seemed to give—just a little—under the weight of my hand.

"Here!" I called out in the softest voice I could manage.

Dex came over with the pickax, kneeling down next to me on the floor. The soft spot was close to the ground, just a few feet away from the door. Dex shoved the edge of the pickax into the small slit between two boards and started to push the handle sideways, wedging the boards apart. One of the boards groaned as it grudgingly moved a few centimeters over. Dex took a deep breath and tried again.

"It's working!" I turned to Dad. "Wait," I said. "How are we going to unchain you?"

Dad's smile vanished. "Kiddo, I've been trying to get out of these things for days. You all go on and get help, then come back for me."

"You want me to just leave you behind? Alone?"

“Not alone,” Dad said, motioning to the unconscious sheriff. “I’ll have some company.”

“But . . .” I shook my head. “Mr. Jameson is out there. If he gets close, this whole building could go up like a matchstick. You’d be trapped.”

“Then you guys had better hurry.” Dad’s voice was stern, but as his eyes met mine, I could see something else in them. Fear. I thought again of our ill-fated Bigfoot hunting trip, and how afraid Dad had been when the bear came after us. I remembered how panicked I’d felt, seeing Dad like that, knowing that he was just as afraid as I was. He hadn’t known the absolute best thing to do to keep us safe; he was just reacting to the situation the best he knew how. He was guessing.

And he was guessing now.

But instead of letting panic overtake me and just taking his lead, I shook my head. Because if both of us were just blindly making our way through every situation with the best knowledge we had on hand, then maybe my guess was just as good as his.

“No,” I said. “I’m not leaving you here alone.”

Dad’s whole face tensed up. “Penelope, this is not up for discussion. You *are* getting out of here—”

I heard something creak behind me and turned around to see that Dex had opened up a small hole in the wall. He tried pulling up another board, his arms straining with the effort, but it wouldn’t budge.

“I think this is as good as it’s going to get,” he said.

"You have to go through it," Dad said. "Now."

"No!" I said back, forgetting to keep my voice low. "I'm not leaving you here alone, and chained. If Mr. Jameson—or whatever he is now—somehow gets inside without burning the whole place down, who's to stop him from attacking you or the sheriff?"

"Pen—"

"I will." Dex stepped forward, looking almost like an action hero with his shoulders squared and the pickax in one hand. Then his eye twitched and I saw Dex again—the boy next door who used to cry when we got too rough playing neighborhood games.

I shook my head, but before I could say anything, Dex made his case. "I won't fit through that hole anyway."

I looked down at the opening his pickax had made and realized it would be tight, even for me. Dex's shoulders probably wouldn't make it through.

"Look at the facts, Penny," Dex said. "Isn't that what you always say?"

Yes. And the facts here I couldn't avoid were that Reese and I were the only ones who would fit through that hole, and there was no way I was sending her through alone. But looking between Dex and my dad, my stomach flipped over on itself. I swallowed against the dry lump in my throat as my gaze landed on Dex.

"I can't lose you," I whispered. I'd meant to say *I can't lose you both* or *I can't lose you, too,* but my voice had faded out at the end, swallowing up the last word.

Dex's eyes widened briefly, filled with an emotion I couldn't place. "Then hurry," he said. "I left my keys behind in the car when we went looking for the sheriff."

I nodded then looked over at Dad. "The faster you go, the better chance we have," he said.

Reese was biting her lip, her eyes on the hole. "What if it's waiting right outside?" she asked.

"Would you rather stay?"

She looked around the barn once before shaking her head emphatically, her blond hair flying around in the darkness. She ducked down and squeezed through the hole. When it was my turn, I looked once more at Dex and Dad, then turned my back on them to leave. When I finally crawled out, there was a fear piercing through my chest, but it wasn't for me.

On the other side, Reese reached down to grab my hand and help me up. The trees around us were still and quiet; there was no more than the faint rustle of leaves in the wind. Still, we spun in a whole circle, alert for any sign of light or movement.

Nothing.

Without saying a word, we took off running toward the road, still holding hands. We raced through the trees, then past the area in front of the barn that was littered with red plastic cups and cigarette butts. Smoke still rose from the fire pit, curling a bit in the air as we rushed past. We ran down the dirt road and hit the street, then turned and sped in the direction of Dex's and the sheriff's cars. Our feet slapped against the old concrete of the two-lane road, and my eyes darted from one side of the woods to the other. I tried not to think about how the shadows in between the gnarled, twisted branches of the trees could be hiding anything inside them.

"Where's . . . the car?" Reese panted out after a few minutes.

"I don't know," I said, fear gnawing at my insides. Then up on the side of the road, we saw the familiar white-and-brown paint of the sheriff's car, still pulled off at an angle. Only this time, it was alone.

Dex's car was gone.

We both pulled up short at the same time. The muscles in my calves were on fire, and I worked to pull air into my lungs.

"Where is it?" Reese shrieked, once again forgetting to stay quiet.

Micah. I hadn't thought before about how he'd get to the agents' storage unit, but now I remembered he didn't have his own car. Had he taken Dex's instead?

The keys are inside. That's what Dex had told me. If Micah had seen them . . .

"It doesn't matter where the car is," I said, shaking my head. "It's not here. So we need a new plan."

I walked quickly over to the sheriff's car and opened the driver's-side door. "Does your dad keep spare keys anywhere in here?"

Reese shrugged, looking nervously into the stand of trees beyond the car. But she still came over to help. We looked under the seats, in the cushions, in the glove compartment. I tore my fingernail when I jammed my hand into the small space between the gearshift and the driver's seat. Every time one of us thought we heard a noise coming from the woods, we whipped around to face the trees, trying to stare through the dark.

"Oh my God, we're such idiots!" Reese suddenly exclaimed, diving up to the dashboard and wrapping her hands around a small, boxy device. A police radio.

Relief hit me like a wave. "Let's call ourselves idiots later."

Reese nodded and held the radio up to her mouth and pushed a button. It connected her right to someone at the police station. A woman's voice, one I didn't recognize, but that Reese did. She explained in a rushed voice that we'd found Ike Hardjoy and the sheriff was hurt and there was someone in the woods.

"Come *now*. Like, five minutes ago now. Send everyone."

The woman on the other side of the radio made Reese repeat herself, but then promised help was on the way. As soon as she said, "Over," for the last time, the radio went silent, and Reese and I both collapsed against our seats—me in the driver's seat, her in the passenger's. The only thing we could do at that point was wait.

"Are the doors locked?" I whispered.

Reese nodded. She still clutched the radio in her hand, her

knuckles going white. She scanned the area around us through the windshield. I thought we would stay like that, vigilant and quiet until help came. But then Reese turned to me, the whites of her eyes shining in the dark.

"Thank you. For saving my dad back there. When Micah wanted to leave him behind."

The comment was so abrupt, so un-Reese-like, that I didn't know what to say.

"And . . . I'm sorry I didn't believe you," she said, her voice rushed and barely above a whisper.

"What?"

Reese made a face like she was annoyed with me, then she sighed and turned to face the windshield, peering out into the night. "My mom's been acting so weird the past few days. Like, much weirder than usual. Any time your dad's name came up, she would just be like *la-la-la* and change the subject."

I stayed quiet, sensing that there was more.

She sighed heavily. "So I pressed her on it, and she finally admitted it, after all these years. What went down between her and your dad. I guess it ended that night—the night you caught them. My dad knew, but he promised to never bring it up again as long as Mom kept me out of it and stayed away from your dad. Isn't that messed up? That they lied to me?"

It was hard to believe what I was hearing, hard to process Reese's words. It had been years since she'd talked to me like I was a person, let alone opened up and told me anything real.

"I think maybe I always knew," she whispered, her eyes dropping low. "Or a part of me did. I just couldn't face what was right there. . . . I mean, they're my parents, you know?"

"Yeah," I finally whispered back. "I do."

"Anyway, I'm sorry. For . . . all that stuff."

And even though "all that stuff" was a pretty lame way of summing up the shitty way she'd treated me back then and this summer, I suddenly didn't have the heart to call her out on it. We'd been so young that night, riding our bikes through the street, believing nothing could ever hurt us.

Reese had just wanted to believe it a little longer.

"It's okay," I said, finding that as the words came out of my mouth, I meant them. "Really."

And she smiled, the smallest of smiles. Then, in true Reese fashion, she flipped her hair, and the moment was over. "God, how long does it take for the cops to get here, anyway? Do they not know what *emergency* means?"

"They're probably . . ." My voice died in my mouth as I caught a glimpse of light out of the corner of my eye, reflected in the car's side mirror. It was moving fast and heading right in our direction, a glaring brighter than a flashlight, brighter than headlights. . . .

Reese screamed.

"Shh!" I said, pushing myself down in the seat. "Stay quiet, stay low. Maybe he won't see us."

Reese threw herself down into the seat. Neither of us dared

to turn around or move a muscle. So we watched as the light got closer and closer, filling up first the side mirror, then the rear-view mirror. The shadows inside the car began to fade, pushed away by the light, as though the sun were slowly rising right outside.

As the light got closer, I craned my neck to look out the passenger-side window. At first the light was too bright to look into directly. But then I squinted—and I saw him. Not just the glowing, moving burst of light, but the figure inside. I saw the outline of a shoulder, hips, legs. His head. I couldn't make out his features, but I knew he was facing us.

Looking right at us.

Or maybe *looking* wasn't the right word. It was hard to believe any human could look out of those eyes, which were more like two black pits surrounded by a brilliant light. They looked like emptiness, like hunger, like wanting. But whatever lurked inside those shadowed holes was definitely aimed right at us.

I pushed myself back against the driver's-side door, and Reese scrambled to get as close to me as possible, her hip digging into the middle console. The light was so bright now that I had to blink against it. But I couldn't look away, not when he was so close.

This Mr. Jameson–like being reached out with one arm—or at least a solid block of light that was vaguely shaped like an arm. Five thin, black shapes that might have been fingers pressed up against the window.

"What is he doing? What is he doing?" Reese whimpered.

"Just stay close. He can't get in. The doors are locked," I whispered back.

"What's that smell?" Reese yelled.

It was burning.

The glass was turning into liquid and dripping away, running at first in small rivulets down the window, leaving only a hole that grew bigger and bigger. I felt the heat then—that oven-intense heat, one that brought up an animal panic inside that made me want to scramble away, away, *away*.

This time, Reese and I both screamed as I fumbled for the door handle behind me. But Mr. Jameson was faster. The light moved inside the window, through the car, stretching out until it landed on skin.

Reese's shriek pierced my skull. There was no longer just fear in her voice—but pain. The light was near her legs, but I couldn't see where it was touching her; it was just too bright. Too hard to see anything. But the burning smell grew worse, not just glass this time, but metal and plastic . . . and skin.

The driver's-side door finally crashed open, and I went tumbling out onto the ground. I reached back up and grabbed Reese under her arms to pull her after me. The heat coming through the window was enough to singe the hair off my arms. But I couldn't focus on that. Reese's screams blocked out all my other senses. I'd never heard a noise like that, not ever.

I squeezed Reese and pulled back with all my might, leveraging my foot against the bottom of the driver's-side door. She finally pulled free, landing on top of me in a heap. Her face crashed against mine, and I could feel hot tears on her cheeks. I looked down at her legs, and even in the dark I could see that one was burned, red welts already rising up just above her calf.

I got up to my feet and tried to get Reese off the ground, too, but she was still crying so hard, one arm wrapped protectively around her injured leg.

The light got brighter again, and I felt the heat before I saw Mr. Jameson moving around the front of the car, toward us.

"Reese, come on!"

She stood up on her good leg, but as soon as she tried to take a step, she buckled, falling against me with a whimper. I tried to take a step back, dragging her with me, but she was too heavy. A prickling feeling of dread spread over me—I'd never be able to carry her away before Mr. Jameson reached us. The car wasn't safe. There was no place to go, nowhere to hide.

I took another awkward step back, Reese essentially a lump of dead weight in my arms. Mr. Jameson was getting closer. I had to close my eyes against the brightness—it was like looking directly into the sun. Through the slits of my eyes, I could still make out some of his burned features, his collarbones, his jaw. The dark space of his mouth opened and closed, opened and closed. Like he was trying desperately to say something, to talk to us.

And then I did hear his voice, low and creaky and barely audible.

"Please," he said, moving closer. "Help."

He reached out an arm, so close that it grazed against the fabric of my T-shirt. I smelled burning cloth, and then after that was the pain, like a hundred sparks flicked against my skin.

"Stop!" a voice screamed.

It wasn't coming from Reese or what was left of Mr. Jameson, but from another figure, one who raced up from behind us, jumping in front of me and Reese like a shield.

"Stop, Dad! Please, it's me—me, Micah!"

The glowing light that was Mr. Jameson paused. Micah held his hands out to him like he was trying to calm an animal. I used that moment to drag Reese another few steps away.

Micah kept his eyes on his dad, but turned his head slightly to speak to us. "I shouldn't have left you in the barn. I'm sorry, I just, I didn't know what to do. But it's okay now. It'll be okay. Right, Dad?"

The light didn't move away, the dark shape inside staying eerily still.

"Please, Dad," Micah pleaded, his voice rising like a child's. "I can still fix everything. You just have to leave them alone and go hide in the woods. I'll come back for you. I will. Please."

The dark mouth in the glowing light opened, and one word escaped—"Help."

Mr. Jameson moved forward again, toward us—and Micah.

"Dad?" Micah asked, taking one unsure step backward. "Dad, it's me—it's *Micah.*"

"*Heeeelp,*" came the voice from the glowing light. Two arm shapes reached out wildly in our direction.

"D-dad?" Micah stuttered. He took another step back, landing hard on my foot. "Stop—please. The fire will fade away eventually, just like always. You have to hide until then, and then we'll leave, we'll go away. No more people getting hurt."

The mouth in the fire opened and closed, opened and closed. If Mr. Jameson was still Mr. Jameson in there, he seemed beyond hearing. Beyond Micah's reach. His hollow features were twisted up with what something I recognized now—pain.

But Micah refused to see it. Another arm reached out for him, and he dodged.

"It's *me*! Dad, stop—"

The glowing arm reached Micah's shirt, burning through it instantly. Micah's whole back stiffened in shock.

"Micah, we have to *run*. Help me with Reese—"

But Micah stood still, transfixed.

"Dad," he pleaded. "Dad . . ."

Mr. Jameson reached out again, this time for Micah's chest. And I knew in that second that Micah wouldn't get away in time, and that Mr. Jameson would burn through him as easily as he'd burned through the glass of the window. I was behind Micah, and the heat from Mr. Jameson was so hot I had to turn my face away. The air so hot I was choking on it.

That's when I saw the gun tucked into the back of Micah's waistband. The sheriff's gun, its handle resting flat against Micah's back. I'd never held a gun before, not a real one. I was still staring at it when Micah screamed. Mr. Jameson had reached him and placed one bright, glowing hand on his own son's chest.

I gripped the handle and pulled it out, aiming it quickly around Micah's shoulder, toward the middle of the glowing ball of light. I put my finger against the trigger, pulled—

And nothing happened.

Micah's screams grew louder, but still he couldn't—or wouldn't—move. But he also couldn't shield us for much longer. I bit my lip, re-aiming the gun. That's when I felt a hand reach up beside me. Reese quickly flipped a switch on the gun—the safety, I realized—before giving me a small nod. She wrapped her hand around mine on the handle. I swallowed hard as she helped me aim again, and we fired.

It took a second for the glowing figure to register what had happened. Through all the light, I couldn't even see if we'd hit him, or where. But then he crumpled, folding in on himself, sucking the light back inside as quickly as turning off a flashlight. For a few moments I couldn't see; the afterimage of the light was too burned into my vision. I blinked heavily and turned away, making out just the outline of Reese beside me in the suddenly dark night.

Micah fell to his knees, reaching down for his dad, for the sprawling figure on the ground. I could just barely make out Mr. Jameson, now free of any light or heat, just an average-size shape holding his hands over his thigh. Through his long fingers, I saw blood.

As my eyes started to slowly adjust to the dark, Micah's dad became more clear. The skin of his face and arms was rippled and puckered, blackened in places. He was completely bald on one side of his face, the ear on that side nothing more than a black hole. The skin of his face was stretched and shiny where it met his neck. Whatever had been done to him all those years ago in the plant's secret laboratory, he hadn't gotten a chance to truly recover, not really. His eyes were closed, his mouth still open and moving, trying to push out words none of us could hear.

Micah ignored his own injuries, reaching instead to place one gentle hand on his dad's head. I thought he might cry, or yell, or ask his dad why—why put him in such an awful position? Why hurt the one person who was still looking out for him? Why? But Micah said none of those things.

"I'm sorry," he whimpered, hunching over his dad, defeated. "I'm sorry."

We heard the sirens then, coming up the road. As they got closer, they blocked out the sound of Mr. Jameson's struggling cry, of Micah's apologies, of the gun slipping from my hand and falling to the ground below.

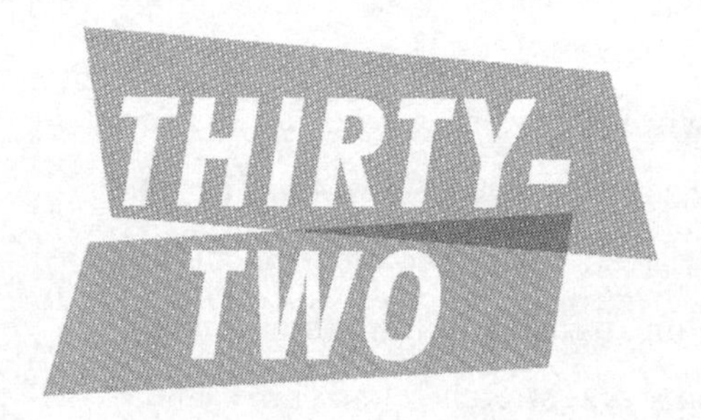

THIRTY-TWO

THE TREES WERE awash in lights: red, blue, white, yellow. Three police cars were pulled up to the side of the road, along with an ambulance, a fire truck, and Dex's car, parked haphazardly where Micah had left it.

A black SUV was parked in the shadows across the street. I watched quietly as agents Shanahan and Rickard loaded two figures into the SUV on stretchers—an unconscious Mr. Jameson and a silent Micah, both with fresh bandages over their injuries, both in handcuffs. A town deputy went to go speak with Rickard, and he looked impossibly young next to the agent, his expression confused and even a little scared in the swirling lights.

Rickard just put one hand on the deputy's shoulder and shuffled him back toward a waiting car from the local station. ". . . federal concern . . . We got it from here," I heard him say as he passed. The deputy tried weakly to protest, but Rickard guided him into the car, then leaned to whisper something in the younger man's ear before firmly closing the car door and walking back to his partner.

I strained to hear, but I was too far away, sitting next to Reese in the back of an ambulance while two medics tended to her burned leg. She was going to be fine, but they still needed to take her to the hospital. Reese jutted out her chin and said she wasn't going anywhere until she saw her dad. One of the medics started to argue with her, and when I saw Reese's eyes go dark in response, I almost pitied him.

My heart jumped into my throat when I saw a group of people moving down the road toward us, and I threw myself out of the back of the ambulance.

There were my dad and Dex, walking slowly but still safe, their faces lit up in the alternating police lights. Next to them, the deputy and two other officers were carrying the sheriff between them.

I started running to meet them, but the two agents swiftly intercepted my dad, blocking my path. But before they could say anything, my dad held up one hand to silence them and turned to me.

"Are you okay?"

I nodded. Next to Dad, Dex gave me a grim smile.

"Ike Hardjoy," Agent Rickard said. "We've been looking all over for you."

"Well, I wish you'd looked a bit harder."

The corners of Rickard's mouth rose just a bit. "Yes, your daughter was telling us about what happened. Horrible thing, for Hal Jameson to be alive all these years, hiding out in the woods while his mental health deteriorated. I'm sure the families of the deceased will be glad to know this is over."

It took a second for the agent's words to register. The agents had arrived at the scene just moments after the local police, and they'd taken over questioning me, claiming jurisdiction. While Micah and his dad were being given medical treatment, I had answered—truthfully—all of their questions about what happened that night. I had explained the glowing light, Mr. Jameson's horrifying ability, all of it.

"His *mental health deteriorated*?" Dex sputtered. "Are you kidding me?"

The other agent, Shanahan, turned to Dex. "He never kids."

"That's not what happened here," I said, my voice level.

"It's all right, guys," my dad said, keeping his eyes carefully trained on the agents. "These agents seem to have their story straight," he added, drily.

"Yeah, until they use their mind-erasing drug on us," Dex spit out.

Shanahan raised one eyebrow. "You're clearly worked up, son. You've all been through an ordeal—"

"He's talking about X10-88," I said.

"Penelope—" Dad warned. But I kept going, fueled by anger

at the smug condescension in the agents' voices. How could they just discredit everything we'd been through, all the pain *they'd* caused with their secret experiments at the plant? With their botched cover-up?

"And you know it," I added. "You know exactly what caused this. You tried to use the meteorite alloy to create a memory-wiping drug, and you wanted to keep it secret. But Mr. Jameson found out. The only thing I can't figure out is whether or not what happened to him was really an accident. He was curious about the basement lab. Did he get too close to the raw alloy and it infected him, turning him into walking fire and almost killing him? Or maybe he got too close to the alloy and then someone else burned the room down intentionally, trying to solve the problem of Mr. Jameson and what he knew, and instead made everything worse?"

Both agents stared at me, their expressions identically indifferent. I realized I'd probably never get an answer.

"No matter what happened, afterward you tried to cover it all up. Not caring how you hurt the Jamesons. Not caring how closing the plant hurt the whole town. And now you'll probably just use X10-88 again on us—"

"Miss, I need to ask you to be calm," Shanahan interrupted. "You're sounding a bit hysterical—"

"X10-88 is gone," Rickard said abruptly. Shanahan whipped his head around to glare at his partner, as if shocked at his reply.

But Rickard kept talking, his steely, appraising eyes on me. "You're a tenacious girl, Miss Hardjoy. With a tenacious father. But if you go looking for a story about a memory drug and its connections to a meteorite alloy, you won't find anything. That project closed years ago, and all records were destroyed. Thoroughly. What happened here was merely an unfortunate remnant of a previous mistake—one we will now rectify. But know this—even if there were still X10-88 floating around in the world—which there's not—there'd be no need to use it tonight. Do you know why?"

The smugness in his tone made me so angry I couldn't speak. I shook my head instead.

"No, I see you do not." Rickard turned to my dad. "But you know, don't you, Mr. Hardjoy?"

"Because no one would believe us," my dad said. His eyes flashed with anger, but also with resignation. "A crackpot journalist and a couple of kids."

"I see you do understand," Rickard said with a small, dismissive smile. "Which means we're done here."

"Wait," I called out just as Rickard was turning around. "What about Micah? What's going to happen to him?"

"We'll question him, of course," he answered. "If what you said is true, he aided and abetted a known killer. Once he's . . . processed, the justice system will sort everything out. He'll face the punishment he deserves."

His tone was level, but his words felt ominous.

"Maybe someday you will, too," I said, keeping my eyes on his.

The corner of Rickard's mouth rose just a fraction before he turned away from me. The agents both climbed smoothly into either side of the SUV, but my eyes were on the back door as it slowly slid away and down the road. Micah was in there; Micah with the big grin and the kind word for everyone. Micah, the pride of Bone Lake, the quarterback with a bright future and a secret so dark it had ensured he'd never get to see that future realized. And even though I still couldn't believe that he'd held my dad hostage, lied to me, wiped my memory, and nearly gotten us all killed, it wasn't anger I felt as the SUV disappeared down the street and into the night. I felt something heavy settle over me instead: a kind of sadness for something lost.

The digital clock in our kitchen had just ticked past midnight, but Dad and I were still wide-awake. We sat on opposite sides of the kitchen table; he was drinking Bud Light from a can while I sipped from a glass of tap water. We both munched slowly on the only food left in the cupboards—a half-eaten carton of Sandies.

Dad looked exhausted, his beard gone straggly, dark circles under his eyes. The skin around his wrists was raw and red. The cops had wanted him to go to the hospital, but he'd firmly told them no.

"I'm taking my daughter home," he'd said. "We can handle everything else tomorrow."

And that was true—with one exception. On the ride back to our house, I'd called my mom and filled her in. Well, not on everything. Not yet. I'd told her Dad was found, and the killer in the woods was caught. I didn't have the energy to rehash the rest of it, not over the phone, not that night. Mom had still wanted to fly back to Michigan, but I'd convinced her to stay in Spain for now. Soon enough, I'd tell her everything.

So now it was just Dad and me, sitting at the kitchen table, neither of us knowing quite what to say. We'd sat like this before many times over the past few years, eating in silence, wary of each other. But I was tired of the silence.

"I'm glad you're okay," I said, trying to break the ice.

"Me?" Dad gave an incredulous chuckle. "Pen, if you'd gotten hurt tonight, I don't know what I would have done. It was reckless, what you did."

"I know."

Dad sighed, then smiled. "Brave, too."

And I couldn't help smiling back. Even after everything, praise from him warmed up my insides.

"I don't know if I should ground you or buy you a car," he said.

"I'd lean toward the second option."

Dad smiled, and we fell into silence again. I felt myself chickening out, like I'd done so many times before. It would be so easy to swallow his praise, to hug him good night, to go to bed, and let everything be the way it'd been before. But Dad's own words kept me in place. *Brave*, he'd called me. I wondered if that was really true. It took one kind of bravery to run off into the darkened woods to save your father from an accidental killer infected with government-manipulated meteorite juice. It took a whole different kind of bravery to look him in the eye and tell him all the ways he'd hurt you, all the ways he'd let you down.

"Dad—" I started.

"Hold on," he said, standing up. He went to the fridge and got out another can of beer. Then, after a moment, he pulled out a second one. He came back down and put one of the cans in front of me.

"Don't tell your mom."

I couldn't help, once again, but smile. I ran my fingers under the cold top of the can, popped it open, and took a small sip.

"I probably shouldn't have given that to you, but after the night we just had . . ."

"It's okay," I said. "I promise not to enjoy it too much."

"I know it's my fault, what happened tonight," he went on, his eyes looking down as he took another sip of his beer. The admission of guilt nearly shocked me into silence.

"Well . . . you didn't make the meteorite land here or make the government experiment on it in our town. You didn't make Mr. Jameson into . . . what he became."

"No, guess not. Government experiments on the meteorite,"

he said, then gave a small chuckle. "There goes my Visitors theory, I guess. Not like anyone believed it anyway."

"I did," I said. "Once."

He went quiet for a minute.

"One thing you could have done differently was tell me about the body you found, the hiker. All these months, and you kept it from me. And then you packed up your camping gear in the truck to go chasing after this story the day before I was supposed to get to town—"

"That's not what the camping gear was for," Dad said, shaking his head. "I was loading up the truck so the two of us could maybe take a trip together. Go camping at the dunes or somewhere . . . like we used to. I was just going to check out the Jamesons' property real quick before we left, and . . . well, you know."

"Oh," I said. So he hadn't chosen his story over me.

"I know things haven't been . . . right . . . between us for a while, Pen. I don't really know what to do about that. I thought if we went camping, just the two of us . . ."

I nodded. "We can still do that, maybe." I hated how vulnerable my voice sounded, how much like a little girl who needed her dad. I cleared my throat. "But . . . I think it'll take more than just camping. I don't want things to go on like they were before. When I was looking for you, I learned so much about you I didn't know. It was like you were this whole other person, one I'd never really met."

Dad looked confused. "I'm not sure I know what you mean."

"Well, it's just . . . everything that happened with Mom, and . . . and with Julie . . . I don't think I ever knew everything that went down with that. So I filled in the blanks myself."

Dad's whole body went still, the tips of his ears turning red. This was the point, right here. The point of no return.

"You were just a kid, Penelope. There was no point telling you all the details. It would only hurt you."

"I got hurt anyway." The words caught around a lump in my throat as I tried to get them out.

Dad closed his eyes then, and I knew that this time I was the one hurting him. He let out a long sigh. "Look, it's really late, kiddo—"

"It *is* late. About five years late for us to have this conversation, I think."

Dad gave a small laugh, but not a pleasant one. "You always were quick with the smart comebacks. I think you got that from your mom."

"No I didn't. And don't change the subject."

"Okay," Dad said, rubbing his eyes and leaning back in his chair. "I won't. I'm not going to pretend that I was the perfect husband or father all the time. And what happened with Julie . . . I screwed up, I know it. And I was never really sure how to deal with that."

"So you just . . . didn't."

"It's not that simple."

"I know that," I said. "But, Dad . . . I can handle 'not simple.' Maybe I couldn't before. But I can now."

Dad looked at me then, really looked at me, his eyes boring steadily into mine. He gave a sad smile. "I guess I can see that." He cleared his throat. "It's hard to explain, Pen. Maybe you'll know when you have kids, but . . . you always saw me in a certain way. Like I was your hero. Like I could catch all the monsters in the world."

There it was again, the lump in my throat. "I know."

"It's hard to go from being the hero to being one of the monsters."

His voice caught, just a bit, and I thought he was going to look away. But he didn't.

"But you're neither of those things," I said, thinking about Micah, and how he hadn't been able to see his dad for what he really was, either. "And I'd rather see you the way you are. No lies. No pretending."

Dad took a shaky breath. "Okay. What do you want to know?"

What did I want to know?

A few weeks ago, I'd wanted to know that every single question in the world had a yes or no answer, and that you could find it if you looked hard enough. My dad was a liar, and I was angry at him—things were as simple as that. But I didn't think that was true anymore. There wasn't a simple answer as to why my parents got divorced, or why my dad did the things he did.

But I knew enough to keep my eyes open now, to keep searching for the answers even when they didn't make sense, even when there was no "right" one. So what did I want to know about him?

Everything.

"I want to know . . ." I said slowly, wondering where to start. The beginning of a thought was forming in my mind. After what had happened these past few days, I didn't think I had it in me to keep writing my Northwestern article on Bone Lake's decline. And I sure couldn't write the truth of what happened tonight, not without verifiable sources or proof. But maybe I could focus my article on something else, something that encompassed both of those stories through a singular viewpoint. A more personal viewpoint, like my journalism teacher had advised. A focus on Ike Hardjoy, professional storyteller. And so many other things, too.

"I want to know why you write stories for *Strange World*," I blurted. "What drives you, when I know you don't believe in half that stuff? Why . . . why do you do the things you do?"

Dad sucked in a breath.

"There's not really an easy answer for that."

"That's okay. I don't need the answer to be easy. I just need it to be true. Even if you think the truth is hard, or that it'll hurt me, or even if it will make you look bad."

Dad was still peering at me. "You want to know the truth."

"I want to know *your* truth." Because that was the best he

could do. The best any of us could maybe do. I could see, now, how the truth wasn't just this one, finite thing. A bear might be just a bear, but people were more complicated. Dad's truth was different from Mom's truth, and mine was different from both of theirs. And that made everything harder; it made the full picture, the full truth, a thousand times more difficult to see. But it made it a thousand times more interesting, too.

Dad gave one slow nod. "Okay, Penelope. We can try that."

"And Dad?" I said, taking one more sip of beer and looking him in the eye. "I want you to call me Penny from now on. It's the name *I* like."

Dad smiled, and this time it reached his eyes. "Okay, Penny. I can try that, too."

MY ROOM WAS completely dark as my head hit the pillow. For the first time in days, I didn't feel a trickle of fear before I closed my eyes, didn't wonder what was lurking around just outside.

Then came the light. I saw it first through the slits of my eyes, a bright light passing right above my head, catching on the opposite wall. I immediately jumped up, heart racing, and spun to the window behind me. There *was* a light out there, one moving slowly past my lawn and toward the trees. But after a few frightening seconds I realized it was just an ordinary flashlight, bobbing along before disappearing around the corner of my house.

I got up, quickly throwing on sweatpants and tennis shoes. There was no light under Dad's door as I passed by and slowly made my way to the kitchen before sneaking quietly out the back. I saw the flashlight as it disappeared up and into the tree house. When I put my foot on the bottom rung of the ladder and started climbing, a head with brown hair sticking up all over shot through the hole of the tree house above me.

"Penny? You scared the crap out of me," Dex said, putting out a hand to help me through the hole.

"Me? You were the one skulking past my bedroom window."

"You mean walking past at a normal pace?"

"Seemed like skulking to me."

We sat down across from each other, cross-legged on the bare wooden floorboards. Dex stood the flashlight up on its end so a circle of light flashed upward onto the ceiling, spilling a dim glow over our features.

I thought about the last time we were in this tree house together and quickly averted my eyes from Dex's.

"What are you even doing out here?" I asked.

"Would you believe that I wanted to finish off those Twinkies?"

I raised my eyebrow.

"Couldn't sleep," Dex admitted. "After everything that happened tonight . . ."

"Yeah, I know what you mean. Did you tell Cindy?"

"Yep. I still don't think she really believes me, though. Not about all of it, anyway. I told her to go down to the station tomorrow and ask for herself."

I sighed. "Yeah, but the sheriff was unconscious for Micah's big confession. All he'll remember is seeing something weird in the woods and then getting knocked out. And the agents fed the deputies their own story. No one's going to believe us."

Dex leaned back against the wall of the tree house, his head hitting the wood with a light *thunk*. "It's not fair. We did this really cool thing—"

"*Cool* is not the word I'd use."

"Well, fine. But we solved this whole mystery and saved your dad, and no one will ever know. For the first time I think I'm getting a small taste of what it's like to be Ike."

"Yeah," I said, hugging my knees to my chest. "I know exactly what you mean."

Dex caught my eye. "So are things . . . okay between you two?"

I shrugged. "Okay as they can be, I think. But there's a very real possibility that things could get . . . better."

"That's good."

"What about your mom? Did you make up from your fight?"

"Honestly, she was so glad to see me okay tonight that I think she might have forgotten about it," Dex said, then added, "For now, anyway."

"Where's the mind-altering space drug when you need it, right?"

Dex smiled. "Do you believe the agents? About the X10-88 being all gone?"

I thought about it, then shook my head. "I honestly don't

know. It'd make a really great story . . . but it doesn't seem likely I'll get my hands on any real evidence."

Dex scrunched up his nose. "Sorry."

"It's okay," I said with a sigh. "It'll make a perfect story for *Strange World*."

"Is Ike really going to write it up?"

"Of course. It's not like *Strange World* has ever needed anything like proof before," I said, half laughing. "He's going to head out to the meteorite site tomorrow to take some pictures, and he asked me to come. He said he'd give me a byline in the story if I helped him."

Dex raised his eyebrows. "Are you going to?"

"Yeah, I think I am," I said. "I've got another angle for the Northwestern article. It's still in its early stages, but I have a few months to work it out."

Dex nodded. "That's cool."

I shook my head, sighing. "I can't believe I'll get my first *actual* byline in a national publication and it'll be *Strange World*. But all I ever wanted to do was find the truth and tell it. And what we'll write will at least be true, even if no one will believe it."

"Kind of ironic," Dex said.

"Tell me about it."

"It's nice, though, that you'll get to work on the story with Ike."

"Yeah," I said softly. Dex was talking about the *Strange*

World story, but my thoughts went to the other one, the more personal one. "I think so, too."

Dex's eyes drifted down, and I wondered if he was thinking about his own dad. The one who wasn't coming back. I wondered if he would find him someday, and if he'd learn for himself all of the reasons why his dad had kept so much a secret. Because now I knew those reasons always existed, if we would just allow ourselves to see them. Dex might never totally forgive his dad, but maybe understanding him could help.

Maybe.

It was strange to not just know, but to really *get* how someone could be more than one thing at the same time. Not right or wrong, not good or bad. But a messy soup of all those things. Julie Harper, Reese, the sheriff. Micah.

Even Dex had more to him than I'd let myself admit. It had been easier to still think of him as the little boy next door. In some ways, that would always be a little bit true. But as I looked across the small tree house at him, his shoulders broad and solid against the wooden planks, his long legs crossing each other so his knees were inches from mine, his hair falling across his forehead in a way that had always seemed unruly but now sent a shiver up my spine . . . there was *more* there. He could annoy me, infuriate me, make me laugh. He stayed in my head when he wasn't around. And there was so much more than that, even. More than I'd been ready to see before.

Dex caught me looking at him. "What is it?" he asked, his

low voice cracking a bit.

I swallowed past the sudden dryness in my throat. "I just, um . . . I wanted to apologize, for what happened last time we were up here together."

Color flared up on Dex's cheeks, and he looked away. "You don't have to—"

"Yes, I do. I just . . . it freaked me out, what almost . . . what *we* almost . . ."

"Yeah, I sort of got that."

"No, but . . . you don't know *why*."

Dex looked up at me, a glimmer of hope in his expression.

"I've known you for so long, Dex. And this summer I've gotten to know you all over again," I started. "And you became—you always were—important to me. And I think I was afraid of messing all that up."

"Messing it up how?"

I thought about all the mistakes I'd made, all the ways I'd gotten things wrong. "I think I started to realize that I'm more like my dad than I ever thought. That I have it in me to hurt someone I . . . care about."

"But we all have that in us, Penny. I don't think you can get around it—accidentally hurting people. It's a part of, well, knowing people. I mean, look at my mom. She's always looking out for people, and her keeping a secret from me, even for the best reasons—it still hurt."

"I know. But *I* don't want to hurt you."

Dex's eyes glimmered as he smiled. He moved closer to me, his knees pressing more firmly against mine.

"What if I told you I'm willing to risk it?"

Bubbles expanded in my chest. A smile stretched across my face. "Just like that?"

"Just like that."

And then everything in my body was leaning forward, seemingly beyond my control. My arms, shoulders, back, neck—everything angled toward Dex, moved across the darkened space between us to be nearer to him.

He was doing the same thing, coming closer in the soft light. There were a few inches between us, and then there was nothing. The instant my mouth met his, I knew everything would change. And I was ready for it. Dex, the boy next door, and Dex, something more—he was everything wrapped into one.

Dex smiled even as he kissed me, and then he put one hand up to the side of my face and pulled me in closer. It felt right, that move. So did the next one, and the next. It all felt so right. All my worries and thoughts flew out the window as the shadows we cast moved across the tree house walls.

Dex was willing to risk it.

And so was I.

Because I couldn't be sure that things would work out, that we'd never accidentally hurt each other, that things wouldn't end badly. Just like I couldn't be sure that Reese and I would ever be friends again, or that Bone Lake would ever thrive again, or that my dad and I would ever really understand each other and be always honest with each other, even if the truth was complicated and messy and sometimes painful.

I couldn't *know* any of this would happen. I couldn't prove it.

But I could believe it.

ACKNOWLEDGMENTS

Thank you so much to Reiko Davis, who has always been the most supportive, encouraging agent a girl could ask for. And many thank-yous to Jessica MacLeish, my incredible editor. When I wanted to swing from portal fantasies to a book about a creature in the woods, you were both on board without any hesitation, and that meant so much.

Thank you also to everyone at HarperTeen for the work you put into making this book a reality. Special thanks to Erin Fitzsimmons, who designed the incredible cover, and Marie Bergeron, who created the amazing illustration. It exceeded all my hopes. And thank you to Tiffany Morris for your valued input and suggestions, and to Sarah Ratner for telling me the beginning of the book needed to be creepier—you were right!

The core of this book would not exist had my dad not spent

a good part of my childhood terrifying me for fun; so thanks, Dad, for convincing me that lake monsters, yetis, and headless horsemen could be real, even if just for a little while. And thanks, Mom, for subsequently allowing me to sleep with a night-light for way longer than was probably appropriate.

Thank you to all my family and friends, old and new, for your support and encouragement—I'd be lost in the woods without you. I also want to thank the YA community in general, for lending support, being awesome, and helping me to learn and grow as both a writer and a human. I'm so glad this space exists, and I feel lucky to be a part of it.

And thanks to Phil, as always, for everything.